The Empress
and
The Acolyte

The Empress and The Acolyte

Lyremouth Chronicles
Book Three

by

Jane Fletcher

2006

THE EMPRESS AND THE ACOLYTE

ISBN 1-933110-60-0
This Trade Paperback Is Published By
Bold Strokes Books, Inc.,
New York, USA

First Edition, November 2006

CREDITS
EDITORS: CINDY CRESAP AND STACIA SEAMAN
PRODUCTION DESIGN: J. BARRE GREYSTONE
COVER IMAGE: TOBIAS BRENNER (http://www.tobiasbrenner.de/)
COVER DESIGN: J. BARRE GREYSTONE

By the Author

THE CELAENO SERIES

The Walls of Westernfort

Rangers at Roadsend

The Temple at Landfall

THE LYREMOUTH CHRONICLES

The Exile and the Sorcerer Book One

The Traitor and the Chalice Book Two

Acknowledgments

I'd like to thank everyone at Bold Strokes Books especially Cindy, Rad, and Stacia for giving me help and support when I needed it, and for standing back and giving me free rein when I didn't.

I'd also like to thank everyone at the Milford Writer's group for their suggestions and comments about the early sections of this book.

DEDICATION

For Lizzy—still

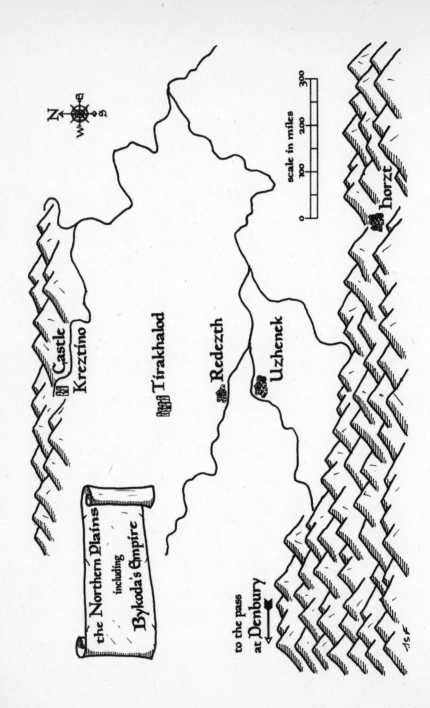

FOREWORD—EMPIRES AND ANARCHY

Magic changes everything

The rare individuals who could directly access the higher dimensions had dictated the history of the world. These workers of magic perceived more than the four normal dimensions of time and space known by the ungifted majority, and thus could manipulate their surroundings in ways that seemed as mystical and unstoppable to the rest of the population as a sighted archer might seem in the world of the blind.

A witch was someone who was aware of just one or two paranormal dimensions. Maybe one person in every hundred might claim this title. Far more uncommon were sorcerers, who could perceive all three paranormal dimensions, including the paradoxical second aspect of time—the realm of soothsayers and oracles.

Nobody knew why some were born with these gifts. Whatever the cause, it did not lie in heredity. Children of the most powerful sorcerer were no more likely to be gifted with magic than those of a common shepherd. And therein lay the source of the chaos that sorcerers had inflicted on the world.

Their powers were vast. One sorcerer, acting alone, could carve out an empire, sweeping aside whatever small culture the ungifted had painstakingly built. Cities and civilisations were created by sorcerers' paranormal abilities, and all fell back to anarchy on their deaths. No empire lasted longer than one generation.

These empire-building sorcerers were as diverse as their empires. Some were tyrants who enslaved entire regions. Some were motivated by concern for others and sought only to enhance the well-being of their people. Some were decadent parasites who exerted no control over their lands other than to claim tribute.

Yet even the worst of these empires were remembered fondly by most of their subjects as a time of stability and safety; a time when a powerful protector kept all other dangers away; a time when a farmer might sow a field with the expectation of harvesting it.

What other option was there? Ordinary, ungifted people could not hope to resist even a witch. Without the structure of empire, what chance was there of ordinary workers gaining any reward from their daily labour? Living by one person's rules was better than living by no rules at all.

Only the founding of the Coven broke this cycle of empire and anarchy, and only for the lands under its control, the Protectorate. On the death of the great philosopher sorcerer Keovan of Lyremouth, his acolytes formed their alliance under an elected leader—the Guardian—and invited other sorcerers and witches to join them. To the ordinary folk of the surrounding region they offered protection in return for the payment of taxes.

For four and a half centuries, the Coven grew in size and power. The territory that it controlled expanded also, by consent rather than invasion. The order and security offered by the Coven was an attractive lure, and bordering territories petitioned to join. In time, the Protectorate of Lyremouth came to dwarf the overnight empires of lone sorcerers.

Like any human institution, the Protectorate was not perfect, but it was generally benign and just. Guilds could manage their own affairs. Ungifted citizens had rights under the law. Folk might grumble at the taxes and distrust the autocratic sorcerers, yet—uniquely in the history of the world—they lived their lives in peace and prosperity, with the hope that their children and grandchildren might do the same.

The advantages of the Protectorate for ungifted citizens were clear, but what inspired sorcerers to join? Why abide by the laws of the Coven, working to the orders of the Guardian, when they could live outside its rule and take whatever they wanted from defenceless ungifted folk?

The answers to this question were also as diverse as the sorcerers themselves. Some were unworldly scholars, eager for the chance to study with others who saw the world in all its multi-dimensional complexity. Some were motivated by moral standards and took satisfaction from working for something that would benefit people for centuries to come. Some had ambitions to rise through the Coven hierarchy and one day have hundreds of powerful sorcerers under their rule.

Or, as with Jemeryl, it could be a case of all three to varying degrees, dependant on what mood she was in that day.

Part One

The Empress

CHAPTER ONE—AN ORACLE OF DEATH

Nails clawed into the tabletop, fighting for grip. The fingers clenched, slowly and laboriously inching the arm forwards. A moment of rest, and then once again the fingers reached out. At the other end of the forearm, where the elbow should have been, loose tendrils of skin dragged across the wooden surface.

Two women stood by the table, watching the sluggish progress. The warm glow of a fire competed with dim light from the leaden sky outside. The only sounds were the crackle of flames and the rain beating against the window. The stone castle walls and thick hanging tapestries blocked out all else.

The younger woman by far was Jemeryl, oathbound sorcerer of the Coven at Lyremouth, still in her mid twenties. Her eyes were fixed in concentration on the animate arm, but her angular features held an impish grin. Light from the flames accentuated the hint of red in her curly auburn hair.

"You know, I think it's going to work." Jemeryl's voice reflected her satisfaction.

"But are you still sure it's a good idea?"

The elder woman turned away and wandered back to her seat by the hearth. Her shrunken body was swallowed by the mound of cushions. Firelight glittered on the gemstones on her fingers and the gold embroidery decorating her robe. It etched deep lines on her face. The wisps of fine white hair on her forehead were almost invisible in the flickering shadows.

Jemeryl raised her eyes to her companion, the Empress Bykoda. "Yes. Why shouldn't I?"

Although the two sorcerers had worked together for many months, Jemeryl knew that the Empress did not share her own enthusiasm for the project. In fact, Bykoda's motives for assisting at all were something that still caused her considerable puzzlement.

Jemeryl returned her attention to the disembodied arm. She picked it up and flipped it back and forth, examining it from both sides. The fingers jerked and flailed about, spider-like, until she made a sharp, cutting gesture above it. Immediately, it ceased to twitch, ceased even to maintain its shape. The object in Jemeryl's hand hung limp, like a half-stuffed stocking. She treated it to a final moment of consideration, then dumped it on the table and also took a seat by the fire.

Bykoda tilted her head. "You haven't had second thoughts? You think it will really benefit your ungifted citizens back in the Protectorate?"

"Only those who've been unfortunate enough to lose an arm or a leg."

"Unfortunate or foolish?"

"Either."

"Might it not make warriors reckless knowing that if they lose a limb your Coven sorcerers will make them a replacement from resin?"

"In my experience, warriors don't feel that indifferently about what happens to their bodies. Keeping themselves in one piece is a major preoccupation because they're always being confronted by people who want to slice them into bits."

"I'll take your word on it. I admit that I've never spent much time bothering about what's going on in their heads."

"I've got Tevi to keep me well informed on the subject," Jemeryl said lightly.

"Your lover? Yes, I suppose you must talk sometimes."

Jemeryl faltered briefly, caught out by Bykoda's pensive tone. Had the Empress never previously considered the idea that she and Tevi might speak to each other? "Um...yes, her. Knowing Tevi so well helps me see that the ungifted aren't very different from you and me."

"And have you never got yourself into an awkward spot because you were overconfident? I wonder if your ungifted warriors might do the same, especially as they won't understand the limitations of the resin."

Jemeryl shrugged. "They'll know that they can't get a replacement head, which should stop them from getting careless. Plus, the ordinary citizens don't trust sorcerers enough to want to rely on us more than they have to."

"You just said they weren't so different from us."

"Do you trust things you don't understand?"

Bykoda gave a laugh. "I don't understand why you're bothered about your citizens' health. But I take it on trust that you are."

"Then just trust that it will be another success to report when I go back, which will make my seniors happy."

Trying to explain was not worth the effort. Jemeryl just grinned and slipped down in her chair, stretching her feet towards the fire. Her casual pose was one of contentment as she considered the successful conclusion of her mission. For over two and a half years she had been a guest at the castle of Tirakhalod, learning as much as Bykoda was willing to teach. The initial invitation came as a surprise, both to Jemeryl and her superiors in the Coven at Lyremouth. Not everyone had been convinced that the isolated Empress would have anything to teach a Coven-trained sorcerer.

Jemeryl however, had been less arrogantly assured of Coven superiority. Admittedly, the Coven's longevity had allowed it to amass vast knowledge and experience. Its libraries held the collected discoveries of thousands of sorcerers. Whereas Bykoda's realm was typical of the normal run of the world. She had built the Empire by herself, using nothing but her own abilities. Her magic lacked framework and support.

To Jemeryl, many of Bykoda's greatest problems were trifling. Bygone Coven sorcerers had long since found the solutions. But in other places, the originality of Bykoda's work was breathtaking. The need to survive had driven her. Every crisis she had overcome by her skill alone. She had been inventive and ruthless, sometimes in ways that did not fit well with Jemeryl's Coven-born ethics. But Jemeryl was not there to offer censure or support and, to her mind, the knowledge that she would be taking back justified her presence. Bykoda would have done the same regardless, and at least the Protectorate citizens would now benefit.

A while passed before Bykoda spoke again. "In all the time you've been here and seen what the Empire has to offer, the challenges, the freedom, no rules, not having to answer to anyone, has your commitment to the Protectorate weakened?"

Jemeryl shook her head. "Not at all."

"It's ironic." Bykoda's tone was serious, even rueful. "When I invited you here, it was partly because I was certain you wouldn't want to take over my Empire. Now I find myself wishing that you would."

"You...what?"

"That day we first talked, I had just learnt that my latest attempt to deal with a certain problem had failed. You asked about the animate resin, how it was done, and I thought it would be a good excuse to get you here. That's why I offered you the chance to study with me here in Tirakhalod. I thought you..." Bykoda sighed and made a vague gesture with one hand.

"You thought I could solve your problem?"

"Not quite. But I thought that you might be useful if no other solution was found."

"It...I..." Jemeryl broke off in confusion. "What is the problem?"

Bykoda gave a wry grimace. "You don't like oracles, do you?"

"No." Jemeryl paused. "Can I assume you've had a foretelling of something that you don't want to happen?"

"You could say that. In eight months' time, I'm going to be murdered."

Jemeryl needed a few stunned seconds to regain her voice. "Yes. I can see that you might be a little upset about that. Um...do you have any ideas how, or why?"

"The how is some form of magical attack that I haven't identified precisely. As for why"— Bykoda gave a shrug—"hopefully just revenge by someone I've annoyed, or an upstart sorcerer planning on usurping my Empire."

"There could be worse reasons?"

"Oh yes. Come with me. There's something I want to show you."

❖

Tevi hugged close to the base of the cliff and looked up. One hundred feet of sheer rock face hung above her. Battlements lined the top, and directly overhead, the watchtower rose higher still. At her feet, the river lapped around her boots. Once the spring rains came, the spot where she stood would be deep underwater, but for now, Tevi could just squeeze by between rocks and river as long as she did not mind getting her feet wet.

The sounds of battle drowned out all else: the crackle of lightning and boom of explosions, and below them, quieter, human voices raised in screams and shouts. Yet, thankfully, none of it was on Tevi's side of the fort.

The stronghold was built atop rocks overlooking a bridge. Triangular in shape, with river-eroded cliffs on two sides, the fort made the most of the defensive potential of the site. Only on the third, landward side could it be assailed by an army. Its purpose was to guard the bridge against any who might seek to strike at Tirakhalod, and in addition to its natural defences, the Empress's powerful magic was imbued in the stone to proof it against paranormal attack—which was more than a touch unfortunate when the fort was being held by a detachment of renegades.

A junior officer witch, a lieutenant, had deserted, taking her troops with her. Commander Ranenok himself had led the force sent to apprehend the deserters before they could cause more havoc. When the fleeing lieutenant realised that she could not avoid a battle, she had bluffed her way into the fort and taken it over. Even so, with all the resources of Bykoda's Empire against her, one lone lieutenant could not win, and she must have known it, yet obviously she was determined to put up a fight. Tevi's task was to bring that fight to as quick an end as possible, with the maximum number of loyal troops left alive.

Ranenok's current assault on the landward side was a diversion, and it seemed to be working. No arrows or other missiles had come Tevi's way as she had snuck along the riverbank. Yet the defenders' oversight was not particularly reckless or negligent. Despite the low water level, the route was not passable for a force large enough to launch a serious attack on the fort. For any ordinary fighter, climbing the cliff would be daunting when not wearing armour, impossible with it. And as Jemeryl had frequently pointed out, even sorcerers did not find flying a viable method of transport.

However, Tevi was not a completely ordinary fighter. The potion she had taken during childhood granted her magically enhanced strength, easily sufficient to tackle the climb while wearing a thick leather cuirass, carrying a sword, and with a shield strapped to her back. Her upbringing on the Western Isles, collecting eggs from the nests of seabirds, had also given her experience of scaling sheer rock faces and a good head for heights.

Before long, Tevi reached the top of the cliff where the battlements began. The man-made wall was not so generous with handholds as the natural cliff, yet the blending of rock into dressed stone was not seamless, and she was able to find a level spot, a foot deep, where she could stand upright without needing her hands to cling on.

From her waist, Tevi unwound a long rope with an iron grapple attached to the end. She whirled it around vertically in a circle and then hurled it upwards. On her second attempt, the grapple caught on the parapet of the watchtower and held. Tevi gave an experimental tug and then waited to see if the sound had attracted any attention, not that there was much she could have done in her exposed position if it had. To her relief, no heads appeared over the parapet. The clank of the grapple hitting stone had obviously gone unnoticed amidst the chaos of Commander Ranenok's magical assault from down the hill. Unsurprising—the noise was enough to have drowned out far more. As she stood there, Tevi could feel the walls vibrating from the volume of the onslaught. After one last tug on the rope, she began to climb.

At the top, Tevi peered cautiously over the parapet. The flat roof of the watchtower was about forty feet across. On the other side, three soldiers were manning a ballista, a form of huge crossbow. Tevi recognised the pile of ammunition just in front of her as exploding spheres. This would be very useful once she had control of the ballista. Of course, getting control was the tricky bit, and outnumbered was never good.

Two of the soldiers were working on the windlass that pulled back the ballista's twin arms. The third was getting another projectile to launch at the attacking troops. Tevi waited a few seconds until his back was to her when he bent down for the sphere, then she hauled herself onto the roof. The slap of her feet hitting the wooden slats made the man look up, but for him it was too late, and he could not hope to match Tevi's strength. She grabbed the soldier, swung him round, and hurled him over the parapet behind her, then she drew her sword and leapt forwards.

At the falling soldier's scream, the other two soldiers jerked away from the ballista, heads turning and hands reaching for their swords. Tevi charged towards the nearer one, a middle-aged woman with a soot-stained face. In clear panic, the woman fumbled at her scabbard, seeking the hilt, but the wild scrabbling was inept and the weapon was only two-thirds drawn by the time Tevi had her own sword embedded in the woman's chest.

Tevi turned to the last of the three soldiers. She advanced a step.

The man's eyes bulged in fear. "You're the...the..." Apparently he recognised her, by reputation if nothing else.

Before Tevi could take another step, he turned and fled from the roof, slipping on the spiral stairs in his desperate haste. Yet surely he would be back soon with support. Tevi knew that she did not have much time.

She glanced into the courtyard of the fort. The magic that had been worked into the stone was holding up against Ranenok's attack and the walls were unbreached. However, the wooden gates were proving more vulnerable to the powers hurled against them. A curtain of smoke was rising, and they were visibly loose on their hinges. The lieutenant witch was standing just inside, bolstering the gates with her magic.

From Tevi's viewpoint, the situation could not be better. Within seconds, she had completed winding back the ballista's arms and placed a sphere in the sling. Fortunately, the projectile stayed in place as she tilted the ballista down and aimed at the gates. Tevi released the trigger.

The fort's defensive magic protected against attacks from outside but not those emanating from within. The gates exploded in a ball of flame. Tevi did not wait to see if the lieutenant survived. The witch had been caught by surprise, and Tevi was fairly sure that she would have been unable to shield herself. Regardless, Tevi knew there was not time to reload the ballista. Already she could hear shouts coming from the stairwell. Now that the gates were gone, Commander Ranenok and his troops would be storming the fort. All Tevi had to do was hang on until reinforcements arrived.

Tevi grabbed her sword and shield, raced to the staircase, and advanced a few steps down. The sound of hobnailed boots was only one spiral below her, and then the first of the soldiers charged into view around the central column. The man had only a split second to register Tevi standing in wait above him before her sword slashed down on his neck, hitting between mail hauberk and helmet. The man dropped back and disappeared around the stairs. Judging by the shouts, he landed on several of his comrades.

Like all spiral staircases in castles, this one ascended clockwise. The design was intended to give an advantage to defending forces, working on the twin assumptions that most people were right-handed and that the attackers would be the ones coming up the stairs. In this case, Tevi was the one with the advantage. The full radius of the circle was empty behind her right shoulder, meaning that she could rain blows down on her opponents, while their answering parries were severely impeded by the central column.

Forewarned, a second soldier came more cautiously into view, with doubt evident in her eyes. She managed to deflect Tevi's first blow on her shield, but her comrades bustling up behind her were ill disciplined and barged into her legs. The soldier lost her footing on the narrow, triangular stair and was unable to counter Tevi's second strike. The soldier fell forwards and then slid away down the stairs. Her place was taken by an older man who kept his shield high.

Jump! a warning voice screamed in Tevi's head. As she did so, her opponent jabbed his sword at her feet. Tevi landed clear of the blade, then braced her forearm on the central column and kicked out as hard as she could. The man flew back into his comrades, taking all those in sight with him as he fell back down the staircase.

While Tevi waited to see what would come next, fresh shouts erupted outside the tower. From the sound, Ranenok and his troops were now inside the fort. The soldiers below her must also have heard and either decided to take refuge or to challenge the new invaders. Whatever their choice, they did not return to fight Tevi.

For another five minutes, Tevi held her ground on the stairs. Tempting though it was to seek out her comrades and join in the courtyard battle, Tevi was too well experienced in warfare to take the risk. She must not allow the enemy to get control of the ballista. Leaving her position would be dangerous. She had no idea where anyone was, and even with her strength, she dare not let herself be surrounded. On the narrow stairs, she could only be attacked one on one.

At last she heard new footsteps at the bottom of the tower. A voice belonging to one of Ranenok's sergeants called out. "Captain Tevirik. Are you there? Are you all right?"

"I'm here."

"We've secured the courtyard, ma'am."

"The roof's clear. I'm making sure it stays that way."

"Right, ma'am. We'll be with you shortly."

The sound of people running up the stairs was followed by that of a short skirmish, and then the sergeant's head appeared around the central column.

"The tower's ours, ma'am."

Tevi nodded and jerked her thumb over her shoulder. "The ballista is up there with ammunition."

A sudden huge grin split the sergeant's face. "You did great with the gates, ma'am."

Tevi smiled back and patted his shoulder. On her way down the staircase she passed three floors filled with friendly soldiers, enemy prisoners, and dead bodies. Most of the soldiers cheered as she passed. The rest brandished their weapons in salute. Tevi nodded in acknowledgement. The prisoners sat slumped and did not raise their eyes.

Tevi emerged into the courtyard. Two dozen of Ranenok's soldiers occupied the space. More were on the battlements. The ruins of the gate hung off its hinges. At the sight of Tevi another riotous burst of cheering filled the air. She responded with a modest half-wave, half-salute, and felt the heat of a blush start on her cheeks.

Smaller towers stood on either side of the gate. Screams and shouts from one spoke of a battle in progress. One of the soldiers pointed towards it. "Commander Ranenok's in there, ma'am."

Tevi looked at the other tower. The door was shut and a group of soldiers were advancing on it holding a thick section of tree trunk, clearly intending to batter the door down. Ranenok would be too busy to take her report, and the battering ram was something that would benefit from her strength.

Tevi took a few steps forwards when suddenly, her internal voice screamed, *Arrow, move!* In blind reflex, Tevi obeyed and threw herself to the right. She had gone a mere six inches when fire shot through her upper arm. The pain exploded in a fresh wave when she hit the ground.

"Look out! Archer in the tower," somebody shouted.

Soldiers in the courtyard dived for shelter. Tevi scrambled behind a low wall and then looked at her left arm. The armour-piercing head of the arrow had gone through the shoulder guard of her cuirass, her arm underneath, and out the other side. A stream of blood was running down to her hand. The wound was certainly not fatal, but without the forewarning and moving those six inches, the arrow would have gone straight through her heart.

Tevi's head started to swim. She leaned back against the wall behind her and concentrated on breathing deeply. Then she heard the crackle of mage fire and Ranenok's voice called out. "Take the tower." Around the courtyard, soldiers moved out from cover.

Tevi struggled to her feet. All the soldiers were charging towards where the door to the small tower had been—now there was just a fire-blackened hole. The archer would have more to worry about than targets in the courtyard.

Commander Ranenok strode over to Tevi's side. "Are you all right?"

"I will be. I was a little careless, sir."

Ranenok frowned. "Get yourself into the watchtower. I'll send Hanno over. Do you need assistance?"

"No, sir."

"I'll be back as soon as we've got this bit cleared out." Commander Ranenok nodded and marched back to join his subordinates in the small tower. The battle would not take much longer.

Despite an annoying dizziness, Tevi made it inside unaided. The ground-floor room of the watchtower was deserted except for two bodies. Tevi leant against the door frame and looked around. The furniture consisted of a table and three rickety stools. Tevi did not think she had the balance required for the stools, so she simply collapsed onto the floor.

Hanno arrived shortly. He was the healer for the troop, based on some natural magical talent and a lot of experience. More soldiers followed him into the room. Some carried in injured comrades, while others removed the dead renegades.

Hanno knelt at Tevi's side. "How are you feeling?"

"A bit light-headed."

He nodded and carefully prodded the spot where the arrow protruded from her arm. "You're lucky. It's not poisoned."

Tevi clenched her teeth and stared over his shoulder. Still more soldiers were entering the room, and curiosity was their only apparent reason for being there. All of them were watching her, and the sound of voices made it clear that others were standing outside the room. The weight of attention was unwelcome. Tevi closed her eyes but could not block out the muttered comments.

"Jed reckoned that arrows bounced off her."

"Do you think she's really bleeding?"

"Looks like blood to me."

The voices died. Tevi opened her eyes to see that Ranenok had entered the room. The Commander glared around and then barked a string of commands. Within seconds, the gawking soldiers had vanished. Tevi closed her eyes again. The shock was ebbing, replaced by a touch of nausea. After the initial flare, the pain had faded to a dull ache, but now the fire was returning.

Hanno moved over to examine the other wounded soldiers. Ranenok stopped him with a harsh whisper. "Deal with Captain Tevirik first."

"This one is more seriously injured, sir."

"And she's worth six dozen like him."

"Yes, sir."

The sharp beat of Ranenok's footsteps left the room.

Tevi licked her lips. "I don't mind if you tend to someone else before me."

"I'm not about to disobey orders." Hanno again knelt by Tevi. For a minute longer, he examined her arm. "Right, first, we'll get rid of this. Lean forwards." He grasped the arrowhead. "Ready?"

Tevi clenched her teeth. The snap of wood triggered an explosion of agony in her shoulder. Before she had a chance to respond, a second quick movement from Hanno yanked the rest of the arrow shaft out. Immediately, the healer's hands pressed hard against the two wounds.

"Fine. That's the second-worst bit over with. We just need to wait for the bleeding to stop a bit." Hanno's voice sounded unnecessarily cheerful.

Fire was washing up and down Tevi's arm, from her neck to her fingers, in throbbing waves. She fought to get her breathing under control. "Does it look like blood to you?"

"Smells and feels like blood as well."

Tevi took another couple of deep breaths. "They don't think I'm really human, do they?"

"Are you surprised?"

"I'd have thought by now that they'd have got to know me."

"What they know is that you're three times as strong as anyone else in the army. And you're only half the size of some."

"I'm taller than most women."

"But not tall enough to account for your strength. They know it's not natural."

"Of course not. It's magic."

"But what sort of magic?" Hanno's tone was lightly teasing.

"It's a potion they brew in my home island."

"No one has ever seen you take it."

"I don't need to anymore. You have a spoonful every day while you're growing up and then the effect stays with you for life."

Hanno pursed his lips. "Well, I must admit I've heard that story about you before. But the other tales are much more fun."

"What other tales?"

"About you and the sorcerer."

"Jemeryl?" Tevi was talking mainly to distract herself.

"Yep."

"What do they say?"

"Well, some say that you're a demon she conjured up. Some say that you're a wild bear she changed into human form. And some say that she made you out of clay and then brought you to life. Since half the troop have seen you bleeding, I guess the bear theory will currently be winning. But overall, the other stories are more popular."

"Why?"

Hanno paused for a moment and looked at Tevi's face, as if judging her mood. "Everyone knows that the two of you are lovers. Demons have a bit of a reputation in that respect. While the clay golem stories allow people to speculate that she might have made various modifications to normal human anatomy."

Tevi's groan had nothing to do with her injury. "I don't think I want to hear."

"No. You probably don't."

"The other soldiers don't treat me like a monster."

"They're far too pleased to have you around. It gives them a nice, safe feeling to think they're going into battle behind an invincible fighting demon. That's why Ranenok said you're worth six dozen ordinary soldiers. It's not just the way you fight. You push up the troop's morale."

Hanno removed one of his hands and examined Tevi's shoulder. "That's the worst of the bleeding stopped. Now we'll get you clean and bandaged."

Going very carefully, so not to break open the wound, the healer removed the shoulder guard from Tevi's cuirass and cut open her undershirt. Then he washed the blood away and examined her arm with his eyes closed, using whatever paranormal abilities he possessed.

As she watched him, Tevi reflected that in the Protectorate, healers were the most respected of witches. In Bykoda's Empire their talents did not even merit a full army commission.

"It should heal fine. No bones chipped or tendons cut," Hanno said eventually. He pulled clean bandages from his bag and also a small flask of liquid. "Remember I said getting the arrow out was the second-worst bit? This will stop infection." His eyes met Tevi's briefly as he removed the cork from the flask. "But it's gonna sting."

Once her wound was treated and bandaged, Hanno wrapped a blanket around Tevi for warmth and studied her face for a few seconds. "You'll be all right. You're looking very pale, but I think it's just the contrast with your hair. You don't normally see anyone quite as dark as you." He patted her good shoulder, smiled, and went to see to the other injured soldiers.

Tevi leaned back carefully against the wall behind her. She felt exhausted, miserable, and bitter. Her black hair was just one more thing that marked her out as different from the rest of the army. In the northern lands, blonds predominated.

For the first few months after arriving in Tirakhalod, she had stayed with Jemeryl in the castle and had found it intolerable. Life had often been difficult in the Protectorate, where the gap between sorcerers and the ordinary ungifted population was a huge social chasm. But no matter how insignificant Jemeryl's fellow Coven sorcerers might think Tevi to be, they had to abide by their oath of allegiance to the Protectorate, which guaranteed the rights of everyone. Citizens could not be subjected to magic against their will. Citizens could not be murdered, mutilated, or enslaved on a sorcerer's whim. Citizens could speak their own mind, elect their own guild masters, live their own lives.

Life for the ungifted was not like that in Tirakhalod. Very soon, Tevi had realised she could not stay in the castle. Her reason for needing time away was not just that everyone treated her as Jemeryl's slave. It was that in allowing Tevi to have her own thoughts and treating her as an individual, Jemeryl was viewed as displaying an amusing yet perverse affectation. Jemeryl's familiar, the magpie Klara II, was taken more seriously.

Yet, Tevi could not abandon Jemeryl. Joining Bykoda's army had been a compromise. Tevi had promised that if she could spend half her time out with the ungifted soldiers, earning her place by fighting against bandits, trolls, werewolves, and other assorted monsters, then she would struggle to put up with the daily humiliations of life in the castle for the remaining period.

Jemeryl had not been happy, terrified of the risks Tevi took each time she went into battle. But in the circumstances, she could not deny Tevi the right to make up her own mind. Tevi grimaced at the thought. Now there would be another scar for Jemeryl to get upset about, and what could Tevi feel had been gained by it?

She clenched her teeth at the irony. She had spent months out with the common ungifted soldiers, people like herself, demonstrating her abilities in her bid to be seen as a person in her own right. She had fought with them, suffered with them, saved their lives. And they still gave all the credit to Jemeryl.

❖

Bykoda led the way down a series of stairs until they were deep underground. The passage had been hewn from the solid rock beneath the castle. Jemeryl could feel a chill radiating off the walls. The air smelt of mildew and mice.

The room they finally entered looked to be a store, either a treasury or an armoury—although, for a sorcerer empress like Bykoda, there was little difference between the two. A row of iron chests lined one wall. Books lay on a desk in the middle of the room. A large bookcase was filled with many more. Shelves held dozens of sealed bottles, crystals, charms, amulets, and some other artefacts that Jemeryl could not even name.

Bykoda unlocked one of the chests and took out a small wooden box, six inches square. Her expression was preoccupied, even wistful. She placed the box on the desk, but rather than open it immediately, she started to trace the carved pattern on the lid with her forefinger. When she spoke, her tone was dispassionate.

"I first received the oracle of my death four years ago. I was actually probing into another matter. It's the annoying thing with foretelling. You only ever find out what you don't want to know. I don't blame anyone for not liking them. I wish I hadn't bothered. It hasn't done me any good, and I never did get the answer to my original question."

"What did you see?"

"The moment of my death. I'm in my council chamber. It has to be one of the meetings I hold twice a year, because I'm sure that all of my acolytes are there, although I can't see them."

"Are you blinded?"

"No. I'm falling forwards out of my chair. My body feels like stone. A fist is squeezing around my heart. My lungs are blocked. And I can't turn my head, say a word, anything. All I can see is the lamplight shining on the floor tiles as they rush closer until I thump into them. The next thing is a crash as the crystal shields drop and shatter. And then someone starts to speak. But the blood is roaring in my ears, so I can't tell whose voice it is. I miss most of it. The only words that I get are '...and now you will die.' My face is pressed against the floor. My eyes are fixed on one of the windows. Through the glass I see the third-quarter moon. Then blue fire bursts over me and...I stop."

"Any other details?"

"No."

"Why do you think that your acolytes are there?"

Bykoda shrugged. "Just part of the foretelling. But I'm sure that they are, and that only happens at the council meeting."

"I imagine you've investigated the oracle further."

"Oh yes."

"What have you learned?"

"Nothing."

Jemeryl pursed her lips while she added up the implication. "Then it's certain."

"I fear so. Of course, I didn't simply give up. I tried everything I could think of, but it made no difference. It was after one of my failed attempts that I invited you here, by way of a backup plan. And I've been continuing with my efforts since, but it's looking inevitable."

"But you think that I can do something to prevent you being murdered?"

"No." Bykoda smiled sadly. "I'm reconciled to it."

Jemeryl frowned. "So what do you want me to do?"

"I'd actually be happy if you became my successor. I'd die that little bit easier, knowing my murderer wouldn't get to take over my Empire."

"Um...I don't think that—"

"It's all right. I know the offer doesn't interest you." Bykoda looked up. Her usual brisk manner returned. "Sight of the moon was the only piece of information that I've been able to make any use of. I spent some time lying on the floor of the council chamber, getting an exact fix on its position in my vision. Then I did a calculation of its phases. I've been able to narrow the date of my death down to three days this autumn. By which time you'll be safely back in Lyremouth."

"Oh, well before then. Tevi and I planned on leaving as soon as the passes over the Barrodens were open. Spring's on the way. We could go in about a month." Jemeryl hesitated. "Do you want me to stay longer? To do whatever it is that you want me to do?"

"No. Because all that I want is for you to take something back with you to the Protectorate."

Jemeryl was bewildered. How could any item be so critical? And how did it link into the oracle? "What?"

"This."

Bykoda opened the box. Lying at the bottom was a stone talisman in the form of a thick disc, carved to look like woven rope. Patterns in silver were inlaid on its surface. An ungifted observer would have seen nothing more to it, but Jemeryl could examine the talisman with all of a sorcerer's extended senses. Deep within the stone were other designs, nodes in the lines of power, links and branches. The talisman was one of the most complex constructions that Jemeryl had ever seen, and its purpose was not easy to discern.

"What does it do?"

"It can change the past."

Jemeryl glanced up sharply. "That's impossible."

"No. Just very difficult. And it's limited in scope. The only thing you can change with it is your own mind." Bykoda gave a wry smile and picked up the talisman. "My father was a carpenter; my mother was a silversmith. From them I got a knack for creating artefacts. This was one of my most ambitious experiments."

"Experiment? Does it work?"

"I believe so."

"Have you never tried?"

"Almost certainly. But then, the futures where I needed to use it never happened, so I have no knowledge of them. The temporal energy of the paradox is stored in the talisman."

Jemeryl took a few seconds to think. "So you can't ever be sure?"

"Not totally. But I know of three specific occasions, when I had fixed on a particular course of action, and then suddenly, for no reason, I did something different. With hindsight, all three of those switched decisions averted misfortune."

"They might just be coincidences."

"They might. Except that I'm not an impulsive person. I'd never have survived this long if I were. You'd have to be me to realise how out of character those spontaneous decisions were. They went in the face of all logic and available information. What I suspect is that, first time around, I went with the planned course of action, and when disaster struck, I used the talisman to reverse my previous decision."

Jemeryl stepped closer and stared at the talisman in amazement. Many attempts had been made to change the past. All had failed. Bykoda's claim was unbelievable, except that the Empress was the shrewdest realist Jemeryl had ever met, and certainly not the sort of person to indulge in wild boasting.

"Why do you want me to take this to Lyremouth with me?"

"Because it's no longer safe. I told you I believe I've used it successfully three times. However, there was one final occasion when I tried to use it and I was not at all successful. The talisman nearly ruptured and exploded in my face. I managed to lock it back down, but it was a close thing. That was over two decades ago and I haven't attempted to use it since."

"Do you know what went wrong?"

"I suspect that it was due to the situation more than the talisman. I had the choice of two candidates. I doubted the loyalty of one and the competence of the other. I made my decision on the basis that suitable threats could solve the loyalty issue, but nothing can be done with a fool. I was wrong, and the candidate betrayed me."

"You tried to use the talisman to change your choice of candidate?"

"Yes."

"So, isn't it poss—"

"I know what you're going to say. Three options: the first, that I'm sure you were going to point out, is that the talisman was inherently flawed all along and never worked. The other times I thought I'd used it were simple coincidence or due to getting a premonition without realising."

"What are the other options?"

"The second is that, rather than just three times, I've used it hundreds, or even thousands of times. So by now, the energy of the stored temporal paradoxes is on the point of becoming catastrophically unbalanced." Bykoda paused. "The third option is a variation on the second. Maybe both candidates produced their own version of a disaster and there was no right answer. Since, in using the talisman, I negate my knowledge of the future, I might have repeatedly picked one and then the other, putting a little more stress on the temporal web with each pass through, until time was at the point of rupture."

"That's your preferred option?"

"Yes."

Jemeryl frowned in thought. "Would the talisman be safe to use now that we're at a different point in the temporal web?"

"I wouldn't recommend trying. Whichever option is the right one, the talisman is unbalanced. I can't think of any emergency that would justify the risk. There's always another solution. Like with my disloyal candidate."

"What did you do?"

"I think you'd be happier not knowing the details. Let's just say that she never betrayed me again."

"Oh. Right." Jemeryl took a breath, forcing her thoughts on. "Why do you want me to take it to Lyremouth?"

"Ideally to have it unmade. But if not, to keep it safe."

"Unmade?"

"If it can be done safely."

"So why don't you unmake it?"

"Because it is going to take more than one sorcerer acting alone. Especially if she only has a few months left to do it in."

"I'm not sure if I ought to take it with me."

"You don't want to learn how I did it? Pry open its secrets?" Bykoda's voice was teasing. "I wouldn't have thought you'd be able to resist the temptation."

"I'm worried that it's too dangerous to have in the middle of Lyremouth. What if it caused a temporal cataclysm in the city? Hundreds of thousands would die."

"It's quite safe as long as you don't try to do anything with it. And I'm sure the Coven will be able to find a secure environment when they start to investigate. Plus, it wouldn't destroy a location so much as a series of causal relationships. *Somewhen* rather than *somewhere*. It's far more dangerous leaving it here. Supposing an errant sorcerer tried to reverse a decision that had a profound effect on the Protectorate? All the miles between Tirakhalod and Lyremouth would be no protection."

"Is there much chance of anyone doing that? Who, apart from you and me, knows about it?"

Bykoda sighed. Her rueful expression returned. "My acolytes. I mentioned it once as a threat. If ever they caused trouble, I'd use the talisman to retrospectively cut their heads off before they became a problem. But I didn't allow for the temptation the talisman presents. I'm fairly certain that I'm going to be murdered by someone who wants the talisman for themself. That was another strong impression I got from the foretelling."

"Have you tried telling your acolytes that the talisman is now unsafe to use?"

"Yes. It made no difference. I suspect my assassin realised I was only saying it in an attempt to stop them from killing me and hasn't worked out that this doesn't necessarily mean I'm lying."

"If somebody made a decision in the past that they desperately want to reverse, maybe your talisman is simply too great a lure. Your murderer won't believe it is unusable because they don't want to believe it."

"It must be something like that. Which means if they get it, they will try to use it." Bykoda took the talisman from the box and pressed it into Jemeryl's palm, making her fingers close in reflex around it. "So much of my life is bound up in the talisman. If it ruptures, I don't know what it would do to me. That is why I want you to keep it safe." The elderly sorcerer looked up and met Jemeryl's eyes sadly. "I can come to terms with dying, but I don't want to risk never having lived."

CHAPTER TWO—THE COUNCIL CHAMBER

Turrets and battlements encrusted the top of the cliff face, grim against the darkening sky. The road leading to the gates ran beneath the heavy walls. Looming over all was Bykoda's keep, a foursquare solid mass devoid of ornamentation. The weight of the tower seemed to crush the spirits of the troops marching along the road.

Sunset was not far off, and the wind had increased its bite, but it was not the chill that made Tevi hunch her shoulders. Her stomach clenched at the thought of entering the castle. She tried to stop herself from glancing up apprehensively, tried to stop herself from brooding on the days ahead. The exercise was pointless. Her mood was falling with each clop of her horse's hooves. The first darts of sleet stung Tevi's face. Yet not even the threat of the coming storm made her look more fondly on the promise of shelter ahead.

The castle was built on a wedge-shaped hill. At the apex, with sheer rock faces on two sides, was Bykoda's keep. The road entered the outer bailey at the bottom end. The column of troops marched beneath the gatehouse in silence. Tevi wondered if they were any more pleased than she was to be back at Tirakhalod. The line of bound prisoners certainly would not be.

The outer bailey occupied the lower, eastern side of the hill. This was by far the largest of the three sections that made up the castle. Barracks, stores, stables, and training grounds were laid out here. Most ordinary soldiers, the lucky ones, would never enter the higher baileys. As she rode past, Tevi looked at one of the barrack buildings. Would she be happier living there with the other ungifted soldiers? But she knew that she did not fit in with them any more than she did with the officers.

Tevi grimaced as she thought again of her anomalous position, the only ungifted officer in the army. But, of course, a sorcerer's favourite could not be treated as a common soldier, even though that was all Tevi had wanted. Many officers clearly resented her status. Everyone else with the rank of lieutenant upwards possessed magical ability. Although, according to Jemeryl, few were anything more than low-grade witches.

The road bent round, climbing towards the inner parts of the castle. The column marched on in formation until a second gatehouse rose above the road ahead. Bands of cloud were swallowing the sunset, hastening the onset of night. The black stone walls were fading into the dusk. Guttering torches marked the entrance.

Commander Ranenok signalled a halt, and the military beat of footsteps stopped. The rush of the wind sounded louder in the following quiet. Ranenok rode back down the line of foot soldiers for a final inspection. Then, at his nod, the sergeants barked commands and the troops broke from the line to drift off into the night in search of food, warmth, and sleep. Tevi watched them go.

Fresh troops arrived to escort the captives to the prison in the middle bailey, but these were markedly different in character from those who had left. Ordinary soldiers did not enter the higher sections of the castle unless they were bound in some way, either by chains like the prisoners or, as with the new guards, by magic stealing their minds. The sight of the ensorcelled thralls with their expressionless faces tightened the knot in Tevi's stomach. She considered that the deserters with their shackles were the less wretched group.

Ranenok and the other captain, Altrun, had dismounted. Tevi likewise slipped down from her horse and handed the reins to one of the thralls. Two others removed her saddlebags and stood waiting.

From experience, Tevi knew that the thralls would follow her and deposit the bags where indicated. She did not know how the thralls received their orders, since spoken commands had no effect on them; nor did she want to know. Some form of magic was involved. Thankfully, Jemeryl refused to have them as servants in her quarters.

Thralls never deserted and never disobeyed orders, but their total lack of reflexes for self-preservation meant that they performed very poorly as soldiers in battle. In overwhelming numbers, they were terrifying. In a tough fight, they would all be dead within seconds. Even asking them to run was hazardous, as they would crash heedlessly into anything that stood in their way. If not for this, Tevi was sure Bykoda would have destroyed the mind of every ordinary soldier in her army.

Captain Altrun had already gone through the gatehouse. Now Ranenok and the line of thralls marched forwards, taking the prisoners with them. Tevi followed on, trailing her small retinue of bearers.

The middle bailey held the more important castle functions: the officers' quarters, the forge, the armoury, the apothecary, and also the prison. The location of this last building in the middle bailey was not for security reasons. Prisoners were only taken so that Bykoda's witches could use them as experimental subjects. If the captives were lucky, they would die very quickly. No trial was ever held. Most likely, they had committed some crime and thus were better candidates to sacrifice than loyal troops or rounded-up civilians, who would otherwise provide the test material.

Captain Altrun had taken word of their arrival, and two witches were already waiting with him at the jail entrance, but before the prisoners could be herded inside, the door to the apothecary opened and a woman emerged.

"Wait a moment." Dunarth, Bykoda's chief alchemist, trotted down the steps. "Good timing. I need someone."

The prisoners were brought to a halt and shepherded into a line. Dunarth dithered her way up and down the row, thinking aloud. "I don't want anyone too small, if they're to—" She broke off in front of a granite-faced man who towered head and shoulders over her. "No, no. I think I'll keep you for...um, maybe..." Her attention shifted to the woman chained beside him.

Dunarth was of middling height and years. Grey was softening her honey blonde hair. Her body tended to plumpness. Her face was round and bland. She looked and sounded like a housewife selecting carrots for the evening meal. And clearly, Dunarth was taking no more sadistic pleasure in her current task than a housewife dropping chopped vegetables into the pot, nor suffering from any greater guilt.

Tevi fought to keep her expression impassive. In her mind, the absence of malice made it worse. Dunarth could not see the prisoners as fellow humans or feel empathy for their plight. Admittedly, it was possible that this current experiment would not be fatal. It might even be harmless, designed to improve the performance of Bykoda's troops, rather then kill her enemies, but there would always be the next test. Before long, all the prisoners would be dead, and they knew it.

At the end of the line nearest Tevi was a young man, scarcely more than a boy, sixteen or seventeen, she judged. His eyes met hers, pleading in wordless terror. Tears trickled down his face. Tevi clenched her teeth, feeling responsible for the role she had played in his capture. What was he guilty of, other than being in the wrong platoon? He could not have defied the renegade lieutenant and lived. Yet Tevi also knew that she had no real choice herself. Judging by the string of sacked villages the renegade lieutenant had left behind, her plans had involved creating a bandit gang on the outskirts of the Empire. Tevi remembered the burnt-out farms and dead families she had seen while they pursued the deserters.

And regardless of justice, there was nothing Tevi could do. She turned away sharply and marched on. Strictly speaking, she had not been dismissed, but she doubted that Commander Ranenok would call her to account, and she could not bear to stand and see which prisoner Dunarth would pick.

The road up the hill reached the last of the three gatehouses. Beyond it lay the inner bailey where Bykoda's keep was sited. Also in this section of the castle were the quarters for her six acolytes and other favoured individuals such as Jemeryl. Thralls guarded the entrance. Few were allowed inside. As Tevi approached, an officer appeared and held up a hand for her to stop.

"What is your business?" The man's tone was curt and contemptuous.

"I'm here to see the sorcerer Jemeryl."

"Has she asked for you?"

"No. She doesn't know I've returned to Tirakhalod yet."

"Wait here. I will send a messenger to find out if she wishes you to be granted entrance."

"I think you'll find—" Tevi bit off her words with a sigh of irritation.

Arguing was pointless. She could do no more than glare at the officer as he went through the charade of dispatching a thrall with the written message. She did not recognise the man but had no doubt that he recognised her. Her notoriety as an ungifted officer and a sorcerer's lover would ensure that.

Jemeryl would want to see her as quickly as possible, and the officer would know it. However, his tabard bore only a lieutenant's badge and that, Tevi judged, was the cause for his confrontational behaviour. So many witches took it as a personal insult to be outranked by someone ungifted like herself. He was clearly one of them, and he was going to make the most of his post as gatekeeper to put her in her place.

Footsteps sounded behind Tevi. Before she could turn her head to see whose, Ranenok's voice rang out. "What's the holdup here?"

The lieutenant snapped to attention. "Sir. I've sent a message to Madam Jemeryl to inform her that Captain Tevirik is here."

"Why not send the captain straight through?"

"Sir, my instructions are that—"

Ranenok cut him off. "Don't bother about that. You should have the sense to use your own discretion. Let her through."

"Yes, sir."

The thralls melted out of their path, yet Tevi saw the venom in the lieutenant's eyes grow. Doubtless he was adding the implied reprimand that he had received to the list of his grievances against her. The fault lay with him and his childishness, not her, but that would not matter.

Ranenok and Tevi emerged from under the gatehouse into the wide expanse of the inner bailey. Although it was the smallest of the three, the hexagonal area was still over two hundred yards across. The gatehouse stood in one corner. Directly opposite, the keep blotted out the last remnants of light in the western sky. Towers marked the other four corners. These were not small, yet appeared so by comparison with the huge keep.

A garden filled the open space in the middle, its beauty incongruous with the menacing surroundings. A wooden summerhouse overlooked a lily pond. Statues stood amid the flowers. Blossom-covered trees lined the walkways. And, thanks to Bykoda's magic, blossoms still covered the trees, even at the end of winter.

Distant thunder echoed over the darkening castle. The scent of roses on the wind was mingled with that of impending rain. Tevi was eager to get indoors. She bid the commander good night and headed off to her left.

"Captain Teverik, if you could spare a moment." Ranenok hailed her.

"Yes, sir?" Tevi turned back.

Ranenok was a tall man with the solid build of a soldier. He looked to be at least sixty, although still fit and forceful. He had clearly led an active life. His left arm ended in a stump at the elbow and a long scar puckered his right cheek, narrowly missing his eye.

As Bykoda's acolyte, Ranenok had quarters in the inner bailey. He was one of the three army commanders. The others were in charge of the army to the north and the south. Ranenok's forces formed the castle guard and patrolled the immediate surroundings. Tevi could admit to a genuine respect for him. She definitely had found serving under him far less difficult than she might. He was competent and fair-minded, and acted as though he seriously believed that he was responsible for the protection of all Bykoda's citizens, rather than just the Empress herself.

"I believe that Madam Jemeryl will be heading back to the Protectorate soon." A hint of a question marked Ranenok's voice.

"I think so, sir. Jemeryl said she was almost ready to go. Just waiting for the passes over the Barrodens to open."

"And you'll be going with her?"

"Oh, yes." Tevi tried not to sound too eager.

"If you wanted to stay, there'd be a place for you among my troops. And you can keep your rank of captain."

"Sir? But I'm just an ordinary, ungifted mercenary."

"Hardly." Ranenok smiled at Tevi's confusion. "I don't hold much hope that you can so easily abandon Jemeryl, but I wanted you to know that the offer was there." He nodded. "Good night."

"Good night, sir." Tevi frowned at his back, retreating into the twilight and then turned towards the tower where Jemeryl had her quarters.

The darkness was now thick enough that the glowing ring of small spheres had appeared above the path around the walls, sufficient to light the way. The promised rain was starting to fall in earnest, driven on the cold wind, though it could not put out the mage lights. The two thralls with the saddlebags continued following Tevi around the outside of the garden, into the tower, and up the staircase.

The lower floors belonged to Mavek, the blacksmith. Tevi hoped she would not run into him—not that she disliked the man, but he would probably want to drag her back to the forge to demonstrate his latest project. Normally, his friendliness and enthusiasm were a welcome change to the cold antagonism of most others. Tonight, Tevi just wanted to see Jemeryl and rest.

Fortunately, there was no sign of the blacksmith and Tevi reached Jemeryl's quarters unhindered. The thralls dropped the bags just inside the doorway at the spot indicated and then left. The sound brought Jemeryl running from another room.

"Tevi. I got the message from the gate. You're back."

There was no need to reply to the obvious statement, nor the opportunity, since Jemeryl immediately flung herself into Tevi's arms and kissed her fervently. Tevi winced as the onslaught twanged the wound in her shoulder. Jemeryl pulled back.

"Are you all right?"

"My shoulder. It's nothing much, but—"

Tevi did not get the chance to finish. Almost before she realised it, she was sitting before the fire with Jemeryl fussing around, bringing cushions, setting out food and drink, removing her boots, inspecting the wound—all interspersed with quick kisses planted on any part of Tevi that was to hand.

The hectic barrage showed no sign of abating. At last, Tevi caught hold of Jemeryl's arm and pulled her down so that they were looking into each other's eyes.

"I'm all right. Honest I am."

"Well, yes, but..." Abruptly, Jemeryl calmed, while her gaze grew more intense. "I've missed you."

Tevi felt her insides melt. She could happily lose her soul staring into Jemeryl's eyes. All the doubts and strains of the previous hour were irrelevant. For the first time since the walls of Tirakhalod had broken the horizon, Tevi felt at peace.

Perhaps I'm wrong to leave Tirakhalod, Tevi thought. *Being outside the castle doesn't help. Perhaps I should just stay in these rooms and not meet anyone else until it's time for us to return to the Protectorate. Jemeryl is the only one I need.*

❖

Jemeryl worked on controlling her reactions while she listened to the details of the battle with the deserters and came to terms with the risks that her lover had taken. She understood Tevi's reasons for wanting time away from the castle. Getting upset would only make Tevi feel guilty, and Jemeryl did not want to use emotional pressure. She was determined to keep tight control of her fears for just a little while longer. Very soon, they would be returning to the Protectorate, and the dangers and stresses of Bykoda's Empire would be behind them.

The fire was burning low, although the room was still warm and cosy and felt all the more so by comparison with the sound of the storm raging outside. Jemeryl sat beside Tevi on a couch, shoulders touching, fingers interlaced. In her free hand she held a glass of red wine. She lifted it up, watching the firelight through its distorting lens. On the armrest, her familiar, the magpie Klara II, was busy preening her wings.

"So how have things been here at the castle?" Tevi asked.

"I've pretty much learnt everything I wanted from Bykoda, although I could easily spend another year here, picking up a few extra bits and bobs." Jemeryl took a sip of wine. "And I did find out something unexpected. Bykoda's going to be assassinated."

"What! Who by?"

"She didn't know."

"But she isn't very pleased about it," Klara added.

Tevi let go of Jemeryl's hand and swivelled to face her. "Bykoda told you herself?"

"Yes."

"Why doesn't she do something about it?"

"She can't. She found out from casting an oracle."

"What difference does that make?"

Jemeryl laughed softly. "It's the temporal paradox. Supposing you cast an oracle and find out about something you don't want to happen and therefore are able to stop it. Then it wouldn't have happened, so you'd have been unable to foretell it from the oracle in the first place. That's what people usually mean by temporal paradox. However, to my mind, the real paradox is that the more useless the information, the easier it is to find out."

"How does that stop Bykoda from protecting herself?"

"She can try anything she wants. But the mere fact she was able to get the information means that nothing she does is going to work."

"What?"

Jemeryl smiled at the confusion on Tevi's face and tried to think of an explanation. "Supposing I were to cast an oracle to find out if the sun was going to rise tomorrow, then it would be very easy to get an answer, because there is nothing that anyone can do with the information to make the prediction not come true. However, the more potential that the oracle has to negate its own accuracy, then the more energy it takes to break through the resulting paradoxes. To get any real, practical advice is virtually impossible."

"So oracles are useless."

"They can be handy for betting on horse races," Klara said.

Tevi ignored the magpie. "I thought some sorcerers made a specialty of foretelling the future."

"They try. But it's mainly done in a negative way. For example—" Jemeryl indicated the door. "Supposing I'm about to go out and I cast an oracle to see if it's safe. If there was no problem, then the oracle should be straightforward, since the information won't affect my actions. But if I couldn't get an answer, it implies that knowing the future would change things. However, I'd have no idea how they would change. If a dragon is outside, then I'd want to stay put. If the building is about to catch fire, then I'd want to get out quickly, rather than hang around wasting time trying to work out what the oracle meant."

Tevi gave a wry smile. "And I guess that most things people consult oracles about are far more complex than whether or not to go outside."

"Quite. The art of professional fortune-tellers is in trying to work out inferences based on what they can't find out."

Klara hopped onto Jemeryl's lap. "Which is how they come up with advice like, *When the third cow crosses the river, listen for the yellow rain*."

Jemeryl stroked her familiar's head with her forefinger. "In my opinion, you're better off flipping a coin."

"Bykoda's found out she's going to be murdered," Tevi said.

"Which only means that the knowledge is useless."

"Except she now knows she needn't put a bottle of her favourite wine aside for her next birthday," Klara said.

Tevi looked at the magpie. "Next birthday? It's going to happen soon?"

"This coming autumn," Jemeryl answered.

"Does she know anything else?"

"She'll die in her council chamber. She's sure the assassin is one of her acolytes, but has no idea which one."

"Then why not kill all six of them? I can't see Bykoda being held back by scruples."

"Her death is inevitable, so one of the replacement acolytes would be her murderer. Removing the original acolyte would merely be the ironic action that allowed the real murderer to get close."

"Or not, if she doesn't do it," Klara added.

Tevi slipped down in the seat, her face knotted in a frown.

"What are you thinking?" Jemeryl asked eventually.

"Trying to work out which of the acolytes I could see as the assassin."

"It's a tricky one. I'd have said that none of them had the strength to challenge Bykoda. She's very careful about who she has around her. The acolytes are the only people in the castle other than her who'd have any chance of being counted as sorcerers in the Coven. They have some awareness of all seven dimensions, but they all have major weaknesses, which is why Bykoda selected them in the first place."

"How about the army commanders? They could use their junior officers to help. The juniors might only be witches, but if they all followed their commander, they might stand a chance."

"Not the way Bykoda has split the army. Anid and Yenneg have to leave their troops behind when they come to Tirakhalod for meetings. Ranenok has people in place here, but his section of the army is by far the smallest. I doubt he could muster the resources to pose a threat."

"Supposing Yenneg rebelled and brought his troops down from the north?"

"It can't have escaped your notice that all three army commanders hate each other. At the first sign from Yenneg, Anid would be leaping for the chance to attack. And the thought of Yenneg seizing power would guarantee Ranenok's help to stop him."

"It can't have been easy to find three people who are so mutually antagonistic."

"I suspect Bykoda's been tampering with their emotions. That's how she makes sure that the army will never unite against her."

"Could Bykoda do that? I thought sorcerers could protect their minds against magic."

"Not those three. From what I can tell, the army commanders can perceive all the paranormal dimensions well enough, but they are very weak in their ability to manipulate what's there." Jemeryl swirled the wine in her glass thoughtfully. "If you want an analogy with the four normal dimensions, it would be somebody who could see where a bell is, and hear it when it rings, but doesn't have the muscles or coordination to pick it up and shake it. They need someone else to build them a rope-and-pulley arrangement. Hence the commanders can command thralls, send messages using orbs, and wield the weapons Mavek and Dunarth make. But they could never challenge Bykoda."

"What about the other acolytes?"

"They have their strengths and weaknesses. Dunarth is very good with the life forces of the fifth dimension but can hardly light a candle using the elemental power of the sixth. Mavek is the opposite. Which is why he's the blacksmith and she's the alchemist."

"And Kharel, the steward?"

"She's probably the best all-round sorcerer of the acolytes. She's pretty rare among magic users in that she's able to make real use of the seventh dimension. The temporal dimension is used for prophesy, which is how she makes sure the castle doesn't run low on supplies."

"Doesn't the temporal paradox get in the way?"

Jemeryl laughed. "You need to set up the system right and be very sharp in monitoring it. Maybe Kharel's big talent is in realising that you should use oracles to warn about running out of flour and not expect them to stop you from making a mess of your life."

"So is Kharel the best candidate for assassin?"

"I don't know. The big problem is that Bykoda has foreseen she'll be murdered in her council chamber, which is possibly the place where she has her strongest defences. Kharel may be the best balanced of the acolytes, but she isn't strong. Bykoda has always been wary about threats. I'm the only really competent sorcerer Bykoda has ever allowed inside the castle."

"Do you know why she doesn't feel threatened by you?"

"She knows I'm not the one who's going to kill her. I'm not one of her acolytes. My ambitions lie with the Protectorate. And I've finally found out why she invited me here in the first place. She wants me to do something for her."

"What?"

"It's another long story."

Tevi yawned. "In that case it can wait until tomorrow."

"Aren't you curious?"

"Of course. But if it's something really vital, I can't imagine you'd have spent all this time talking about everything else."

"And you don't want to wait until Tevi's too tired to do anything except sleep before you go to bed," Klara said.

Jemeryl laughed and pushed the impertinent magpie off her lap.

❖

The council chamber was on the ground floor of Bykoda's keep. Tevi and Jemeryl stopped just inside the large double doorway and looked around. The room was about forty feet square. From the floor to the rafters was at least thirty. On the opposite side of the room, the morning sunlight fell through three tall, clear glass windows and lay in gleaming oblongs on the marble floor. The stone walls were bare of paintings, tapestries, or carvings.

The lack of furniture increased the feeling of austerity. Six wrought-iron chairs for the acolytes stood in a line to the right. Facing them was Bykoda's throne. All the chairs were placed close to the walls, so that a clear thirty feet of tiled floor would separate Bykoda from her acolytes at meetings. A balcony ran the length of the room above the row of chairs. The only other items in the room were two large green crystals suspended by chains from the ceiling. They hung five feet in front of Bykoda's throne and a little way out on either side.

Four thralls stood guard in the corners, unmoving. Their glazed faces showed no response to Tevi and Jemeryl's arrival. Tevi looked at one, shivered, and looked away. Jemeryl advanced to the centre of the room.

Tevi joined her by one of the suspended crystals. "You said that Bykoda has herself well protected in here. Can I assume these crystals are part of her defence?"

"Yes. They project a shield in front of them."

"Can you see through it?"

"Oh yes. It's completely invisible. In fact, it's in place at the moment."

Tevi frowned and waved her hand back and forth through the space between the crystals. "It doesn't seem terribly effective."

Jemeryl smiled. "It's actually rather sophisticated. Have you got a projectile to hand? A coin would do nicely."

Tevi nodded and dug one out of the purse on her belt.

"Right. Now stand by Bykoda's throne and pretend you're her, throwing a weapon at one of the acolytes."

Tevi obliged. The coin bounced off one of the central iron chairs. Tevi treated Jemeryl to a sideways look. "You're not playing games with me, are you?"

"No. Now go and pretend you're one of the acolytes throwing a weapon at Bykoda. And be ready to duck."

Tevi walked a dozen paces across the tiled floor and bent to retrieve the coin. After another bemused frown at Jemeryl, she tossed the coin. Halfway across the room the coin hit a barrier and came hurling back, with three times the velocity that it had before. Tevi just managed to get out of its way.

"And it isn't just ordinary missiles. The crystals would do the same to any sort of magical attack as well. I'm sure you won't mind if I don't demonstrate," Jemeryl said cheerfully.

"So she can lob whatever she wants at her acolytes, and they can't do anything to retaliate."

"Uh-huh."

"She doesn't trust them, does she?"

"Well, one of them *is* going to murder her."

"Is it possible to punch through the shield with enough force?"

"I couldn't. Which means that none of the acolytes stand a chance."

Tevi walked back to the throne. "So whoever hits her has to be standing in this end of the room."

"Except Bykoda isn't going to blithely sit here and let one of the acolytes walk through the shield to kill her. The assassin would be smoking ash before they'd taken five steps."

Tevi studied the room thoughtfully. Only bare stone surrounded the throne. The door and all the windows were on the other side of the shield. "Could she be attacked between here and the door?"

"No. Because she gets safely in place before the acolytes are allowed in."

"How about some sort of booby trap in the chair?"

Jemeryl tilted her head to one side, thinking. "I don't know."

Tevi lay down and examined the underside of the chair, but before her eyes had adjusted to the dark, Jemeryl spoke with a warning note in her voice. "Um...Tevi. Unless you have something definite in mind it might be a good idea to stop that."

Tevi pulled back and glanced around. All of the thralls were staring in her direction, swords drawn. She stood up. "They didn't like me doing that?"

"They certainly didn't. If I hadn't held them back, you'd currently have several rather serious perforations."

Tevi took a deep breath and grimaced. "Right."

"I'd guess that the possibility of a booby-trap has already occurred to Bykoda, and she's set the thralls to respond to anyone who looks like they're tinkering."

"But you were able to restrain them. Couldn't the acolytes do the same?"

"Not without alerting Bykoda. She will have felt me blocking the thralls just now. When we've finished here, I'll find her and explain what we were doing and why."

Once Tevi was standing away from the throne, the thralls went back to their original pose. Jemeryl stood in front of the nearest one, staring into the blank eyes.

"What are you thinking?" Tevi asked.

"I'm wondering just how comprehensive their instructions are. There are good and bad points to using thralls as guards. They don't get distracted, or fall asleep, or lose concentration. However, they are limited to doing exactly what they're told and nothing else."

"The instructions wouldn't need to be complex."

"But it's easy to leave holes. For example, these thralls might have been told to attack anyone they see tampering with the throne. Which means they would completely ignore someone who hid themself and the chair under a blanket before fitting the trap. Or if they're supposed to monitor everyone who comes through the door, they wouldn't bother with anyone who climbs through the window." Jemeryl sighed. "They have no initiative whatsoever."

Tevi's lips twisted as she fought to control her disgust. "It's immoral. They're worse than slaves. It would be kinder to kill them."

"I tend to agree with you. If it's any consolation, it's one of the things that Coven rules specifically forbid in the Protectorate."

Tevi grunted, unconsoled. She had not before even considered the idea that the Coven would need to ban its members from enthralling citizens and was unhappy that Jemeryl did not seem to fully share her disgust at the barbarism. Partly to distract the uncomfortable thought, Tevi paced back to the acolyte's chairs and turned around. "Does the shield go all the way across the room?"

"How do you mean?"

"I was wondering about using a ricochet to get around it."

Jemeryl came to stand by Tevi and considered the crystals. "There's a gap of a foot or two at either side, and a slightly smaller one at the top. It reaches the floor completely. It would be hard to bounce anything off with enough force to hurt her. Quite apart from being a very tricky shot."

Tevi pointed up. "What about the chains? Could you hit them and bring the shield down?"

"Oh. There's a thought." Jemeryl stood on tiptoe, then on the seat of one of the iron chairs, and finally jumped up and down. "Maybe. But I think you'd need to be about ten feet in the air."

"I don't suppose Bykoda would be likely to overlook someone climbing a ladder in the middle of a council meeting." Tevi sighed and looked up. "Or supposing they were standing up there." She pointed to the balcony above the acolyte's chairs. Without waiting for Jemeryl's answer, Tevi headed for the door.

From the outside, Bykoda's keep looked like a solid cube of stone. In fact, the middle was hollow. Tevi emerged into the enclosed central courtyard. Immediately to her left, a single flight of stairs ran up the side of the wall. Tevi climbed the steps and opened the door at the top. When she stepped through, she found herself back in the council chamber, looking down from the balcony. A few seconds later, she was joined by Jemeryl.

"What's this balcony used for?"

"Various things. I've sat here to listen to the meeting, if it's something Bykoda doesn't mind me hearing."

"I thought she trusted you."

"Don't be silly. Bykoda doesn't trust anyone. However, I suspect that the bits she hides from me are the things that might trouble my conscience."

"You aren't tempted to find out what they are?"

"No. I want to sleep at night." Jemeryl rested her shoulder against the wall and looked down on the chamber. "The other things this balcony is used for is when people other than the acolytes need to give reports. Or occasionally she has a prisoner up here when she's using the council for a trial."

Tevi was surprised. "Bykoda bothers with trials?"

"Very occasionally. Usually for ulterior motives."

A bench ran along the wall at the back. Tevi sat down. "I don't envy you having to spend so much time with her."

"We get on all right. She's not bad company as a person and..." Jemeryl frowned, choosing her words. "I respect her. She has phenomenal ability. She's utterly ruthless, but she'd never have carved out her Empire if she wasn't. You've seen the worst of it here at Tirakhalod, but for most of her realm, the ordinary people get on with their lives in safety. Her army keeps out trolls, bandits, and werewolves. Much of her magic goes to improving harvests, if only to feed the troops. When she dies, people around here will be a lot worse off until another strong sorcerer comes along to build the next empire. Bykoda can be cruel, but she never hurts people simply for amusement. The next emperor may have a different idea of entertainment."

Tevi shrugged. She was not convinced, but rather than pursue the topic she pointed at the chains holding up the crystals. "So, could someone up here break the chains?"

"Not easily."

"Why not?"

Jemeryl hauled Tevi to her feet and positioned her so she was looking along the length of the balcony rail. "There. Can you see the faint shimmering?"

"Oh yes."

"It's a good old-fashioned, let nothing through either way type elemental barrier. This one I could smash my way through. Mavek probably could as well, although I doubt any of the other acolytes would be up to it. But Mavek couldn't break through if he's sitting downstairs at the time."

"Mavek's adept at creating magical weapons. Couldn't he make something for an accomplice to break the field and then the chains? Once it's down he could hit Bykoda from below."

"They wouldn't have time. Even if the accomplice was able to break through from the balcony, Bykoda would have got them before they had a chance to launch a second attack on the chains. It's a question of timing, it won't—" Jemeryl broke off suddenly.

"What is it?"

"Thinking about timing. I've just remembered something Bykoda said. Her vision had her in pain and collapsing. But only after she'd hit the floor did she hear the crash of the crystals dropping. Which means she must initially be attacked while the shield is in place."

Although Tevi could not understand the magic, she was able to pull a simple conclusion from what Jemeryl had told her. "The only option is that the chair is booby-trapped."

Jemeryl shrugged. "The only other possibility is that one of the acolytes is pretending to be far weaker than they really are. But I don't want to think about what sort of power it would take to punch through the crystal shield. I don't know whether to be relieved or disappointed that we'll be back in Lyremouth by then and may never find out."

"I think I'll settle for *relieved*."

"That's because you don't have my professional curiosity on the subject." Jemeryl smiled. "Come on. Let's go. I need to explain to Bykoda about you, the throne, and the thralls."

CHAPTER THREE—AN ANTISOCIAL GATHERING

The room was lit by mage lights which had been adjusted to cast a warm hue. If the hope had been to engender a welcoming atmosphere, it was failing miserably. The twenty or so guests were emanating waves of frosty antagonism. The hall was large enough to have taken ten times the number with ease. This allowed the little groups to form like islands, with only glares crossing the gulfs between them.

Tapestries made the room less austere than others Tevi had seen in Bykoda's keep. Dark wood panelling showed in the gaps between the hangings. The chairs dotted at the edges were elegantly carved, with velvet cushions, but none of them were currently in use, possibly because nobody wanted to be at the disadvantage of looking up at everyone else.

The social gathering held no prospect of being fun, and the presence of thralls did not help Tevi's mood. Armed guards stood at strategic points around the walls in their solemn black armour. Their faces were lost in the shadow of their helmets, but Tevi imagined their lifeless eyes, watching the room but seeing nothing. A row of domestic thralls with platters of food and drink waited to one side.

Jemeryl and Tevi were among the last to join the gathering. Kharel, the steward, stood at the doorway to greet new arrivals. She was a tall, skeletally thin woman of about sixty. Like several other sorcerers Tevi had met, Kharel had the unsettling habit of never truly focusing on the person she was talking to. On the few occasions that Tevi had needed to speak with the steward, she'd had to fight the continual urge to look back over her shoulder to see what was going on behind her.

Kharel gave a small nod of greeting. "Jemeryl. Please allow me, on behalf of the Empress Bykoda, to welcome you to this gathering." Her voice was stilted, as if she were quoting from a script.

"It was gracious of Bykoda to invite us."

Tevi controlled a scowl that might have undermined Jemeryl's tactful reply. *Command* would have been a better word than *invite*.

Kharel continued. "I'm sure you will excuse Bykoda for not being here in person."

"Of course."

"Food and drink are available. Bykoda hopes that you will enjoy yourself."

"Thank you."

"And I'm sure that you are eager to make merry with your fellow sorcerers."

"Er...yes." For a moment, Jemeryl looked lost for words.

Tevi decided that the steward's last remark could be taken as terminating the conversation and, discreetly but firmly, towed her partner away. She suspected that Jemeryl had been fighting the urge either to laugh or indulge in blunt honesty, and neither would have been wise. At the best of times, the other sorcerers were not people who made you think of the word *merry*, and this was certainly not the best of times.

On a daily basis, the acolytes conspicuously avoided each other as much as their work would allow. Large social events were a rare occurrence in Tirakhalod. However, the army commanders, Anid and Yenneg, were at the castle for a briefing with Bykoda. Normally they were stationed at their regional headquarters many miles away. The Empress had decided to take advantage of their presence by holding a reception for all six acolytes.

Jemeryl and a few others had also received invitations, phrased in such a way as to let the recipient know that refusal was not an option. Although there had been no direct mention of Tevi, Jemeryl had been given permission to bring two associates with her. However, the prospect of the gathering had been so grim that Tevi required several hours of pleading before she had agreed to keep Jemeryl company.

After helping themselves to wine, they wandered to a clear patch of floor. A few eyes tracked their movement, but the attention did not stay on them for long, and the hostile stares soon reverted to more deeply disliked, long-standing rivals. If looks could kill, the gathering would have been over in seconds with a total absence of survivors.

Tevi leaned closer to Jemeryl and whispered, "When do they break out the fiddle and start the barn dance?"

Jemeryl half choked on her wine. Once she had recovered, she grinned back at Tevi. "I'm so pleased you're here. I wouldn't want to be on my own. Thanks."

"You could have brought Klara."

"Talking to your familiar would be rather childish in a situation like this."

"Do you think they view talking to me as any more mature?"

"Who cares? And if it all gets too much, we can just stand in a corner and suck face. And it really wouldn't be acceptable if I did that with Klara."

Tevi could not stop herself from laughing. "Well, just remember. You owe me for it."

"I don't want to be here any more than you do."

"I think it says something that Bykoda herself isn't showing up."

"Oh, she's probably here, just not in person."

"In what way?"

Jemeryl nodded towards the guards. "I'd guess she's mind-riding one of the thralls. That way she gets to eavesdrop but can't be assassinated."

Commander Ranenok left his two junior officers and came over to join them. Once the bland exchange of greetings was over, he turned more purposefully to Jemeryl. "I'd like to thank you for the use of Captain Tevirik's services over these last two and a half years."

"Nothing to thank me for. It was her decision."

Ranenok's nod gave the impression that he did not fully believe her. "Well then, thank you for not withholding your permission."

Tevi clenched her jaw. She respected Ranenok as much as she did anyone in Tirakhalod, and she knew that he valued her as an officer. Yet he still clearly viewed her as Jemeryl's possession.

"Tevi doesn't need—"

"I'm a free citizen of the Protectorate, and a member of the Guild of Mercenary Warriors. Only my guild masters could refuse me permission to take any given military employment. And Jemeryl isn't a guild master."

Tevi had interrupted Jemeryl deliberately and saw with satisfaction the surprise on Ranenok's face. His eyes shot to Jemeryl as if looking for signs of outrage. Instead he saw her calmly sip her wine. Tevi wondered if now Ranenok might believe that she was truly a free agent. Or would he just assume that Jemeryl was playing games with him?

"Um...You've no idea how great an asset she is." Ranenok continued more hesitantly, although still addressing Jemeryl.

"As I said before, I'm just an ordinary mercenary." Tevi further unsettled him by being the one to reply.

"Her...er...your effect on troop morale shouldn't be underestimated. Quite apart from your own fighting ability. The soldiers trust you in a way they'll never trust someone gifted with magic." Ranenok at last was speaking to her. Tevi smiled, chalking it up as one small victory.

"Tevi's not completely ungifted," Jemeryl said.

Ranenok looked surprised. "What?"

"It's a very minor gift. She has prescience, working less than a second into the future, about life-threatening events."

"Oh, so that's why you don't wear a helmet in battle."

"Jemeryl has told me the iron in the helmet would block the forewarning. I decided that I was safer without one," Tevi said.

Ranenok nodded. "But the troops don't know about it. From their viewpoint, you're an ordinary soldier. One of them."

"They know my strength is magical."

"But it's a type of magic they can relate to. Believe me, I see the difference when you're their officer. The soldiers fight harder and fiercer."

Dunarth had been drifting closer while they were talking. Unlike everyone else, the alchemist had made no attempt to wear her best clothes. Even Jemeryl had discarded her usual loose-fitting and well-creased overshirt for a dark green robe. Tevi had dressed head to foot in black, to match both her hair and her mood. But she had to concede that Dunarth's stained work clothes had the edge. They gave the unmistakable message that the alchemist thought the reception was an unwarranted waste of time.

"You could get the same effect from the courage potion I made for you...the one you never use." Dunarth's irritation with Ranenok was clear.

"That's because there's a difference between high morale and suicidal recklessness," he snapped back.

"So you say."

"In an impossible situation, you need troops to retreat in good order. With your potion they just got slaughtered where they stood."

"What does it matter? Either way they'd lost the battle."

"With good morale the troops will regroup and carry on fighting from a better position. Dead soldiers can't fight and I get left shorthanded."

"It's not my fault if you don't have enough reserves with you."

Jemeryl touched Tevi's arm. "I'd like something to eat."

Tevi gratefully went along with the excuse to escape the growing argument.

Mavek was by the domestic thralls, refilling his glass. The blacksmith was Tevi's clear favourite among the acolytes. He had a barrel chest and huge hairy shoulders. As a sorcerer, he did not need muscles for his work. His magic would suffice. However, he looked the part, and his appearance helped Tevi feel at ease in his presence, as did his enthusiasm for his work and his welcoming smile. Although right now his face held an uncharacteristic scowl. The apprentice standing with him looked equally cheerless.

Mavek did not waste time on a polite greeting. "You got roped into this fiasco as well?"

"Bykoda kindly invited us," Jemeryl answered pleasantly.

Mavek made a contemptuous noise.

Tevi caught Jemeryl's eyes flick towards the thralls and remembered her guess at Bykoda attending in spirit. If the possibility had occurred to Mavek, he was not letting it censor his words. Then she noticed him sway slightly and realised he had come to the gathering already half drunk. His sense of caution was clearly dulled. Tevi hoped that he would not end up paying for it.

Mavek gestured with his glass towards the middle of the room where Yenneg and Anid had come face to face. "I don't know why Bykoda has them as acolytes. They're both useless. I bust my guts making things for them. They'd be sod all use if I didn't...incompetent witches...and I never get a word of thanks out of either. Ranenok's no better. And every time one of them makes a cock-up, they go running to Bykoda saying my work let them down."

He took a gulp of wine and was about to go on. However, he was interrupted by raised voices. Yenneg and Anid clearly agreed with his opinions in as far as they related to the other one.

"I don't think you're in any position to say that." Yenneg crackled with fury.

"Why not? It's true," Anid snapped back. If her tone sounded any less angry, it was probably due to the satisfaction of having nettled her rival.

Tevi led the way to a quiet corner where she and Jemeryl could have a respite from the hostility.

Jemeryl looked thoughtful. "You know, I think I've worked out the answer to something that has been puzzling me."

"What?"

"Why Bykoda called this gathering."

"And what is your answer?"

"It's so that everyone will be reminded of just how much they hate all the rest."

❖

As the evening wore on the arguments fizzled out, if only because all the acolytes were now too angry to talk to each other. The exchanges had been heated at times, although the nearest thing to a violent assault was one of Ranenok's officers receiving a glass of wine in the face.

Jemeryl had managed to stay clear of the squabbling, although she was increasingly irritated by the raised voices and repetitive insults. Dunarth was apparently the acolyte with the greatest stamina for verbal sniping. Well after everyone else had shut up, the alchemist was still haranguing Kharel about some supplies she wanted. Jemeryl thought that the contrast of style might have been interesting had it not been at the end of a tedious evening. Dunarth dug in with the determination of a terrier while Kharel was responding with aloof sarcasm.

"I asked for it four months ago."

"I don't suppose you've noticed that it's winter at the moment. How did you think I was going to get it over the Barrodens?"

"I thought that's what you used your foresight for. You order things when you can get them and before they're needed."

"Yes. But you need to tell me your requirements. I use foresight, not mind reading. And even if I could get into your mind, I don't think I'd want to." Kharel's tone suggested that crawling through sewers would be a suitable analogy.

Jemeryl stood with Tevi in a corner, wondering when it would end. Surely the gathering would not last until dawn. She considered her empty glass, but decided against a refill. There was enough potential to make enemies without getting drunk.

"Can't we go soon?" Tevi asked.

"That's just what I was thinking. I'm hoping Kharel is going to make a sign that the party is over."

"In which case someone needs to drag Dunarth off her."

"As long as it doesn't provoke a bigger argument."

"So why don't you try?"

"Why me?"

"Because you're the only sorcerer here who hasn't been involved in a shouting match yet."

"And I have no intention of starting."

Mavek staggered over. By now, he was very drunk. "Tevi. You've seen my...my lightning star. It worked. Ranenok's a fool. He just can't see...and..." Mavek straightened up slightly and began using his hands to illustrate his words. "The enemy is coming like this, and you've got the clouds here. Then what you need is..."

Jemeryl backed off a step. She had already heard the explanation once that evening. It had not made much sense to her then and, judging by the deterioration in Mavek's speech, it was unlikely to be any more comprehensible the second time around. She caught Tevi's eye and nodded in the direction of Kharel. The gathering had to end soon. There was a limit to how much more she could stand. Facing Dunarth's wrath was a small risk by comparison.

Tevi stayed talking to the blacksmith, possibly to keep him out of trouble. Jemeryl slipped away and was halfway across the room, still trying to think of a suitable opening gambit, when she was intercepted by Commander Anid.

Anid was a short, solidly built woman of about fifty. She had a flat face, etched with lines that made her look permanently unhappy. Her blond hair was cropped short. She was in command of Bykoda's army to the south, which also meant acting as Bykoda's deputy for the region. As such, she had more autonomy than the acolytes based in Tirakhalod but had to renounce it when outside her area. The two junior officers and a dozen foot soldiers were all the support she had been allowed to bring with her to the castle.

"Jemeryl. I understand you will be returning to the Protectorate shortly."

"Yes. In under a month."

"And you'll be taking your...Captain Tevirik with you?"

"Of course."

"I wonder if you could be persuaded to part with her?"

"Pardon?" The question had Jemeryl floundering.

"The army grapevine. We get news from other regions. I've heard about how useful Ranenok has found her. It sounds like she's a real asset, and I'm sure he's made you an offer. Whatever it is, I'm prepared to top it."

"You think you can buy her?" Jemeryl's voice rose as the first kick of anger hit her.

"I wasn't hoping that you'd give her to me for free." The way Anid's tone implied that she was being reasonable and friendly only made things worse.

"She's not for sale."

"You haven't asked what I'm prepared to pay yet."

"Tevi is not a possession. I don't own her." Jemeryl was furious.

"What is she, then? You must have created her somehow."

"I didn't create her. She doesn't belong to me."

Anid thought for a moment. "Does that mean she's up for the taking? There's nothing to stop anyone who wants from claiming her?"

"How dare you! Tevi is a free citizen of the Protectorate."

"Oh yes, I know. You've got all these rules about rights for the ungifted. But she's been serving in the army here. You could tell your Coven authorities that she'd been killed in action. Who'd know? I'd make it worth your while."

"Tevi is a free woman. No one owns her, and no one ever will." In the back of her mind, Jemeryl was aware that the room had gone silent. Heedless, she carried on, her voice as loud as anything that had been heard that night. "I take my oath to the Coven seriously, to uphold the laws of the Protectorate. It isn't meaningless claptrap. And one of the rules is about preserving the freedom of its citizens. I swear, if you try to lay one finger on her, you'll end up as a heap of smouldering cinders."

Anid took a step back. She shook her head in bemusement and turned away, obviously realising that she was not going to change

Jemeryl's mind. Yet she could not resist one parting shot. "You get very emotional about her. She must be good in bed."

Jemeryl did not know how she found the willpower to stop herself from blasting Anid where she stood. She spun around and stormed off to a corner where she was soon joined by Tevi.

"Um. Do you want me to remind you about not getting into a shouting match?"

"She wanted to buy you."

"I gathered."

"Aren't you angry?"

Tevi shrugged. "I've been living with that attitude since we got here. I've sort of got used to it."

"But surely not that blatant?"

"Sometimes. You could have asked how much she was prepared to pay. It might have worked out as a compliment."

"Tevi!"

"I'm joking. Anyway, the good news is that your set-to with Anid gave Kharel the chance to escape. Perhaps she can now call the evening to a close."

Even as Tevi spoke, fresh voices rose behind them, Ranenok and Kharel accusing each other of making a mistake with the provisions for the castle troops.

❖

Mavek was the one who finally put an end to the gathering when he threw up and then passed out in the middle of the floor. Six of the thralls were needed to carry the huge blacksmith away. Dunarth immediately stomped off, without exchanging further words with anyone. Among the people remaining, there was a slow but unmistakeable drift towards the door.

Tevi sighed with relief, happy that they could now go. "Good old Mavek. He's obviously been to these sort of events before. I'd been thinking he was drinking so much to blot out the surroundings, while all along, it was part of his escape plan."

Jemeryl merely grunted in reply. She was showing no sign of regaining her good humour after the quarrel with Anid.

"And thankfully, we won't have to attend any more."

"One is more than enough. Come on. Let's go." Jemeryl drained her glass.

"We could wait for the scrum around the doorway to ease."

However, Jemeryl had already set off across the room. Tevi was about to follow when a voice hailed her.

"Captain Tevirik. May I have a word?"

The speaker was Commander Yenneg, the leader of Bykoda's army in the north. He was the youngest of the acolytes, not yet forty, tall and good-looking in a rakish way. He stood with loose-limbed ease. The smile on his face looked genuine, while his eyes met Tevi's in friendly candour.

"Yes, sir?"

"I don't want to keep you. But I wondered if you would come over to my rooms tomorrow evening. There is something I wish to discuss with you."

"Concerning what?"

"This isn't the place, and there isn't the time. I know you are about to leave."

"Um..." Tevi glanced over her shoulder, but Jemeryl was out of earshot, marching towards the door. She looked back. There was no easy way to refuse the request, and no real reason why she should. It was a definite point in his favour that he was asking, rather than ordering. "Yes, sir. At what time?"

"Wait until after the watch calls seven. I ought to have finished the briefing by then."

"All right, sir." Tevi smiled back. "I'll see you then."

Yenneg gave a small nod of acknowledgement and then wandered back to his supporting officers.

❖

Yenneg's quarters were situated in the corner of the inner bailey diagonally opposite the rooms allocated to Jemeryl. At the appropriate time, Tevi exited the door of their tower and set off around the lit perimeter. The central gardens were in darkness, but the scent of flowers drifted on the breeze. By the gates, she passed the thralls standing guard. Tevi wondered if the mind-dead slaves could still smell the roses' fragrance. And did anyone in Tirakhalod know or care about the answer?

When she arrived at her destination, a servant thrall silently escorted her to Yenneg's ground-floor study. Bookshelves lined the walls and a desk covered with maps and reports stood in the middle of the room. Logs blazed in a large stone fireplace, complementing the mage lights hanging in midair. Above the mantel was a shield bearing Yenneg's crest, a silver griffin on a blue background. Two comfy chairs were positioned beside a low table in front of the fire. Yenneg sat waiting, with a bottle of wine and two glasses laid out ready.

Tevi hesitated at the sight of him and the informal setting, recalling some of the rumours she had heard on the army grapevine. She wondered if she should have brought Jemeryl. Yenneg had not specifically asked her to come alone, but it was too late now.

Yenneg beckoned her to the empty fireside chair and indicated for her to sit. The thrall poured wine for them both and left. Yenneg settled back, took a sip of his drink, and then looked thoughtfully at Tevi.

"I was very impressed by Jemeryl's remarks last night. Not just the threat to reduce Anid to cinders, although it's a nice thought. But the assertion that she's willing to treat you as a free individual who can make her own decisions."

"She wasn't just saying it, sir."

"She wouldn't stop you doing as you wish?"

"No, sir."

"Jemeryl is taking you back to the Protectorate with her?"

Tevi hesitated over the word *taking*, but replied simply, "Yes, sir."

"Did she ask you if you wanted to go?"

"She didn't need to, sir. She knows how I feel about returning."

"If you said you wanted to stay here, she'd accept your decision?"

"I'm sure she would." Actually, Tevi hoped that Jemeryl would be upset enough about them separating to put up a fight, but she did not want to complicate the issue.

"So, what would it take to make you want to stay?"

Tevi took a mouthful of wine to cover the pause while she worked out how to phrase the answer. "I won't leave Jemeryl. We are..."

"Lovers. I know."

"Yes, sir." The word was not strong enough to describe the bond, but it would do.

"You've been together for some time."

"Over four years."

"And neither of you is getting tired of the relationship?"

"No, sir." Tevi felt a familiar irritation. Even in the Protectorate, so many assumed that a mighty sorcerer could have no real long-term interest in an ungifted mercenary fighter. The anger loosened her reticence. "Is this a preamble to offering me a place in your army?"

Yenneg laughed. "I admit I'm considering it."

"Why, sir? First Ranenok, then Anid, and now you. I'm not that special."

"Ranenok thinks you are. And I've heard rumours. Last year, one of his garrisons was transferred to my section. The officer spoke very highly of you."

Tevi shook her head. "I don't see it."

Yenneg stood up. "Let's put it to the test. Come with me."

He led the way to a room across the hallway where a large table took up three quarters of the floor space. The table was bare. Its top was covered in a metallic material that shimmered in the mage light. Apart from it, the room was empty. Yenneg put his glass down on a windowsill and then waved his hand over the table.

Immediately, the tabletop turned green. The change was not limited to colour. The surface shifted like grass seen from a distance, rippling in the breeze. Tevi looked closer. It was grass. Then hills bulged up on either side. These in turn sprouted a miniature forest of trees. A tiny silver river flowed down the valley, broadening briefly into a marsh in the upper reaches, with reed beds swaying along the edges.

Miniature troops appeared on the scene at the bottom of the valley. Cavalry rode on tiny horses and a column of archers and pikemen marched beside the river. Tevi heard a bugle faintly sound the command to stop, and the soldiers formed up in a line with banners waving in the wind.

New figures then emerged up by the trees, three dozen trolls in battle array, brandishing their weapons. Tevi bent closer to study them. In her duties with Bykoda's army, she had already encountered the demi-human warriors. Trolls were, on average, slightly taller and a lot heavier than humans. Their mottled grey skin was so tough that many did not bother with any other form of armour. Their movements were slow and lumbering, but their strength more than made up for this in terms of their fighting abilities. Added to which, they had a natural resistance to many forms of human magic.

Trolls were mainly found in the mountains, where they lived in anarchic cave-dwelling clans. When they came down to the lowlands, it was to loot, kill, and destroy. They took no prisoners. Neither would they surrender, but instead carried on fighting until their last breath. They never rode on horseback, which left them especially vulnerable to cavalry on the plains. But in their home territory, they were masters of ambush. They could wait for hours, motionless, and their skin could subtly shift in tone for camouflage. Doubtless this was what gave rise to the legends that they could turn themselves into stone at will.

Tevi viewed the animated tabletop uncertainly. After four years with Jemeryl, displays of magic no longer surprised her. However, it was obvious that Yenneg was expecting something from her. She glanced up to see him watching her intently.

He smiled. "You're the commander of the human troops. What would you do?"

Tevi looked back to the table, this time evaluating it as a tactical problem. The humans outnumbered the trolls, three to one. The battle should have been straightforward, but something did not feel right. "Is this based on a real encounter?"

"Yes. It was a skirmish that took place eight years ago."

"If I'd been the officer in charge at the time, what would I have known about the enemy chieftain?"

"Not much. The trolls had raided the town of Crezata. They were intercepted as they were on the way back to their burrows in the Luzkonin Hills."

"That must be at least eighty miles." Tevi frowned.

"What are you thinking?" Yenneg asked after nearly a minute of silence.

"I'm thinking it's a trap. A war band wouldn't go that far from their burrow unless they were following a chieftain with a lot of prestige. And you don't get prestige among the trolls without winning battles. Yet it looks like a beginner's mistake. They've got their line between the trees on one side and the marsh on the other, so they can't be outflanked by cavalry, except the river looks like it should be easily fordable above and below the marsh. It's tempting to move my archers forwards with the pikemen to pin the trolls down, while the cavalry go around the marsh on the other side of the river and fall on them from behind."

"And where's the trap?"

"Crezata isn't a large town, but there still aren't enough trolls here to have sacked it." Tevi pointed to a hillside. "I'd bet that they've got more fighters hidden in the trees over there. It's very narrow between the marsh and the forest on that side of the river. The cavalry could be ambushed as they go past. They'd be trapped between the trees and the bog with no room for manoeuvre. They'd be sitting targets. And once the cavalry was slaughtered, the trolls could come back around and outflank my archers, just like I'd been hoping to do to them."

"So, what would you do?"

"I'd use my pikemen to protect—"

"No. Don't tell me. Tell them." Yenneg smiled as he spoke.

Tevi hesitated before realising what he meant. She looked down on the table and took a deep breath. "Pikemen, form up in threes on either wing." The tiny soldiers marched into position.

The miniature battle swung into action. On her order, Tevi's cavalry charged and broke the centre of the trolls' line. The intended ambushers in the woods, seeing their trap foiled, emerged from cover and attempted the outflanking manoeuvre anyway, only to be met by ranks of pikes as they forded the river. Archers peppered the enemy as they tried to regroup. Within twenty minutes the battle was over and Tevi's troops were victorious.

Tevi grinned. She did not even need to feel guilty about the casualties.

"Would you like to see how the battle actually went, eight years back?" Yenneg asked once it was over.

"Oh, um. Yes."

The scene reverted to the original lines, and the battle began again, but this time the cavalry forded the river. The resulting ambush went every bit as badly for the humans as Tevi had expected. At the end, only a handful of troops were left, fleeing the field.

Yenneg sighed. "And the real horror is that the officer was one of the more gifted witches. She'd have been quite capable of scrying the hillside, but it never occurred to her to look. No doubt this defeat would have made her much more cautious next time, except for her, there never was a next time. She'd been leading the cavalry."

"I'm sorry to hear that."

"It was one of the reasons I had Mavek make this table. So that my officers can get some experience without losing their lives. But you don't need it. You've got a good tactical head. You fight with the strength of ten men. You inspire the troops you lead. You're going back to the Protectorate with Jemeryl." He met her eyes with an ironic grin. "And you can't see why all the army commanders would like you to stay?"

"It's nothing against life in Tirakhalod." This was not strictly true, but Tevi was feeling in a tolerant mood after playing on the battle table. Her eyes returned to the tiny celebrating trolls. "And I'm not sure that I'm that good tactically, it was just..." She let the sentence trail away in a modest shrug.

"Do you want me to prove the point? Look, here's another skirmish, only this one—" Yenneg also cut off his sentence mid-flow. "But it's getting late. I won't be around tomorrow evening, but if you come over, one of my officers will set the table up for you. I'll leave instructions."

"I'm afraid I'm off on patrol for a few days, starting tomorrow."

"Then when you come back. I'm going to be staying in Tirakhalod, so my quarters will be staffed. The next council meeting is in twenty day's time, and I've decided against going to my region only to have to turn straight around and come back here again. You're welcome to come over and use the table whenever you want."

"Thank you." Tevi was delighted with the offer.

"I have ulterior motives. If you should change your mind about going back to the Protectorate, I'm hoping to be your first choice for commanding officer." Yenneg's eyes again met hers in an open, comradely smile.

❖

Tevi's bags were packed and she was ready to leave. She sat eating breakfast while Jemeryl kept her company. Klara stood on the edge of the table, scanning the plates in the vain hope of something she might consider edible. Human breakfasts were often a big disappointment for the magpie.

Jemeryl swallowed the last of a roll and leaned back in her chair. "I'm pleased you had a good time at Yenneg's."

"The battle table was great. Do you think you could make something similar when we're back in Lyremouth?" Tevi had talked about little else since returning.

Jemeryl smiled tolerantly. She found the enthusiasm for a war game hard to understand, but was happy to indulge her partner. "Probably. I'll ask Mavek for details next time I see him."

"I'd been worried when I got there. Yenneg has a bit of a reputation. Although not as worrying as Anid."

"In what way?" Jemeryl was still angry with Anid and not surprised to learn that she had made a bad name for herself.

"Stuff you hear on the army grapevine. Mainly about sex. The stories say that Anid has slept with every officer in her command."

"Has she?"

"I doubt that she's slept with every last one. There have to be some she doesn't like the look of, but you don't get that sort of reputation without doing something to set it off. The latest talk is that two of her officers were involved with each other. Anid broke up the relationship by claiming one of them. Then she tired of him and moved on to his ex-partner."

"And Yenneg's the same?"

"Not quite. He doesn't touch his officers, which is better for morale. He goes for the ungifted, which is why people are so keen to tell me about it. To let me know I'm not the only one involved with a sorcerer. I've heard he'd recently picked up a lad from a village, so he shouldn't be on the lookout at the moment. But it did leave me worried when I saw the wine and the cosy setting."

"He behaved himself?"

"Perfectly. He wanted me to join his section of the army, but he took it well when I said no. And then we just played on the battle table."

Jemeryl was inclined to be more suspicious but did not want to push the issue. "Who else do the soldiers talk about?"

"All the sorcerers. Ranenok used to have a steady partner, one of his captains, but she was killed four years ago, and he's not been involved with anyone since. Some people reckon that Kharel and Bykoda have something going on, but since neither has any contact with ordinary soldiers I don't see how anyone could know. And most soldiers think Bykoda only has sex with thralls. Mind you, some say that about all the sorcerers."

"Including Jemeryl?" Klara asked.

"Possibly. Although no one has dared say it in my hearing. The nastiest rumours are about Dunarth. The soldiers hate her."

"How nasty?"

"It starts with reanimating corpses and goes downhill from there."

Jemeryl shook her head. "That wouldn't work."

Tevi laughed. "I didn't really need your opinion on the magic. I just assumed it was a stupid rumour."

"Are there any non-stupid rumours about her?"

"Some reckon that Mavek and her are lovers. Did you notice that those two were the only couple who didn't have an argument at the gathering?"

"I hadn't kept count. But they have to work together. Bykoda can't afford to set them at each others' throats. With the rest, she deliberately stirs things up."

"Divide and rule."

Jemeryl leant her head to one side. "I wonder..."

"What?"

"Mavek and Dunarth. None of the acolytes on their own is strong enough to challenge Bykoda. But if you combine the talents of those two, they'd make one very competent sorcerer." She thought for a moment. "No. It's too obvious a threat. I'm sure Bykoda is on the watch for any sign that they are getting on too well together."

"You have no idea who the assassin is?"

"No. And I don't think we have any way of finding out. We know that we can't stop it, but it doesn't really concern us. By the time it happens we'll be back in Lyremouth. All we can assume is that one of the acolytes must be far more powerful than they seem. It could be any of them."

"But they've all been here for years. If they are so much stronger than her, why wait until now? Why put up with years of being pushed around by Bykoda?"

"I don't know."

Klara hopped forwards. "After they've done it, you could write a letter to whoever it is and ask."

Jemeryl looked at the magpie and sighed. "You know, it's a sad thing when Klara is the one coming up with the most practical suggestions."

❖

Jemeryl spent the day making notes in Bykoda's library. She returned late in the evening. Why rush back when Tevi was not there? The rooms always seemed so empty without her. The only comfort was that this would be Tevi's last sortie with the troops. Soon both she and Tevi would be back in the Protectorate. Jemeryl did not know what new post the Coven would assign to her, but she was sure it would be possible to find an associated job for Tevi so that they did not end up spending so many days apart.

Crumbs from breakfast still littered the table. She looked at Klara who was riding on her shoulder. "If you were a sparrow instead of a magpie, you'd have eaten that, so it wouldn't need cleaning up."

"And if I were a woodpecker, I'd have eaten the table."

Jemeryl brushed the magpie off her shoulder and looked around. Assorted small jobs needed doing, but it could all wait until the next day. Now that she was alone in the rooms, she could feel her mood dipping. The first day after Tevi left was always the worst. An early night would be a good idea. She wandered into the bedroom.

Tevi's clothes lay where they had been dropped the night before. Seeing them, a wave of affection swept over Jemeryl. She bent to pick up the shirt, intending to give it a hug before putting it away, but then something shiny caught her eye. On the ground a few inches to the side was a jewelled brooch.

The item was not one that Jemeryl had seen before. Around the outer edge were set diamonds and sapphires. In the centre was a silver griffin on a blue enamel background—Yenneg's emblem. Jemeryl frowned. Tevi had not mentioned him giving it to her, and surely something so valuable would not have been overlooked. Although on second thought, Tevi had been so excited about the battle table that anything else might have been forgotten.

Jemeryl put the brooch in a drawer. Tevi would be back in a few days. Questions could wait until then.

CHAPTER FOUR—LINKS IN THE ETHER

From the baffled expression on Tevi's face, Jemeryl could tell, even before she spoke, that she had not seen the brooch before. Tevi studied the griffin design for a few seconds and then flipped it over, as if hoping the reverse side would be more enlightening.

"No. Yenneg didn't give it to me. But it has to have come from him. The silver griffin is his emblem." Tevi handed the brooch back.

"Then how did it end up on the floor of the bedroom?"

"Maybe it caught on my clothing while I was playing on the battle table and dropped off when I was getting ready for bed."

Jemeryl lay the brooch in the palm of her hand and rocked it back and forth pensively, feeling the weight. Candlelight glinted on the diamonds and rippled over the silver griffin. The same candlelight was reflected in the black glass of the windows. In daytime, these gave views over the inner bailey on one side and the plain below Tirakhalod on the other. Currently, clouds blanketed the stars and moon, and nothing could be seen outside. Most of the room was hidden by shadow.

The army patrol had arrived back at the castle a few hours earlier, allowing enough time for Tevi to wash, eat, and give an account of her exploits. While they ate and talked, Jemeryl had sat beside Tevi in the warm firelight, feeling snug and relaxed. She was thankful to have Tevi back safe and would have liked to forget about the rest of Tirakhalod for the evening, but the brooch raised issues that had to be discussed.

Jemeryl shifted around so that she was nestled more comfortably against Tevi's body and held up the brooch. "I don't think so. There's nothing that could snag on clothing well enough so that it wouldn't drop off while you walked around the bailey. The pin is locked in its clasp."

"How else could it have got here?"

Klara gave a derisive squawk. "Are the pair of you having some sort of contest to see who can act the densest? Obviously, Yenneg came snooping around while Jem was busy in Bykoda's library."

Jemeryl frowned at the magpie. It was the simplest option, and one that had already occurred to her in the previous four days while waiting for Tevi's return, but it was not an answer that she was happy with.

Tevi spoke first. "It's a bit much to swallow. Yenneg comes in here for some unknown reason. He's so careful that he leaves no sign at all that he's been around except for dropping one highly identifiable item. You've got to admit it's unlikely."

"I agree. It's too blatant a clue. It's more likely that someone with limited imagination planted it to make us think that Yenneg was snooping."

"Why?"

"Who knows? Maybe Ranenok or Anid did it. They heard that you'd been to see him and wanted to sow some mistrust."

"I think it's too unsubtle even for that."

Jemeryl thought for a moment and then sighed. "You're right. It's actually a bit insulting if anyone thought we'd be taken in so easily."

"Oh well, if we're talking insults, they're never in short supply around here."

"But neither is plotting and scheming."

Tevi grinned. "True."

"I just can't think what sort of plot it might be part of."

"Maybe it's supposed to be a warning."

Klara hopped up onto Tevi's knee. "You mean a bit like slipping a note under the door that says, *Don't trust Yenneg. He's a conniving bastard.*"

An unsettling idea was tiptoeing around at the back of Jemeryl's mind. It was going to have to be faced. "It might be a threat."

"Threat?"

Jemeryl nodded. "I'm just worried that this has happened so soon after Bykoda gave me the talisman. We've been here over two and a half years, and this is the first time something like this has happened."

"As far as we know."

"Oh, I don't mean about someone coming in here. We've probably been searched on dozens of occasions. This is the first time that someone has deliberately let us know about it."

"But who, apart from Bykoda, knows that you have tl talisman?"

Instead of answering, Jemeryl slipped from under Tevi's arm an went to the adjoining room. An iron-bound chest stood at the foot c their bed. Jemeryl lifted the lid and took out the box Bykoda had give1 to her. She returned to Tevi.

The flickering candles were good for creating an intimate atmosphere but not for seeing by. Jemeryl conjured a mage light foi better illumination and examined the outside of the box, using not only her eyes and fingers, but also her extended sorcerer's senses. The carving on the lid was intricate and cast strange perturbations through the upper dimensions, but it was not the sort of magic she was seeking.

Jemeryl opened the box, which was reassuringly empty. The talisman was far too dangerous, in her opinion, to be left lying in their rooms, and she had it on a chain around her neck, even while sleeping. She was relieved, though, that their visitor had not placed one of the nastier totems in its place.

The bottom of the box was lined with red silk padding. This came out after a little experimental tugging and beneath it, embedded in the wood, was a small silver disc like a coin.

"Stupid. I should have checked before." Jemeryl was angry with herself.

"What is it?"

"A tracer charm."

"It lets you trace the box?"

"Not me, but whoever's got the other matching half of the charm. Tracer charms come in bonded pairs. They have an unbreakable link between them in the ether."

"Can you use this part to trace it back and find out who has the other part?"

"No. It only goes one way. This half is the caller, not the hearer."

Tevi frowned. "So you mean that whoever has the mate of this charm will be able to tell that Bykoda has given you the talisman?"

"Yes."

"And if that person is the assassin?"

"That's what I'm afraid of. Bykoda thought the assassin was aftei the device. She'd wanted it to come as a surprise to her killer after sh(was dead that the talisman was no longer in Tirakhalod."

Tevi slumped down in the seat. Her eyes were fixed on the fire. "This changes things, doesn't it? We're going to have to find out who the assassin is. We can't save Bykoda. To tell the truth, I'm not sure if I want to, but now the assassin will be after us as well."

"Maybe not. I see two possibilities. One is as you say, that the assassin knows I have the talisman and searched our rooms. All they found was the empty box, but they decided to leave a message. If that person was Yenneg, the message is one of bravado. He wants me to know that he's after me." Jemeryl frowned. "And if it was someone else it's a bit harder to decode."

"Don't you wish they'd just written a note. Why do sorcerers have to make everything so complicated?" Klara said.

Tevi pushed the magpie off her knee and asked her own question. "You think there is another possibility?"

"Yes, if we're lucky. Bykoda herself may have put this tracer charm in the box. The talisman wasn't something that she wanted to lose. I'm going to be seeing her tomorrow morning. I'll ask."

"Do you want me to return the brooch to Yenneg? If he's the one who left it, we'd be sending our own message back."

Jemeryl held the jewel up in the firelight, thinking. "No, we'll hang on to it a little while longer. We don't know if he was the one who left it, and even if it was, I'd rather keep him guessing."

❖

Jemeryl's footsteps echoed loudly along the stone hallway in Bykoda's keep. A line of narrow windows overlooked the central courtyard on her left. From them, parallel bars of morning sunlight striped the flagstones ahead of her. At the far end, the entrance to Bykoda's private rooms was flanked on either side by a silent thrall.

Just as she was approaching, the heavy wooden door opened and Kharel backed out, clasping a couple of rolled scrolls. The steward turned around and acknowledged Jemeryl with a dignified nod.

Kharel did not look surprised to see her, but seers rarely looked surprised. They never laughed at the punch line to jokes either. Foresight was not reliable enough to be the reason, and Jemeryl suspected that seers deliberately cultivated a stone face to create the facade of all-knowing wisdom. She was sure that there was no good reason why they

could not focus on the face of the person they were talking to. Their eyes were no different from anyone else's.

"You are here to see Bykoda." Kharel said it as a statement, not a question.

Jemeryl mentally notched up yet one more irritating habit of seers. "Yes. Is she available?"

"For now." The steward gave another regal nod and started to walk away.

"Before you go..."

Something in Kharel's tone had set Jemeryl wondering whether the seer knew about Bykoda's impending death. Kharel certainly would if she were the assassin. Yet, even if she was innocent, her foresight might have given her a warning. Also, Bykoda had admitted to casting oracles to find out more about the assassination. If she had needed help, Kharel would be the best qualified person in Tirakhalod to give it.

"You wish something from me."

"Um...I was..." Jemeryl hesitated, suddenly feeling foolish and wishing she had thought before speaking. How could she broach the subject? Bluntly asking, 'Do you know that Bykoda is going to be murdered?' was not an option.

"Yes?"

"I just wanted to ask if you had any plans for after Bykoda...er, for what you might do in the future, if you weren't needed as Bykoda's steward anymore."

"I trust that Bykoda will not seek to replace me. I certainly have no plans to leave Tirakhalod. Where do you think I might want to go?"

"Lyremouth. To...er...look in the library there. There's a whole section about divination. And there's lots of other seers in Lyremouth, if there was anything you wanted to talk to them about. Anything um, unsettling. And so I just thought maybe you might be interested." Jemeryl stopped talking before she made herself sound even more inane than she already had.

Kharel's expression was a touch more condescending than normal. "I have been Bykoda's steward for forty years. After all this time, I will not leave her."

"But she's getting old, and she won't live forever. After she dies, there is no saying what will happen at Tirakhalod."

"I also am not young."

"You're still younger than she is."

"Even so, I will not long outlive her." Kharel gave another of her dignified nods and turned away.

Jemeryl let her go. Of all seers' irritating traits, by far the worst was that after talking to them, you were always left feeling more confused than before. Was Kharel's prediction accurate? And if so, did she know how ominous the implication was for herself? The nearest thing to worthwhile information was that if Kharel was telling the truth, it made it rather less likely that she would be the assassin.

After one last look at the departing steward, Jemeryl pushed open the door and stepped through.

Bykoda's private quarters occupied half of the keep. The accommodation was extensive, and from what Jemeryl had seen, largely unused. The old Empress mainly kept to a few of the smaller rooms on the lower floors. Did the large halls start to seem too lonely with only the thralls for company?

The first room a visitor entered was the audience chamber, noticeably more austere and imposing than the other areas that Jemeryl had seen. Bykoda was standing by a window, staring out pensively. She turned around at the sound of the door closing.

"Ah, Jemeryl. I've found the diagrams you were after. They're on my desk in the study."

"Thank you."

"And while I was looking for them I came across something else that I thought you might be interested in. Come along. I'll show you."

Jemeryl felt a grin spread across her face. Anything Bykoda thought she might be interested in was certain to be well worth seeing. Jemeryl knew that Tevi disliked the Empress and understood the reasons why but could not fully share her partner's view.

Bykoda was ruthless and autocratic. She had no qualms about killing, yet neither did she take pleasure in it. She seized what she wanted, without regard to ethics, and accepted that others would be playing by the same rules. Even though her own life was now forfeit, Bykoda was not calling foul. And Jemeryl was sure when her subjects came to look back on Bykoda's rule, they would reckon that the peace her Empire brought had done more good than harm.

On the way to the study, Jemeryl thought to ask about the charm before she got distracted. "Bykoda, I was examining the box the talisman was in last night, and I saw there was a tracer charm in it. Do you know anything about it?"

"Oh yes. I'd had Mavek fit it many years ago. I'd forgotten it was still there." Bykoda smiled. "I might as well give you the other half. I have no use for it. It should be in my study as well. I'll dig it out for you."

"Thank you."

Jemeryl felt a knot of tension inside herself dissolve. The question of Yenneg's brooch was still unanswered, but it was the lesser of her concerns. Bykoda's assassin must be someone extremely powerful and adept, and Jemeryl would rather not have that someone pursuing her on the way home to Lyremouth.

The study doors closed behind them. Bykoda walked over to her desk. Jemeryl followed, smiling. Now she could concentrate on the promised entertainment.

❖

Tevi was not around when Jemeryl returned to their rooms. Most likely, she was over at Yenneg's playing on the battle table. Jemeryl shook her head at the thought. She could no more understand Tevi's fascination with pretend wars than Tevi could understand her interest in the study of magic.

Jemeryl wandered through to the fireside and sat, stretching out her legs. The talisman box was where she had left it the night before beside the hearth. She fished the half of the tracer charm that Bykoda had given her from her pocket and examined it. The engraved pattern was like a flat cord looped around in an elaborate knot. The only difference from the half in the box that anyone ungifted would notice was that grooves in one were ridges on the other. If pressed together, the two would fit seamlessly.

To a sorcerer, the differences were far more conspicuous. Idly, Jemeryl lifted the silver disc and aligned it in the energy currents of the sixth dimension. Soon the disc started to grow warm between her fingers. Once it was ready, she waved her hand over it, an incidental gesture caused when her aura in the fifth dimension tripped the forces into play. Instantly, the disc was ice cold, and the energy congealed into a thin link through the ether.

At the sight, Jemeryl's mood of relaxed satisfaction evaporated. The link did not go to the talisman box. Instead it streamed off, out of the room. Jemeryl sat up straight. Was it possible that Bykoda had made a mistake and given her the wrong charm? She slipped from the chair and retrieved the other half from the box, then held the two up side by side. Seen together, it was obvious that the charms were not identical. The loops and twists did not form the same knot-work pattern.

Jemeryl sat back on her heels, thinking furiously. She did not know what was going on, but the first thing was to find the other half of the charm that Bykoda had given her. The caller from the box was inert and useless to her, but this new half was a hearer, still bonded to its mate, and could lead her to it. She stood up and began following the link, reeling it in like a fisherman.

The ethereal trace led her from the tower, through the garden, and out of the inner bailey. At the gatehouse, Jemeryl paused and looked around, confused. She had expected the trail to take her back to Bykoda's keep, or even to one of the acolytes' quarters. Where was it going? The nature of the link provided no clue as to its length. She could only hope that the caller was close at hand.

Jemeryl turned her back on the inner bailey and continued following the line in the ether. The guards at the gate stood impassive as she went by. She passed the officers' quarters in the middle bailey, the prison, and the apothecary. And then, just when it seemed that she would be led farther on to the outer bailey, the trail turned aside and brought her up sharply at the entrance to Mavek's forge. Jemeryl looked up at the black smoke overhead belching from the huge chimneys, then she opened the door and stepped inside.

Mavek's main workshop was a cavernous hall. Chaotic activity filled the space. Daylight from high windows sifted through rising smoke and steam. Blue mage lights hung in midair, and red flickering from forges glinted over the workers. Showers of sparks erupted under blacksmiths' hammers. And yet, despite all this light, the hall was like the gloomy interior of a cave. Tools and half-built equipment lined the walls and hung from the ceiling like stalactites. In the middle of the workshop, a construction was taking shape resembling a large armoured scorpion twice the size of a man.

Mavek and a half a dozen of his apprentices were busy on the creation. His voice boomed over the sounds of hammer and fire.

"Careful now. Lower the forward plate."

No one had noticed Jemeryl's arrival. In fact, she suspected she would have to shout and wave her arms to have any hope of getting anyone's attention. And still the tracer charm pulled her on. Quietly, she sidled around the edge of the hall, keeping to shadows. A corridor led off from the commotion of the main hall. As Jemeryl slipped away down it, she was followed by the sound of Mavek's shouts. "Towards me. Towards me. Keep it steady."

The ethereal trail ended in a small side room. A long workbench filled one wall. Moulds, files, and shapeless lumps of metal were scattered across it. Other tools, mainly hammers, hung on the walls. The bench marked the end of the link, but only at the last moment did Jemeryl realise that the trail ended not on it, but under.

She knelt and crawled beneath. Where the flagstones of the floor met the wall was a thin crack. In the light of a summoned globe, Jemeryl could just about make out the edge of a silver disc hidden inside it. Extracting the charm was awkward, even with telekinesis. Whoever put it there had clearly not been concerned about retrieving it again.

Jemeryl shuffled out from under the bench and stood up, frowning. Why hide the charm? And why in this room? She looked around thoughtfully. The mysteries of the blacksmith's craft could be difficult for the untrained to comprehend. Yet, even to her eyes, it was obvious that some of the moulds on the bench were for making tracer charms. Further confirmation was found on the shelf above. Three new pairs of charms were lined up, ready for use.

Jemeryl considered the matching pair in her hands, the charm she had got from Bykoda and the one she had found under the bench. Her mind bounced around through a series of half ideas, none of them completely satisfactory. She needed to talk to Tevi. Jemeryl dropped the charms into her pocket and left the room.

The scene in the workshop had changed while she had been away. The noise had dropped to a low rumble and Mavek was standing by the exit, apparently trying to get a perspective view on the metal scorpion. The apprentices were also keeping back, awaiting the master blacksmith's judgment.

Creeping away unnoticed was not going to be easy. Jemeryl decided not to try. A few steps away was a low cabinet that would serve as a seat. She shifted over to it and then sat, trying to give the impression that she had been there for some time, awaiting a suitable break in the activity.

At least a minute passed before she was spotted. An apprentice trotted over to her. "Can I help you, ma'am?"

"I want to talk to Mavek, but I don't want to disturb him in the middle of what he's doing."

"I think he's nearly finished."

Jemeryl nodded as if he had confirmed what she already suspected. "I've been watching you with the scorpion. I assume it's some sort of weapon."

"The weapon is inside. A poison dart shooter. The case is just for show. But it never hurts to frighten the enemy before the fighting starts." The apprentice grinned. "I'll tell Mavek you want him."

"It's not urgent. Whenever he's got a minute will do."

Mavek did not take much longer to finished his appraisal of the scorpion and join her. What clothes he wore seemed mainly for protecting his more vulnerable parts from sparks. Sweat beaded on his face and rolled through the forest of hair on his chest and thighs.

"Do you need help?"

"I've come to ask a favour. You know that I'm returning to the Protectorate soon. I was hoping I could have a tour of your workshop before I go." This was not merely an improvised excuse. Jemeryl had intended to make the request next time she saw the blacksmith.

"Sure. Why not now?"

"I wouldn't want to interrupt your work."

Mavek gave a broad smile and gestured over his shoulder with his thumb. "Now's as good a time as any. I've got to wait for that to cool down."

He led the way to one side of the workshop where an assortment of artefacts were at various stages of assembly. Their first stop was by a black metal breastplate. Mavek rapped it with his knuckles.

"We been trying to create some fireproof armour. Well...fireproof isn't that hard. You don't come across much on a battlefield that will melt dwarf steel, apart from dragon breath. The problem is the people inside still get cooked. With this, we've been building up the metal in layers. In the middle is a grid of powdered fire agate. It links into the conduits of the sixth dimension and carries away the heat instantly."

Jemeryl stepped forwards, intrigued. Like so much she saw in Tirakhalod, it was both deceptively simple and breathtakingly imaginative. "Wow. Does it work?"

"Unfortunately it works too well. The problem we have now is that the person wearing it freezes to death."

The tour continued through the workshop. Most of it made sense, although there were some items she was going to have to ask Tevi about later. The golems she understood, but Jemeryl had no idea of just how impressive it was for a crossbow to shoot a bolt through one eighth steel at four hundred yards, or why you might want self-destroying caltrops. Some of the inventions she found frankly horrifying. She had never realised that there might be so many ways to disembowel an opponent.

At last, as the tour was reaching its end, she was moved to ask, "Don't you ever wish your work might do more to make people's lives better, rather than killing them?"

Mavek carefully placed the war axe he had been demonstrating back on the rack. For a few seconds he stood staring at it, then he turned and looked down at her. His eyes held a sober intensity.

"Yes. Sometimes. But the easier Bykoda's soldiers win, then the less of them that get killed. And if they don't win there's an awful lot of people whose lives would become an awful lot worse." He shrugged. "And some of my work is harmless...like over here."

He went to another bench. On it were a row of cushions with assorted weights balanced on top.

"What are they?" Jemeryl asked, confused.

"Inflatable cushions." Mavek grinned. "Bykoda's council meetings can go on forever. With the current stuffed cushions, after four hours, you can feel the imprint of each individual straw in your arse. I was hoping these would be more comfortable. But I'm having to sort out issues. At the moment they tend to deflate, and you get seasick if you shift around too much. I'm thinking about dividing the inside into dozens of individual compartments."

Mavek turned away from the bench and sighed. His gesture took in all of his workshop. "But you're right. The cushions are just a diversion. Nearly all my life has been spent working out better ways to kill people. Maybe I should have moved to your Protectorate when I was younger.

Then I could have worked on designing a better ploughshare." He shook his head sadly. "But it's too late now."

"It's never too late."

"Maybe." Despite what he said, Mavek's voice held no hope.

Jemeryl patted his shoulder in encouragement. "Believe it. But I've taken up far too much of your time. Thank you for showing me around. It was very kind of you."

A ghost of a smile returned to Mavek's face. "Anytime."

❖

Tevi lay sprawled on the sheepskin rug before the fire, staring at the ceiling. Running through her head was the last skirmish from the battle table. Her troops had won, but at a high cost. She needed to work out better tactics that would mean fewer lives lost. The sound of the door cut short her musing.

Jemeryl entered, stripping off her cloak. She smiled at Tevi in greeting. "Have you been back long?"

"Just a few minutes. How did you know I'd gone out?"

"You weren't here earlier when I stopped by."

Klara II had been riding on Jemeryl's shoulder. The magpie swooped across the room, landed on a perch above the fire, and then buried her beak under her wing. Tevi watched her settle and then turned back to Jemeryl. "I was over at Yenneg's. Playing on the battle table."

"I guessed. How did you do?"

"I won. Twice." Tevi sat up and was about to go into more details, but then she noted Jemeryl's distracted expression. "Is everything all right?"

Jemeryl joined her by the fire. "I asked Bykoda about the tracer charm."

"From your face, I'm guessing that the charm was nothing to do with her."

"Not quite. She had one put in the box. But somebody made a swap." Jemeryl quickly summarised her morning.

"So what does it all mean?" Tevi asked once the account was finished.

"Somebody got a new set of charms and made a switch. I'd guess they took the half from Bykoda's study. The talisman box was locked up in her storeroom and a lot harder to get at."

"Getting in the study without her knowing still can't have been easy."

Jemeryl wrinkled her nose. "Well, Kharel would be best placed. But over the years, I'd bet that all the acolytes have had a chance."

"I still don't see how it works out."

"I've been thinking it through. What probably happened is that someone went into the workshop, got a pair of charms, and hid the caller in the nearest spot. They took the hearer away and kept hold of it until the opportunity arose to make the swap. Once they'd done that, they then had the hearer that was linked to the box, so they could trace the talisman. And all Bykoda had was a useless charm that would just lead her back to the forge. But unless she looked carefully, or tested it out, she wouldn't know."

"How hard would it be to get the charms from the forge?"

"Really easy. A couple of spare sets were just sitting in the work-room. Anyone could walk in and pick them up. Nobody noticed me."

"So it doesn't help us narrow down the suspects?"

"Nope. No help at all."

A knock at the door interrupted the conversation. Tevi went to answer. One of Yenneg's officers was outside holding a small glass bottle.

"Captain Tevirik. Commander Yenneg sends this as a token of his admiration for your victories this morning."

Tevi took the offered item. "Please thank the commander for me."

"Yes, Captain Tevirik." The officer went.

Tevi wandered back to the fire and carefully removed the stopper from the bottle. The scent of sweet musk filled the room. "Perfume?"

Jemeryl took the bottle and examined it. "I know this. It comes from the islands out on the eastern ocean. And it's the genuine stuff, not magic. It must have cost Yenneg a fortune to get."

Tevi frowned. It was not the sort of gift she would have expected from a commanding officer, but then the casual acceptance of bribery at Tirakhalod always felt alien to her. "I guess Yenneg is hoping to impress me."

"Oh yes, he must really want to have Captain Tevirik in his army."

Tevi put the stopper back and placed the bottle beside the talisman box. She gave her lover an accusing look. "It's bad enough all of them calling me Tevirik. There's no need for you to start."

Jemeryl smiled, unrepentant. "It's your own fault for telling them what Tevi was short for."

"Somebody asked me, but I never said it was my name."

"But Tevi is such a blatant diminutive. People clearly didn't think it was the right thing to call an officer. But if you like, I'll let people know even Tevi is just a nickname, and that you should really be called *Strikes-like-lightning*."

Tevi's glare only had the effect of sending Jemeryl into a fit of giggles. The women of the Western Isles had unconventional ideas about suitable names for warriors. Her real name was something that Tevi had been very pleased to leave behind. Jemeryl was the only person on the mainland in whom she had confided. Some days, Tevi even regretted telling her.

❖

Bykoda's face was dispassionately thoughtful as she examined the twin tracer charms laid on her desk. "So someone has outmanoeuvred me. It's about time that one of them managed it." Her tone even sounded admiring.

"Do you have any idea who might have done it? Or when?"

"No. Mavek brought me the box with the charm in it. I tested it out to make sure I was happy with the workmanship. Then I put the hearer in the cupboard over there and haven't touched it since. There's been no need. And at one time or another, all of them have been left alone in here. Anyone could have made the swap." Bykoda drummed on the desk with the fingernails. "A quite unforgivable oversight on my part."

"You understand that I'm worried."

"Oh yes. I am too. The chances are far too high for comfort that my killer is the one who wanted to trace the talisman. And I don't like the thought of them getting their hands on the talisman any more than you like the thought of being ambushed on the way back to Lyremouth." Bykoda left her desk and went to stare out through her study window.

"I'm afraid that finding out about it hasn't really told us much."

Bykoda turned back to face Jemeryl. "On no. It has told us a great deal. On a practical level, it has told us that we need to take much more care over your return to Lyremouth than we had supposed. Also it tells us that my killer is working to well laid-out plans, rather than merely seizing an opportunity. And that they are capable of subtlety and inventiveness. Which I find rather satisfying. I would so hate to be murdered by a lucky fool." She sighed. "I only wish that circumstances would allow me to make a decent fight of it."

Jemeryl felt a half smile touch her mouth, but then she looked again at the expression on Bykoda's face and it died. Beneath the placid exterior was a cold-blooded resolve, far more dangerous than any screaming rage.

❖

Except for Klara dozing atop a bookcase, their rooms were empty when Tevi returned from a ride beyond the castle walls. The magpie was such a constant companion of Jemeryl's that Tevi was surprised to see her.

"Where's Jem?"

The magpie lifted her head at the sound of the door closing. "She's talking to Bykoda."

"Why didn't she take you along?"

"She didn't tell me."

"Did she say when she'd be back?"

"No."

"Any idea what it's about?"

"No." Klara's beak twitched petulantly. "Nobody tells me nothing. A bird of my talents and I might as well be a blackboard." She pointedly tucked her head back into her breast feathers, still muttering indistinctly.

Tevi grinned. The sarcastic ill-humour that Jemeryl had bestowed upon her familiar was not meant to be taken seriously, although Tevi suspected Jemeryl often used her alter ego to vent her own irritation.

The familiar was little more than an extension of the sorcerer's own intellect. Jemeryl described the link as being so close that she was literally performing some of her own thinking in the magpie's head. The practise was not without hazards. If anything happened to Klara, Jemeryl would also be at risk. Tevi assumed that the benefits of a familiar justified it. Magic, and the worlds that Jemeryl saw, were not something she could ever understand.

Tevi dumped her riding gear by the door and wandered across to the window. Apart from horse riding and reading, not much in the way of entertainment for the ungifted was available in Tirakhalod. Boredom had been yet another reason for joining the army. Tevi idly picked up a book that had been left on the window seat. She could read while waiting for Jemeryl to come back, or she could go and try a new skirmish on the battle table.

Tevi caught the corner of her lip between her teeth. She knew that Jemeryl was questioning just how much time she was spending on the battle table. But Jemeryl had other things to do, and the battle table was fun. Tevi's expression changed to a grin as she headed back towards the door.

Was it not poxy bad luck that she would only start to enjoy herself in Tirakhalod when it was nearly time to leave? Yenneg was also a pleasant surprise. Previously she'd had little to do with him, but he was proving to be easygoing and considerate. He had even asked whether Jemeryl was showing signs of objecting to being left alone so much.

"Klara. I'm nipping over to Yenneg's battle table. If Jem returns, tell her I won't be long. I'll be back before nightfall. I promise."

"Would you like me to find a piece of chalk so you can write that on my back?"

Chapter Five—Star-crossed Lovers

Two dozen ogres ploughed ahead in a fury of fists and feet. The shield wall crumpled before the onslaught and broke. Howls of triumph drowned out the screams of the dying. On the other side of the field, phalanxes of enemy pikemen pushed back Tevi's forces, step by step. Defeat was imminent.

The ogres chased after the fleeing swordsmen, stopping only to tear fallen soldiers limb from limb—gruesome to watch, but ultimately their undoing. Within minutes of breaking through the shield wall, the ogres were no longer a cohesive force. Individual monsters were scattered across the right side of the field, spread out and vulnerable.

The cavalry charge put an end to their triumph. One by one the ogres went down. But the day was not yet won. Tevi's outnumbered swordsmen could hold out against the pikes no longer. They fled back to the ridge, where those who had survived the ogres were regrouping. The enemy phalanxes marched forwards, pikes lowered.

Fortunately, the cavalry had the discipline that the ogres lacked. Having driven their enemy from the field, they broke off the pursuit and wheeled around. A second cavalry charge hit the pikemen in the rear where they were most vulnerable. The tightly packed phalanxes began to disintegrate. With fresh hope, Tevi's infantry went on the offensive, and at last, the enemy, assailed to both front and rear, faltered and fled.

Tevi contemplated the scene. A victory, but not a very good one. Scarcely half of her troops had survived. The ogres were the problem. Tevi studied the twenty-foot-tall behemoths, wondering what deranged sorcerer had created them. She would have to ask Yenneg about the history of the battle. But in the meantime, maybe if she started with a cavalry charge on the ogres, they could be routed early on. The combined infantry should be capable of pinning down the phalanxes until help could arrive.

Tevi was about to go in search of a witch to reset the table when she spotted the candle in its holder on the wall. Only a stub of wax remained. Hours had passed. Tevi's shoulders slumped in disbelief. Where did the time go? She had promised Jemeryl that she would be back early, but she was going to be late. And this was the fourth time it had happened in the space of eight days.

Angry with herself, Tevi grabbed her cloak and dashed from the room. She paused on the steps outside. Night had long since fallen, and a ring of mage lights lit the path around the perimeter of the bailey. The setting moon was only a thin sliver above the battlements, casting the weakest glimmering. The shortcut across the unlit central gardens would be hazardous. Tevi was about to go the long way round, but then she took another look at the moon's position and realised just how late she was. She bounded down the steps and hurdled over the box hedge that surrounded the garden.

By the time her eyes adjusted to the dark, Tevi had already acquired a range of minor injuries. She had tripped twice, encountered a particularly thorny rosebush, and got a wet foot from misjudging the leap across a pond. She was just thinking that things were getting better when she ran up against a tall hedge of conifers.

Rather than detour around the obstacle, Tevi dropped to her hands and knees and crawled through where the network of branches was thinnest, at the base of the trunks. Her head emerged on the other side. She was about to drag herself out onto a gravel path running parallel to the hedge when she froze. Someone was creeping stealthily along the path towards her. From Tevi's low vantage point, the figure stood out in stark silhouette against the stars.

Even with the darkness, the person was evidently worried about being spotted, or followed, and hugged close to the firs. Yet Tevi was able to make an identification. As the figure turned to look behind, the clear outline of half a left arm was displayed briefly, ending at the elbow. Ranenok.

Tevi pulled her head back into cover as the army commander passed. Ranenok showed no sign of knowing that she was there. He carried on cautiously up the path without pausing.

Hunting a sorcerer was dangerous. Tevi had no illusions about being a match for him if events should lead to conflict. Regardless of how weak Ranenok's magical abilities might be, they were more than sufficient to deal with one ungifted opponent. However, Tevi could not let the chance go by. Ranenok was engaged in some illicit activity, else he would not be creeping around in the dark. She had to learn more.

Once the soft sound of footsteps on gravel had faded, Tevi reversed through the branches and snuck along the outside of the hedge. The row ended on the banks of a large lily pond. Tevi crouched in the shelter of the last of the firs. The moonlight was just sufficient for her to see Ranenok climb the steps of a wooden summerhouse overlooking the water.

Tevi crept back a few yards, then wormed her way beneath the hedge, crossed the path, and slipped into a patch of bushes on the other side. The most likely explanation for Ranenok's behaviour was that he was meeting someone in the summerhouse. Tevi wanted to get close enough to hear what they were saying.

An open patch of lawn lay between her and the wooden building. Tevi worked her way around the edge, although she knew that keeping out of sight was pointless. If Ranenok was looking out for her using his sorcerer senses, she would not be able to keep hidden. Yet being under cover made her feel safer.

The last few yards were through a high border of delphiniums and foxgloves. As she got close, the low murmur of voices confirmed her guesswork. At least two people were in the summerhouse. Tevi crouched beside the back wall and pressed her ear against the wooden slats. Immediately it was clear that the soft whispered tones were not due merely to the need for secrecy.

"I wish we were snuggled up in my bed. I could warm you properly then."

Tevi bit her lip to stop herself from laughing. Nothing sinister, just a lover's tryst, although the clandestine venue and Ranenok's behaviour implied that whoever he was meeting was not free of other entanglements. Tevi was about to slip away and allow the commander privacy for his liaison, when the second voice made her stop.

"I agree we'd run less risk of splinters. But if Bykoda found out, splinters would be the least of our problems." The speaker was Kharel.

"I wish there was some way we could get free of her."

"There isn't."

"You should be more positive."

"I know what I've seen."

"But is that an oracle or your own fears talking?"

"It isn't...I don't..." Kharel sounded distressed.

"Oh, come now. I didn't mean to upset you." Ranenok spoke even more gently. His words were followed by the sound of kissing.

Noises from the summerhouse grew unmistakeably more passionate. Tevi backed away through the ranks of tall flowers.

At the gravel path, she stopped and looked again at the summerhouse. No alarm had sounded. Sometimes even sorcerers could let their guard down. Tevi pursed her lips in an expression of sympathy. Ranenok should be free to pick the lover of his choice without fear of whoever else might object. It was something that everyone deserved.

Tevi raised her eyes to the sky. The moon had slipped below the battlements. The shortcut through the garden had not proved quick. Tevi swallowed. Her own relationship was about to hit a temporary rough patch. Jemeryl would not be happy.

When she opened the door to the main room of their quarters, Tevi caught a brief glimpse of Jemeryl pacing back and forth in front of the fireplace before her partner spun to face her, hands on her hips.

"Tevi! Where have you been?" Jemeryl both looked and sounded angry.

"I'm sorry. I was playing on the battle table and I got carried away."

"This always happens."

"I know. But I swear, one minute it was daylight outside, and the next time I looked up it was night."

Jemeryl was not placated. "I was worried about you. I thought Dunarth might have kidnapped you for a few experiments."

Underneath the anger, Tevi could hear genuine fear in her lover's voice, and a pang of guilt hit her. She stepped closer and pulled Jemeryl into a hug. "I'm sorry. There's nothing else I can say. I don't know where the time went."

"I sent a message over to Yenneg's rooms an hour ago."

"I never received it. Whoever took the message must have forgotten to pass it on."

A little of the anger left Jemeryl's stance. Her body softened into the embrace, although Tevi could tell that she was not yet ready to forgive.

"You think you can just give me a hug and I'll let it drop?"

"No. I know you better than that."

"That's not a good answer."

"Would you like me to rephrase it?"

Jemeryl pulled away. She plucked a twig off Tevi's cloak and held it to the light, then she stepped farther back and considered the state of the rest of Tevi's clothing. Her frown shifted to one of confusion. "Are you sure you've just been playing at battles all this time?"

"Not quite. I got delayed on the way back. By Ranenok and Kharel."

"How?"

"I spotted Ranenok tiptoeing through the garden so I followed him. He met Kharel in the summerhouse."

"Do you have any idea why?"

"Um...yes. They're lovers."

"Oh." Jemeryl sank back into Tevi's arms. Surprise had clearly swept all other emotions away. "Do you think Bykoda knows?" she asked after a long pause.

"From the bit I overheard, Ranenok and Kharel don't think so. They were worried about what might happen if she found out."

"They're probably right. Two acolytes forming a relationship is the last thing Bykoda wants. It's why she puts so much effort into setting them at each other's throats. Individually, she's more than a match for any of them."

"Could Ranenok and Kharel together challenge her?"

"I wouldn't have thought so, but Bykoda doesn't take chances. Did you know that the council meeting is the only occasion where she is ever in the presence of more than two of her acolytes at once?"

"So it's a good place to kill her if you want a big audience."

Jemeryl lay her face on Tevi's shoulder. Tevi held her close, feeling the angry tension slowly drain from the body in her arms. She was going to have to do something to make it up to Jemeryl, but for now they were in harmony.

"I wonder..." Jemeryl said after a long silence.

"What?"

"I'd been thinking that the council room was an odd place for the assassination. Why tackle Bykoda where she's strongest? Why make things difficult? But it would make sense if you wanted to be sure that the other acolytes knew who'd done it."

"Would they do that? Most murderers want to hide their crime."

"If they take over the Empire they get to make up the laws. Maybe they want to kill Bykoda in a spectacular fashion for the intimidation factor. The assassin wants the other acolytes to sign up as recruits for the new regime and knows they won't do it willingly on account of them all hating each other's guts."

"Except for Ranenok and Kharel."

"And maybe a few others we don't know about." Jemeryl yawned. "We can talk more tomorrow. It's too late now." She pulled back and directed an accusatory gaze at Tevi. "Try to be earlier next time."

"I will. I promise." But as she kissed Jemeryl's lips, Tevi wondered if it was a promise she could keep.

❖

Herbalism had always been Jemeryl's least favourite branch of magic. The discipline involved too much careful measuring of unpleasant substances for unspectacular results. It also brought back memories of working in hospital wards—the smells, sounds, and sights. Jemeryl knew that for ordinary citizens the healers were the most admired of Coven sorcerers. On a daily basis, people's lives depended upon the cures that herbalism provided, but that did not make it fun.

Jemeryl looked at the façade of the apothecary with distaste. The subject held even less appeal for her here in Tirakhalod where it was used to kill more often than cure. She had avoided the apothecary whenever possible. However, this far north, plants grew that were unknown in the Protectorate, and Dunarth was the expert in them. Not taking samples back would be unforgivably remiss. Jemeryl took a deep breath and climbed the steps to the door.

The first room she entered was an office. Ledgers filled a long shelf on one wall. Two clerks were working at a desk in the middle. A blackboard with scribbled notes was by the door. Jemeryl assumed the clerks would both be witches, magic users with access to only one of the paranormal dimensions. For witches assigned to the apothecary, their extra dimension would certainly be the fifth, where the life forces of animals and plants were held.

"Can we help you, ma'am?"

"I'd like to see Dunarth."

"She's through there." One of the witches pointed to a door.

Even without the body on the slab, it would have been obvious to anyone that the room Jemeryl entered was used for dissection. Knives and bone saws lay ready. The air was thick with the smell of blood. On either side, shelves were lined with jars containing organs: some human, some animal, and some Jemeryl could not even guess at.

Dunarth and a young witch were working on the body. The alchemist glanced up as Jemeryl opened the door but continued with her task.

"Do you want something?"

"I was hoping for a few samples."

"Animal or vegetable?" Dunarth's voice was conversational, even cheery.

"Vegetable."

"Can it wait a few minutes?"

"Yes."

Dunarth nodded and carried on slicing. The corpse was a middle-aged woman of thickset build. A few old scars crossed her shoulder and upper arm. The hair had already been shaved from her head. Her skin was white. Jemeryl noted the severed jugular and surmised that the body had been drained, but no visible cause of death was apparent.

Jemeryl turned away. She did not want to know more, but a displeased snort made her look back. Dunarth's expression had changed to annoyance. She discarded her knife and stepped back.

"There's no point going on. Waste."

The witch gave a questioning look. "Ma'am?"

"You can tidy up. Throw the blood out."

"Yes, ma'am."

Dunarth stomped over to a basin to wash her hands.

Jemeryl joined her. "The experiment failed?" She could not help herself asking.

"Wasn't an experiment. One of the soldiers got blind drunk and fell off the battlements last night. Broke her neck. I was hoping for a few samples. But from the state of her liver, she can't have spent much of the past ten years sober. All her organs will be affected. Even the blood is useless. The bones might be all right, but I've got plenty of those in stock."

"Excuse me, ma'am," the witch interrupted. "What shall I do with the body?"

"Put it out for burning with the rest of the rubbish."

"Might the woman have some friends who'd want to bury her?" Jemeryl asked.

Dunarth stared at her in confusion, much as a cook might if it were suggested that the inedible parts of a sheep should be returned to the flock for a ceremony. "Why bother?"

Small wonder that she was so hated by the ungifted troops, Jemeryl thought, but said nothing.

"Now, what did you want?" Dunarth asked.

"I wonder if I could have specimens of some local herbs."

"Which ones?"

"These for starters. But basically anything you think we might not have back in the Protectorate." Jemeryl pulled out the list she had prepared.

Dunarth scanned it briskly. "Hmm. I don't have any of that, or that. They don't come into season until summer. But I can let you have all the rest and some other stuff. Follow me."

The alchemist led the way to another room, where arrangements of jars, pipes, and funnels covered the benches. Jemeryl recognised the equipment as being for the preparation of potions. Judging by the sound of soft dripping, several were currently in distillation. Well-stocked shelves filled the rear wall of the room. Dunarth marched over and started taking down bottles and pouches.

"Watch what you touch in here. Most of it is poisonous."

The warning was unnecessary. Dunarth's potions had a deadly reputation, and Jemeryl would have had better sense than to prod around. She looked at the nearest bench. Green liquid was being filtered through sand. With morbid curiosity, Jemeryl examined the aura, expecting to be shocked, but to her surprise, it was faintly familiar.

"This one isn't. And I feel that I ought to know it."

Dunarth glanced over her shoulder. "Why? It's a pointless waste of time."

"Then why are you making it?"

"I was asked to."

Jemeryl frowned. "Couldn't you refuse?"

"Doing a favour can be a good investment."

"So what is it?"

"A love potion."

The reply was the last thing Jemeryl had expected, but at least she could account for the familiarity. Her apprenticeship in the Coven had seen its share of adolescent pranks. But why was Dunarth making one now? Surely nobody over the age of sixteen would bother with such a thing. Yet who, apart from the acolytes or Bykoda, would have the authority to request a potion made? And who would Dunarth think it worth currying favours with?

"Who's it for?" Jemeryl had to ask.

Dunarth stopped measuring out the herbs and treated her to a long hard stare. "How long have you been in Tirakhalod?"

"Just over two and a half years."

"And you haven't yet learnt not to ask questions like that?" The alchemist gave a bark of laughter. "Let's just say, someone who should know better."

The description did not help. It covered all the possible suspects.

Dunarth carried on collecting the samples. Watching her, Jemeryl wondered whether by doing it in person rather than delegating the task to one of the witches, Dunarth might be trying to make another small investment. And if so, what repayment the alchemist was hoping for.

The answer to this question came as soon as the samples were finally bagged up.

"Um...your servant, Captain Tevirik."

"She isn't my servant."

Dunarth brushed the objection away. "I'm intrigued by the potion you made for her, the one for strength."

"I didn't make it. It's brewed on the island chain she comes from."

"Does she have any with her?"

"No. As I understand it, the potion needs to be taken throughout childhood. It affects muscle and bone development. After the person is fully grown, there is no need to take it again."

"Really." Dunarth looked impressed. "I've tried making strength potions. The trouble is that the heart is a muscle like any other. People who took it ended up bursting blood vessels in their brains. I was never able to sort it out. Do you know that—"

"I'm familiar with the problems." Dunarth was not the only one to be intrigued. Until Tevi had shown up in the Protectorate, every sorcerer in the Coven had believed that strength potions were impossible.

"I wonder..." Dunarth began cautiously. "If you would allow me to examine her. I promise I won't do any permanent damage."

Jemeryl restrained the first angry words that rose to her lips. Instead she settled for the one answer that she knew would cause the most confusion. "It's not for me to say. You'll have to ask Tevi."

❖

"It's time to go."

The magpie's strident voice made Tevi jump. She glanced over her shoulder at Klara, perched on the windowsill. The beaklike eyes could not display human emotions, but Tevi felt the smugness radiating. She turned back to the table. The battle before her was reaching its climax. The first of her soldiers had breached the walls. If they could claim the gatehouse then the city was hers for the taking.

"Um...I want to see..."

"It's on your head. You know what Jem will say. Just don't blame me."

Tevi sighed ruefully. Indeed, she did know what Jemeryl would say. And in truth, there was no need to continue. The defenders were falling back. Now that they had been routed from their positions, the battle was effectively over. It would have been nice to see it through to its conclusion, but what was the point in having a talking alarm if you ignored it?

"All right. I'm going."

Tevi collected her belongings and headed for the door. Klara fluttered over and landed on her shoulder. Bringing her along to keep an eye on the time had been Jemeryl's idea. So far, it was working well.

As she passed the door to his study, she met Yenneg coming out. The army commander gave a warm smile and adopted an informal pose, leaning his shoulder on the door frame.

"Ah, Tevi. Are you going?"

"Yes, sir. I'd promised Jemeryl that I wouldn't be late this time."

Another broad smile lit his well-formed features. "And it's so easy to lose track of time."

"I know. That's why I brought Klara with me."

Yenneg's eyes flicked briefly in the magpie's direction. A pensive expression flashed across his face. "How did you do today?"

"I won the battle of Rezecha Ford. And took the city of Tracheck."

"You did well."

"But I think I could do better. I'm not making the most of my cavalry."

Yenneg nodded. "It's all a question of timing. If you can wait a minute, I've got a book that you might find interesting."

"Certainly." Being a few minutes late would not matter. It was the few hours that had been testing Jemeryl's patience.

Yenneg strolled back into his study. From her position at the door, Tevi saw him scanning along one of the bookshelves. He disappeared from view as he moved on to a second set. "Aha. Here it is." Tevi heard the sound of rustling and then he was back at the door, holding out a thin volume.

"There you go. You can take it with you to read. Dravin's thesis on the deployment of cavalry. It's the classic text on the subject, a couple of centuries old, but it's never been beaten. The language can be hard to follow in places, but I'm sure Jemeryl can help you out."

"Thank you, sir."

❖

After the evening meal, Tevi got the chance to look through the book that Yenneg had given her. Reading and writing were unknown on the islands of her birth. The skill was one that Tevi had acquired only after coming to the mainland as a grown woman, and she was happy to admit that her standard of literacy was open to improvement. Even so, she thought that "hard to follow" was definitely an understatement for the text.

It did not help that the book was written in an archaic version of the local dialect. After more than two years living in Tirakhalod, and with a little magical assistance from Jemeryl, Tevi was able to speak the standard form fluently, but the outdated terminology in the book was a struggle to understand.

Tevi glanced across to where Jemeryl sat transcribing loose notes into her journals, ready to take back to Lyremouth. A sorcerer's work required much scouring of ancient texts, and Jemeryl was by nature a far more enthusiastic scholar than she was.

"Um...Jem. What does *Giggynge of sheeldes and helmes bokelynge* mean?"

"What?"

"I'm trying to read this book that Yenneg lent me. But I'm having trouble."

Jemeryl left the table and came to sit beside Tevi on the couch. As she leafed through the book her shoulders started to shake with laughter. "Yenneg certainly wants to broaden your education."

"It's supposed to be about making the best use of cavalry."

"It probably is. But I'd struggle to read it. And even if I could make sense of the words, I wouldn't understand the context, although it might mean something to you. Um...*Giggynge of sheeldes*, that sounds like it's something to do with adjusting the straps on shields."

"Well, obviously you'd have to do that immediately prior to battle."

"Oh yes, obviously." Jemeryl put her arm around Tevi's shoulder, still laughing. "I'm teasing you. I'd have assumed the straps would have been at the right adjustment to start with."

"No. When you're travelling, you—" Tevi broke off. A folded slip of paper had dropped from the book and landed on her lap.

Jemeryl picked it up and opened it flat, revealing a handwritten note.

> *My darling,*
>
> *I love you so dearly, and it fills my soul with joy to know you feel the same about me. This current time is a trial to us both. It pains me that we can only have snatched moments together, but soon she will be gone. Hold true to our love. Once Tirakhalod is free of her detested presence then nothing will stand in the way of our happiness.*
>
> *Your loving*
> *Yenneg*

"Who do you think he's writing to?" Jemeryl asked.

"I've no idea. His current lover is one of the peasants from the nearest village. It can't be him. There's nothing keeping them apart, and the lad can't read anyway." Tevi paused, thinking. "Of course, we don't know how old this note is. It could be someone he was involved with years ago. And there have been enough of them."

"Except he says *soon she will be gone*. Bykoda's still here."

"Maybe he was being overoptimistic."

"Or maybe the peasant is a ruse to cover an affair with one of the other acolytes. He does sound certain that Bykoda is about to make a permanent exit."

Tevi shook her head in bemusement. "First Ranenok and Kharel, and now you think Yenneg and one of the others."

Klara was perched on the back of the seat. "Who'd have guessed that Tirakhalod was such a haven for star-crossed lovers? Maybe it's something in the water."

Jemeryl looked thoughtful. Klara's words had clearly sparked a memory. "It might indeed be something in the water. Remember Dunarth was making that love potion. If you want an ally for an attack on Bykoda, what better way to get unquestioning support?"

Tevi slipped down in her seat, staring at the paper. Everything they learnt only made the problem more complex. Even if this note was part of the plot to kill Bykoda, it still left one big question. "But which one's the victim, and which one's the assassin?"

"Yes. Now that's what we need to find out."

❖

One of the lieutenants met Jemeryl just inside the entrance of Anid's quarters. "Can I help you, ma'am?"

"I'd like to see the commander."

The statement was not strictly true. Jemeryl needed to talk to the woman. *Like* did not come into it. Anid had returned to Tirakhalod in advance of Bykoda's next council meeting, scheduled for two days' time, and regardless of how much Jemeryl might dislike her, it would be foolish not to get the most up-to-date information concerning travel to the south of Tirakhalod.

"I'll see if she is available."

The lieutenant reappeared a few seconds later. "The commander can see you now."

The room that Jemeryl was shown into was small and comfortably furnished. Firelight and wood panelling made it feel welcoming, even though the decoration was mainly of weaponry and hunting trophies. Crossed swords were the dominant motif, Anid was relaxing in a chair by the fire. The remains of a light lunch were scattered across a table in one corner, and a wineglass was in her hand. She gestured with it as Jemeryl took a seat.

"Would you like some?"

"No, thank you."

Anid waited until the lieutenant had gone before continuing. "What can I do for you?"

"I was hoping that you could give me current information about the state of the passes over the Barrodens."

"Which pass do you intend to take?"

"I haven't made my mind up yet." And even if she had, Jemeryl would not have said.

Only two passes crossed the Barroden mountain chain, one at Horzt in the east and one above Denbury in the west. If Anid was the assassin and after the talisman, why make her job easier by letting her know the route in advance?

Anid pursed her lips. "The pass at Horzt will be first to open. I left Uzhenek four days ago. We'd had no news about it then, but it won't be closed for much longer. It might even be open now. Spring looks to be coming early. Seeing that it will take you at least twelve days to get there, you could set off tomorrow. If you want to go via Denbury, it might pay to wait a little while longer."

"How is travel on the plain?"

"Snow's all gone. The roads are a bit mushy underfoot, and the rivers are swollen with the runoff, but they should be fordable. Avoid the lower reaches of the Rzetoka River, and make sure you've got rope with you, just in case."

"Is there anything else I need to know?"

"No trouble that I know of."

"Then I won't take any more of your time." Jemeryl made to stand, but Anid waved her back.

"You're definitely returning to the Protectorate?"

"Yes."

"What does Bykoda think about that?"

Jemeryl frowned. "How do you mean?"

Anid treated her to a long, searching stare. "Just an odd idea I have. Ever since you've been here, I've been wondering why Bykoda invited you. She's never allowed a halfway decent sorcerer to get within blasting distance of her before. And then she starts teaching you all her tricks. And the more it goes on, the more I've been asking myself, *Why?*"

"And what conclusion have you reached?" Jemeryl said, more as a challenge than a question. She had no patience for the acolytes' petty political intrigue.

"Maybe she's grooming you to take over."

Jemeryl shook her head. "You're way off target."

"So why do you think she's been doing it?"

"You'll have to ask her."

Anid laughed without rancour. "You don't like me, do you?"

"No." Jemeryl had no reason to be sparing with the truth.

"Because I wanted to buy your little sweetheart?"

"Is there any point to this?"

"Yes. There is." Anid met her eyes steadily. Suddenly the taunting façade was gone, replaced by something that seemed far more sincere. "I've got some advice for you. I'm not bothered over how you feel about me. I couldn't survive in Tirakhalod if I let those sort of things get to me. But you"—she pointed at Jemeryl—"aren't that ruthless. If Bykoda offers to make you her successor, turn her down. You'll never make it."

"And are you hoping that she'll nominate you instead?"

"Me? No. I'm not up to it. I'm a decidedly third-rate sorcerer. If I was in your Coven, I'd be at the level of third assistant dishwasher in Lyremouth. It's only because I'm no threat to her that I get to be in charge of half the Empire. Believe it or not, what I just gave you was honest, friendly advice, and that's a very rare thing to find around here."

Jemeryl wondered if the commander was drunk, although there was no trace of slurring in her voice. "So why the spirit of generosity?"

"Because I'm in a generous mood, and despite what you might think, I'm not a callous bitch." Anid swirled the wine in her glass. "You and your ungifted captain, you love each other?"

"Yes."

"Then run back to the Protectorate and live happily ever after, because you won't do it here. Your heart makes you way, way too vulnerable." Anid paused. "Did you know that I had a couple of kids?"

"No."

"Two sons. Both totally ungifted. I got them a place in the army. Yenneg's predecessor arranged for an *accident* to happen to them." Anid's eyes were fixed on her glass, as if hypnotised. Her voice was softer than Jemeryl had heard it before. "And Bykoda's children didn't do much better. Although she got the satisfaction of dealing in person with the bastard who killed them. Your captain is the only ungifted officer who's ever lasted more than a year in the army. And that's simply because no one hates you enough to get at you through her."

"It's...I...that's awful." Jemeryl struggled for words. She gazed in sympathy at the army commander, for the first time considering the personal cost of living within the ruthless power games of Tirakhalod. The Coven had its internal conflicts, but there were rules. There was justice. There was security. In Bykoda's Empire, the higher you got, the more precarious your position. What would life be like when love was only a weapon that could be used against you?

"Yeah, well. It was my own fault. I knew my sons were in danger. When they were babies, I thought about taking them somewhere safe. I even thought about joining the Protectorate. But I didn't fancy washing dishes. I thought I could protect them. I was wrong." Anid's voice dropped. "And that's the risk you take in Tirakhalod when you love someone ungifted."

"I'm sorry."

Anid shrugged and tossed back the contents of her glass. "It was a good few years ago. I don't think about them now...more than once or twice a day. Mostly, I try not to love anyone. And if I can't stop myself, I make sure that nobody else knows about it. It's safer when you're caught up in the sort of games Bykoda plays. Yenneg's predecessor, the bitch who had my sons killed, she didn't really have any cause to hate me. It was just Bykoda messing with her head. That didn't stop me from getting her in the end, though."

"What did you do?"

"You don't want to know." Anid got up and collected the wine bottle from the corner table. While she poured a refill, Jemeryl watched her. She had the feeling that the army commander was using the diversion to clamp down on her emotions. The moment for heartfelt revelations was past.

Back in her seat again, Anid picked up her glass. "Anyway, Yenneg has taken over now, and he's a fool. He's going to do something really stupid."

"In what way?"

"He's too new at the game. Ranenok and me, we can't stand each other, but we know it's not real. We're not on different sides. We go through the ritual of swapping insults, but we make sure we keep a grip on our common sense. If ever I'm tempted to do something serious, I step back, count to ten, and let it drop. But Yenneg...he's going to do something nasty before he realises that he's being strung along by Bykoda."

"Ranenok feel the same as you?"

"I'm sure of it. He's on to Bykoda's tricks. He and his partner never had children. They knew the chances of them being gifted were no higher than for the peasants in the village, so they took precautions. But when his partner died, you could see the fire go out of his eyes." Anid gave a snort of amusement. "Mind you, there's a bit of a sparkle back these days. I think he's having an affair."

"Any idea who with?" Jemeryl kept her tone innocent.

"I guess it has to be Kharel or Mavek."

"Not Dunarth?"

Anid laughed. "Haven't you spotted that Dunarth is a little bit odd?" She tapped the side of her head. "There's some connections missing up here."

"I've not noticed."

"You must have. She understands her plants and potions. But she hasn't got a clue about other people. She doesn't realise that the things she says and does will have an effect on others. Probably because other people have no effect on her."

"She was telling me about the advantage of trading favours."

"Oh, she's learnt about manipulating people, but it's just an exercise in logic for her. She doesn't understand *why* some things work. She can't put herself in other people's shoes. And if there's nothing she wants from you, she'll ignore you. She doesn't have friends, and she certainly doesn't have lovers. No, it's got to be Kharel or Mavek that Ranenok's playing with."

"Who do you favour?"

"Fire or ice? It's a hard call. Kharel acts the cold fish. I'm sure there's life underneath the frost, but would she let her guard down? Plus, I've always suspected that she has a bit of a thing going for Bykoda, which I'm sure isn't reciprocated. I wouldn't put it past Bykoda to have had a hand in sowing the seed with a spell or two." Anid took a sip of wine. "And on the other hand, there's Mavek. But I didn't think he was looking for anyone new. He's been burned in the past, but he won't let the flames go out. He's been fanning the embers all these years. You need to know how to let go of the pain."

"Maybe he's finally moved on."

"I'm not sure. Mavek's the same as you. He wears his heart on his sleeve. If he had an affair going, he couldn't keep it hidden."

"Ranenok might have something going with one of his officers."

"In which case why not let everyone know? I never keep my affairs secret. But I never let anyone think it's serious." Anid's eyes fixed back on Jemeryl. "But you have. You've made it obvious to everyone how they can get a handle on you. Take my advice. Get back to the Protectorate as soon as possible. It's the only place you'll be safe."

CHAPTER SIX—THE RUNE SWORD

Tevi lay sprawled on the couch grimacing at the open book. Dravin's cavalry thesis was starting to make some sort of sense to her, but it was not easy going. She had worked out that by *carte* he meant *chariot*, and thought she understood the point he was making in the section that she was on, although she was sceptical about the example given. Was she reading it right?

Tevi took a few more seconds, clicking her thumbnail across her bottom teeth, and then raised her head. "Jem. Do magic spells bounce off mirrors?"

Jemeryl was sitting at the table. She put her pen down. "Depends on what it is. Some do. Most don't. Why?"

"It's this bit in the book. Dravin is going on about the stability of a four-wheeled chariot and tells the story of an ungifted warrior who had a mirror shield. He charged up in his chariot, and when a witch lobbed a spell at him, he was steady enough to reflect it back and kill her. At least, I think that's the story."

"It's possible with the right sort of spell."

"Or the wrong sort, if you're looking at it from the witch's point of view," Klara added.

"But not most spells?"

"No."

"I wonder if I'm reading it right."

"What does it say?"

"*Widen hes mirer sheelde.*"

Jemeryl left the table and perched on the arm of the couch by Tevi's head. She leant over to study the page and then pointed to a word. "*Mirer*. It can mean mirror, but the root of the word means to look at or to admire. I suspect what Dravin means is an admirable shield."

"It's just some sort of enchanted shield?"

"That's my guess."

Tevi nodded. "It would take a spectacularly stupid witch to see someone coming at her with a mirror shield and still pick a reflectable spell."

"Er...I'd have, er...yes." Jemeryl sounded distracted.

Tevi shifted around on the couch, and twisted her neck to look up at her lover's face. Jemeryl was staring at the windows. However, it was night and nothing could be seen outside. Suddenly, Jemeryl's expression changed from preoccupied to excited.

"Have you thought of something?" Tevi asked.

"Yes. Look." Jemeryl pointed at her reflection in the window.

"What is—" Tevi did not get the chance to complete her question.

"I'll bet anything that it will work. Come on."

Jemeryl grabbed Tevi's hand and dragged her from the room. They left the tower, rounded the outer edge of the bailey, went under the arch into the courtyard of the keep, and finally ending up in the council chamber.

The room looked exactly the same as the last time that Tevi had seen it. The thralls in the corners might even have been the same individuals—if individual was a word that could properly be ascribed to thralls.

Jemeryl trotted over to the acolytes' iron chairs and faced the side wall. Tevi stood by the door and watched her indulgently. She did not know where it was all leading, but she was happy to go along with Jemeryl's enthusiasm.

"Right, let's see then." Jemeryl bobbed her head from side to side, then took a step backwards and repeated the action. She ducked briefly to a half crouch, followed by three paces forwards. Then, to finish, she took a long step to the side and three vertical jumps.

"If this is a new dance, I hope you're not expecting me to remember the steps," Tevi said.

Jemeryl glanced back. Judging from her expression, she had lost on the bet with herself about whatever it was working. She waved her hand in the general direction of the wall. "It was the windows."

"What about them?"

"The reflection. As I said, most spells won't bounce off mirrors.

But some do. And unlike the stupid witch, the assassin would want to pick a reflecting spell."

"You thought they could bounce a spell around the edge of the crystal shield?"

"That's what I hoped."

"And it won't work."

"See for yourself."

Tevi went to Jemeryl's side. It was night, and nothing could be seen in the windows except the reflections. The problem with Jemeryl's idea was immediately apparent. The bottom of the windows was at head height, and from the acolyte's chairs, only the image of the upper walls and ceiling floated darkly in the glass.

"The windows are too high." Jemeryl stated the obvious. "I can't even see the canopy over her throne."

Tevi stood on her toes. "I can just about see the top of it. But I'm a few inches taller than you."

"Mavek is the tallest of the acolytes," Jemeryl said thoughtfully.

"Easily. He's at least nine inches taller than me."

"So what could he see?"

Tevi looked at her, amused. "I don't know. I'm not tall enough."

"Jump."

"That's hardly going to be accurate. Why don't you try standing on a chair?"

Jemeryl's eyebrows drew together in a pantomime of a hard-done-by frown, but then she clambered onto a chair. "No good. I'm too high."

"Crouch down."

"Is this right?"

Tevi stood beside her, judging the eye height. "Up a bit...there. I think you're about right now. What can you see?"

"The very top of the back of the throne." Jemeryl shook her head. "It won't work. Bykoda is too short. She'd have to be standing up, with a tall hat on, and he might just be able to set fire to the pom-pom on the tip."

Jemeryl hopped down from the chair. "We might as well go. I'm sorry I dragged you away from your book."

"That's all right. I was in need of a break. Although I'm starting to get a feel for the words."

"You've got a knack for languages."

Tevi was surprised. "You're better at them than me."

"No. I've used magic to acquire everything I know."

"It's the same with me. I wouldn't be able to make myself understood in Tirakhalod if you hadn't helped with magic. And I didn't even know that more than one language existed before I reached the mainland."

"I brought with me the necessary components for the spell so we could learn the main language used in Tirakhalod. And that accounts for everything that I can say or understand. Meanwhile, you've picked up bits of half a dozen different dialects without any more help."

"Only because I need it with the troops. They come from all over Bykoda's Empire. It's better if you can shout commands in their native tongue. But I couldn't hold a proper conversation."

Jemeryl patted her shoulder. "Don't underestimate yourself."

Suddenly Jemeryl's hand tightened in a grip, immediately claiming Tevi's attention.

"What is it?"

Jemeryl was staring at the ceiling. "The chains."

"What? Oh...can you hit them using a reflection?"

Jemeryl took a pace to the side, craning her neck. "It's tricky with the shield in front of them, but...yes. Yes. You can. I think. I want to try. Can you go and hold the crystal on the right? I don't want it to smash when it hits the floor."

Tevi walked over and grabbed the chain just above the crystal. Jemeryl took a few more seconds to check angles and then hurled a ball of silver lightning at the window. Tevi saw the reflected bolt hit the chain above her head, but even to her ungifted eyes, the power of the shot on the rebound was greatly reduced. The chain vibrated in her hands, but did not break. Jemeryl tried a second and then a third blast. Yet still the crystal mounting remained firm.

"It's no good," Jemeryl conceded at last. "The windows look like mirrors at night, but they don't reflect all the energy. Most of it goes straight through. I can't put enough power into the bolt to do any serious damage to the chain."

Jemeryl's shoulders slumped in defeat. She glared at the chain fixture as if it had just insulted her personally, then turned and slouched back to their rooms. Tevi followed behind in a far more cheerful manner.

After four years together, she knew that she did not need to worry about her partner's dejection. It would not last. Jemeryl could be obsessive when stumped by a magical problem, but she was naturally optimistic. No setback could demoralize her for long. Soon she would be chasing the next idea.

Tevi was aware that her own personality was far more prone to negative brooding and a willingness to give up and let fate take over. Jemeryl was ambitious, with an eye to her future in the Coven. Tevi was content to take each day as it happened. As long as she was with Jemeryl the rest did not matter. Although some things could still get her wound up—like her current problem with a gang of crossbowmen holed up in a mine. After three attempts on the battle table she had failed to shift them. The problem was starting to cost her sleep.

When they reached their rooms, Jemeryl threw herself into the chair by the fireside, but already her frown was easing. "I know we can't save Bykoda. But it's frustrating that I can't see how the killer is going to do it."

Tevi dropped down beside her. "The *how* I don't worry about. I probably couldn't understand even if the killer tried to explain it. It's the *why* that confuses me."

"They want the talisman."

"Not the killer. Bykoda. Why is she there?"

"In what way?"

"Bykoda knows roughly what day she's going to be killed and where. Why will she walk into the chamber? Why not barricade herself in the top of the keep and not come out until after the danger time is over?"

"Because it isn't going to work out like that. For some reason she's going to hold her normal autumn council meeting at the normal time." Jemeryl's tone sounded less confident as her sentence progressed.

"But why? Does the oracle remove her free will?"

"No. It gets very hard to phrase in normal words. But basically the oracle tells her what her free will is going to make her do."

"Bykoda doesn't strike me as the sort of person who would freely walk to her death. The only way I could see her going into the council chamber on that day is as a prisoner."

"Oh." Jemeryl's eyes opened wide. "I hadn't thought of that. Why didn't you say something before?"

"It only just occurred to me." In truth, she had not been giving much thought to Bykoda's impending fate. The unavoidable death of the ancient despot after they had left her lands was not something Tevi could bring herself to care much about. The suggestion had popped into her head unbidden.

Various ways existed to inhibit a sorcerer's powers. By far the easiest was an iron collar. Some years before, Jemeryl had explained how iron distorted the forces of the paranormal dimensions. The sorcerer had likened the effect of wearing an iron collar to that of fireworks continually going off in your face. It completely blocked out access to the higher dimensions until the wearer had learned to see through the commotion—an adjustment that could take months.

"Would Bykoda have noticed in her vision if she'd been wearing an iron collar?"

"Probably," Jemeryl replied after some thought. "But there are other sorts of magical restraints she might have been held by. Something like that would tie in with the feeling of paralysis that she reported."

"So maybe the critical time is several days beforehand, when she's defeated and captured. Maybe Bykoda is in the council chamber on that day because her killer wants to use the room for a public trial and execution. The crystal shield wouldn't be able to protect her if her attacker could stand wherever they wanted."

"That's worrying."

"Why? What difference will it make to Bykoda?"

"I meant for us. Bykoda is confident that we'll get back to the Protectorate safely. She won't let the assassin take the talisman without a fight, and since she knows she won't die until autumn, she assumes she'll be able to defeat any challenge before then. But maybe the killer will first imprison her and then come after us."

Tevi frowned in thought. "For what it's worth, I don't think so. Bykoda is far too dangerous a person to keep under lock and key for six months. If the person who captures her has any sense, they won't let her live six days. Six minutes is more than I'd risk in their place."

Jemeryl chewed on her lip. "I just wish we could feel more secure. With the talisman at stake, I don't want to take a gamble."

"Just how dangerous is the talisman?" The question was one Tevi had worried about.

"I don't know, and nor does Bykoda. And that's the frightening thing." Jemeryl rolled her head around to look at Tevi. "Why don't you get me a drink while I try to think of a good explanation?"

"A feeble excuse." Nonetheless, Tevi smiled as she went to open a bottle of wine. On her return, she passed a glass over and snuggled up beside her partner on the couch.

Jemeryl adjusted her position to take account of this and slipped her arm around Tevi's waist. "When you change time, you have to store the energy of the temporal paradox. Think of it like storing water behind a dam. With everyone else who's ever tried, the dam burst immediately. Bykoda's achievement is that the dam has held for years. And despite all the other people who've failed, we don't have much more than guesswork about how the dam burst goes because all the information has been lost with them. However, we do know its power."

Jemeryl swirled the wine in the glass thoughtfully. "Sorcerers who've played around with time have tried to do something like burn a piece of paper and then change time so that it is unburned. Unfortunately for them, the temporal dam has burst. What we think happens is a bit like how water in a normal burst dam finds its own level. The released temporal energy tries to resolve any paradoxes. It doesn't change the past any more than water flows uphill, but it tries to make it so that the present is in such a state that it doesn't matter which way the events went. For the sorcerer with an unburned piece of paper, the easiest resolution is for everyone who knows what had happened to drop dead, and for the room it happened in to explode. But we don't know for certain because anything that could tell us gets destroyed in the process of resolving the paradoxes. So far, the biggest attempts to change time have left some rather large craters behind."

"How much energy is stored in the talisman?"

"Again, I don't know. We think that a temporal dam isn't like a dam on a river, in as far as energy doesn't continually build up over time. It *is* time. But that's guesswork. No one has ever had a dam hold long enough to test. But the more I think about the talisman, the more frightened I get. By now, the string of causal relationships must be affecting just about everyone in the world."

"Everyone?"

"Consider. Bykoda changes time so that a man who would have bought a new pair of boots doesn't. Everyone who would have seen him in the boots is affected. If the energy in the temporal paradox is enough to kill all those people, then everyone who would have met them is affected. And so it goes on. There have been decades for the temporal paradoxes to build up, and we can be sure that Bykoda's tinkering with time will have changed more than just somebody's footwear."

"Would there be enough energy in the talisman to kill everyone in the world?"

"There might. My gut feeling is no, but I suspect that's mainly wishful thinking. Bykoda is very worried, and she knows far more about it than me. Remember I said that a temporal rupture won't change the past, like water won't run uphill? Bykoda thinks there might even be enough energy to cause a sort of back-surge and remove her from history. But even if the temporal rupture can't kill everyone, I don't want to think about what sort of chaos would be left behind, the unresolved paradoxes bouncing around. It's never happened before. That's what's frightening."

Tevi stared thoughtfully at her glass, adding it all together. "We can't let the killer get the talisman."

"I know."

❖

Tevi marched into Ranenok's main briefing room and snapped to attention. "You wanted to see me, sir?"

The summons had arrived just after breakfast. Tevi had dashed over, even though she had formally resigned her army commission in advance of leaving Tirakhalod, and so was no longer subordinate to the commander. The message had contained a worrying lack of information on what he wished to talk about. However, from Ranenok's expression, it was not trouble. He smiled and gestured towards two chairs positioned in the warm spring sunlight by the window, clearly intending an informal meeting. No one else was in the room.

Ranenok opened the conversation once they were both seated. "I wanted to congratulate you on your performance as an officer. You've been an asset to my command."

Tevi ducked her head modestly. "I was just following my profession as a mercenary."

"The Protectorate Guild of Mercenary Warriors has a formidable reputation. If you're a typical representative I can understand why."

"Well, admittedly they're not all as strong as me."

Ranenok laughed. "If they were all as strong as you, your guild would rule the world."

This, Tevi knew, was mere flattery. "I think not. I know I couldn't hope to compete with anyone using magic."

"Don't be so sure. We're not invulnerable. And I have something for you that might help even the odds a little." Ranenok rose and went to his weapon rack. He returned carrying a sword in its scabbard. "I would like you to accept this as a gift from me."

Tevi took the offered weapon and half drew the blade. Even to a first glance, the workmanship was clearly of the highest order. From the sheen of the metal, she could tell that it had been worked to give the rare combination of a hard edge and a supple core. Strange letters were engraved in a pattern down its length.

"Thank you," Tevi said, both gratified and a little surprised.

"It's a rune sword. Jemeryl mentioned that you have prescience. This blade is forged to cause the minimum disturbance in the temporal currents. It may allow you an extra fraction of a second at a crucial moment." Ranenok spoke with warm sincerity. "I hope it will serve you well."

"Thank you, sir," Tevi repeated, although this time her surprise was sufficient to have half robbed her of her voice. A rune sword was an exceedingly valuable item. Most mercenaries would never earn enough in their lifetime to buy one, even if they had the gift to make use of it.

"You'll need some final adjustments so the blade will harmonise with your own aura. I've made arrangements with Mavek to do it. He said that he'd be free just after lunch today, if that's convenient for you."

"Thank you." Tevi really could think of nothing else to say. She slid the blade back into its scabbard and smiled at the commander.

"You'll be leaving Tirakhalod within the month?" Ranenok's tone made it a question.

"Yes. I think so."

He hesitated and then said, "I suppose there's no chance of you going on one last mission?"

"I didn't know that anything was planned."

"It wasn't. I've just received news of a raiding party of trolls just fifteen miles north of here. It's anyone's guess how they've got so close.

Mark it down to Yenneg's incompetence for letting them through. I'm sending out troops at dawn tomorrow to hunt them down, but I can't lead the platoon myself, since the council meeting starts then. Dealing with the trolls shouldn't take much more than a day or two, and I thought that if the passes over the Barrodens aren't open yet, you'd be back well before Madam Jemeryl was ready to go."

"I'd have to discus it with Jem."

"Of course."

Tevi felt a faint flicker of anger. She did not have to ask permission and she wanted to explain. "We need to make a joint decision about when we leave. I can't just say—"

Ranenok held his hand up. "It's all right. Just a faint hope on my part. You've more than fulfilled any obligations to me." He tilted his head to one side. A questioning expression crossed his face, with a hint of underlying amusement. "Jem? Is that what you call Madam Jemeryl?"

"Er...yes. When we're alone together." Tevi thought it best not to admit that "Jem" was the least of the soppy endearments.

The smile on his face strengthened. "I fear I had initially misunderstood your relationship. It was only seeing you together at the gathering that made me realise."

"In what way?"

"I'd assumed that she was the sorcerer and that you were her plaything with very little say in the matter. It's the way such things would run around here."

Tevi shook her head vehemently. "Jem sees me as her equal."

"And you love her."

"Oh, yes."

"That's good, although love can be very dangerous." Ranenok turned his head to gaze out of the window. The smile was swallowed by a bleaker expression. "It leaves you vulnerable. It makes you take insane risks. It can hurt like nothing else. But I don't think life is worth living without it."

His eyes scrunched closed, as if in response to the bright sunlight on his face, but Tevi suspected that was not the only reason. "I tend to agree with you, sir." Once again the words let her down and she could think of nothing helpful to say.

Ranenok looked back sadly. "Wherever your future takes you, Tevi, I wish you well."

❖

Clear blue skies hung above Tirakhalod. Jemeryl stood by a window overlooking the plain below. The last traces of snow had retreated from the grasslands. A mat of green rippled in the wind from the south. She turned and drifted to the windows on the other side of the room. Unlike the thin arrow slits on the outer facing walls, these were wider, giving a good view of the entire bailey.

Spring was on the way. Soon, Bykoda's magic would not be required to maintain the blooms in the garden. Several people were visible out in the warmest day so far that year. Kharel was one, taking a midday stroll between the flowerbeds and doubtlessly reviewing various intimate memories of the summerhouse. At least, that was what Jemeryl would have been doing in her place.

The sight of the steward reminded Jemeryl of something she had wanted to try out, a test for detecting the influence of love potions. She had already made the necessary preparations. Jemeryl grabbed an outdoor coat, dropped the tincture with its prognostic wrapping into her pocket and trotted down the stairs.

When she reached the garden, Jemeryl wandered along an avenue between borders of red hot spikes set against a background of white trailing vinery. She then turned onto a paved way beneath a canopy of cherry blossom and finally joined up with a circular path around the lily pond.

This seemingly aimless sauntering actually had her on an intercept course with the steward. As they got close, Jemeryl considered the other woman. Kharel was not someone you would suspect of a steamy love affair. Not because of her age or looks—Kharel wore her years well—but her emotions were under such tight control that it was easy to be misled into thinking that she did not have any.

"Ah, Kharel. I was hoping to see you." Jemeryl hailed her when they were still several paces apart.

"Jemeryl." The steward acknowledged her with a nod of the head.

"I need to talk to you about supplies for the journey to Lyremouth."

Unbidden, Jemeryl fell into step beside the steward. Her hand in her pocket wrapped around the tincture. She needed Kharel to say Ranenok's name. How difficult could that be? Was there a person in the world who did not want to talk about his or her lover? But, if there was an exception to the rule, then Kharel was very likely to be it.

"You will be leaving soon."

"In ten days or so."

"If you give a list of your requirements to my clerk, I will see that they are ready. I will tell him to treat them as a priority."

"Thank you."

"It is what Bykoda would want."

"She has been very generous." Jemeryl wondered how to turn the conversation to Ranenok. Kharel was offering no openings to exploit.

"You have benefited from your time here."

"Oh yes. We both have. I know that Tevi has found her experience serving under Ranenok most instructive."

Kharel avoided the bait. "I'm pleased for you."

"And equally, he asserts that Tevi has been of great use to him."

"I'm sure." Kharel sounded completely disinterested.

The two of them strolled on farther.

"Do you know how he lost his arm?"

"I believe it was an encounter with werewolves nearly a decade ago."

Jemeryl needed to work at concealing her frustration. Was Kharel deliberately avoiding her lover's name? "When I get back to Lyremouth, if we get the replacement limbs to work, perhaps he might be interested."

"That is something for you to discuss with Rane—"

At last. The instant that Kharel started to say the name, Jemeryl crushed the resin case of the tincture between her fingers. The liquid soaked into the prepared parchment wrapped around it.

"—nok."

"Maybe I will, next time I see him."

Jemeryl gave a smile to terminate the conversation and turned away onto another side path that took her back to the lily pond. Soon Kharel was out of sight. Jemeryl extracted the damp parchment from her pocket and held it in the sun to dry. The test was a well-known standard. If Kharel was the victim of a love potion given to her by Ranenok, the prognostic wrapping would turn red. If she was the one who had administered the potion to him, it would turn blue.

The minutes passed while the darker tinge caused by dampness faded. The parchment stayed obstinately white. Jemeryl looked at it thoughtfully. It was an answer of sorts. Neither Kharel nor Ranenok had used a potion on the other. Their affair was genuine on both sides.

Jemeryl stared vacantly at the lily pond while she tried to unscramble her thoughts. Yenneg's note might have nothing to do with the love potion and even less to do with Bykoda's assassination. But if it did? Jemeryl frowned. The trouble lay in finding a suitable candidate among the other acolytes.

Mavek felt like the best bet in the role of victim. Jemeryl wanted to trust Anid, although she knew that she should not, and it was interesting to speculate on the idea that Anid might be using the potion to ensnare a hated rival. Ranenok and Kharel would not be carrying on their affair if either were magically enamoured of somebody else, although invoking unrequited love in Yenneg might have political uses. Dunarth was too eccentric to make any judgement about.

The sound of footsteps interrupted Jemeryl's musing. She hastily thrust the strip of parchment back in her pocket in case it was Kharel returning. However, when Jemeryl looked up, she saw Bykoda ambling alone through the gardens.

The Empress smiled and raised her hand, beckoning. Clearly she wished to talk. Once they were standing side by side, Bykoda slipped her arm through Jemeryl's. "I trust you won't mind giving a little support to an old woman for a turn around the garden."

The linked arms surprised Jemeryl, not so much for the familiarity as for the way it drew attention to how frail the elderly woman was. Bykoda appeared so dominant in her keep that you never noticed her great age. In the springtime garden it was all too obvious. A touch of self-mockery had underlain Bykoda's words, but the description *old woman* was accurate. Even without the assassin's help, Bykoda did not have much longer to live.

"I've been giving some thought to your departure. We need to make sure that you're well on the way before the assassin knows you've left Tirakhalod."

"What do you propose?"

"Have you made enquiries about the route, and when you can leave?"

"Yes. I spoke to Anid yesterday afternoon. She thinks the pass at Horzt will be open within days, and that I could leave now."

Bykoda nodded. "Then I think that now would be a very good time to go. Or more precisely, tomorrow. My acolytes are all here for the council meeting, which means that they aren't sitting in ambush on the road ahead of you. Wait until the meeting is underway and then go. They'll all be fully occupied, so nobody will have time to notice that you've left Tirakhalod for a few days."

"I'll need provisions and to pack in secret."

"I can help you with that. Come to the keep this evening. I'll have everything you need ready. And I'll try to make sure that you have a good head start. Normally the council meeting goes on for four to five days. I'll keep them hanging around the castle for as long as I can. But..."

"But?"

Bykoda sighed heavily. "You've examined the council room?"

"Yes."

"Then you must have realised that my killer is a formidable sorcerer. I fear one of my acolytes has been hiding their talents. If it comes to a battle, I might lose."

"I hope that you don't."

"I hope so too. But one comfort I can take from the oracle is that I know it won't be fatal this time. The moon is in the wrong phase and the wrong position."

Bykoda came to a halt in front of a bed of roses. She bent her head to smell one, and then straightened again, smiling. "Do you know the oracle has been something of a blessing to me?"

Jemeryl was surprised. "I'm not sure I'd have looked at it that way."

"Do you see the towers and all the windows around us?"

"Yes."

"Has it occurred to you what an easy target I am standing here?"

"Er...no."

The two women strolled on farther, passing down a walkway

beneath a pergola. Pendants of purple wisteria dangled above their heads. The breeze carried the scent of the flowers.

"I hadn't dared leave the keep openly for decades. Imagine. I'm the Empress of a mighty Empire, and I've been a prisoner in my own keep. But now, I know I won't die in the garden, so I can walk out in the sunshine and stop to smell the flowers. It has been a great blessing for my final years."

A shiver ran through Jemeryl as she remembered Anid's revelation about Bykoda's children, dead at the hands of someone who wanted to hurt the Empress. And now, Bykoda lived alone in her huge empty keep, with just the company of mindless thralls. She was utterly alone. It was a high price for being ruler of an Empire. Anid's warning against becoming Bykoda's successor was unnecessary. The price was not one that Jemeryl would ever be willing to pay.

❖

Snakes of green light wreathed the rune sword. The shimmering continued up Tevi's arm as far as her shoulder. Mavek lifted the tip of the blade level with his eye so that he could squint along the length, and shot a succession of sparks from his fingertips. The green bands rippled where they were hit and then reformed in a different alignment. Although there was no detectable effect on the hilt, it seemed to fit more naturally in Tevi's hand. Mavek grunted and picked up a glass knife.

"It's a beautiful piece of work." He offered his opinion as he carefully sliced the knife along the length of the sword blade.

"Is it one of yours?"

"No. I'm not sure where Ranenok came across it. Probably retrieved it from raiders."

Tevi studied the play of light on the rune sword. The metal gleamed with a crystal purity. "Strange to think of brutes owning it. As you said, it's beautiful."

"It's a shame that its only purpose is to cause hurt." Unmistakeable regret underlay his words.

"Are you sorry that so much of your work does the same?"

The muscles in Mavek's jaw stood out as his teeth clenched. He sucked in a breath. "Sometimes I tell myself that I just make the things and I'm not responsible for how they're used, but I can never quite get myself to believe it. There's a good many folk lying in their graves, and my hand put them there, as surely as if I'd slit their throats."

Tevi shook her head. "You have to allow people responsibility for their own actions. A lot of those killed by your weapons had set themselves on the path to their grave when they decided to loot and steal and were stupid enough to think they could get away with it in Bykoda's lands."

Mavek's eyes met hers. "Is that what you tell yourself?"

The question got under Tevi's guard like a blow to the stomach. She raised her eyes to the ceiling while she composed an answer. "The same as you. Sometimes. Other nights I lie awake wondering if I should have done something different, and whether there is another person lying awake that night crying for somebody I've killed. But that is my guilt on my head. You don't need to carry it as well."

"Hey, that's too heavy a load not to share. I'll do my bit." Mavek grinned in a friendly fashion.

For a while he continued to work with the glass knife in silence. Tevi watched him. He and Ranenok were her favourite people in Tirakhalod. They alone seemed to view her as a person rather than as an appendage of Jemeryl.

"I appreciate Ranenok giving the sword to me." Tevi moved to a less awkward topic of conversation. "I've only been doing my job. I don't know why he was so generous."

Mavek snorted. "I asked him the same thing when he came to see me about doing this alignment for you. He said he wanted it to go somewhere it could be used properly. For most people this is just a heavy sword. There aren't many with the strength and skill who can also benefit from the temporal harmony."

"Couldn't Ranenok use it himself?"

"He's getting old for hand-to-hand fighting, and only having the one arm doesn't help his balance. He'll be passing over his command before too long."

"That will be a pity. He's a good commander."

"Maybe. I don't like him. I know that's partly due to Bykoda's tricks. But don't get taken in by him. He's out for himself, like the rest of us." Mavek tapped on the blade. "Yes, he knew that you could use the temporal alignment. But I got the feeling he was hoping it might induce you to do him one last favour and go on a mission he was talking about."

"The trolls?"

"Yes. Did you say you'd go?"

"I said that I couldn't. Jemeryl wants us to leave soon."

Mavek nodded. "Oh, right. Well, as a sorcerer, she'd get to make the call."

"No. It isn't that. I'm..." Tevi ran out of words. She did not want to get into the real reasons for refusing. Jemeryl had told her at lunch about their plans to go the next day when the council meeting started.

"I understand. I used to have an ungifted partner, years and years ago. It's so hard to get the balance right between you. I used to try to make sure that I always listened to her wishes. But I know that sometimes we'd argue, and I'd just make up my mind about what I wanted and do it. It's so easy, especially when that's how the rest of the world assumes it is anyway."

"Jem doesn't do that."

"No?" Mavek looked surprised. "Well...Ranenok's not to know. There's no way he'll blame you for ingratitude if he thinks you've been given orders by Jemeryl."

"I'm not ungra—" Tevi stopped. She could not deny it. She was being ungrateful and it was not necessary.

Tevi felt her lips tighten in resolve. As soon as Mavek had finished the alignment, she would go and tell Ranenok that she was able to lead the platoon out. Jemeryl would just have to accept it. After all, they were partners, and she had as much right as Jemeryl to decide when they left Tirakhalod.

❖

Jemeryl put down her pen and dismissed the mage light. Only then did she realise how late it had become. Apart from the firelight, the room was in thick shadow. Through the window, the sky was turning pink with the beginnings of sunset. And Tevi had not yet returned from the forge. Was aligning the rune sword taking so much longer than expected? Or had Tevi been unable to resist this last chance to play on the battle table and gone straight to Yenneg's quarters? Although surely she would have dropped the sword off first.

Regardless, it was now time to collect the journey provisions from Bykoda. Jemeryl closed the cover of her journal, stood up, and walked across the room. Just as she was reaching for her cloak, she heard the sound of the door and Tevi entered with the rune sword in her hands.

"There you are! I was wondering what had happened to you. Did the aligning take a long time?"

"Um...a bit. But I went over to see Ranenok afterwards. To thank him again, and..." Tevi finished with a lopsided shrug, clearly ill at ease.

"Are you all right?"

"Oh, yes. I'm fine."

"You sure?"

"Yes."

"Really sure?"

Tevi just gave a tight nod.

Jemeryl frowned. Something was bothering Tevi, but it did not seem to need immediate action, and if Tevi was not going to volunteer the information, sorting it out would have to wait until after the provisions were collected. Maybe if Tevi took her time calming down in their rooms, she would find it easier to talk.

Jemeryl gave Tevi a quick reassuring hug, and then grabbed her cloak off the peg. "Sit down and relax. I've got to collect the stuff for the journey from Bykoda and sort out the details of us leaving. We'll talk when I get back."

Tevi's expression tensed still further. "Er...we're going to have to change our plans a little."

"Why?"

"Ranenok wants me to lead a platoon out to deal with a band of trolls tomorrow. I've told him that I will."

"But you know we're leaving for the Protectorate tomorrow."

Tevi turned away and walked towards the fireplace. "We can change our plans. It will only take a day to deal with the trolls. I've worked it all out."

"Not with me you haven't."

"Was I supposed to?"

"It would have been nice." Jemeryl felt a mixture of confusion and anger.

"You didn't discuss it with me when you told Bykoda we'd leave tomorrow."

"There didn't seem to be any need to."

"Because I don't get a say in it?"

"Tevi!"

Tevi deposited the rune sword on a table and turned back. Her expression was of somebody who was consciously working on sounding reasonable. "Look. This is what I've thought. The trolls are only fifteen miles away. Ranenok has scouts pinned on them, so they won't take any hunting down. If I leave at dawn, I'll get to them by early afternoon. There's only fifty trolls, and I'll have over two hundred troops, so the battle won't take long. Once it's over, I'll leave the troops and ride back alone. We need to sort out a secret rendezvous outside Tirakhalod. The moon won't set until after midnight, and I can be with you before then. So we'll only delay leaving Tirakhalod by one day."

"And when did you work all this out?"

"While Mavek was doing the alignment."

"You didn't want to talk it over with me first?"

"Ranenok was making his plans for the trolls, so he needed to know as soon as, er... There wasn't ti..."

Tevi's voice died. She was, Jemeryl thought, a lousy liar. Anger started to overtake the confusion. "We're going to be running for our lives from an assassin who's strong enough to punch through a crystal shield. And you want to start playing games on a whim?"

"It's not a whim. It works out best for avoiding trouble as well."

"How?"

"Because even if the assassin knows that you've got the talisman, they won't be watching you quite so closely while I'm away. They won't expect you to go and leave me. Also I know that you can put all the provisions into one of your trick sacks, but you can't do it with horses. I can bring you a spare one from the platoon. And you'll find it a lot easier to slip out of the castle unnoticed if you don't have to take a horse with you."

Jemeryl chewed on her lower lip while she glared at Tevi. To be fair, the plan was not without merit, but Tevi seemed to be acting in a deliberately provocative manner. "You should have discussed it with me first."

"Why?"

Jemeryl dropped her cloak and paced forwards until she was within arm's reach of Tevi. "Because we work best when we work together."

"Not that we worked best when I just..." Tevi's voice died again, and her head sank.

"What?"

Tevi raised her head and met Jemeryl's eyes. "It's not that you prefer if I just blindly follow your lead?"

Jemeryl turned around and marched back to collect her cloak. "Right. Fine. You go and fight your trolls. I agree that it works all right as a plan. I'd have liked to have been involved at some stage, but it seems you had some reason for ignoring me." She flung the cloak around her shoulders and faced back into the room. "Have you sorted out where we can meet up after you've finished playing soldiers?"

Tevi swallowed. "There's a guard post by a bridge about two miles south of here. It's unoccupied at the moment since it's still too early in the year for trade caravans. I thought it would be a good place."

Jemeryl nodded. "I'll ask Bykoda to have the supplies left there. As you say, the less I have with me, the easier it will be to slip out of Tirakhalod unnoticed. I'll go and see her now. And maybe when I get back, we can discuss this a bit more calmly."

"I've told you everything."

"You haven't told me why. What have I done to upset you? Because I feel that you're getting at me over something, and I'd like to know what it is."

Jemeryl left the room and slammed the door shut behind her.

CHAPTER SEVEN—PLOTS AND POTIONS

Tevi sank down on a chair and rested her head in her hands. Had she been wise to insist on the change of plans? Had she been right? The doubts threatened to crush her. She never had any problems when it was just her and Jemeryl alone together. Why had she let other people get under her skin and put them in conflict?

And yet, Jemeryl had given in and let her decision stand. Tevi bit her lip, feeling perilously near to tears—not from guilt or regret that she had annoyed Jemeryl, although both might come later. But until that moment, she had not realised how desperately she needed the reassurance that Jemeryl also saw their relationship as a joining of equals.

The last three years had been tough. Now that it was nearly over, Tevi could let herself relax. As the tension ebbed away came the realisation that not for a second, not with all the temptation, not by word or action, had Jemeryl ever treated her as a possession. Of course, Tevi had known it, but not until then had she let herself consciously think about it.

Tevi berated herself. She had been unfair, and she owed her partner an apology. But more than that, she needed to tell Jemeryl just how much she loved and valued her.

Klara had been left sitting on the back of a chair. The magpie stared at her with black beady eyes, radiating disapproval. Was it worth talking to the familiar? Trying to explain things? Jemeryl would know what she said, and it might be easier than talking face-to-face. But Tevi felt that she had already acted like an idiot. There was no need to act like a coward as well.

Jemeryl had been gone for about five minutes when a knock roused her. When Tevi opened the door, a blank-faced thrall stood outside on the landing, holding out a note. As soon as Tevi had taken it, the thrall turned and left. Presumably a reply was not required. Tevi closed the door and broke the seal on the paper.

Tevi,

Please come and see me. I must talk with you. There are things we have to settle. I need to know where you stand. You know that this situation cannot continue.

Yenneg

"I do?" Tevi spoke aloud, her face screwed into a confused frown.

If it had not been for her name at the top of the page, she would have wondered if the thrall had made a mistake and delivered the note to the wrong person. In fact, even the name was curious. Her rank was not given as Captain, and it was the first time she could remember Yenneg not calling her Tevirik. Something odd was happening.

Tevi opened the door again. She wanted to be ready for when Jemeryl returned, so that they could talk, but that was all the more reason to deal with Yenneg as quickly as possible. Surely, whatever he wanted to discuss would not take too long. Tevi trotted down the stairs.

Outside, sunset was past and the inner bailey was fading into the gloom, but the light was still just strong enough for the shortcut across the garden to be safe. Tevi jogged along the gravel path through the central garden while her thoughts snagged on barbed recollections of the argument with Jemeryl. She was desperate for the chance to explain why she had needed to assert her own will.

Tevi was still juggling with feelings of self-reproach when she arrived at Yenneg's quarters. However, once she had arrived, memory of the peculiar summons squeezed its way back, claiming her attention.

Like on the first occasion when she had visited him, Tevi was shown into Yenneg's small private parlour. The atmosphere in the room was subtly different though. The only light came from the fire and a couple of candles. The scent of sweet lavender filled the room. Yenneg also seemed to have taken more care than normal with his appearance.

His clothes were casual, yet clearly expensive. A blue silk shirt matched his eyes and contrasted with his blond hair, while the cut of the collar drew attention to his well-formed features. Two glasses of wine stood ready on a table.

"You wanted to see me, sir?"

Yenneg smiled broadly. "Yes. And thank you for coming so quickly. I'm sorry if the message was a little...cryptic. But I will explain all. Please, take a seat." Once they were both in their chairs, he picked up a glass of wine, indicating for Tevi to do likewise. "A toast. To the future."

Tevi took a sip of the wine, to cover her surprise as much as anything. Yenneg's behaviour was definitely unusual.

Yenneg watched her closely, still with the broad smile spread across his lips. "What do you think of the wine?"

Tevi took another mouthful, this time considering the rich flavour filling her mouth. "It's very good."

"I'm pleased you like it. It's my favourite vintage, but expensive. We import it from your Protectorate."

"Oh. Right...um." Tevi's confusion was growing. "And what was it that you wanted to talk about, sir?"

"Well, the wine is not completely unrelated. I wanted to show that we get some of the benefits of the Protectorate, even here. In fact we can have as much as we want of the best on offer." Yenneg took another thoughtful sip. "I know my summons was abrupt, but I wanted to see you before the council meeting starts tomorrow. I've been away from my region for too long and will have to rush back as soon as the meeting is over, so we won't have a chance for another talk before you leave Tirakhalod. I'm worried that you have not considered all the things you should have."

"What do you think I've overlooked, sir?"

"Please, for tonight, forget the *sir*. Call me Yenneg." He put his glass down. "I've been reviewing your results on the battle table. They're very impressive. And I've been wondering if it might be sensible to pick army officers who are gifted with tactical rather than magical ability. So I want to repeat a question that I asked you before. What would it take to make you stay in Tirakhalod?"

"I um...want to return to the Protectorate. I don't think I..." Tevi took a gulp of wine, desperately trying to come up with a tactful way to explain. Was Yenneg even aware that to be ungifted in Tirakhalod was to live as a sub-human?

"In the Protectorate, your position is...what?"

"I'm just an ordinary mercenary."

"No special status?"

"No."

"That's a waste of talent. Here you could be so much more. You could command hundreds of soldiers. I would promote you to sub-divisional leader with your own castle. You could have wealth, luxuries, slaves, whatever you *desire*."

Tevi glanced up sharply. Yenneg had put a distinct emphasis on the last word. His eyes were fixed on her. In the flickering firelight his face shifted in and out of focus, melting. Tevi blinked and shook her head to clear it. Yenneg's features settled down. Yet still they seemed to be subtly different than before. He carried on talking, describing the army post he had earmarked for her, but Tevi found his words hard to follow. Her gaze fixed on his lips. As it did so, her stomach jolted uncomfortably, like a failed somersault that ends in a fall. She took another few sips of wine to combat the wave of nausea that struck her.

At last, Yenneg finished speaking. "So what do you think?"

Tevi swallowed. It was a good question. What did she think? Could she think at all? Yenneg's presence a few feet away was sending a whirlwind through her head. She felt as if chains were binding her to him, pulling her close. Yet every time she tried to evaluate the effect, the chains melted like ice in a furnace. The constant flux intensified the nausea in her stomach.

"Er...I'm sorry. I don't feel too well. Maybe the wine has...gone to my...my head." Tevi struggled to get the words out.

"Oh, my apologies. Have you not eaten yet this evening? The wine is rather strong on an empty stomach. I should have thought."

Yenneg stood and put his hand on her shoulder. For a second, the touch sent a sparkling wave rushing beneath her skin before it fizzled out in a soggy anti-climax. Was she drunk? Or had Yenneg poisoned her drink? Tevi was sure that she had not had enough wine for the first option, yet the other made no sense. Perhaps she was suffering from a delayed reaction to the spells Mavek had cast on her while attuning the rune sword.

"My head is..."

"Why don't we go outside? The fresh air might do you good," Yenneg suggested quickly.

Tevi nodded her agreement.

They paused at the doorway to the tower, while Yenneg dispatched a thrall with a note. Tevi stood with her eyes fixed on the battlements, gulping air. The stars were out. More time had passed than she had thought. The cold evening breeze cleared her head, but the world was out of kilter. Tevi was sure that the epicentre of the disturbance was Yenneg. Yet the harder she tried to pinpoint the feeling, the less certain she became. Somebody draped her cloak around her shoulders.

The thrall with the note marched away. Yenneg took Tevi's arm and steered her towards the garden. A small amber mage globe bobbed above their heads, lighting their way. Gravel crunched beneath their feet. The soft dusk was full of the scent of roses and the trill of insects.

As they strolled between the flower beds, Yenneg carried on talking about all the things Tevi could have if she stayed in Tirakhalod, but Tevi paid little attention to his words. The touch of his arm was unsettling. Whenever she looked away, she was overwhelmed by the idea that it was Jemeryl beside her, and arousal swept over her like a cavalry charge. Whenever she looked back at his face, the charge collapsed in chaos. By the time they reached the lily pond, Tevi was certain that some sort of magic was being used against her.

The summerhouse loomed before them, the scene of Ranenok's rendezvous with Kharel. Yenneg led Tevi up the short flight of stairs into a hexagonal room, twenty feet or so across. An ornate gilded seat ran along the wall facing the door. The narrow bench did not look suitable for an amorous encounter, and the remembered comment about splinters suggested the floor. Tevi's eyes fixed on the wooden planks, imagining what had taken place there. The train of thought was definitely interacting with the magic being used against her, sparking it off with new impetus.

By now, Tevi had strong suspicions about the exact nature of the spell and knew that she should get away from Yenneg, but the magic was sapping her will and her knees were weak. She staggered and sat heavily on the bench. Immediately, Yenneg was beside her. He raised his hand to her cheek and gently turned her face towards his. Their eyes locked, with bizarre effects. On one level, Tevi found herself enraptured by the deep blue depths, but whenever she tried to put the eyes into the context of Yenneg's face, the attraction exploded in a stomach-wrenching surge.

Judging by his expression, Yenneg was not suffering from similar problems. "Admit it. You'd like to stay here with me."

Yenneg's face was getting closer. He was going to kiss her, Tevi knew, but she lacked the strength to resist. She was no longer sure if she wanted to. Their lips met. To her amazement, Tevi felt herself responding, her mouth opening, her tongue caressing his. It was almost like passion, but an odd disembodied passion, as if Yenneg were not really there.

Yenneg was burrowing beneath the folds of Tevi's cloak. She felt one of his hands rub along her thigh then move up, past hips and stomach, towards her breast. Was it his hand or Jemeryl's? Tevi was unsure. Then a movement of her head brought her chin into contact with the roughness of his shaved face and the confusion was routed.

She pushed him away. "No."

The disparate parts of Yenneg's face coalesced into an expression of astonishment, followed by fury. He leapt to his feet. "The bitch! She *has* got you under a spell."

Yenneg's hands moved, unmistakeable spell casting, weaving patterns in the air that left faintly luminous traces. Tevi braced herself for the magical assault, yet nothing happened. The speed and style of Yenneg's gestures changed to sharp cutting motions, and his expression grew fiercer.

"What spell is it? Do you know?"

Tevi shook her head. She had no idea what he was talking about. Sparks drifted from Yenneg's fingers towards her, giving off a thin, humming whine. Tevi watched them get closer and fade. Yenneg's hands moved again, but then a new sound from outside distracted them both. Footsteps crunched on gravel.

Yenneg jerked towards the door and then back. A look of desperation swept over his face. Without warning, he launched himself onto Tevi, knocking her flat on the bench, his body half covering hers. Tevi summoned her will, desperate to break through the bonds and shove him off. Yet her spellbound limbs would not obey.

"What the..." A voice shouted.

To Tevi's relief, Yenneg scrambled away. In the mage light by the doorway stood Jemeryl and, beside her, the smaller figure of Bykoda.

Tevi tried to rise, but her body was helplessly uncoordinated. She slipped off the bench and ended up sitting on the floor with her back braced against the edge of the seat.

Jemeryl advanced into the room. "What is going on?"

Bykoda was the first to reply. "I think, my dear, that's a rather naive question, especially from a woman of your intelligence." The elderly Empress had not left her position by the door.

Tevi was vaguely aware that Yenneg was making a show of straightening his clothes, well in excess of anything justified by their minimal disarray. However, it hardly registered. Jemeryl stood before her, filling the world. The entire weight of the spell hit Tevi in a onslaught of sensation. She could scarcely breathe. Her body was shaking. She could not move her eyes away, not that she had any wish to.

Yenneg spoke next, in tones of bravado. "I don't know who told you we were here, but you would have soon found out anyway."

"Tevi?" Jemeryl's voice held nothing but disbelief.

Despite the chaos that was tearing her head apart, Tevi understood what scene Yenneg was attempting to play out, with herself as a conscripted actor. She needed to force out an explanation or denial, but no words could get past her lips. Jemeryl's presence was paralysing her, an effect far more irresistible than anything Yenneg had achieved.

Tevi watched Jemeryl take another few steps forwards and then crouch down so that their eyes were no more than a foot apart. Tevi thought she would die from the shock. Yet somehow, she forced her mouth to shape the words, "Wine. Love potion."

Her voice was not loud enough even to count as a whisper. Certainly nobody else in the room would have heard, yet Tevi could not control her breathing to manage anything else.

At first Jemeryl showed no sign of comprehension, but then suddenly, the bewilderment on her face transformed into fury. She leapt up, her arms moving in a blurred aggressive swirl. The gesture ended with an action like hurling a ball. Blue fire erupted from Jemeryl's hands and shot towards Yenneg.

The other sorcerer had obviously recognised the gesture and made an effort to protect himself. A shimmering shield sprung up before Yenneg, but it was not strong enough, and the shockwave knocked him off his feet. His shoulders slammed into the wall behind him and he crumpled to the floor. Jemeryl had been telling the truth when she claimed to vastly excel the acolytes in magical ability, not that Tevi had ever entertained doubts. Jemeryl's hands moved again, and this time Yenneg was sprawled on the floor and in no state to mount a defence. A second bolt of blue fire burst in his direction.

Lightning in the form of a whip snapped across the room, intercepting Jemeryl's attack before it struck. The diverted fireball hit the wall of the summerhouse two feet from Yenneg's head and smashed through it, as if it were a stone going through wet paper.

"Jemeryl." Bykoda's voice crackled like her lightning whip. "I understand that you're angry, but I have uses for Yenneg. If you must take it out on someone, I'd rather you did it on your two-timing mercenary slut."

"Tevi had no part in this."

"That wasn't the way I saw it. She wasn't fighting him off."

"He's drugged her."

Meanwhile, Yenneg had clambered to his feet and was edging around the room towards his defender. "I haven't. Tevi...darling, tell her how you feel about me." He neither looked nor sounded as confident as his words.

Tevi shook her head, partly in rejection, partly hoping to clear the paralysing fog.

"Tevi. You needn't be frightened of her. I'll protect you."

His words were so absurd, they were almost funny. What Tevi would have liked to say in reply was, *You're a filthy gutless maggot who isn't worthy to breathe the same air as Jemeryl*, but all she managed to get out was, "Bastard."

"He's drugged her," Jemeryl repeated.

"Why do you think that?" Bykoda asked.

"When I visited Dunarth, she complained about wasting her time making a love potion."

"She told you it was for Yenneg?"

"No. She wouldn't say."

"I suppose we could ask her." Bykoda spoke lightly.

"There's no need. Tevi would never be interested in that turd-eating mongrel if she wasn't under a spell."

Yenneg had reached Bykoda's side and clearly felt safe enough to rejoin the argument. "You're just jealous."

"I'd tend to take Yenneg's part in that." Now that Bykoda was no longer at imminent risk of losing one of her acolytes, she appeared to find the situation amusing. "He's not so unattractive. If I were fifty years younger, I might be interested myself."

"Tevi wouldn't be. What he doesn't know"—Jemeryl stabbed her finger at Yenneg, who flinched noticeably—"is Tevi's background. On the islands she comes from, they have strange taboos. One is about choice of lover. All the people from Tevi's home have an exclusive interest in either men or women. Never both."

"Really? How perverse. Most folk have enough trouble finding a suitable lover without cutting their options in half." Bykoda laughed as she spoke.

"There's nothing rational about it. It's the way they're brought up and it gets ingrained. No man would ever stand a chance with Tevi."

Yenneg's composure was unravelling again. "That's nonsense. Of course I haven't drugged her. Why would I be so desperate for an ungifted grunt?"

Jemeryl turned on him. "It's easy enough to prove. When I heard about Dunarth's potion I made a diagnostic tincture. It's in my room. We could send a thrall to get it."

Abruptly, the defiance went out of Yenneg. His shoulders slumped, but a little-boy smile blossomed hopefully on his face. "Oh, well. It was worth the try."

Bykoda looked at him. "You admit drugging the mercenary?"

"Just a simple love potion. Branon's red infusion."

"Why?"

Yenneg gestured vaguely towards Tevi. "She's got a real talent for leadership. I wanted her in my part of the army, but she wasn't going to leave Jemeryl. So I thought if I could get Jemeryl to ditch her first..." He let the sentence trail off and nodded towards the hole in the wall. "Anyway. No harm done. She missed me."

Jemeryl's hands started to move in the build up to a fireball.

"Jemeryl. Stop that." Bykoda snapped out the command.

"He's a—"

Bykoda glared at her acolyte. "Yenneg. Leave us now. And no more stupid tricks."

"Yes, my Empress." Yenneg gave a nervous half bow and slipped away from the summerhouse.

"I'll kill him," Jemeryl whispered.

"You most certainly won't." Amusement had left Bykoda's voice "This is the sort of thing my acolytes get up to all the time. Usually for bigger stakes than one ungifted warrior, whatever her talents. Accept it as the price for what you've gained in your time here. I've granted you a lot of privileges. Don't overstep the mark. Yenneg is worth more to me than a thousand like her...or you." Bykoda let the words hang in the air for a few seconds. "I suggest you take your mercenary to Dunarth for the antidote. And then go back to your quarters and calm down." The Empress turned around sharply and followed her acolyte off into the night.

Tevi had watched throughout as a passive observer. The ferocity of her desire for Jemeryl rendered her body helpless. But now she was in the situation she most wanted—they were alone together. When Jemeryl knelt by her side, Tevi reached out, ready to drag her lover into her arms. She must have Jemeryl right that second, or she would die from the pain.

However, her coordination was hampered by the potion and Jemeryl evaded the clumsy grab. She caught hold of Tevi's hands and held them securely and then stared into Tevi's eyes.

"Poor love. You're pretty deep under the spell, aren't you?"

"Please...Jem...I need to...I need." Tevi had never felt desire like it in her life. She was not sure if she could live another minute without release. Her body felt ready to explode. Her skin ached.

"I'm sure you do." Jemeryl stood up, hauling Tevi to her feet and pulling her towards the door. "But when I make love to you, I want it to be you, not Yenneg's filthy potion. Come on."

Tevi was too disorientated to resist being led into the garden, but she made one last appeal. "Where are we going? Can't we stay here, just a little...please?"

Jemeryl was unmoved. "I'm taking you to Dunarth for the antidote. You may not like Bykoda's ethics, but her advice is always very practical."

❖

"People think I've got nothing better to do than sort out their juvenile pranks."

Dunarth sounded just as angry as Jemeryl felt, although with less obvious cause. She turned and trudged off down the corridor like a spoilt four-year-old in a sulk. Jemeryl followed after, still with Tevi in tow, while battling the urge to point out that if the alchemist had not made the love potion in the first place then they would all have been spared the aggravation.

In the potion preparation room, Dunarth directed Tevi to a chair and then held a dosing rod over her for a few seconds. She looked at Jemeryl. "Are you sure you want the exact antidote? I've got another potion here that'll—"

"I want the exact antidote." Jemeryl did not wish to hear what Dunarth thought might be suitable compromise for Tevi.

Dunarth slammed the rod down on a bench. "Right." She stomped off again, the maturity level of her behaviour having dropped by at least another twelve months.

Tevi sagged in the chair, her head slumped forwards. From the way she had her hands clenched around each other, Jemeryl guessed that she was struggling with the effects of the potion. She fought her own temptation to give her lover a hug. It would only make Tevi's ordeal harder.

"Don't worry. Once you get the antidote, things will settle down."

"Soon, hopefully." Tevi's voice was strained. "And I'm sorry about the trolls. I should have asked you first."

"It's all right." In fact, Jemeryl needed a few seconds even to remember what Tevi was referring to. Her anger with Yenneg had driven all else from her head.

"It's just that everyone else here thinks of me as a possession. I just needed to do something, even though it was stupid, just to prove that I could do what I wanted."

"It really is all right. And for what it's worth, Bykoda thought it was a good plan."

"I won't do it again."

"We're leaving soon. You won't have a chance."

Tevi nodded and her head sank even lower. "I'm so pleased you turned up when you did. What made you come to the summerhouse?"

"I was just about to leave Bykoda when we got a note from Anid saying events were taking place that we ought to know about. I've got no idea how she knew."

"Are you sure it was from Anid?"

"That's who the signature said. I didn't do any tests to make sure. There didn't seem any reason to at the time."

"I'll bet it was from Yenneg. He sent a note off just before we entered the garden."

"Oh...of course. Yenneg wanted me to discover you. And it was wise of him to arrange for Bykoda to be there as well, else I'd have killed him." Jemeryl drew in a deep breath. "I still might if I get the chance."

"Not a good idea to upset Bykoda."

Jemeryl let the breath out in a sigh. "It's all right. I'll probably have calmed down by tomorrow." Without thinking, she reached out to pat Tevi's shoulder, but then restrained the gesture.

Around them the benches held a similar number of distillations to the last time Jemeryl had been there. The faint sound of dripping marked their progress. At the other end of the room Dunarth was thumping around. Amazingly, no glassware had yet been broken.

Jemeryl's thoughts jumped around in her head, stringing events together. "You know, this plot of Yenneg's explains a lot."

"In what way?" Tevi asked without looking up.

"Like the brooch we found after your first meeting with him. Yenneg snuck into our quarters and planted it so it looked like the thing had dropped from your pocket. He knew you were out on patrol, so I'd be the one to find it. I was supposed to think he was giving you expensive presents that you weren't telling me about. And you losing track of time on the battle table. I bet he did that to you so you'd be coming back late from his quarters with no good explanation of what you'd been doing."

"The love letter in the book?"

"That too. He picked a book he thought you wouldn't be able to read and probably hoped that by then, I'd be suspicious enough to be checking all the things you got from him. I was supposed to find the note and think that the *she* in *soon she will be gone* referred to me."

Tevi shook her head. "It never even occurred to me to read it that way."

"It didn't occur to me either."

"It's nice to know you trust me so much."

"More a case of Yenneg being male."

"And if it had been Anid playing tricks?"

"I don't know. Maybe not even then. I do trust you."

Tevi gave a snort that was probably as close to a laugh as she was capable. "So you're saying I needn't be particularly furtive when I want to indulge in some misbehaviour?"

"I hope that's just the love potion talking." Jemeryl was also teasing, although on further thought, she surprised herself at how much she did trust Tevi. She would never have considered the idea that her partner might be unfaithful. *I'm just too arrogant about my own charms,* she derided herself.

Tevi groaned. "I don't know. I'm all over the place at the moment. I thought love potions were supposed to make you fall for the person who gave it to you."

"Most do. But the one Yenneg used was one of the subtler potions that works on existing sexual responses."

"He thought that I was already keen on him?"

"Not exactly. But he assumed that there'd be something for the potion to inflame. It needn't be full attraction, just an awareness."

Tevi lifted her head. "When I said no to him, in spite of the potion, I think he got the idea that you have me spellbound."

"That's understandable. Normally magic is the only way to put in the sort of emotional block that your culture has given you. You didn't start with any feelings for him that the potion could work on."

"Was that why I felt attracted whenever I didn't think about it, but as soon as I focused on him I felt ill?"

"I don't know. He makes me sick as well."

"Could a different sort of potion have made me fall for him?"

"Oh yes. But they're easier to spot and harder to control. Yenneg was too confident of his own allure to think he needed it."

"I find it hard to imagine."

"Anyone can become besotted with anything. We used to play games with potions when I was an apprentice in Lyremouth...young enough to think it was funny. We got one of my friends to fall head over heels for a table in the refectory." Jemeryl paused, considering the memory and then smiled. "Actually, that time was rather amusing."

Dunarth reappeared, huffing as if she'd had to run three times round the castle. She banged a pottery beaker on the table with as much force as she could without breaking it. "There's your antidote. Leave it to settle for five minutes before drinking, though I don't know why I bother saying it. Nobody ever listens to me." She jerked her thumb at a nearby set of funnels and tubes. "Do you know what that is?"

"Poison?" Jemeryl guessed.

"Make it stronger. Make it stronger." Dunarth affected an inane jabber. "That's all I get asked. With that coating a weapon, just one scratch, and you're dead in seconds."

"Sounds effective."

"But why? It's too effective. Soldiers expect their comrades to die. Rather than simply dropping dead, it would be much more useful to have the victims screaming and thrashing about for a couple of hours. Destroys morale and breaks up formations. Makes sense, doesn't it, Captain?"

"Er...yes," Tevi agreed with a catch in her voice.

"There. Even an ungifted warrior agrees with me, but nobody else does." Dunarth turned and stamped away. "Do what you like with the antidote. Wash your hair with it. I'm going to find something useful to do."

As the door shut, Tevi groaned. "I'm so pleased you're here. I wouldn't want to be alone with her."

"So am I. I wouldn't trust Dunarth not to try a few experiments out on you. She's interested in your strength."

"It's not that. I'm starting to think she's sexy."

❖

Tevi collapsed onto the couch and closed her eyes. Relief washed over her, just to be back in their own rooms and feeling more in control, even though Jemeryl had said that an hour or two might pass before the antidote completed its work. Tevi was content to wait it out. The evening had held more than its fair share of unpleasant experiences. For the moment, things were getting better and all she wanted was to relax.

Jemeryl did not immediately join her on the couch. Tevi heard footsteps and then a faint rustle of paper.

"Is this the cryptic note Yenneg sent?"

"Has it got the bit about *this situation cannot continue*?"

"Yes."

"Then that's the note. It was odd enough that I went to see him at once."

The couch moved as Jemeryl sat down. Without opening her eyes Tevi shifted closer, so that their shoulders were touching. The contact sparked ripples through her.

Jemeryl said, "He wanted you to visit him while I was still with Bykoda. But he must have hoped you'd leave the note behind. I bet it was intended to inflame my jealousy so that if his messenger thrall missed me at the keep, I'd still see it and come looking for you."

"He's been very busy scheming."

"True, and he's totally thrown us out with all those events that have absolutely nothing to do with Bykoda's murder."

"So we've got less idea about who kills her than the complete blank we thought we had?"

"That sums it up. Except we'd be even worse off if Yenneg hadn't left his brooch back at the beginning. Because then I might never have thought to check the box and we would not have found out about the tracer charm swap."

"But it still hasn't got us anywhere, has it?"

"Not really."

Tevi opened one eye and watched Jemeryl screw the note into a ball and toss it onto the fire. The shape of Jemeryl's hand drew her gaze, transfixing her with memories. Tevi felt her breathing become fast and shallow. Desperately, she tried to distract herself. "How about that new poison Dunarth was talking about?"

"The shield blocks normal missiles as well as magic. An arrow or dart couldn't get through."

"Perhaps the murderer coats Bykoda's throne with it. All it would take is one scratch."

"When did you last scratch yourself on a chair?"

"It happens."

"Not often enough to rely on. And there can't be any sort of hidden device. The room is searched, inch by inch, before each council meeting." Jemeryl shifted around on the couch. Their shoulders rubbing together made Tevi's insides kick.

"So you...um, don't have any ideas?"

"To tell the truth, at the moment I'm not feeling that bothered about whoever kills Bykoda."

"I thought you liked her."

"That was before she implied that I should overlook somebody trying to rape you as suitable payment for a few spells."

Tevi scrunched her eyes shut, but not due to distress over Yenneg's intentions. In fact, she found it hard to think about him at all. Awareness of Jemeryl, sitting beside her and discussing sexually charged matters, was blasting all other thoughts from her head. Tevi forced herself to concentrate. "For what it's worth, Yenneg backed off as soon as I said no. Although I think it was more from surprise than respecting my wishes."

"You were ensorcelled and in no fit state to say yes or no."

"And I think he was intending to get caught before things went that far."

"Even so, I still want to kill him." Jemeryl scooped up Tevi's hand, interlaced their fingers, and pressed Tevi's knuckles against her lips. "You're mine."

"Always." Tevi could hold back her desire no longer. She rolled her head round so that she was staring into Jemeryl's eyes. "I want to make love to you right now."

Jemeryl looked unmoved. "You're still feeling the effects of the potion."

"Maybe. But it doesn't take a potion to make me feel this way about you."

"You can't be sure of—"

Tevi did not let her finish. She wrapped her hand around the back of Jemeryl's neck and pulled her forwards. Their lips touched in a kiss, gentle at first, but growing in passion. Her hand slipped lower, pulling Jemeryl more closely against her. Tevi felt as if her existence was defined by the contact of their mouths.

Eventually, Jemeryl struggled back, pulling free. "I don't know if we should."

"Why not?"

"Because I don't want to think that Yenneg is playing any part."

"He isn't. This is the last thing he intended."

"But it..." Their eyes locked and Jemeryl's voice died.

"And who really cares?" Tevi asked softly. She shifted her hold on Jemeryl, easing her around on the couch. "As you said, no matter what, I'm yours."

Jemeryl was now facing Tevi, her knees curled on the seat and most of her weight pressing against Tevi's legs. Their noses were mere inches apart. Tevi felt her pulse racing. She pulled Jemeryl into another kiss, longer and more forceful.

When Jemeryl drew back a second time, Tevi did not give her the chance to speak. Without letting their eyes meet, Tevi caught the ties on Jemeryl's shirt and began tugging them loose. At the sound of a drawn breath, Tevi hesitated a second, dreading that she would be told to stop, but the only response was a sigh.

Once the last of the ties were undone, Tevi pushed back the loose fabric. Beneath was a thicker, close-fitting undershirt—necessary in the chill northern spring. The fastening on this was a score of tiny buttons. Tevi struggled with the first and gave up on the second. Need surged through her. Unable to bear any more delay, she seized the shirt by the collar in both hands and ripped it open.

"Tevi!" Jemeryl gasped her surprise.

Tevi was too overwhelmed by desire to care. She pulled Jemeryl to her. Her face burrowed through the remnants of the undershirt until her lips made contact with the warmth of Jemeryl's skin. The soft touch flooded through her in a wave of sensation, fuelling her desperate hunger. The strain of the evening of denial combined in that moment, and shattered. Tears started in Tevi's eyes.

She stood, effortlessly lifting her lover's weight, took one step forwards, and then lay Jemeryl down on the sheepskin rug before the fire. Tevi pushed back the torn undershirt, exposing more of Jemeryl's skin to the amber light. The sight transfixed her eyes. She spread her hand over the firm stomach muscles, then swept up to cup the fullness of Jemeryl's breast. Her thumb rubbed over a nipple that enlarged and hardened at her touch.

Tevi lowered her mouth to Jemeryl's throat and traced the line of collarbone with her tongue, while her hands loosened the clasp on Jemeryl's belt. Jemeryl's breathing turned to gasps and her arms around Tevi's shoulders tightened. The sound and the touch and the taste washed over Tevi, inflaming her senses, and at the same time relaxing her. She was safe, secure, and loved. And, more than anything else, she knew she was where she ought to be.

Tevi broke free of Jemeryl's arms and twisted up onto her knees. Gripping the material around Jemeryl's waist, she peeled the clothing down. In the flickering light, the triangle of auburn curls at the top of Jemeryl's legs seemed to dance as if they also were flames. The soft glow accentuated the flush on her skin.

Jemeryl plucked at the cloth of Tevi's shirt sleeve. "You too."

Tevi obeyed clumsily. She felt drunk, swimming through the liquid weight of her desire. Her actions were slow and heavy, but so essential and inexorable. Her conscious will had gone, and she was there only as observer.

Soon they were both stripped of all clothing. Tevi let her gaze travel the length of her lover's body, drinking in each detail. The potion was coursing through Tevi, driving her beyond the bounds of mere lust. The desperate need would have been more than she could have borne, were it not that now release was so close. Already, Tevi felt her climax start to build just from the act of looking. When Jemeryl touched her, she would explode.

Magic lay outside Tevi's knowledge, yet it would coil through every fragment of her life, and this had been inevitable since the day that she and Jemeryl became lovers. Plots and potions were symbolic of all the things from Jemeryl's world that Tevi would be powerless to withstand. As long as she was with Jemeryl, the direction her life took would be subject to events that she could not comprehend and could have no control over. She would be like a rider clinging helplessly to the back of a wild horse.

How to accept what she could not understand? Her only answer was easy. Tevi raised her head so her eyes locked with Jemeryl's. For a moment, she paused while the rest of the world ceased to exist. "I love you."

❖

The sound of shifting logs woke Jemeryl from a light doze. She raised herself on one elbow. She and Tevi still lay naked on the rugs by the hearth, but now the fire had burnt down and the air in the room was chill. Her shoulder had gone numb.

The temperature was something she could rectify by magic, but not the hardness of the floor. They should move to their bed—especially since there would be more than enough nights spent sleeping on the ground before they reached Lyremouth.

Sight of the moon through the window caught Jemeryl's attention. The crescent floated in the black sky, just off the first quarter. With luck, they would be over the Barroden Mountains and back in the Protectorate before the new moon. Her eyes moved on to the woman lying beside her.

Tevi's face was soft and flushed in sleep. Jemeryl felt her stomach flip. A smile crossed her face. After four years together, Tevi could still make her feel like an adolescent in the grip of her first crush.

Jemeryl's smile faded. A nagging fear danced around at the back of her mind. She did not want Tevi to go on the troll hunt, but what could she do? Life in Tirakhalod had been a constant bout of humiliation for the ungifted warrior, and coming here had been solely at Jemeryl's wish. She was the one who had wanted to study magic with the aging Empress, and Tevi had put up with it for her sake. The least she could do was accept Tevi's right to make her own decisions.

Her gaze fell on the rune sword. Jemeryl also understood Tevi's sense of gratitude. The sword's value was far more than just monetary. With it in her hand, Tevi would get a fraction of a second more warning of anything that might kill her. It increased the chances of Tevi returning alive and unharmed, not just now, but for as long as she had the sword. Thinking about it, Jemeryl felt pretty well disposed towards Ranenok herself, or would if it were not for the trolls.

And something about the coming sortie worried her. Of course, no battle was without risk, but surely Ranenok would dispatch enough troops to deal with the trolls easily. For a moment, Jemeryl toyed with the idea of trying to change Tevi's mind. She could not demand, but she could beg, grovel, even cry. Jemeryl dismissed the thought contemptuously. It fell far short of what she considered an adult standard of behaviour.

She dropped a soft kiss on Tevi's lips and shook her shoulder. "Come on, Tevi. We can't stay here all night."

Tevi's eyes batted open. Her arm snaked around Jemeryl's waist for a quick hug before she wordlessly got to her feet and staggered towards their bedroom.

CHAPTER EIGHT—THE COUNCIL MEETING

The moon was slowly sinking and stars shone in the clear night sky. Jemeryl walked across the central courtyard of the keep towards the door of the council chamber. Just before she reached it, a voice hailed her.

"Jemeryl. If you have a moment. I have a message for you."

Jemeryl stopped and waited until Ranenok joined her. "Yes? What is it?"

"It's from Captain Tevirik. She wanted you to know that the battle with the trolls is over. It finished a short while ago. The message arrived just as I was leaving my quarters."

"Thank you." Jemeryl gave a tight smile. On one level she was relieved to know that Tevi was safe, but the message meant that the fighting had taken longer than had been expected. Tevi would not be joining her at the guard post until midday tomorrow at the earliest. Yet nothing could be done about it, and another day's delay in leaving would not matter—probably.

Ranenok gave a small nod of acknowledgement and passed through the doorway to the council chamber, ready for the evening session. The other acolytes filed in after him. Jemeryl turned right and climbed the staircase to the balcony door. Apart from Ranenok, nobody had paid her the slightest attention. With luck, nobody would notice when she was not there on the following days.

At the top of the stairs Jemeryl paused and looked across the gravel courtyard. A nagging sense of foreboding teased at the edges of her mind, unsettling her stomach. But what was there to worry about? The moon cast a blue light over the statues in the middle. A few thralls were visible. Two stood at either side of the archway leading to the inner bailey. Others guarded the various doors and stairways opening onto the courtyard, symbols of Bykoda's control. What could threaten her here?

Jemeryl's eyes fixed on the moon, hanging high in a clear sky directly in front of her. It was at first quarter—something of a relief in her current state of agitation. Bykoda's vision of her murder had the moon at the third quarter. But even if Bykoda, in her death throes, had been mistaken about the phase, it would not matter. With its current position, the moon would not be visible through any of the council chamber windows. They were all on the outer wall of the keep, overlooking the garden.

Jemeryl took another few breaths of the crisp night air to quiet her nerves and then opened the door behind her.

Mage lights illuminated the floor of the room below, although the balcony was in darkness. Everyone was in place. Bykoda was waiting on her silver throne, her eyes fixed on the floor by her feet. Her aging body looked birdlike, yet imposing—an imperial eagle. Her expression was autocratic and uncompromising. The acolytes had also taken their seats, ready to begin the session. Jemeryl looked down on them sitting directly under her.

One of them was going to kill Bykoda, and Jemeryl did not have the first idea who, or how. Anid had a map partially unrolled on her lap and was sketching lines across it. Ranenok's fingers were drumming on his knee. Twice Jemeryl caught him restrain a glance at the woman beside him, though for her part, Kharel was as motionless as one of the statues in the courtyard. Dunarth was scratching dirt out of the embossed pattern on her armrest with her fingernail. Yenneg sat indolently, with his legs stretched out, crossed at the ankle. Mavek was shifting around in his chair, transferring his weight from buttock to buttock, possibly evaluating his inflatable cushion.

Jemeryl eased back on her chair. It was going to be another long session. Already that day, she'd had cause to be grateful for Mavek's new cushions, a vast improvement on the previous stuff-straw type. Everybody had one, she noted, even Bykoda, although this might mean that the elderly woman would feel less inclination to cut short the reports than she might have otherwise.

Jemeryl was tempted to quit the meeting early and go back to her room, but all her preparations were complete. She would not leave the castle until after the moon had set, which was not for another three hours. Spending the time pacing around her quarters would be even less entertaining than the council meeting. And if she ignored the reports and speeches, she could use the occasion for one last attempt to spot holes in Bykoda's defences.

Bykoda raised her head. "Anid. Can we have your report on troop numbers in the south?"

❖

One hour later, the meeting had moved on to Yenneg's report. The sound of the man's voice set Jemeryl's teeth on edge. After ten minutes, she had decided that she could not stay. Pacing her room would be far more entertaining. Even banging her head on a wall would be an improvement. She stood and took a step towards the door, but then stopped. The realisation hit her that once she left the balcony, she would never see Bykoda again. If, in the years to come, she returned to Tirakhalod, any of the acolytes might still be there, but not the Empress.

They had spent so many hours together, and Jemeryl had gained so much. Despite the events of the previous evening, and the reaction to Yenneg's plot, she could not deny a soft spot for the old woman. She was not blind to Bykoda's faults. Jemeryl fully understood the reasons for Tevi's dislike of the Empress. Yet still, Jemeryl had a sincere admiration for Bykoda, for her ability, intelligence, and determination. She wished there was some way she could say good-bye.

Jemeryl moved to the centre of the balcony, hoping to catch Bykoda's eye. However, the Empress' attention was fixed on Yenneg.

"By the end of the month, we will have horses and equipment ready to commence training three hundred new cavalry recruits. These will be sufficient to patrol the region west of Zetovna by late summer."

Judging by Bykoda's expression, she thought something in Yenneg's statement was highly questionable—the numbers, the timing, or the effectiveness. She was leaning forwards in her seat, elbows pressing down on the armrests of her throne, her chin resting on her interlaced fingers. Yenneg's voice did not waver, and he carried on with his report on training.

"After reallocating divisional resources, the garrisons at Tetezch, Khatonya, and Zrebona are now back at full strength."

The nature of Bykoda's frown changed from scepticism to outright annoyance. She threw herself back in her chair, impatiently. Her eyebrows flicked. The momentary expression of surprise was gone in a flash, but then, a second later, her eyebrows rose again, higher this time and in unmistakeable shock. Her eyes opened wide. Her jaw dropped.

At her vantage point in the gallery, Jemeryl felt her insides clench. She stepped forwards until her hands were brushing against the balcony railing. Bykoda raised her head slightly, and her eyes met Jemeryl's for one last time, in disbelief and horror. None of the acolytes seemed yet to have noticed. Yenneg's voice droned on.

"Three dozen archers have been—"

An eruption of white hot sparks shot up, cutting off Yenneg's words and dazzling everyone. For an instant, the crystal shield in the centre of the room shimmered like sunlight on water. Simultaneous with this was a cry from Bykoda, short, sharp, and agonised, gurgling off to silence. As the afterimage of the sparks cleared from her vision, Jemeryl saw the Empress pitch forwards, crumpling to the floor. She did not wait to see more.

Jemeryl leapt for the balcony exit. She wrenched the door open and hurtled down the stairs. Before she had reached the bottom she heard the crash of the crystal shield falling. The sound echoed around the courtyard from the open door behind her. The thralls outside the main door had collapsed as Bykoda's hold on them failed. Jemeryl jumped over their bodies, through the door, and into the council chamber.

Bykoda was lying on the floor, her head turned towards the windows. Five of the acolytes were still frozen in their chairs, but one had risen and now stood in the centre of the room. Mavek.

Ripples of green flowed over his huge frame. Yellow light shone from his eyes. His bass voice boomed out. "For too long have you held this Empire in your grip. At last, I am ready to make my move. I have learnt all your secrets and have no further need for you. Your strength is outmatched. Your Empire is mine, and now you will die."

Mavek's hand moved, swirling in the same pattern that Jemeryl had used the night before against Yenneg. The bolt of blue fire crashed down on the powerless Empress, engulfing her, and then all was still. The echoes were broken only by the hiss of static and cracking ice. Soon, this too faded away, leaving utter silence in the chamber.

Jemeryl rushed forwards and dropped to her knees at Bykoda's side. Blue fire burnt cold, not hot. Faint tendrils of condensation drifted away from Bykoda's frozen body. Ice crystals glittered in her hair. Exploded veins made a tracery under her skin. A few feet away, the shards of the crystal shield lay scattered across the floor. Everything matched Bykoda's vision, except for the moon.

Mavek was still talking. The rhythm of his words suggested a prepared speech, but Jemeryl was not listening. Her gaze fixed on the windows. With the darkness outside, nothing was visible, except soft, smoky images in the glass. From her position on the floor, Jemeryl could see reflections of the ceiling, upper walls and balcony, including the spot where she had been standing, but certainly no trace of the moon.

Then one window pane caught Jemeryl's eye, where the reflection was clearer and firmer. With the dim light in the upper reaches of the chamber it was not so very conspicuous, but now that she had spotted it, the difference was unmistakeable.

Trying to look as if she was making a futile attempt to listen for breath from the dead Empress, Jemeryl lowered her face to beside Bykoda's, although careful not to touch the frozen skin for fear of frost burn. Through the reflection of the open balcony door, left by her own frantic departure, the back to front image of the first quarter moon hung sharp and clear in the anomalous window pane. Jemeryl sat back on her heels.

Mavek still held the floor. He strutted back and forth across the chamber, chest thrown out and hands striking the air, as he declaimed in august tones about the justice of his cause in removing Bykoda, his strength and power, and the wisdom that all would show by submitting to his rule. The other five acolytes sat in stunned shock, listening to him.

"Those of you who wish to serve me may keep their current rank. Those who do not can join Bykoda. This Empire is now mine, unless there is someone here who wishes to challenge me, now that you have seen the extent of my power." The ex-blacksmith paced to the middle of the room. His eyes dared each one to answer. None did.

After five seconds of silence, he turned around. "Jemeryl. There is one position of acolyte now vacant. Perhaps you would like to take it?" The tone of his words made it sound more like a threat than an offer.

Jemeryl stood up slowly. Maybe rushing into the council chamber had not been the wisest move. She did not want to get drawn into any confrontation. Extricating herself from the situation was now her main priority, and the first thing was to stop Mavek before he offered any direct threats against her that he might feel obliged to back up with action. Offering a few implied threats of her own might not hurt.

"Thank you. But I am already oath-bound to the Coven at Lyremouth and will be returning there soon." Jemeryl forced her voice to stay firm, matching Mavek for confidence. "Relations between the Protectorate and the previous Empress were always cordial. I'm sure that you will want this to continue. And I will be happy to carry any communications from you back to Lyremouth with me. Perhaps you would arrange for your dispatches to be sent to my room. But I will take no more of you time now. I know you have much to discuss." Jemeryl gave a gracious nod and turned to the door.

It was a bluff on her part. The Protectorate was powerful, and doubtless the Coven would take the murder of one of its sorcerers very seriously. But the truth could so easily be concealed. If Mavek made good the threat to send her to join Bykoda, who was there to carry the true report back to Lyremouth? And no matter what happened, outright war between the two states would not be an option. However, Jemeryl had the strong suspicion that Mavek was also bluffing, and to a far greater extent than herself.

She heard him clear his throat. "Thank you. I will come to see you shortly."

Jemeryl reached the door, turned, gave a brief formal bow to the room in general, and then stepped out into the night, not daring to let her composure slip. She was still far from safe.

The dead bodies of the thralls lay on ground. They had not survived the break from Bykoda. Jemeryl spared them one pitying glance. Tevi would say they were better off like that. The only sound was the crunch of her footsteps as she crossed the gravel courtyard, heading for the archway out.

Once she emerged from the keep, the changes that had come over the castle were far more conspicuous. The plants in the garden were already withered and dead. No lights shone from the rooms in the towers, and outer bailies resounded with shouts and screams. Flames were rising in the direction of the forge. Mavek would have to move quickly to re-establish control if he was to have any hope of holding on to the Empire. With luck, it would tie him down long enough to give her the chance to escape from Tirakhalod, rendezvous with Tevi, and get safely across the northern plains.

❖

Klara swooped low over the battlements of the outer bailey. Few even noticed her in the darkness. With the general chaos, one small bird was of little concern. She would probably not have received much greater attention even if it had been obvious that Jemeryl was looking out through the eyes of the magpie.

The sorcerer was mind-riding her familiar. Transferring her senses to the bird was the quickest and safest way to scout out her escape route. It was an easy trick, although not without risk. While her mind was inhabiting the magpie, her own body was unconscious and vulnerable back in her quarters. However, she had a watch ward set on the door, which would give notice if anyone came visiting, and she should not be away for long.

No traffic was moving on the road, although a few bands of soldiers and peasants were camped at the side. Jemeryl noted their locations and flew on. The bridge and guard post came into view. Jemeryl was relieved. So many buildings in Bykoda's Empire were not real, only an illusion projected by her magic. Now that she was dead, the disguise would be gone. Jemeryl had feared that the guard post might be revealed as no more than a straw hut, or even an outline drawn with magic symbols. However the building looked to be stone-built and secure. Presumably, it had played a part in the magical defences of the Empire. Illusions were of use only to impress the ungifted.

Jemeryl circled the guard post once. Tevi would not be there until the next day. Jemeryl was tempted to fly north and try to find her. In the wreck of Bykoda's Empire, who knew what dangers might be running wild? But Jemeryl dared not leave her body unprotected for so long, and Tevi was far from helpless. In fact, she was probably in a less precarious situation than Jemeryl herself.

Before returning to the castle, Jemeryl spared a look for the road south. Uzhenek lay two hundred miles away. It was the southernmost town of Bykoda's Empire, as well as being Anid's army headquarters.

Given the likely chaos breaking out down there, the town would be a good place to avoid.

Another two hundred miles beyond Uzhenek were the Barrodens— the mountain chain that lay between the Empire and the Protectorate. However it would not be possible to cross there by the direct route. Due south of Tirakhalod the chain was at its highest and widest. The pass at Horzt lay nearly four hundred miles to the east, while the pass above Denbury was even farther to the west, over one thousand miles away. However, the longer route might be the quicker one. Once they were over the mountains, they could take a boat down the River Lyre to the city at its mouth.

Jemeryl still had not made up her mind on which way to go, but the decision about the route could wait. She wheeled around and flew back up the road. Within minutes she was over the gatehouse of the outer bailey. Here was where the greatest change was apparent. The barracks and other buildings for the ungifted soldiers had been pure illusion. The area had been utter mayhem earlier that night. But at last, three hours after Bykoda's death, the situation was calming down. Many of the common soldiers had fled, and all of those who remained were now drunk. The beer in the stores had been real, and no walls were left to keep it secure. Jemeryl was pleased to see that nobody was keeping sentry duty. Avoiding the ungifted warriors would have presented no problems for her, but the officer witches were also gone, and this would simplify her task of slipping out unnoticed.

Jemeryl's path veered up the hill, over the middle bailey. The bodies of dead thralls lay in small, pathetic piles by the gates. The fire that had broken out in the armoury was now under control. Here, several witches were in evidence, but equally, they would all be far too busy firefighting to notice her passing.

To a first glance, the inner bailey was deserted, but then Jemeryl saw a figure crossing the derelict remains of the garden. The size made him easy to identify. Mavek was heading in the direction of her tower. Possibly he was merely going to his own rooms on the lower floor, but Jemeryl doubted it. She snapped free of Klara and returned to her own body lying on the couch. By the time the door to her quarters opened, she was fully restored to her normal state of consciousness.

Mavek strode imperiously into the room. His shoulders were thrown back, his head held high. His normally easygoing expression was fixed in an arrogant mask of disdain. He was clearly still trying to play the bluff, but Jemeryl was fairly sure she had all the answers. She stood up, matching his attempt at intimidation with calm self-assurance.

At first he tried to glare her into submission. When this did not work, he crossed his massive forearms and said, "I'm sure you know why I'm here."

"I could make all sorts of guesses. Why don't you tell me?"

"I want the talisman."

Jemeryl sighed. "Yes. I thought you might. I'm afraid I can't let you have it."

"You dare defy me? After you saw what I did to Bykoda!"

"Yes."

"I could kill you where you stand."

"I don't think so."

"Do you have any idea of the power it took to strike Bykoda down through her crystal shield?"

"I dread to think of what sort of power it would take." Jemeryl paused. "But that wasn't what you did."

The first chink in Mavek's bravado showed in the set of his jaw. "What do you mean?"

"I know how you killed Bykoda, and the level of magical ability it took wouldn't have strained the powers of a third-rate witch."

"Third-rate witch? I smashed aside a crystal shield and you doubt my magic?" With each exchange, Mavek's assurance was slipping.

"You didn't go through the shield. And the magic that killed Bykoda was all due to Dunarth, although she doesn't know it."

"You don't know what you're talking about." Although he was still using defiant words, his voice sounded waveringly insecure.

"I think I do. You killed Bykoda with a pin coated in Dunarth's strongest poison that you'd fixed inside her deflating cushion." Jemeryl gave a rueful smile. "I'm stupid not to have guessed before when I visited you in your workshop and you showed me the trial cushions with the different weights. You said you were trying to stop them from deflating. But then why the different weights? You're the heaviest of the acolytes. Why not make sure that the cushion was all right for you? Then it would be bound to hold out for all the rest. You were testing the rates of deflation. Obviously, it had to be safe for when the room was searched. Somebody might have even sat on it to test it for comfort, and you wouldn't have wanted any of the thralls to drop dead and spoil your plan."

To illustrate her point, Jemeryl picked up a cushion—an ordinary one with tassels—and waved it around. "The council chamber is searched before the start of proceedings, and after that, nobody is allowed in on their own. You weren't able to change the cushion during the day, so it had to have exactly the right deflation rate for Bykoda's weight to hold out until after nightfall. In the break before the evening session you fixed a mirror outside the window. You couldn't have done it during the daytime; the mirror would have been too obvious. And then you sat there and watched Bykoda. When you saw her react to being pricked by the needle, you stood up and put on the light show to distract everyone and make it look more spectacular than it really was. Then you bounced a shot off the mirror to bring down the crystals. But, as I said, a third-rate witch could have done it." Jemeryl tossed the cushion back onto the chair.

While Jemeryl was speaking, Mavek's expression had gone from surprise to fear. His eyes flicked towards the door as if he was thinking of fleeing. "What are you going to do?"

"I'm going to go back to the Protectorate. And I'm going to take the talisman with me."

"I need to use it."

"You can't. It doesn't work."

"That's what Bykoda told you? She was lying. I've seen her notes. I couldn't do it myself, but I know how she made it, and it would work."

"It may have worked once. But the temporal forces have become unbalanced. It's too dangerous to make the attempt."

A new resolution came over Mavek's face, while shades of his old friendliness returned. "Maybe if I tell you why I need it."

"It will make no difference."

He showed no sign of hearing. "I had a partner once, like you, ungifted. We lived over to the west, near the mines. We had three children. The oldest was eight. I was mine foreman. I had the gift for a more important job, but I was happy as I was. One day I went into town for a meeting. It wasn't urgent. I could have left it. But I woke up on a sunny morning and thought it was a good day for a ride, so I'd get it over with early. While I was gone, a band of thieves picked that day to raid the mine. The workers fought them off and they fled...straight past my home, and they thought they'd hole up in my house." Mavek's face crumpled. "They murdered everyone there. My partner, my children, even my dogs. But it didn't help them. When I got home I..." Mavek shrugged, clearly struggling. "But it didn't bring my family back. And ever since Bykoda told us about the talisman, it's all I've been able to think about. I want to go back and change my mind. I want to wake up on that sunny morning and think, '*What a good day to spend with my family.*' I want to be there when those bastards arrive."

Jemeryl stared down at the floor, trying to think of suitable words to say. "I...I'm sorry for you. I really am, but you can't have the talisman." She made her voice as gentle as possible. "Have you thought of what might happen if it ruptures? Think of all the other families it could ruin."

"*If.*" Mavek's tone made his scepticism clear.

"Bykoda wasn't a woman to scare easily. And she was frightened of the danger."

"It's as much for Bykoda's sake that I need the talisman."

"Why?" Jemeryl frowned, confused.

Mavek stepped forwards, eagerly. "Don't you see? If I get the talisman and save my family, then I'll never become an acolyte and I'll have no need to kill her. I'm not a murderer. If it wasn't that I knew that once I'd got the talisman, I could undo what I'd done, I'd never have killed her. You have to let me have the talisman. It's the only way to put things right."

Jemeryl sank onto the couch, fighting with her pity for the man. She wished she could think of some way to help him, yet there was only one possible answer to his request. "I can't risk it. It's far too dangerous. I can't give the talisman to you."

"That's your last answer?"

"Yes."

Mavek stared at her for a long time. "It won't end here."

"It has to."

He retreated towards the door, shaking his head in an action that looked like a nervous twitch. "I'll be back."

"I won't have changed my mind."

"Then I'll make you."

"You're not strong enough. We both know that."

"I won't be alone."

Jemeryl got to her feet. "You're not wise to threaten me. I could strike you down, here and now, when it's one on one."

"But you won't." With his eyes still on Jemeryl, Mavek reached behind him and opened the door. "You're like me. Neither of us are killers." Only at the last moment did he break eye contact and slip away.

Jemeryl followed him to the stairway, but she made no attempt to let loose a magical assault. Mavek was right. She could not kill in cold blood—not while the hope of some other solution remained. His footsteps faded away down the steps.

She shut the door firmly and turned back to the room. How long did she have before he returned with support? And what should she do about it?

Mavek was adept in the sixth dimension, and very weak in the others. As a sorcerer, he was no match for either her or Bykoda. He would never be able to control the Empire on his own. The obvious interpretation for why he had staged Bykoda's death in such a dramatic fashion was to intimidate the other acolytes into supporting him. Jemeryl pursed her lips—exactly the same game that he had tried playing with her. Yet Mavek had made it clear that he had no long-term interest in the Empire.

Why did he need the support of the acolytes? Was it just to hold the Empire together long enough to give him time to investigate the talisman? Alternately, it would be surprising if working the talisman did not require skill in the seventh dimension, the second aspect of time. Was Mavek hoping to get Kharel's help, and wanted the seer to be too scared to ask question about what they were doing? Jemeryl's expression grew more sombre. Or did Mavek want their help to overpower her and take the talisman if she could not be coerced into handing it over?

Jemeryl considered her options. She could go and tell the acolytes the truth about Bykoda's death. But how would they respond? There was the risk that they would collectively decide that they wanted the talisman anyway and still gang up against her. Or they might simply turn on Mavek. Even if events went that way, Jemeryl was unhappy with the likely outcome. The pain in Mavek's voice as he had spoken of his family still echoed in her ears. She did not want to be in any way responsible for his death.

Klara had returned and was in her normal perch on the bookcase. Jemeryl spoke to the magpie, voicing her thoughts aloud. "We go now and hope that Tevi gets to the guard post soon."

The bags for the journey to Lyremouth should be waiting in the guard post. All that Jemeryl needed to do was go. After edging the door open, she waited, searching for any sound or other sign of activity in the stairwell. All seemed clear.

She had to leave before Mavek had the chance to summon allies against her. He would not know of her readiness for departure and would calculate that she needed to gather supplies. Mavek would therefore think he had more time than he did. With luck, he would leave it too late. But her first step was to get out of the castle unnoticed.

Jemeryl pulled the door shut behind her and crept down the stairs.

≈≈≈

PART TWO

The Acolyte

CHAPTER NINE—THE RUINS OF EMPIRE

Even though she had travelled slowly and cautiously, dawn was still hours away as Jemeryl approached the guard post. Her primary concern had been to avoid detection. Not that she felt overly worried on her own account, but it would be better if Mavek did not know where she was. Tevi would shortly be making her own way there, and sneaking through a magical cordon might prove tricky for the ungifted warrior.

A wry smile crossed Jemeryl's face. The guard post had turned out to be a better choice of rendezvous than either of them had known, back when Tevi pushed the plan on her. When Mavek found out that she had fled the castle, he would assume she was either racing south, back to the Protectorate, or north, in search of Tevi. Surely it would not occur to him that she was staying put a scant two miles from the gates of Tirakhalod? Or that she did not need to seek out Tevi?

A waist-high clump of bushes grew a stone's throw from the guard post. Jemeryl crouched in its shelter and considered her goal. The guard post was a one-story building, about twenty feet long and twelve wide. It stood beside the road a few dozen yards from the bridge. A door and a single window were on the side overlooking the road. Rough mortar filled the spaces between the stones, and slate tiles covered the roof. Although no sound came from the building, a faint light shone through gaps in the window shutters and the scent of smoke wafted on the night air. The clear implication was that someone currently occupied the guard post.

Jemeryl's first thought was that Tevi was there already. She almost rushed up to the door, but then she remembered Ranenok's message. If the battle with the trolls had not finished until sundown, it would be impossible for Tevi to have got to the guard post so soon. Whoever was in the building was unlikely to be a friend, and should be dealt with cautiously.

Tirakhalod's fires and furnaces had long since claimed the few trees to be found in the region. Now only long grass and shrubs covered the land. Grazing horses had removed even this from around the guard post. Nothing would hide Jemeryl's approach from anyone watching. She could, if she wished, turn herself invisible, but this would only work for the ungifted. To anyone with magical ability, the effect would be as subtle as jumping up and down, screaming, "Look over here. I'm a sorcerer!"

A chill breeze blew from the north, sighing through the grass. An owl whooped in the distance. The rush of the river drowned out all other sound. The sky overhead was clear, but the moon had set hours before and starlight was too faint to see much of use. Fortunately, Jemeryl's sorcerer senses were not so limited.

With her eyes closed, she studied the fluctuating life forces of the fifth dimension, trying to learn more. She picked out traces of deer in the grassland, birds in their nests, fish in the river, but the building was a blank. Somebody had sealed the walls against magic.

Jemeryl chewed her lip. Was that same somebody inside? Or was it the remnant of Bykoda's magic? She shifted her attention to the sixth dimension, searching the elemental forces for traps and alarms. This felt clear, but was it also masked? Finally, unwillingly, she probed the seventh dimension. At first no sense of foreboding rose in her, but then disquietening tendrils seeped in, as if from a distance.

Jemeryl clenched her hand in a fist and broke off her probes, angry at herself. To her mind, fortune telling was too haphazard a game to count as proper magic. She was wasting time in attempting it. She certainly could not rely on any results. Common sense and a little reasoning would be a better guide.

That people were sheltering in the guard post was not a surprise. With the collapse of Bykoda's power, one-third of her army had deserted. Gangs of soldiers were everywhere. Predictably, some had chosen to take shelter in the building for the night, rather than sleep in the open air.

But were any of them witches? Jemeryl did not want rumours of a sorcerer in the guard post to circulate. Before long, the report would get back to Mavek. Jemeryl had to make whoever was in the guard post leave without revealing her own presence. To that end, the ungifted would be so much easier to deal with.

Jemeryl fixed her attention back on the building. After a moment more thought she was sure that the creator of the wards was not there. Anyone powerful enough to block out a sorcerer's probes would rank too highly even to consider lodging in the guard post. But Jemeryl would still have liked a better idea of who, and how many, she had to deal with. Were any of the deserters standing sentry? Were they awake or sleeping, sober or drunk? A grin then grew on her lips, as she imagined Tevi, telling her that experience would bet on the latter option in both cases.

Jemeryl left the bushes and crept close. She had to take a chance and hope it would not come to a direct fight. As a last resort, she could take everyone prisoner until she and Tevi were ready to go. Carefully, she opened the door and peered in.

The main room occupied two thirds of the building. It held a fireplace, a table, and a set of bunk beds. Another doorway led to a second room. Four soldiers were sleeping, top and tail, in the bunks. Two less fortunate comrades lay on the earthen floor. The fire in the hearth had burnt down, but still gave off heat and dull red light. Nobody stirred.

Jemeryl smiled, slipped inside, and closed the door behind her. From the uniforms, she was sure that none of the soldiers was any sort of officer, and hence no witches were present. And now that she was in the warded building, there was no harm in displaying a bit of her own magic.

Jemeryl tiptoed to a dark corner where she should be out of the way and grabbed a handful of sixth-dimensional tensors. Within seconds, she had used the energy to realign the links between the life forces of the fifth and the temporal currents of the seventh. The result was that anyone who looked in her direction would see only how the corner had been before she stood there—which was close enough to being invisible for her needs.

The simplest option would be to take over the soldiers' minds and fill them with the urge to go. However, direct tampering left residual traces that would be apparent for days to come, should anyone with the gift chance to look. As this might well happen if the deserters were captured and interrogated, a little indirect action was safer.

The first thing was to wake somebody up. With a ripple in the sixth dimension, Jemeryl set icy fingers stroking the cheek of a rough-faced soldier on the floor. The woman's eyelids flickered open. At first she brushed her weather-beaten skin, as if thinking to wipe away drops of water, and then rubbed more forcefully. Jemeryl brought sound into play, projecting footsteps, soft and unmistakable, pacing the room.

"Who's there?"

The shout roused several of her comrades. "What's up?"

"There's someone here."

A bull-necked man on the top bunk sat up and stared around in the dim firelight. "No." He frowned. "You're dreaming."

Jemeryl repeated the footsteps. Someone swore. Both soldiers on the ground sprung up and backed away. Now, everyone was awake and tense. They stared about, wide eyes darting, ready for the next sound. Jemeryl let them wait. She did not want to overdo things. The fewer unusual events they had to talk about, the better, but gradually, she made the temperature in the room drop.

After two minutes of silence, one man laughed. "It's nothing. We're too edgy."

The women who had woken first rubbed her hands on her arms. "It's cold."

"Toss something on the fire."

Another soldier, the youngest there, scrambled from his bunk and picked a log off the pile beside the chimney. Three seconds after he threw it on, Jemeryl caused a loud pop and a shower of sparks to erupt. She drove the sparks around the room in a swirl, just suggesting a figure of fire, and then, before anyone could be certain what they saw, she let it disperse. Everyone had jumped at the explosion, and Jemeryl hoped, got a good dose of adrenaline and a racing pulse. Now they looked unnerved.

"Poxy sap."

Jemeryl repeated the footsteps, but this time from above.

"What's that?"

"Only a bird on the roof."

"Go and check."

"I'm not chasing sparrows in the dark."

The youngest soldier had retreated until his back was against a wall. Now he jerked around. "Something touched me."

Jemeryl smiled. That last bit had been nothing to do with her. Suggestion and nerves were doing their job.

The man on the top bunk jumped down. Using his heavily muscled frame, he barged through his comrades around the hearth. "It's nothing. We just need to keep our heads screwed on. The bitch is dead. That's what they say. We don't have anything to worry about." He knelt, scowling, and held his hands out to the flames. "What's wrong with this frigging fire? I'm freezing."

Jemeryl channelled airborne moisture into a droplet a few feet above his hands, coloured it red, and let it fall.

"Shit! Blood!"

A few more red drops fell, hitting his comrades and the ground.

"It's raining blood."

Already, the youngest soldier had grabbed his gear and was heading for the door. Two others were close behind. Within ten seconds, the room was deserted.

Jemeryl stepped from her corner, grinning. In broad daylight tomorrow, what would the soldiers make of the events? The cold before dawn had woken them. A bird had been walking across the roof. Water had condensed on the ceiling and dripped, and in the firelight it had looked red. And the battle-hardened warriors had fled. With any luck, they would feel too embarrassed to tell anyone—especially since their clothes would show no trace of bloodstains in the morning.

Jemeryl shut the door that had been left open in the soldiers' flight and sealed it with a spell that would allow only herself and Tevi access. Now that she was inside, the masking ward in the walls would prove very useful. She was free to work her magic, without fear of detection. But what was the source?

Searching for the answer took Jemeryl no more than five minutes. A charm was built into the chimney breast, unmistakably Mavek's handiwork, although Bykoda must have commissioned it. Jemeryl also discovered a secret store containing several other devices, some defensive and others deadly—quite hideously so. For what sort of dire contingency had they been stashed away here? The building had been constructed from real stone and imbued with magic that had outlived the Empress. Who had been intended to use it? And who was the intended victim? Jemeryl shook her head, grateful that she had not been privy to all the dark secrets of Bykoda's Empire.

Memories of the last three years made Jemeryl pause, staring into the fire. Bykoda was dead. The old woman had been tyrannical, unfettered by any moral restraint. She had taken people's land, their lives, their minds, as if it were her right and in return had given them stability. And now the Empire was ended. Jemeryl could not condone all that Bykoda had done—far from it—yet the world was unlikely to be a better place for her passing.

Jemeryl turned away and continued her search of the building. The door to the other room was locked, and the soldiers had wisely not tried to force it. Or maybe one had, and the rest had taken note of their comrade's fate—a trap was set in the sixth dimension. Jemeryl disarmed it and looked inside. The room was either used as a store or a prison, and maybe as both, dependant on need. Currently all it held were the supplies from Bykoda.

Back in the main room, the soldiers had left remains of their supper behind. Jemeryl doubted that they would be coming back for it. The packs from Bykoda held plenty of food, but it seemed a shame to waste what was there.

She sat by the fire and picked up a loaf of bread and a wedge of rich white cheese, but then a wide yawn surprised her. On second thought, she was not very hungry. What she needed most was sleep. The food would keep for breakfast. Jemeryl pulled a blanket from one of the packs and crawled onto the lower bunk. There was little else for her to do, except wait for Tevi.

❖

A yellow haze touched the eastern sky, rimmed with the first hint of pink. Dawn was close. Three birds called from the top of a nearby pile of rocks, but they were not songbirds welcoming the new day. The raw complaints of the carrion crows were as cheerless as the icy air, a fitting fanfare for the dead. There was plenty to attract them to this spot.

Tevi stood on the gravel slope and fixed her eyes on the horizon. She remembered a conversation from her early months on the mainland, after the first time she had killed somebody. An older, experienced mercenary had spoken to her, trying to help her through the doubt and guilt.

"At the end, you don't know what it was about, or what was gained, or where the right and wrong of it lay. You just wake up in the morning, spare a thought for those who can't, and thank whatever god watches over you."

The words often came back to her at dawn, especially ones like this, in the aftermath of battle. She walked down to the gravesite, dug wide enough for three. The dead soldiers already lay at the bottom. Two men and a woman, the youngest barely eighteen. Tevi looked at his face. He had trusted her leadership and followed her commands, and now he was dead. Tevi could feel the muscles in her jaw clamping. The guilt was hard to take. The thought that far more would be lying there if she had made the wrong decisions was a poor sop to her conscience.

The rest of the platoon gathered around, shuffling uneasily. The nervous expressions and agitation in their ranks was due to more than grief for the dead. Tevi knew she would need to address the problem very soon, but for now, the funeral came first. The other officers, a junior captain and two lieutenants, stood a short way off, making no attempt to hide their expressions of boredom.

Tevi knew that few commanding officers in Bykoda's army would bother attending a funeral for common soldiers. Most would consider themselves generous just in allowing time for the troops to deal with their lost comrades in whatever fashion they thought fit. Some would even have ordered the corpses stripped and thrown on the pile of dead trolls.

Tevi would not let the witches' disdain stop her from doing what was right. She would honour her fallen subordinates. She would even have treated the trolls with respect, except that trolls never showed any reverence for their own dead. Maybe they did not care, or maybe they considered it tactless to draw attention to defeat. In the absence of better information, Tevi could do no more than follow the trolls' own example and leave their bodies to the crows and foxes.

The soldiers were a different matter. They left behind friends, lovers, and family. They had been her responsibility and she had failed them. To speak over their graves was the least she owed them. They had come from the southwest of the Empire. Tevi had a rough idea of their beliefs—enough, she hoped, to say the right things at their funeral.

She raised her eyes from the bodies and began to speak. "Yesterday, three new heroes went to the halls of their ancestors. We will not forget them, their laughter or their tears. The world was brightened by their presence, and our hearts are now darkened by their loss. But they can go with their heads held high. Fate rolls the dice and we are the stakes. They were not cowards to argue the call. They faced their challenge. They passed their test with loyalty and courage..."

❖

By the time the sun had cleared the horizon, the grave was filled and a cairn raised over it. The troops assembled for inspection. In all, nearly two hundred soldiers were lined up across the rocky hillside. Tevi chewed her lip as she considered them. Daylight made glaringly obvious the overnight changes to army equipment.

The tabards emblazoned with Bykoda's crest that used to shine like silk had turned to plain sackcloth. The untarnished blades were already showing signs of rust. Leather was disintegrating. In the background, the war dogs howled and whined. Inspecting the troops was a sham. Their kit was falling apart as they stood there, but the routine drill gave Tevi a better chance to gauge the mood. Something had gone wrong with Bykoda's magic. The fact was obvious to everyone. The common soldiers eyed each other with fear and uncertainty. Even the officer witches were not hiding their disquiet.

Tevi could guess the cause, but she was not about to share the information. She knew Jemeryl had no trust in oracles, and here was the justification. Despite confident predictions of date, Bykoda had clearly been overthrown sooner than expected. But this was not Tevi's concern. All she wanted was to rejoin Jemeryl and return to the Protectorate. Already she had been delayed more than she had intended.

Yesterday's encounter had not been the straightforward battle expected. The trolls either had good luck or good scouts. By the time Tevi's platoon reached them, they had retreated into crags on top of a hill. The position was well suited for defence. Even so, Tevi had the numbers for a frontal assault. Yet she would have taken heavy losses in the fighting, far more than three.

She had played a bluff. The trolls had no way of knowing that she wanted the affair over with quickly. For several hours, her archers had peppered the hilltop from a distance. The trolls were too well protected to take serious casualties, probably no more than one or two over the course of the afternoon, but it inflamed their volatile tempers.

Then Tevi had sent a squad of soldiers to dig ditches and ramparts, in full view of the trolls, as if she meant to blockade the hilltop. A drawn-out siege did not fit with the trollish idea of warfare. They had come roaring down from the crags, hoping to overwhelm the isolated ditchdiggers, and had run straight into an ambush. Tevi had been using the cover of archers to deploy her troops. A few of the trolls had managed to fight their way back to the crags, but their reduced numbers had been insufficient to hold out. Tevi's soldiers had followed, scouring every crevice. Yet night was falling before they had been sure that every troll was accounted for.

Tevi had thought about leaving as soon as the fighting was over. The moon was up, and there would be enough light to travel for a few hours. She could get halfway to the guard post, then rest and continue at dawn. But she had seen the bodies of her fallen soldiers. Staying for the funeral was a small enough payment to set against their sacrifice. And regardless of when she left, she would not reach Jemeryl that night.

She sent news of the battle to Ranenok, asking that he let her lover know she was all right. She could not ask directly, but with luck, he would also give enough information for Jemeryl to work out about the delay to their plans. As soon as possible, Tevi would make her excuse to leave the troops and hurry to the rendezvous. If she could get there for mid afternoon, they would have a few hours to rest the horses, and then she and Jemeryl could set out for the Protectorate under the cover of dark.

After setting up camp on the hilltop, her troops had bedded down for the night. Tevi was just about to seek her own bed in the officers' tent when an indefinable wave had swept across the camp. Everyone felt the change, though none could explain what it was. War-dogs had started howling. Equipment had degraded in the soldiers' hands. The contents of several packs had burst into flames.

Tevi had sent one of the officers to contact Tirakhalod using a message orb, while she and the other two worked to maintain discipline in the platoon. The high morale of the triumphant soldiers had aided in this second task, but the orb had been less successful. Despite repeated attempts, no contact could be made with the castle.

By morning, the mood of the platoon had fallen. Something was wrong, and everyone knew it. Tevi felt torn. She wanted to stay, watch over her troops, and return them safely to their barracks, but she could not. She had to leave and rendezvous with Jemeryl. Plus, if her guess was correct, the barracks might not be the safest location.

Tevi finished walking along the last line of troops and moved up the hill to a spot where everyone could see her. She was not going to lie to them, but neither could she tell them the whole truth. Fortunately the whole truth was not required, and her plan should work out for the best for everyone.

She raised her voice. "You did well yesterday. You don't need me to tell you that. And you don't need me to tell you that something odd happened last night. I wish I could tell you what it was, but nobody has any definite information. It might be some residual magic the trolls sparked off. It might be some sort of attack. It might even be something strange with the phase of the moon. But one thing we do know is that we stayed here last night and nothing bad happened to us. So rather than dash off into a trap, we're going to carry on staying here until we know what's going on. The trolls thought they'd found a nice defensive position. But they forgot all about how to make use of a defensive position—you stay put in it. We're not going to make the same mistake. We're going to fortify this hilltop and see if anything thinks it can get us out." Tevi's gaze travelled over the ranks of soldiers. Some were smiling; all looked happier. Safety and defence were what they wanted to hear. Even the officers looked more at ease. "All right. Parade over. To your posts."

The soldiers dispersed. As expected, the three officer witches hovered nearby. Tevi summoned them over. They had been the most troublesome part of her command. Their attitude made it clear that they did not appreciate serving under an ungifted leader, although only Captain Altrun had raised objections.

He was the youngest of the officers but the most adept at magic. Unlike the other two, he made no attempt to keep in good physical condition, as if boasting with his sagging waistline that muscles were not the source of his strength. He was the one to speak now, his round bland face fixed in an insubordinate sneer.

"That's it? We're just going to sit here?" Tevi glared at him, until he added, "Ma'am."

"No. We're going to send someone back to Tirakhalod to find out what's happening."

"Do you want me to ask for volunteers?"

"No. I'm going."

The witches looked surprised. "Are you sure...ma'am?"

"Yes." Tevi hesitated. She needed to pick her words carefully. "I was here for the tactics of the battle with the trolls. That's over. The current problem is something to do with magic, and I can't help with that. We need to send someone to Tirakhalod. If there is anything out there waiting to ambush us, then one person alone has the best chance of slipping through unnoticed. But if that person does get noticed, then I'm the one who stands the best chance of fighting a way through."

Captain Altrun frowned. "Wouldn't one of the lieutenants be better? They could defend themselves with magic."

"Do you have any idea what has broken our link with Tirakhalod?"

"No."

"Do you have any idea what *could* have broken our link with Tirakhalod?" Tevi glared at them, noting the jitters. She had spent enough time talking to Jemeryl to know what witches and sorcerers found unnerving.

"No," Altrun conceded at last.

"Then the chances are that you can no more defend against it than I can. What chance there is lies in all three of you staying together and combining your powers to fight it. You three are needed here and I'm not." Tevi knew she would win that point. Easy to convince someone of something they already believed. "While I am gone, Captain Altrun will be in command." That was the final ploy. Altrun's eyes lit up. "If you don't hear from me in three days, it will be up to him to decide what to do next. Any other questions?"

Of course, there were none.

Tevi left them and made haste to pack her belongings. Most of what she needed for the journey to Lyremouth was with Jemeryl, but it was up to her to bring a second horse. She could claim she needed it for change of mount, and as security should one go lame.

The sun was now rising higher in the sky. Tevi spared it a glance, estimating the time. Another few minutes should see her on the road and well on schedule to reach Jemeryl before dusk.

A shout claimed her attention. "Captain Tevirik."

"What is it?"

"Captain Altrun wishes to speak with you, ma'am. He's in the command tent."

Tevi tossed her bag aside and returned to the tent at the centre of the site. All three witches were waiting for her.

"Has something happened?" Tevi asked as she ducked through the opening.

"The message orb, ma'am. It's not yet fully functional, but it seems to be returning to life."

Tevi swore under her breath. If they received countermanding orders, she would have to delay her departure. How long would it be before she had the chance to sneak away? Why could the thing not have waited another hour before stirring? Small consolation that Altrun looked just as displeased as herself.

The orb's silken wrapper was spread open on a table. Unlike the lifeless pearl surface of the previous night, mist swirled deep within. She did not need the gift of magic to tell that the orb was interacting with something. One of the lieutenants was waving her hand over it, sculpting its energies to her bidding. This was the part that Tevi, ungifted, could not do, although she could speak via it, once a witch had coerced it into life.

The lieutenant spoke. "The harmonic ether is responding, ma'am. Another globe has bound to its resonance. I heard the summons. Commander Ranenok wishes to speak with the four of us."

Tevi braced herself to look into the orb. Island born and bred, she had never suffered from seasickness, but the sensation she got when peering into the orbs gave her sympathy with those who did. For a moment her stomach flopped around like a beached fish, her eyes refused to focus, and then cleared. She was watching two scenes at once, the tent and somewhere else. The scenes were not superimposed. They were both present at the same time. The sickness came whenever Tevi tried to work out where she was.

Jemeryl had explained that the orbs worked by directly interacting with the watcher's brain. Eyes and ears were not involved in the process but tried to play a part out of habit. Jemeryl had also said that the direct mental link was open to misuse, and in the Protectorate would only be permitted with strict safeguards. The absence of these safeguards was no surprise to Tevi. In her opinion, the potential for abuse was deliberate, as it was with every other form of magic in Bykoda's Empire.

Ranenok was standing in one of the rooms of the keep. He was clearly on edge. The fingers on his hand were clenched as tightly as his jaw. His feet were making continuous small movements, as if fighting the urge to shuffle. Sensing the watchers, he looked up. His eyes met briefly with Tevi's and something like guilt flickered there.

He drew a deep breath. "Good morning. I'm afraid I have very serious news to impart. Late last night, the Empress Bykoda was murdered in her council chamber. And by the common consent of the acolytes, Mavek is now emperor. I am acting on his orders."

Tevi's own surprise was such that she barely registered the gasps from the other three. Bykoda's death she had expected. Mavek's name she had not. Did this mean that he was the assassin, or had he merely stepped in opportunistically?

Ranenok went on. "There is more I must tell you. The Coven sorcerer, Jemeryl, has fled from Tirakhalod. Emperor Mavek wishes to speak with her most urgently. If anyone gains knowledge of her whereabouts they should contact Tirakhalod at once. She is not to be trusted and may prove very dangerous to anyone who tries to tackle her. Furthermore, her associate, Captain Tevirik, is to be arrested and must be taken to Castle Kreztino without delay. She will be questioned once she gets there."

Kreztino was on the northern edge of the Empire, as far from the Protectorate as it was possible to get. Instinctively, Tevi took a half step back, but with three witches surrounding her, flight was impossible. Ranenok's eyes met hers again, sad and apologetic. "In case there is some clue in her belongings, all her possessions must be brought to Tirakhalod at once. However, she is not to be mistreated. It is imperative that she remains alive and well until other orders are issued."

❖

The moon was three days past the quarter and thickening to the full. With each successive night its rays fell more strongly. It would not set until well after midnight. The guard post stood serene in its light. The gentle rush of the river matched the whisper of the grass.

The figure paused beside the last thicket. Its head twisted back and forth as if seeking, and something in the movement hinted that scent was as important as sight. The figure was human in shape although taller than a man, and its outline quivered in the breeze. Even under moonlight, it seemed strangely devoid of detail, soft and dark, like smoke.

After a few seconds more, it continued its advance. The progress was silent, smooth and unhurried, flowing rather than walking. At the door it stopped again, but this time with a suddenness that suggested it had received a jolt or run into an unexpected block. It wavered, appearing even more smoke-like in its twisting distortion, and then dissolved, sinking to the ground in a formless puddle.

Inside the guard post, the remains of the fire lit the room with a muted red light, revealing the scattered possessions littering the floor. Debris had accumulated over the three-day wait: boots, books, scraps of paper, and half-eaten food. Jemeryl lay asleep in the lower bunk, curled beneath the blanket. The even sound of her breathing and the faint shifting of logs in the fire were the only sounds.

In the dim, flickering light, the smoke seeping under the door was not at first apparent. But more and more of it flowed through—creeping tendrils, like mist off a marsh. Still it seemed to be hunting, stalking its prey. At the centre of the room it began to coalesce, rearing up to regain its original height.

Now there was detail. Red eyes gleamed in the face and fanged jaws opened. Knotted muscle bunched across shoulders and back. Clawed hands reached towards the sleeping woman.

"Er, Jem. I think you might want to wake up." Klara gave the alarm.

Jemeryl jerked bolt upright in her bunk. Her gaze raced wildly around the room until it fixed on the phantom lurching towards her. Confusion and surprise surged across her face, followed swiftly by resolve. The thing was a simulacrum, nightmarish in form and deadly to the ungifted, but no more than a minor nuisance to a sorcerer. Jemeryl's hand flew out in a warding gesture, sending stars of ice leaping from her fingertips. Where they hit, they sucked the figure in, so it was swallowed by ripples of implosion. For an instant the outline glowed white and then vanished, leaving only a rain of ash drifting to the floor.

Jemeryl sighed and pulled her feet out of the bed. She staggered to the fireside. The flames were nearly out. After adding another four logs, which she ignited with a fire spell, she sat with her arms wrapped around her legs and her forehead resting on her knees. The fire was not necessary for warmth, her magic could have provided that, but there was something comforting in its living presence. She was in need of comfort.

"Where is Tevi?" She voiced her frustration.

"She'll be here soon. She's probably having to avoid gangs of deserters and things. You don't need to worry. She can take care of herself."

Jemeryl twisted her head to look at the magpie. She could put no faith in the bland reassurance. Lying to yourself rarely worked, even if you got your familiar to say the words aloud.

"She should have been here today, at the very latest. The trolls were no more than twenty miles away. It shouldn't take her three days."

Jemeryl's eyes returned to the flames. Her pulse began to calm after the shock awakening, but her thoughts continued to churn. The first day in the guard post had been tedious but otherwise stress free. She had been sure that Tevi would get there that night. The next day had been one of growing anxiety. When another night passed with no sign of her missing lover, Jemeryl's fears had crept to the fore. This was now the third night, and she could no longer avoid the conclusion that something had gone seriously wrong. She was going to have to make new plans, although her options might soon become limited.

In a burst of activity, Jemeryl rattled through the items by the fireplace, finding a pan and a flask of water. Herbal tea might calm her fears. And if not, at least making it would give her something to do rather than worry. She balanced the pan over the fire.

Klara watched with beadlike eyes. "Do you um...think Mavek has captured Tevi? And made her tell him where you are, and hence the...?" The magpie jerked her head towards the circle of ash.

"The simulacrum?" Jemeryl sat back, sombre in thought. The possibility had to be faced, but after a short while, she shook her head. "No. I suspect it came here by chance. Or more likely, Mavek has now got the situation in the castle under control and is checking the surroundings for trouble. He's probably sent out a dozen or more of them. Simulacrums look far more dangerous than they really are—as long as you know how to deal with them. They might take care of any deserters stupid enough to try fighting, but they wouldn't give the slightest problem even to a third-rate witch."

The water in the pan started to boil. Jemeryl made her tea, but then put it aside, untasted. Her eyes fixed on the fire.

"Mavek wouldn't insult me by sending a simulacrum after me. I shouldn't think he had the first idea that I was here." Jemeryl rested her chin on her knees. "But he does now."

CHAPTER TEN—THE GAME OF
THREAT AND BLUFF

S orcerer Jemeryl. I am here on behalf of the Emperor Mavek to speak with you." The shouted words were delivered with enough volume to not only be heard inside the guard post, but to have woken Jemeryl had she still been asleep.

In fact, Jemeryl had been awake since before dawn, considering her options. The final decision, to let Mavek make the first move, had not been easy, but she was fairly sure that he would begin by talking rather than fighting, and that she would win out on any information exchange. Mavek already knew where she was. Staying put would tell him nothing new, whereas Jemeryl felt she could do with some fresh news from the castle.

She wandered to the window. Oiled cloth, rather than glass, kept out the wind while allowing in light. Somebody—possibly a deserter—had torn a small hole in the fabric. Through it, she could see one of Mavek's assistants standing alone on the other side of the road. He was among the older blacksmiths, nearly fifty, with a lean, wiry build. Soot and grease etched the lines on his face and darkened the fringe of white hair over his ears. Jemeryl had seen him about the castle, but they had never spoken before. This was their chance to get better acquainted.

"You can come in. The door's not locked," she called out.

"Will you promise me safe passage?"

"No."

Jemeryl grinned and strolled back to the fireside. It was extremely unlikely that she would want to harm the envoy, but there seemed no reason to start out by limiting her options, and she doubted that he would run back to the castle with his message undelivered, regardless of how she answered.

Two minutes passed before the door opened and Mavek's envoy sidled in, looking ill at ease. A bag was slung over his shoulder. He deposited it on the ground by his feet.

Jemeryl remained leaning against the chimney, holding a mug in her hand. She gestured with it. "Would you like some tea?"

"No, thank you."

"I don't think we've been introduced."

"My name's Cluthotin."

Jemeryl nodded her head in acknowledgement. "I take it you have a message for me."

"Yes." Cluthotin stood up straighter and pushed his chest out. However, the attempt to project confidence was marred by the trouble he was having in finding his voice.

"What is it?" Jemeryl prompted.

"Sorcerer Jemeryl. You have murdered the previous Empress, Bykoda, and are now trying to flee the lands. Mavek demands that you return to Tirakhalod to answer for your crimes."

Cluthotin licked his lips nervously, waiting for her reply. Jemeryl let him wait. She sipped her tea in silence while she considered the implications of what he had said.

That Mavek was blaming her for the murder was not a complete surprise. The acolytes would know it was false, but they were too frightened by what they thought they had witnessed to defy him and tell the truth. Nor would they press him to explain his motives. However, the accusation of murder was a good excuse for everyone else, explaining why he would devote the entire resources of his newly gained empire into tracking her down.

From Mavek's point of view, the biggest danger was if she made contact with any of the acolytes and told them how the murder had been committed. Hence, one lone, low-grade witch was being used as envoy. Jemeryl could tell Cluthotin the full story, but with the six most powerful people in the Empire as eyewitnesses against her, it was very doubtful if she could even convince Cluthotin that Mavek was the killer, let alone produce any sort of interest in her theories of how and why.

The demand that she return to Tirakhalod was the interesting bit. Did Mavek really want to force a confrontation? Surely he could not risk tackling her with witnesses present. Was it all just part of a bluff? Did Mavek think she would not comply, so there was no risk in demanding? Was it a pretence to cover a different message? And of course, there was no mention of the talisman.

Cluthotin's composure was slipping. The pulse in his neck beat rapidly, like a bird's. He clearly had more to say and was fearful at how it would be received. Jemeryl deliberately said and did nothing to make his task any easier. Eventually, he bent down and dug around in the bag he had brought with him. When he stood, he was holding out an iron collar.

"In view of the dangerous nature of your actions, the Emperor Mavek demands that you wear this before you enter the castle."

"Mavek is being over-ambitious in his demands." Jemeryl kept her voice low and deadly.

The iron collar was more that just an insult. Iron distorted the flow of energy in the higher dimensions. The effect of a complete circle so close to the brain and main sense organs was devastating in its effect on awareness of the upper dimensions. The intensity of the forces would blanket out all else. If Jemeryl obeyed the instruction she would be handicapped, reduced to below the level of ungifted. What game was Mavek playing, even to make the suggestion?

"You refuse?"

"Of course."

Cluthotin swallowed and reached into his bag again. "The likelihood that you would respond in this way was considered. I am therefore authorised to show you these."

He pulled out a grey shirt, a tooled leather belt, and a broad rune sword—Tevi's shirt, Tevi's belt, and Tevi's sword. Jemeryl tried not to stare or react. The possibility had been growing at the back of her mind with each hour of Tevi's non-arrival. It was one of the reasons she had waited for the expected envoy.

Cluthotin licked his lips. "You do recognise these?"

"Yes."

"As you can tell from these tokens, your accomplice has been apprehended already. If you obey the Emperor Mavek's orders and submit to custody, you are both guaranteed a fair trial. If you do not, then your accomplice will be executed immediately."

Jemeryl gave a humourless laugh. "Do I look stupid?"

"Ma'am?"

She treated the envoy to a condescending appraisal. Attempting to explain matters to him was pointless. "If I give you a message to take back to Mavek, can you deliver it word for word? You won't understand what it's about, so if you try to abridge it or change the words around, you'll get it wrong. But if not, I could write it down for you."

"I'll try."

"Don't worry, it isn't long. Tell Mavek..." Jemeryl paused, picking her words. "I'm very disappointed in him. No, he cannot have the talisman. And if he hurts Tevi, then I will make sure he ends up wishing that he'd sat on the cushion himself. And we both know I can make good on that threat."

"So you're defying him?"

"That's about it." Jemeryl drained the last of her tea and put down her empty mug. "You can go now, but leave Tevi's things behind. And you better pray that I get the chance to give them back to her soon. If I come after Mavek, there won't be much hope for any of the obstacles he tries to put in my way, and the chances are that you'd be one of them."

Cluthotin pushed the whole bag in her direction with his foot and then backed towards the door. Jemeryl waited until he was gone before moving. Only then did she let herself sink down with her hands pressed to her head. Both she and Mavek were bluffing. Whose nerve would break first?

Revenge would be no substitute for losing Tevi, and Mavek would know it. But equally, Tevi was Mavek's best protection and the only thing that could keep Jemeryl and the talisman in the northern lands and within his grasp. Executing Tevi would leave him with no cards to play. He had to keep Tevi safe from both death and rescue. He would undoubtedly have a watch on the guard post, ready to track Jemeryl if she left.

On the other hand, if Jemeryl had put on the collar, then Mavek would have been able to take the talisman and use it. Which would almost certainly result in the death of Tevi, Jemeryl, and a vast number of others. Whatever the threats, Tevi was safer with Jemeryl unconstrained.

Jemeryl was also aware that the possessions were not absolute proof that Mavek had Tevi. The items could have been stolen from her—or stripped from her body. Jemeryl squeezed her eyes shut. That last possibility was one she would leave until she had proof. But if Tevi was dead, and Mavek had played any part in it, then the time for bluffs would be over.

❖

Herds of wild goats scattered at the riders' approach. The trail wound through the windswept foothills, climbing steadily. Traces of snow clung to hollows on the north facing slopes. The mountains before them were getting close, a jagged line of rock and ice filling the sky. From maps, Tevi knew that Castle Kreztino lay at the foot of the double-peaked mountain straight ahead. At their current rate of progress, they would be there on the next day.

Captain Altrun had set a punishing pace. Presumably he had got the implied threat in the warning about Jemeryl and worked out the possibility that the dangerous sorcerer might be on their heels. Most common soldiers had been left at the first garrison post they reached. The remainder of the platoon had been put on horseback. Four further changes of mount had allowed them to average more than sixty miles a day. Currently, the troops were more exhausted than the relay horses. Many soldiers were nodding as they rode.

Ironically, despite being a prisoner, Tevi was in a better state than most. Her hands and feet were tied to her saddle, which meant she could not fall off. This had allowed her to catch some sleep on the journey. That night would be her last chance to escape before they reached Kreztino. Over the previous days, she had noted which guards were more keen on gossip than keeping an eye on her, and who would furtively swig rough spirits to drive away the chill on night watch.

This northern part of the Empire had been under Yenneg's control, and Tevi was unfamiliar with the terrain. Her knowledge did not go much beyond the location of a few major features, such as castles and large towns. Any hope of escaping on the previous nights had been thwarted when they had stopped at small forts and Tevi had been locked in a cell. However, now they had reached the sparsely populated outskirts of the Empire, and she was positive no similar military posts were nearby. That night they would have to make camp in the open.

Her chances were boosted by the attitude of the three officers. They were venting their resentment at being required to follow her orders before by treating her with exaggerated contempt now. None had taken personal charge of her. She was watched over only by the ordinary soldiers. No special measures were being taken against her escaping. In their eyes, she was clearly just an ungifted and overrated fighter. Tevi did not think she was being immodest in taking this as proof that magical talent was no guarantee against stupidity.

Despite her known strength, the rope around her wrists was no thicker than normal. At the morning break she had found a sharp stone that she had been able to hide in her boot. From her experience of Jemeryl, Tevi was sure the witches could have controlled her mind and prevented such activity. Their laxness meant she could be free of her bonds within seconds.

Furthermore, none of the troops thought of Tevi as a mere ungifted fighter—not with stories of the conjured demon circulating. When it came to the crisis, Altrun might be surprised to find out that the soldiers were no more frightened of him than they were of her, and no more keen to engage her in combat.

The sky was clear, except for high wisps of cirrus. The moon would be bright enough to light her way. Unfortunately, it would also assist anyone who chased after her. Simply leaping on a horse and pelting off would not do. Altrun and the other witches might not have anything close to Jemeryl's level of ability, but their magic was still formidable and deadly. However, as Jemeryl had often remarked, even sorcerers did not find flying a viable method of transport. Before making her escape, Tevi had to find a way to deprive them of their horses.

The detachment consisted of Tevi, the officers, and a dozen other soldiers. When she added in the spare pack horses, this gave her twenty animals to deal with. She did not think she would be able to kill them all silently before the alarm was raised—not that she liked the idea anyway. Driving the horses off would most likely not work either. Two or three would be bound to drift back within minutes, and Captain Altrun only needed one.

Her best option was to lead the horses away with her—just as long as none decided to be uncooperative. Tevi was certain that restraining spells had not been laid on the animals. The trouble was that Tevi did not know enough about the witches' capabilities. Would they be able to exert mental control over the fleeing beasts and command them to return? From Jemeryl's disparaging remarks about the level of skill and training found in Bykoda's officers, Tevi thought the answer was no, but with her life at stake, a tad more certainty would be nice. She would feel a lot happier once she was out of the witches' line of sight.

Tevi looked around for any sign of available cover, trying to work out her chances. The sun was sinking low on the horizon. Soon they would be stopping. As if on cue, a shout rang out. One of the lieutenants peeled away from the head of the line and rode back, giving the order to dismount. The weary soldiers obeyed with obvious relief. One soldier made a half-hearted attempt to tie the reins of Tevi's horse to a bush.

The site chosen was on the side of a hill, sheltered from the cold north-westerly wind. A river ran along the bottom, with wide grassy banks that would provide food and water for the horses. No trees grew in the grasslands, but a low hill rose on the other side of the river. If Tevi could get behind it she would be safe from attack by arrows or fireballs. In the distance, a huge herd of shaggy wild cattle, stretching a mile or more in length, ambled across the grassland. Setting her route via them should take care of any tracks she might leave.

A gully washed down the hillside a little way off. Once she had got rid of her bonds, she could creep down it, out of sight of any sentries who were managing to keep their eyes open. The sound of the river would cover her loosing the horses from their hobbles, and it would be darkest of all in the shadow at the bottom of the hill. The first anyone would know was when she rode up the opposite hillside. By the time the officers had woken and got out of their tent, she would be away.

Of course, that was if everything went well. But the situation was looking as good as she could have hoped. Tevi tried to suppress any undue animation on her part. Not all her guards were as overconfidently blinkered as the witches, although nobody was paying her any attention at the moment.

Captain Altrun and one lieutenant had ridden to the top of the hill from where they appeared to be surveying the terrain. Tevi watched them in scorn. Why did they bother? What did they think they were looking for? Neither had shown the first understanding of how to use land features to their advantage. From her knowledge of other officer witches, Tevi suspected that they surveyed the campsite solely because it was what they had been told to do.

The rest of her guard were preparing the camp. The unsaddled horses were hobbled and set to graze by the river. The first puffs of smoke were rising from campfires made using knots of grass and dried dung, both of which were in abundant supply. Four soldiers had been detailed to erect a tent for the officers at a spot suitably removed from the ungifted subordinates. Others were laying out their gear. Judging by the soldiers' exhausted movements, it would be amazing if most did not fall asleep on sentry duty.

Apart from the two officers on the hilltop, Tevi was the only person still in the saddle, probably because everyone was too tired to remember about her. With luck, the sentries that night would be equally neglectful. Still, she would have liked to be untied and let off her horse. The saddle was leaving its impression on her.

"Get the prisoner down." The lieutenant snapped the order as she passed by.

One of the soldiers put aside his bedroll and moved to obey. He kept his eyes averted while he untied the rope around Tevi's ankles. Only when he moved to her wrists did he look up. For a moment he held her eyes, then he turned his neck to glare at the lieutenant's back, cleared his throat, and spat.

Tevi pursed her lips, taking some consolation from knowing that she was more popular with the troops than the witches were.

The soldier fumbled at the binding around Tevi's hands, his thick fingers made clumsy by tiredness, but eventually he finished loosing Tevi from the saddle, although her wrists were still bound together. He took a half step back and raised his arm, offering her help to dismount. Suddenly his expression froze. A shadow swept over the camp, and for an instant, Tevi was in shade. She jerked her head up, but missed whatever had gone overhead. Then somebody screamed.

The look on the face of the soldier at her side had turned to horror. He stumbled away then turned and ran, crashing heedlessly through the campsite.

From higher up the hillside, Captain Altrun called out, although his words were garbled and distorted. "You...get the...don't..." The panic in his voice was what made Tevi forget the fleeing soldier and look at him.

Altrun and the second lieutenant were about twenty yards away. They must have been on their way back, but now they were fighting with their mounts. The horses had clearly seen and recognised whatever had gone overhead. Altrun was hauling on the reins, trying to pull his horse's head towards the camp, but then he appeared to give up the battle. He slipped his right foot from the stirrup and swung it over the horse's rump, about to jump clear. He looked up. Shock transformed his round face, followed by terror. He opened his mouth to yell, but he did not get the chance.

Fire crashed down on him, a waterfall of flame, deluging both horses and riders. Grass crackled and flared at the edges. A huge shape was falling from the sky, swooping low over the burning pool. This time Tevi saw it. The beast was immense, covered in green-brown scales. Bat-like wings sliced through the air. Fire poured from a mouth set in a lizard's head that was as long as a man.

A single beat of its wings pulled the dragon from its dive. The draft caused the dying fire to re-erupt in fury, hurling clumps of burning grass and flesh into the air. A barbed tail whipped inches above the ground, parting the flames. And then it was gone, leaving the charred remains of horses and humans, crumpling to the blackened earth.

Tevi's horse had been frozen in terror. Now it bolted, tearing the bush it had been tethered to from the ground. Tevi grabbed at the horse's neck with her bound hands, fighting to stay in place. Across the campsite, soldiers were running, screaming, searching for cover. Her horse ploughed through anyone and anything that got in its way. It left the soldiers and their scattered possessions behind and raced up the hill. Tevi was not sure that being an isolated target was wise, but neither was waiting for the dragon's return—not that she had any choice.

A crescendo of screaming broke out behind her. The dragon was back. Tevi heard the roar of flames. Her horse surged forwards in intensified panic. Tevi looked over her shoulder but could see nothing except a wall of fire and smoke. And then above the screams and the fire and the pounding of her horse's hooves she heard a new sound, the rush of wind over wings, growing closer. She flung herself low over her horse's neck—a futile gesture. The image of Altrun, engulfed in flames, was all she could think of.

The dragon's shadow swept over her. With the sun so close to the horizon, the dragon had to be low, and right on top of her. Tevi could feel the draft from its wings, and then huge claws drove in on either side, impaling her mount. She and the dying horse were lifted clear of the ground. A monstrous reptilian mouth came down. She had a glimpse of rows of saw-like teeth before the dragon bit off the horse's head, ending its pathetic struggling. The ground fell away below as the dragon rose up into the evening sky, carrying her away.

❖

In the fading light, six metal golems clanked towards the guard post. They were fearless, twenty feet high, and had the strength to smash through stone. They were naturally impervious to arrows, swords, fire, or anything that might hit them weighing less than a ton. They were some of Mavek's most fearsome creations. Their combined strength was enough to challenge even a sorcerer. Yet, watching them bear down on the guard post, Jemeryl was unbothered—mainly because she was hiding under the bridge.

In fact, seeing the golems was something of a relief, confirming her guesswork. Jemeryl remembered them from her tour of Mavek's armoury. They were the obvious choice to send against her. True, Mavek had other weapons that could have proved more dangerous, but the golems offered the best chance for capturing her alive. She liked to think that Mavek would not have killed her unnecessarily, but either way, he would not want to risk damage to the talisman.

Sunset was over. The grasslands were being swallowed by gloom. Jemeryl shivered in the chill wind. She had been waiting for hours, and accommodation under the bridge was far from comfortable. Why could Mavek not have acted a bit quicker? Although, from her knowledge of him, it was perhaps more a case of luck that he had not left it until the next day. Mavek was overcautious by nature. His instincts were all wrong for seizing the moment. He would never be able to keep control of Bykoda's Empire.

However, he was an inspired craftsman. The devices made by him that Jemeryl had found in the guard post were impressive and very useful—to her. The masking ward in the chimney meant Mavek was unaware that she was no longer inside the building. A short-acting charm had allowed Jemeryl enough time to move to the bridge without being observed, although regrettably not enough to flee the area. A third defensive shield would, she hoped, protect her over the next few minutes. The more dramatic offensive charms were all primed and set waiting in the guard post.

Five of the golems formed a loose ring around the building. The sixth plodded heavily up to the door. Its metal hands reached out, grasping for the frame. At the moment they touched the wood, lightning leapt out, wreathing the figure in trails of sparks. The golem jolted as if stung. For a moment it swayed, but then righted itself and took two steps to the side. It clenched its huge steel hand into a fist. Jemeryl shifted back further under the stone arch of the bridge, anticipating what was to come.

The golem punched the wall. Chips flew off and the whole building shook under the impact as if it were made of straw. On the fourth blow, stones fell away, leaving a two-foot gap. The golem stretched its hands in, gripping the edges of the hole, ready to pull the wall apart and complete its demolition.

The guard post exploded.

The ground shook. Stones and timbers hurtled into the sky. Smoke billowed out in an instant, shrouding the golem that had broken the wall. The others were knocked from their feet. Shrubs were torn out by their roots and blown away. Grass was whipped up and ignited in a storm of black ash. And then the roar faded away across the grasslands, to be followed by pounding as chunks of rock and broken tiles came crashing back to earth.

Under the bridge, grit and small chipping rained down on Jemeryl, stinging her skin. The ground had bucked so violently that she had banged her arm on a stone. Her ears rang and dust made her eyes water, but her shield ward had held, and apart from the bruised elbow, she had taken no injury.

Once the smoke cleared, Jemeryl looked back to where the guard post had been. A few stones were still standing, but mostly the site was a rubble-filled crater. Three of the golems had regained their feet. One was lying motionless, and another was repeatedly trying to stand, despite now having only one leg. Of the golem that had punched the wall, there was little left apart from twisted junk.

Jemeryl was impressed. The device had been even more powerful than she expected. Golems were notoriously hard to damage. When she had first seen the metal constructs in the armoury, she had been surprised that Bykoda allowed anything inside the castle that might pose such a threat to her. However, controlling the golems required great concentration, and it would be beyond the ability of anyone to manage more than two at a time. Conversely, for a powerful sorcerer, two golems were beatable odds. In order to have used them against Bykoda with any surety of success, Mavek would have needed at least one, and preferably two other acolytes as accomplices. Jemeryl guessed she should feel flattered that he was treating her with the same degree of respect.

But one thing it did mean was that some other acolytes were nearby. Only they would have the ability to control the half-living machines. But who? And was it worth the risk of trying to talk to them?

Three minutes passed before Jemeryl got answers to her questions. Mavek emerged from the dusk, hurrying to the site of the ex-guard post. He had just reached the edge of the crater when two more figures appeared, converging on the scene from different directions. Jemeryl was not surprised to see Yenneg and Anid. The two army commanders were the most likely acolytes to have had previous experience with golems.

"What was the explosion?" Yenneg asked once he got within hailing distance.

"Bykoda." Mavek's voice was taut.

"She left a booby trap here?"

"Yes. Something she had me make for her a few years back."

Anid stood surveying the scene with her arms folded. "Bykoda? Are you sure?"

"Of course I'm sure," Mavek snapped. "Do you think I can't recognise my own signature? And I didn't go making stuff like this for anyone else."

"Did you know it was here in the guard post?"

"No, I didn't know. Otherwise I wouldn't have—" Mavek broke off, sounding too angry to continue.

"I guess she left a little surprise for anyone who tried tampering with the remains of her Empire." Anid kicked at a loose stone. "The bitch always was one step ahead of anyone else."

"What do we do now?" Yenneg asked.

Mavek drew a deep breath, clearly trying to gather his composure. "You can both go. I wish to conduct experiments on the site."

Anid looked surprised. "What for?"

"That is none of your concern." Mavek spoke as if to an impudent child. "Go, and take what's left of the golems with you."

The golem that had lost a leg was now lying still. Yenneg moved towards it while gesturing to one of those still standing. Obediently the huge metal figure clumped to his side, bent, and effortlessly picked up its fallen cohort. The other inert golem was similarly dealt with.

"I'll take these." Yenneg jerked his head at the lumps of metal strewn about and grinned at Anid. "You can do the scrap collection."

He strolled away before there was time to argue. The two golems with their burdens lumbered along behind him. Anid glared at the departing figures before summoning the remaining intact golem to the task. Within ten minutes it had gathered all the broken pieces big enough to worry about. Anid then set off on the road back to Tirakhalod.

Jemeryl waited until she was out of sight before turning her attention to Mavek. He was sifting through the wreckage of the guard post in the light of a conjured globe, no doubt searching for the talisman. Given the state of the devastation, he would be at the task for days. He was so weak in the fifth dimension it might take him that long before he realised that she had not died in the building.

Jemeryl had four options. She could talk to Mavek. She could kill him. She could take him prisoner or she could ignore him. The first two options she dismissed immediately. Talking was pointless, and he had been quite right about her; she could not kill in cold blood.

Taking him prisoner needed more thought. She could try to exchange him for Tevi—but who would she have to negotiate with? If she overpowered him, it would ruin his pretence of having exceptional powers. Who would care about him enough to want him back? The acolytes would be free to pursue their own ambitions. Without Mavek to stop her, Dunarth might decide to investigate Tevi's strength by dissection. Or Yenneg might try some more of his recruitment techniques. Jemeryl wanted to get to Tevi as soon as possible. She hoped that Tevi was a prisoner in the castle, but a longer journey might be necessary, and lugging a useless hostage around would only slow her down.

The first thing was to find out where Tevi was being held. Mavek was unlikely to volunteer the information. Anid would be a more willing talker, especially once she learned that the new Emperor did not have phenomenal magic at his command. But what else might she do? From what Jemeryl had overheard, Mavek was acting like an arrogant dictator. Given that the acolytes had not started out with fond feelings for each other, it was likely Anid would want revenge on Mavek for his contemptuous treatment.

Jemeryl caught her lip in her teeth. She had hoped to avoid getting involved in the inevitable power battles between the acolytes. Neither had she wanted to play a part in anyone's death. Yet Mavek had left her with few options. If he had not taken Tevi prisoner and threatened to harm her, then Jemeryl would have left him alone to do whatever he wished in the crumbling Empire. Now she needed an ally. Telling Anid the truth about Bykoda's murder ought to get her one, and Mavek had no one to blame but himself. Jemeryl just hoped that she would get to Tevi before everything fell apart.

Mavek's attention was fixed on the piles of rubble. Jemeryl slipped quietly from her hiding place and followed after Anid. Soon Mavek and the guard post ruins were lost in the dark behind her, while ahead, Anid had conjured a light globe, making her easy to spot even were it not for the thumping of the golem. Jemeryl overtook her half a mile along the road.

"Anid."

She spun around. "Who's there...who...Jemeryl?"

Jemeryl walked into the circle of light. "Yep. Me."

"But—"

"I wasn't in the guard post."

Anid's face shifted through several phases of confusion before settling into a grim smile. "Obviously. Did you know it would explode?"

"Yes. I rigged it to. Bykoda had left a cache of Mavek's devices there. I made use of a few."

Anid's gaze shifted back along the road, obviously sizing up the situation. When her eyes returned to Jemeryl, a narrowing revealed more than a shade of concern. "What do you want?"

"Just to talk. You don't need to worry."

"About what?"

"I want to tell you how Mavek killed Bykoda."

Anid shook her head, but as an expression of confusion, not refusal. "I still can't get over him doing that. I never guessed that he had that sort of power."

"He hasn't. It was all a trick."

"I was there. I saw—"

"So was I. But I know how he did it. It was his new inflated cushions. Except Bykoda's wasn't. It was deflating. There was a pin fixed inside, coated in some of Dunarth's new poison. Once the cushion had gone down enough, when Bykoda sat back, it pricked her, and that was all it took. Oh...and he had another trick planned. He'd positioned a mirror outside one of the windows. While everyone was watching Bykoda fall out of her chair, he bounced a bolt off the mirror to bring the crystals down. The rest was all acting."

While Jemeryl was talking, Anid's expression went from disbelief to surprise to a stunned daze as she tried to keep up. "It was all a sham?" she said at last.

"Yes."

Anid drew in a deep breath, frowning. "Bykoda always said he was a pain in the arse."

"She was more correct than she knew."

"But he must know that he can't get away with it for long." Anid's thoughts were clearly moving on. She looked up. "And why is he after you?"

"Um..." Jemeryl would rather not get into the details. "He thinks I have something."

"Do you?"

Jemeryl shrugged.

"Come on. You can't expect me to take this on trust if you're going to hold back," Anid spoke angrily.

"It's nothing much."

"Something of Bykoda's?"

"Yes."

"What?" Anid's face cleared. "Her talisman to change the past?"

"Why do you say that?"

"Because I know Mavek. He wants to get his family back."

Without answering, Jemeryl edged away, ready to react if needed. Anid also had lost her children.

"You think I might want to do the same?" Anid asked.

"The talisman won't work anymore. The temporal forces have become unbalanced. That's why Bykoda gave it to me. She wanted me to take it to the Protectorate."

Anid shook her head. "It wouldn't matter to me whether it worked or not. I don't want it. I'm not that sort of coward."

Jemeryl studied the other sorcerer. Anid seemed sincere, but Bykoda's acolytes were all used to playing games of deception. Jemeryl was not about to take the disavowal on trust. "Does courage come into it?"

"It does where I come from. In the far southwest, we have a saying.

Fate rolls the dice. We are the stakes. And only a coward calls cheat.
I've seen the roll of the dice. I haven't always liked it, but it's my life.
It's how I've lived it. It's what makes me who I am, and it's what I'll
answer for. My mistakes are as much a part of me as my successes, and
I won't give either up."

"That isn't how Mavek sees things."

"No he's a coward and a fool and a cheat and..." Suddenly Anid's
expression hardened. She started to march back towards the destroyed
guard post. "And that bastard's been treating us all like—"

Jemeryl caught hold of her arm. She was certain that Anid's last
angry outburst had been completely genuine and that Mavek, not the
talisman, was her goal. But before Anid charged off, Jemeryl wanted
some information. If possible, she would also like enough time to get
to Tevi before Mavek was challenged.

"I'm not going to stop you doing whatever you want, although
you might like to take an hour or two to think things through first. But
before you go, I want you to tell me where Tevi is."

Anid stopped. The anger faded into awkward sympathy. "I...I'm
sorry. It's bad news."

Jemeryl felt her insides clench. "He's hurt her."

"No. Not Mavek, at least not directly." Anid's lips tightened.
"He had troops taking her north—as far from you as possible. We got
news via the message orb an hour ago. The troops were attacked by a
dragon."

"She..." Jemeryl could not find the words.

"I know. There used to be some dragons in the mountains, but
there's been no sign of them for decades. One must have come back to
its old hunting grounds. Over half the party were killed. Only one of
the lieutenants and four soldiers survived. I'm really sorry. Tevi wasn't
one of them."

Jemeryl could not believe it. "You're sure she didn't escape?
She's resourceful. Maybe she used the attack to get free? It isn't easy to
identify a body after a dragon has burnt it. And she—"

Anid gripped Jemeryl's upper arm, breaking her flow of words.
"Are you sure you want to know it all?"

"Yes."

"She was still tied to her horse when the dragon hit them. Her
horse bolted. The dragon had incinerated most of the troops, but as it

flew away, it grabbed her and the horse for its meal. The lieutenant saw it eating them as it flew off."

"Someone's lying."

"Believe me. I know how you feel, but no—I swear I'm not lying, and neither was the lieutenant. Mavek was furious. He virtually sucked her brains out through the orb. That was why he attacked you this night. He'd planned to go in at dawn tomorrow, but he was frightened that you had Tevi bound to you in the ether—though you'd always denied it. He thought you might sense she was dead when the bond was broken."

"No. It's not true. She can't..." Jemeryl felt as if her soul were ripped in two.

Anid's eyes met hers in pity. "I'm sorry. I'm so very sorry."

"I... It..." Breathing was agony. Jemeryl could not frame the words. She sank down onto the road.

Anid knelt beside her. "Ideally I'd take you back to the castle, keep an eye on you, get you drunk, whatever. But we don't have that option. You need to get to the Protectorate as quickly as possible. Regardless of what you or I do about Mavek, there isn't anyone strong enough to hold things together now that Bykoda's gone. There's going to be chaos here soon, and the talisman needs to be somewhere safe. Bykoda was a bitch, but she wasn't any sort of fool. If she thought you should take the talisman to the Protectorate, then I'm prepared to bet that it's a good idea." Anid's hand rested briefly on Jemeryl's shoulder. "I'll sleep on what you've told me and deal with Mavek tomorrow. Thanks for letting me know about him, and"—she stood up and stepped back—"good-bye."

Numb, Jemeryl sat staring at the road long after the acolyte had disappeared into the night.

CHAPTER ELEVEN—THE MOUNTAIN LAIR

Jemeryl had spent a long time sitting on the ground. At some point, there had been shouts and the sounds of fighting from the north, enough to catch her notice but not her attention. Now there was only the whisper of wind through the grass.

Tevi was dead.

"No."

She did not know how many times she had said the word, in denial more than disbelief. She could not accept it, even if it were true. Her world was not big enough to contain such a loss.

Midnight was past. In a few more hours the sun would rise for a day that Tevi would not see. Somehow, Jemeryl had to get through it, and the night that followed, and all the days that would come thereafter. Tears rolled down her face.

At last, Jemeryl lifted her head. Klara stood nearby in silence. No comfort could be gained from the familiar. No words would help. Jemeryl's legs were numb. She thought it likely that she was cold. The pain of a stone pressing into her knee was a welcome distraction. She had to move. With the thought came a change of mood. Not only did she have to move, she wanted to move. To do something—any action that she could throw herself into as a substitute for thinking and feeling.

Jemeryl pushed herself to her feet, staggering as the blood returned to her legs. She took a few seconds to stamp some life back and then turned towards the south and the Protectorate. Klara took the habitual perch on her shoulder, yet nothing else was as it should be.

Jemeryl's footsteps beat a fast march on the road, taking her into a future without Tevi. Before long, the ruins of the guard post came into view, where one solitary figure scrabbled through the rubble, too intent on his search to hear her. Mavek. The person who had sent Tevi to her death. The person who knew what had really happened. Jemeryl came to a stop and watched him, her breath shuddering in her lungs.

Conscious thought played no part in Jemeryl's actions. She reached through the fifth dimension where Mavek was too weak to sense her attack and blasted into him. The full force of her grief directed the flow of energy through his aura. Mavek's scream was cut off as he collapsed. By the time he came round, Jemeryl had him bound by the strands of the ether.

His eyes fixed on her face. Surprise gave way to guilt and fear. "Jemeryl. I—"

She cut him off. "What has happened to Tevi?"

"You must believe me. I never—"

"Where is Tevi?"

"I never meant it to happen. I swear I didn't mean it."

Lightning shot from Jemeryl's fingertips, crackling into the helpless prisoner. Mavek cried out while the spasms shook him.

When he was again still, Jemeryl said remorselessly, "What have you done to Tevi?"

Mavek's expression was now pure panic. "A dragon. There haven't been any for so long...I never thought that one would...please...I didn't mean it to happen."

Jemeryl knelt and grabbed hold of his hair. She pulled his face closer to her own. "Anid told me, but I don't believe her. Tevi can't be dead."

"It's not my fault. I swear it. I wouldn't have hurt you. That's why I used the golems. But you..." He was a man drowning in terror. "Please. I'm sorry."

Mavek's aura was open and vulnerable. Coven rules forbade certain forms of assault via the fifth dimension, but Jemeryl did not care. She ripped apart the strands of his aura, tearing and slashing in search of the truth, dissecting his mind.

She shredded the core of his being. Pain was irrelevant. This attack went far deeper. Mavek retreated, a small wounded animal, screeching as it gave up its hold on the world. Memories burst open. Dreams and desires burned and scattered, like embers on a gale. Nothing of him was left unscoured.

At first Mavek screamed, then his voice changed to moans and choking, and then to sounds unrecognisable as human. The stench polluted the night air as his bowels and bladder emptied. His heels scrabbled desperately on the ground, but his feet could not carry him away to safety.

Not until she had clawed through the last fragments of his soul did Jemeryl stop her invasion. Mavek lay twitching but silent. He would live, although there was no saying what incurable damage had been inflicted.

Jemeryl stood and looked down at him, feeling sick. Full awareness of the crime she had just committed flooded through her. Guilt and horror churned in her stomach as she fought back the urge to vomit. She should not have done to him what she had just done. Already she regretted it deeply. Mavek was not a Protectorate citizen, but the Coven rules still put limits on how he might be treated as a prisoner and as a human being.

Jemeryl had broken the rules and gained nothing from it. Mavek had been telling the truth, and so had the eyewitness he had questioned. Her conscience was not eased by the knowledge that his interrogation of the lieutenant had not been gentle either.

And Tevi was dead.

Jemeryl's shoulders shook with sobs. She flung her head back to the night sky, but the scream would not come. It would not ease her pain.

At her feet, Mavek's breathing became more regular. He was truly unconscious now. Who could say what state he would be in when he awoke? Jemeryl loosened the ethereal bonds that had held him secure. Maybe he would recover, and if he did not, then Anid's job the next day would be made easier.

The road south led over the bridge and off across the plains. Jemeryl knew she had to go that way and take the talisman to the Protectorate. She clenched her teeth. The task was one that she could cope with, a reason to wake up tomorrow morning. And when the talisman was safely delivered, then she could work out how to deal with the rest of her life.

❖

The world below was laid out in the moonlight. As a child, Tevi had watched seagulls circling high overhead and had dreamed of being one, sweeping through the sky and looking down on tiny trees, huts, and people. Her current view was everything that she had imagined, but she was in no state to appreciate it. They were flying through the mountains and snow glittered blue in the moon's rays. She was shivering violently, more from cold than fear.

Her initial blind terror had faded. She knew that she was going to die soon. She had come to terms with the idea. More painful was the knowledge that she would never see Jemeryl again. The hardest thing of all was the guilt. She should not have gone on that last mission. She was going to leave Jemeryl alone, and she would not even have the chance to say sorry.

The dragon's claws were not holding her directly. They had impaled the horse with her still sitting in the saddle. During the early part of the flight, Tevi had been ready to dive off if she spotted a lake or river that would give some hope of surviving the fall. Unfortunately, their route had not passed over a waterway big enough to make a feasible target, and any they crossed now would be hard ice. Even so, Tevi still considered throwing herself off the horse. It would be quicker than freezing to death.

But at the back of her head, insane optimism would not let her give up. Maybe when they landed, the dragon's hunger would fix on the larger horse, giving her time to...run? Hide? Attack it? Tevi did not know, but she could not give up yet, not completely.

Countering this hope was another vision, that of a mother bringing home food to a brood of ever-hungry babies. The image of an eagle dropping a half-dead rabbit into its nest would not go away.

The cold was getting worse. The icy wind was bad enough, but in addition, the dragon was steadily taking her both farther north and higher into the mountains. Tevi curled forwards over the horse's neck, but the animal had been dead long enough to have lost all heat. Her clothes were completely inadequate. Captain Altrun had interpreted the orders to send her belongings to Tirakhalod as meaning to strip her completely. By way of replacement, she had been given the minimum of clothes, scavenged from other soldiers' kits. The shirt and boots were too big and the leggings were too short, leaving her ankles exposed. Yet the poor fit was not the problem so much as the threadbare thinness. She had no undershirt or cloak. By the time they reached their destination she would be frozen solid. She hoped that the dragon broke a few teeth on her.

For the past few miles, the dragon's flight had kept to the bottom of a winding valley, with bleak crags rearing above them, but now a looming mountain blocked the way ahead with no route through. They would have to go over the top. Tevi's eyes lifted to the towering peak. How cold was it up there? But a moment later she realised that her fears were misplaced. They were descending, and ahead was a cave entrance with a broad and reasonably flat ledge projecting in front of the opening, big enough for a dragon to land on. The monster was approaching its lair. Panic tried to make a reappearance, but Tevi was too cold to care.

The smooth action of flight ended in a jolt and the scratching of the dragon's rear claws on bare rock. Huge wings beat once more and then folded. The dragon released its hold on the horse and its front claws dropped down on either side of the carcass.

As the limp body of her mount hit the ledge, Tevi fell off and rolled away. She finished up a few feet from the cliff's edge, face down, her head cushioned on her arms. The heavy landing had knocked the breath from her body. Combined with the life-sapping cold, she lacked even the strength to raise her head, but her ears were attuned, dreading the sound of baby dragons, eagerly descending on their supper.

There was nothing.

The silence brought a feeling of peace. The icy wind no longer clawed and buffeted her. The rock she was lying on felt soft and safe. She could almost forget the cold and the dragon, and simply drift off to sleep where she was. Almost, but not quite. Fighting back the weakness, she lifted her head and looked at the monster. It was staring at her attentively. So much for her hope that the horse would be first on the menu.

The dragon advanced until the great jaws hung over her. She felt its breath stirring her hair. "I don't know what will happen." A faint smell of sulphur accompanied the words.

Tevi shrank back while she fought to muster a coherent thought. Surely she had misheard.

"I don't know what will happen," the dragon repeated.

Was she hallucinating? Did dragons speak? And why couldn't this one make sense? "Wh-wh-w-w-" Tevi's teeth were chattering too much to get the words out.

"You're cold." The dragon's head rolled from side to side in a gesture that, on a human, would indicate indecision, but then it stopped.

"This I should deal with in order."

Abruptly, the dragon turned and leapt skywards. The draft from its great wings blew ice and grit into Tevi's face. Within seconds, the sound of slow flapping had faded away into the night.

Tevi struggled to her knees and looked around. This was her chance to escape. On one side, the cave shaft plunged into the mountain. The mouth was easily large enough for the dragon to enter. Its depth was impossible to tell. Moonlight penetrated no more than a few yards. Presumably it would eventually narrow to a gap that the dragon would be unable to follow her through. But what would that gain her? Starving to death underground was not a good plan.

On the other side, the cliff dropped away for one hundred feet or so, until it levelled out into the pine forest. The way down looked climbable—or would have, if her fingers had not been too cold to uncurl. And even if she reached the valley floor, there was little chance that she would survive the night in the open.

Tevi turned back to the cave. It was the better of the two choices... probably. She tried to crawl forwards, but managed only a few feet before sinking down onto the rock. Easiest of all was to stay where she was and sleep. Now that she had stopped shivering, she felt very peaceful. Hypothermia was setting in. Tevi recognised the symptoms even as she lost the will to fight them. Everything would be so much nicer if she just let herself float away.

The sound of the dragon's return barely registered, as did the cracking, snapping, and roaring that followed. What finally pulled Tevi back to awareness was the sudden heat that flowed over her. She rolled onto her side and looked towards the source. The dragon had built a fire, and fire was not something that dragons did by halves. Tevi guessed that one massive pine tree had gone into making it, or maybe three small ones.

With the warmth, her shivering returned, along with painful pins and needles in her hands and feet. The stinging on her nose and cheeks was either frostbite, or she was too close to the blaze. Tevi shuffled away slightly and lay on her back, staring at the firelight on the rocks above her head. Her blood and bones felt as if they had turned to ice, but they were starting to thaw. Her heartbeat had not faltered. She was going to be all right, she thought. Or as all right as anyone could be within breathing distance of a dragon.

"Food is a good thing."

Tevi lifted her head and looked towards the dragon. It was definitely speaking. Its voice had a dry, reptilian sibilance. The pitch was surprisingly high for such a large beast. Its intonation was too inhuman to judge whether it was friendly. Should she take the words as an offer or a threat?

This question was answered immediately when the dragon ripped a foreleg off the horse and held it in her direction. Tevi noticed something like a dewclaw on the dragon's front paws that was in opposition to the rest, giving it a crude yet powerful grip.

With enormous effort, Tevi hauled herself into a sitting position. Possibly her distaste for the bloody limb of her former mount showed, because the leg was quickly withdrawn.

"You prefer cooked?"

Tevi met the dragon's gaze. "Er..."

The dragon thrust the horse's leg into the fire, held it there for a dozen seconds and then pulled it out. The smoking remains were deposited before Tevi. After a long hesitation, she pulled it towards her and began to peel off the blackened skin. The meat would be burnt on the outside and raw in the middle, but some of it should be edible, and refusing to eat would not help the horse.

The unreality of the situation sparked her sense of the absurd. Unexpectedly, a grin pulled at her lips. The dragon had gallantly rescued the distressed damsel and was now doing its best to play the gracious host, although its domestic skills could stand some improvement. "Nobody is ever going to give you a job as a chef."

The dragon had been making short work of the rest of the horse. It glanced up. "You don't know that."

"It's a safe guess."

"Guessing." The dragon waved its head from side to side in the gesture Tevi had seen before. "You humans do it so much. I don't know how you manage."

"Don't you?"

"No. But it so happens that I'm trying to learn."

Maybe the dragon would make more sense when she was fed and warm. Tevi shook her head and turned her attention back to the food. Hot fat squirted over her fingers and she raised them to her mouth. "I don't suppose you have a knife around here?"

"Look in the back of the cave. Take anything you want. I can collect more."

After an aborted attempt to stand, Tevi settled for crawling. Her legs were like rubber and her head spun. Light from the fire now pierced the deeper recesses of the cave, glinting and sparkling. The rear was filled with something that shone, Tevi noted, even as her hand slid into the first pile of coins. Of course—gold and gems. What else would you expect in a dragon's lair?

The mounds of treasure were heaped halfway to the roof in places. Weapons and armour lay scattered among the hoard. Finding what she needed did not take long—a small hunting knife that must have belonged to somebody important. A jewelled design inlay the sheath. The hilt appeared to be solid silver.

As she was about to return to her dinner, something else caught Tevi's eye. A fur cloak made of white fox, lined with pale blue silk. Tevi was feeling better with each passing minute but the extra warmth would be welcome, and it would be something to wrap around herself when she slept. She pulled it over her shoulders and picked up the nearest brooch to fasten it in place.

The dragon had finished its meal and now watched her as she ate. Its huge chin rested on its front paws, like a dog. Nothing more was said until she pushed the unwanted parts away, cleaned the knife, and returned it to its sheath.

The dragon's yellow eyes were still fixed on her. The pupils were vertical slits. "Now is the time to talk."

Tevi nodded. She was looking forwards to getting some idea of what was going on. Maybe the dragon would make more sense now that she was in a better state for dealing with conversation. However, the dragon simply continued to stare in silence. Presumably, it wanted her to start things off.

"Why have you brought me here?" Although not original, this seemed like a good opening question.

The dragon lifted its head. "We have to sort it out so that I'll know again."

"Know what?"

"You've forgotten already, haven't you?"

Tevi shook her head in confusion. "Forgotten what?"

"What's going to happen."

"I don't know what's going to happen."

"That was the answer."

"It was—" Tevi broke off and rested her head in her hands. She was fairly sure that her difficulties were not a reaction to nearly freezing to death and that she would not have been able to keep track of this dialogue, regardless of her state of mind.

"And I don't either. Which is the problem," the dragon added.

"I'm not coping with this."

"I'm finding it difficult as well."

Tevi studied the dragon. "Couldn't you be a little bit clearer about what you mean?"

The dragon laid its chin back on it paws, and its shoulders slumped. The posture implied that it too was resigned to a long, frustrating conversation. Eventually it said, "I don't think so. But if it's any comfort, if everything works out, you'll know in the end."

"Great. Look—" Tevi stopped. "I don't know your name."

"Do you want to?"

"Yes."

"You're sure?"

"Yes." In truth, Tevi was not particularly bothered, but at least she thought she understood what they were talking about.

"Klathi borthar azdenothash ano kaesh a dothe ith ano kral bur a anthi."

"That's your name?"

"Yes. I suspected that you wouldn't really want to know."

"It's not the knowing. It's just that I don't think I can remember it."

The dragon tilted its head to one side. "It means, 'Shards of daybreak pierce the cloak of night and slice its remnants into soft shadows.'"

"In your language?"

"No. The quote is from a dwarven poet my mother once ate."

"Oh. Right. Uh...can I call you Shard?"

"If you think it will help."

Tevi pinched the bridge of her nose between her fingers, trying to summon the strength to continue. "Right, Shard. Can we go back to step one? Why have you brought me here?"

Shard stared at her and then sucked in a great breath, as if it was putting a lot of effort into working out how to take the conversation forwards. "You mean that you want to know the answer from your point of view?"

"Yes...probably." It could not be any worse than the last reply she had got to the question.

"So that I can take you back to meet with the sorcerer you want to find."

"Jemeryl?" Tevi's head shot up in hope.

"There isn't another sorcerer you'd want to find, is there?"

"No. But why?"

"Don't you know why there isn't another sorcerer?"

Tevi slapped her hands down on the rock floor in frustration. "No. Why do you want me to meet up with Jem?"

"For you to sort it out so that I'll know what's going to happen."

"You want our help?"

"Yes."

"What do you want us to do?"

"Take it away."

"The talisman?" Tevi said in sudden inspiration.

"Yes."

At last something made sense. Tevi wiped her hand over her face and focused on Shard. The dragon had raised its shoulders off the ground and was again swaying its head from side to side. Muscles in the forelegs bunched and flowed. The action was pronounced enough that the heels on its front paws lifted a fraction off the ground with each roll and its claws scratched on the rock. A faint rumbling came from its throat.

The gesture indicated some strong emotion, Tevi was sure—but how to interpret it? The dragon's thought processes were obviously very different to anything she was used to, although something about the action put her in mind of a nervous cat. Then Tevi looked into Shard's eyes, inhuman but intelligent. With the contact came understanding. Maybe dragons could project what they were feeling, because Tevi was suddenly quite certain that she could name the emotion. The nervous cat analogy did not go far enough. The dragon was terrified.

❖

The sounds of another mighty pine being shredded into firewood woke Tevi the next morning. She rolled over to watch. The meticulous actions suggested that Shard was giving its entire attention to the task, maybe as a way to avoid thinking about whatever was frightening it. Or maybe she was witnessing a rare dragon tree-shredding ceremony. Who could say?

Tevi disentangled her feet from the cloak and stood up. The view from the mouth of the cave was impressive. Dawn was just past. The tops of trees rolled away before her in waves of dark green. White-capped mountains stood proud against the dusky pink sky. A cold breeze carried the scents of pine and snow.

Shard heaped the last splinted branches onto the pyre and ignited it with a puff of breath. The heat was welcome, but Tevi flinched at the memory of Captain Altrun the day before, encased in flames from that same source, writhing in agony and dying. She had not liked the man but had not wished quite that much harm on him.

To one side of the fire lay the body of a stag, presumably for breakfast. Tevi picked up the hunting knife. "If you don't mind, I'll cook my own food."

"Yes."

Tevi guessed that the dragon was agreeing, rather than minding. Certainly, Shard made no objection when she sliced a generous steak from the haunch and then went in search of a long spear to use as a toasting fork. Nothing in the way of drink was available. Tevi was not sure if she would have wanted vintage wine or brandy for breakfast anyway, and she could not imagine anything else being worthy of the dragon's hoard. She settled for filling a large golden bowl with snow and leaving it close enough to the fire to melt.

While waiting for the venison to cook, Tevi examined her fingers. No trace of frostbite could be seen. The dramatic rescue from her captors had left her uninjured, and if she had understood Shard correctly, she was to be reunited with Jemeryl more quickly and with less effort than she could have managed alone. Tevi frowned, wondering what the chances were that she had understood Shard's intentions. Far too little that the dragon said had made any sort of sense.

Tevi looked at the dragon. "How do you know about the talisman?"

"I don't know what's going to happen. I don't know my life."

"But you do know about the talisman." Tevi persisted.

"My life has changed. How could I not know?"

"How has your life changed?"

"It isn't what it should be."

"There are a lot of people who could say that." Tevi could not stop the rueful laugh. "But it doesn't tell me how you have found out about what Bykoda did."

"It changes things. Dragons know when things have changed."

"You mean you can tell when time is..." Tevi stopped. If she was correct in interpreting Shard's head swinging as fear, then this was definitely the subject that upset the dragon.

"You will take it away." The dragon's intonation made it impossible to tell whether this was an order, a question, or a plea.

"We'll try." Tevi gave her best assurance. "Can you help us? If you can pick up Jemeryl and the talisman, you could fly us back over the Barrodens."

"No."

"It would be much quicker and safer if we—"

"No."

Apparently, the issue was not up for negotiation. Tevi sighed. "Can't you do anything else to help us?"

"I will take you as close as I can. And when you can get him away from it, we will all come."

"All? More dragons?"

"Yes. This is what I've had to guess." Shard's shoulders slumped and it stared into the flames. "I don't know how you humans cope with it. But even though I've not had much practice at guessing, I think I know where you'll be once you've sorted it out."

"Do dragons always make this much sense?"

"You'll probably find us easier when we know what we're saying. Of course, we don't often try talking to people. And most people are too busy running away to listen."

Tevi shook her head and pulled her food back from the fire to inspect. The meat was cooked well enough. Eating would definitely be more profitable than talking to Shard.

The breakfast was far from being the worst she had eaten, and equally far from being the best. The meat was tough. The stag had obviously had a long happy life, bounding over the mountains, and the melted snow had an unpleasant metallic tang, but it was better than nothing. At least there was no shortage of either.

With the meal over, Tevi stood on the rim of the ledge and looked out over the view. "When do we leave?"

"When you're ready."

"I'm ready now."

"No, you're not."

"What else do I have to do?"

"We're going to be fighting once we arrive. You need to get yourself suitably equipped. You can help yourself to anything you like."

Tevi wandered into the cave. In daylight, she was better able to evaluate the extent of the treasure that Shard had amassed. The piles were slightly smaller than she had thought, but not by much. Weapons and armour would be easy to find. Warm clothing might be more of a challenge.

A chain-mail hauberk lay a few feet away. One of the thick woollen tunics worn underneath to stop the links chafing at the wearer's skin was still inside. Tevi bent and picked up the tunic. As she did so, a collection of bones dropped out. A quick glance at the condition of the cloth told her that someone had not merely died, but decomposed in it.

Tevi dropped the tunic and took several deep breaths. Shard was a dragon. Dragons killed people. The only reason that she had not been killed too was that Shard needed her help, and she should not have allowed herself to forget it. Tevi looked back over her shoulder. Shard was watching.

"There should be some cleaner clothes if you hunt around." The dragon was clearly unbothered.

Tevi could not let the issue go so quickly. "Why did you kill this person?"

"Why not?"

"That isn't a reason."

"How about, it was her time to die?"

"That isn't a reason either."

"Then I can't answer your question. It was the way it was going to be. We dragons know this...or we should. That's why I need you to sort it out."

Tevi faced the dragon. "Will us taking the talisman away mean that you can kill more people?"

"More than what?"

"More than you would if the talisman stayed here."

Shard rested its chin on its paws and seemed to give the question serious consideration. "I don't think so," it said at last.

"Don't you feel any remorse for the people you kill?"

"Do you?"

"Yes."

"Why?"

Tevi bowed her head. "Because I know I've caused harm to someone, and I worry that I didn't do the right thing."

"That's the difference, then. I also know that I've caused harm, but I know that what happens is right."

"Wantonly killing people can't be right."

"Why not?"

Tevi turned around. Talking was pointless. She was tempted to refuse to take any of the stolen loot, but if the dragon was right about there being fighting where they were headed, then it would be foolish and dangerous to make a stand on principle.

In a short while she was fully arrayed. A bundle of clean clothing had been half buried at the back of the cave. In it had been another padded tunic and also a black silk shirt and leggings to wear beneath and stop the rough wool from scratching her skin. A mail hauberk of the finest dwarven bronze was too good and too rare to ignore. Somehow the dwarves could get bronze nearly as hard as steel, yet it would not affect her prescience like iron. Tooled leather boots reached to her knees, with matching gauntlets for her hands.

Tevi wanted to keep the fur cloak for warmth on the journey. The lining was soft sky blue. When she found a silver embroidered surcoat that complemented the colour perfectly she hesitated. Was she being greedy? She pulled it on over the mail anyway and secured it with a jewelled belt. Tevi was sure that the original owners would rather she had the items than their killer.

For a weapon, Tevi selected a well-made long sword. The scabbard and hilt had been decorated with engravings and inlayed ivory, but the blade was strong, unadorned steel. The blacksmith had not let artistry get in the way of the military requirements. The sheath of the hunting knife fitted on her belt. Tevi also took the long spear she had used to cook breakfast. On a final impulse, she picked up a shield, because she liked the woven geometric designs embossed around the rim. As these were in blue and black, they matched her shirt and surcoat perfectly.

She walked back to the dragon. "Am I ready to go now?"

"You don't have a helmet."

"I never wear one."

"You should protect your head."

"I'm safer without one. I have limited prescience. It only runs about a second into the future and only gives me information about life-threatening events, but it still gives time to duck. An iron or steel helmet would block it out."

"Doesn't have to be steel."

Shard lumbered into the cave. The sounds of scrabbling followed. When the dragon returned, a winged helmet was in its mouth. It dropped the offering before Tevi. "This is made from dwarf bronze, like your mail. It won't affect your prescience."

Tevi picked it up. "It's not a good design." She pointed to the flared wings on either side. "If you get hit over the head with a sword, you want it to glance off. These wings would give the blade something to catch on. A serious helmet is as round and smooth as possible."

"A serious helmet is also made from steel," the dragon countered. "This is the best you're going to get."

Apart from the wings, the helmet also had a crest in the form of spikes. The cheek and nose guards had been shaped to form an eagle's beak. Whoever it had belonged to had clearly been mainly concerned with show. The inside was extra padded for comfort. Tevi smiled. If nothing else, it would keep her ears warm. She slipped it over her head.

"Now am I ready to go?"

"Yes."

Shard extended a foreleg. Tevi realised it was an offer to climb on the dragon's back. A saddle, or something to provide a secure seat would have been nice. In its absence, Tevi shifted up until she was just behind Shard's head. Here, the dragon's neck was narrow enough for Tevi to grip with her legs. The backward-projecting horns between its ears could also be grabbed in an emergency.

"Are you settled?" Shard asked.

"Just about."

The muscles under Tevi bunched. For a second, the dragon held the crouch, and then it launched itself off the ledge. Treetops skimmed by beneath Tevi's feet. The huge wings powered down, causing a wind that roared through the branches. And then, beat by beat, the dragon climbed into the morning sky.

CHAPTER TWELVE—FIRE, DEATH
AND DESTRUCTION

The thick sheet of cloud stretched unbroken from one horizon to the other, heralding the start of the spring rains. The sky to the south was already streaked brown. Before long, the downpour would reach her, though Jemeryl could not muster the energy to care. She lay on her back, staring at the grey sky. The sun was hidden, but the time must be somewhere in midmorning.

The night before, she had walked until well after sunrise. Sticking to the road meant that she did not need to worry about direction. She would have continued walking all day, except she knew that she ought to rest. An isolated patch of thicket offered the best shelter available on the windswept plain. Judging by the small burnt circles from campfires, others had thought so before her.

Jemeryl had not set up camp, just dropped her backpack and lay down between the bushes, knowing that she needed to sleep. But she had doubted that she would be able to, and she was right. The seething emotions would not let go. Eventually she drifted off for a few minutes, only to wake from nightmares filled with Mavek's screams.

Groaning, Jemeryl sat up and hugged her legs. She rested her forehead on her knees. Tears squeezed from beneath her closed eyelids. Tevi was dead.

"Why don't you eat something?" Klara's voice jarred on her ears.

"I'm not hungry." Jemeryl felt as if she would never be hungry again.

"Have a drink, at least."

Jemeryl gave in and pulled the cap off the water-skin. The liquid hit her stomach like lead, but it loosened the tightness in her throat. Her gaze travelled through the waving screen of branches to the road, thirty feet away. She should get moving. Or she could stay where she was and rot. Both options sounded equally appealing.

Images danced through her head: Tevi looking up from a book, her head tilted slightly at the interruption and an indulgent smile on her lips; Tevi walking through a doorway, shaking rain from her hair and stripping off her cloak; Tevi standing a few yards away, locked in conversation, unaware that she was being watched, until she turned slightly and their eyes met. Jemeryl summoned the more intangible memories: how she felt when Tevi held her hand, the warm, safe sense of belonging, the strength of knowing that she need never face anything alone. Except she did now.

Another memory teased her—the last night Tevi had spent in Tirakhalod. Jemeryl remembered waking up on the floor with Tevi beside her. She recalled the happiness of watching dim firelight on Tevi's sleeping face, and also the nagging fear squirming inside her. She had not wanted Tevi to go on that last mission. With hindsight, it might even have been her sorcerer's senses giving her a premonition of tragedy. Why had she not acted on it? Why had she decided not to ask Tevi to change her mind?

Surely getting Tevi to agree would not have been hard. After Yenneg's stupid games with the love potion and Bykoda's indifferent reaction, Tevi could not have been feeling much loyalty to the regime at Tirakhalod. Why should she undertake dangerous work on their behalf?

Jemeryl scrabbled through the pack at her side and pulled out the sword and shirt she had claimed from Cluthotin. They were the only keepsakes she now had of Tevi, and she hugged them to her.

If only she had tried to make Tevi stay. They could have left as soon as the council meeting started and been well on the road before Bykoda had been murdered. By now, they would be halfway to the Protectorate and safety. Tevi would be by her side, warm and breathing. Jemeryl's face twisted in a grimace. If only she had made the right decision on that night.

Without conscious thought, her hand travelled to the chain at her throat. This situation was the result of exactly the sort of mistake that Bykoda had created her talisman to rectify. Jemeryl pulled the talisman free from her shirt and let it swing before her eyes. The carved patterns on its surface seemed so much more evocative than the last time she had looked at them.

Bykoda had been sure that the device was no longer safe. Bykoda had also understood how to work the thing but had not dared to use it. Jemeryl knew that her own chances of successfully altering the past were too small to risk. If the talisman ruptured, it would cause massive destruction. She would be responsible for the deaths of thousands of people. Her own life would undoubtedly be lost with them. But she would not be in pain any more, on her own, missing Tevi.

And supposing it worked?

Jemeryl rested her head back on her knees and sobbed. Until that moment, she had not fully understood the awful temptation of the talisman.

❖

Once she had got over her initial apprehension, Tevi enjoyed the flight. Sitting on a dragon's back, wearing a thick fur cloak, was definitely preferable to freezing in its claws. She knew that she was just a passenger, but the feeling of power was inescapable and exhilarating. The whole world lay beneath her like a giant version of the battle table.

She tried to spot landmarks she knew, but everything looked different from the air. Shard was flying higher than the eagles. The contours of the land were lost, so that hills, rivers, and forests were little more than variations in colour. Also, as the morning progressed, Tevi had the growing impression that their route was purposely avoiding the region that she was familiar with.

The circumstances of her journey to Shard's lair meant that she had paid little attention to direction and had only a vague idea that they had headed north. Yet, on leaving the cave, Shard set off due east. After some hours, Tevi noted that their bearing had swung south. Then, with midday approaching, Shard again altered course and turned to the west.

As far as Tevi could judge, and if she was right about the location of Shard's lair, they would end up passing some way south of Tirakhalod. The impression was that Shard had made a wide detour around an obstacle, except Tevi could think of nothing the dragon could not have simply flown over. She even began to wonder if it was all part of the dragon's perverse mentality, that they would travel in a huge circle and arrive back at the cave again that night.

A blanket of low cloud soon cut off her view of the land and she lost all sense of progress. After another hour went by, Tevi was toying with the idea of asking Shard to land for a while so that she could ease her aching muscles and at the same time ask the dragon just where they were headed. She was about to speak when she noticed that they were descending. The featureless bank of cloud was getting steadily closer. Wisps of white curled up towards them, getting thicker, and then they plunged in.

Tevi was disappointed to discover that the inside of a cloud was exactly like dense fog. She could see no farther than the length of Shard's wings. Maybe the lack of visibility also disturbed the dragon. Shard dived steeply and soon emerged beneath the layer. The land below was flat, without trees or hills. Tevi spotted a mixed herd of deer and the shaggy cow-like animals that grazed the northern plains.

A river meandered across the grasslands. They were now low enough that Tevi could make an estimate of its size. At last, Tevi was fairly sure of where they were. The river had to be the Kladjishe, thirty or so miles northeast of Uzhenek. Tevi frowned. Surely Jemeryl would not have abandoned her and set off for the Protectorate alone?

"Why haven't we gone to Tirakhalod? Jem is most likely still there waiting for me." Tevi leaned forwards to shout in the dragon's ear, but Shard made no reply.

Perhaps dragons found it hard to fly and talk at the same time. Questions might have to wait until they landed. Which, if Uzhenek was their goal, should not be much longer. At the dragon's rate of progress, Tevi estimated that they would reach the city within minutes.

For the first time, Tevi noticed people on the ground below. And they, in their turn, had clearly seen the dragon. Tevi watched them inch across the ground in what was probably a flat-out dash to escape. Luckily for them Shard was not currently hostile. Watching their pathetic attempts to flee made her realise just how little chance a normal person stood against a dragon—as if more example than Captain Altrun were needed. However, Tevi would happily have staked her life that Jemeryl would be able to blast Shard from the skies if she wanted. Which was in turn a worrying thought. Tevi could only hope that, if Jemeryl were waiting ahead in Uzhenek, she would not take any pre-emptive action against the incoming monster.

The Kladjishe had etched a wide valley through the otherwise featureless plain. Shard's path lay parallel to the river. The dragon was flying low, barely fifty feet above the brink of the escarpment on the southern side. Finally, Tevi spotted the outline of Uzhenek in a bend in the river ahead, although it was very different from the city that Jemeryl and she had passed through on their way to Tirakhalod. Back then, Jemeryl had told her that the ethereal towers and imposing defences were purely an illusion projected by Bykoda. The Empress was now dead and the citadel had vanished, but the surrounding slums remained.

A mile before the city, Shard veered off to the left, away from the river, and then looped back, heading straight for the point on the valley wall that would be overlooking Uzhenek. Ahead of them the smooth field of grass ended in a ragged line where it dropped away to the flood plain beyond.

Just before they were about to shoot over the edge, Shard made a sharp dive and landed. The sudden cessation of movement came with a thump. For the moment, Uzhenek was out of sight, although it could have been no more than a quarter of a mile away. The area was deserted. Anyone who might have been around had already fled.

"You should get off here. No one should see that you were on me."

Tevi jumped down, pleased to be able to stretch her legs. She also had questions she wanted answers to. "Why? And where's Jemeryl? You said you were going to take me to her."

"I said I would take you to where she was going to be. Which I have."

"Why not take me straight to her?"

"I can't guess how to explain. Just wait for her and tell her what I've told you about us coming when you've sorted it out."

"But you haven't told me anything."

"I've told you all sorts of things. You just haven't understood."

"But—"

Shard cut her off. "No. You will need to run to the city."

With a mighty beat of its wings, the dragon leapt into the air. Tevi was a fraction too late in shielding her eyes from the cloud of grit and grass. By the time she could see again, the grey sky overhead was empty, but she caught a glimpse of Shard's tail vanishing as the dragon swooped over the edge of the escarpment. Tevi raced after, drawing breath to shout one last question. She reached the brink and looked down.

Already, the dragon was far ahead, hurtling on towards the city. The people would be terrified. Tevi decided that she might as well follow the instruction to run, if only so that she could allay the inhabitants' fears.

Tevi launched herself down the slope. The need to watch her footing meant her eyes stayed fixed on the ground, rather than on events in the city, but by the time that she was a third of the way to the bottom, the first faint screams were carried to her on the wind. Why was Shard scaring the townsfolk? It had put her down where it said she needed to be, so why not go straight home now? Did dragons enjoy the fear they caused?

The steep gradient levelled out. Tevi's progress changed from bone-jarring bounds to an even run, and she was able to look up safely. However, when she did so, the sight made her stumble and fall to her knees.

No more than a hundred yards away, the nearest huts were wrapped in flames. The twisting columns of smoke spiralling up into the grey sky were matched by others from more distant parts of the city. Blackened figures lay on the ground, some still moving.

Remembered words echoed in Tevi's head.

"Wantonly killing people can't be right."

"Why not?"

The screams rose to a new crescendo. Tevi saw the way people were running and looked in the other direction. Shard was approaching again, up the valley. The dragon's wings beat a slow, unhurried rhythm, graceful and unstoppable. Tevi watched in horror as the dragon's mouth opened and a fountain of fire erupted. Another line of blazing death was scored across the city.

Tevi was too shocked to think, but her body moved instinctively. She pushed back up onto her feet, shrugged the shield off her shoulder, and slipped her left arm through the grip. Her right hand tightened on the shaft of her spear. She did not know what Shard was up to, but had the nasty hunch that it was her fault. Equally, she did not know what she could do, but she had to do something.

Shard had stopped spewing fire and was lazily circling the city. It soared a few hundred feet up, then rolled into a dive and came down right in the heart of Uzhenek. The huge shape disappeared behind the burning buildings. The dragon had landed.

Tevi charged into the city. People were fleeing blindly. Tevi ducked and barged her way through the oncoming torrent. Bands of smoke rolled across her path, obscuring vision and making her eyes sting. She fought her way onto the main east-west thoroughfare and turned in the direction of where Shard had landed. The road she was on climbed gently. Tevi remembered that Bykoda's magical citadel had occupied the centre of Uzhenek, raised on a low hill on the valley floor.

The number of people surging past her dwindled as she raced nearer to the middle of the city. Over the crackle of burning thatch, Tevi listened for the sound of the dragon. An outbreak of shrieks and wild shouts seemed a likely guide. The burning remnants of a thatch roof blew across her path. Tevi hurdled over and charged on. She dived through a wall of smoke and found herself suddenly in the open.

She had been right. This was the spot where Bykoda's phantom towers had stood. Of the previous ethereal beauty, all that remained were a few dilapidated stone structures scattered across the otherwise empty hilltop.

Shard was there, less than a knife throw from where she stood. While Tevi watched, the dragon ripped the side off one building. From the clamour of hysterical voices raised, it was packed with people.

Why did they take refuge there? Tevi wondered, and then answered her own question immediately. Uzhenek was a city made of straw and hide. No other building materials were available on the grasslands. Even wood was a rare luxury. Bykoda had imported the stone for a few vital buildings that she did not want tied to her magic, and the terrified townsfolk had seen them as the best protection from the dragon's breath. But they were no protection from the dragon's claws.

People were scrabbling free of the broken building. Some tried to run, but most seemed frozen in fear. One figure, a woman, fell at the dragon's feet. Shard pawed at her with its claws and hooked out a tiny squirming shape wrapped in a shawl—a baby. The woman leaped up and made a futile attempt to get back the wailing infant. Shard hoisted the baby out of reach, and the woman collapsed back to her knees, shouting incoherent threats. The dragon ignored the woman and swung the prize up to its huge jaws. Clearly it was now time to eat. Tevi did not wait to see more. She took three long steps and hurled her spear at the dragon.

The spear had not been designed for use as a javelin, and was not weighted for throwing. It wobbled and twisted in flight, and hit the dragon's flank broadside on. Even had it flown straight, the chances of the point piecing the dragon's thick scales were not good, but it was enough to get Shard's attention. The dragon dropped the baby and leapt towards Tevi. It landed a scant twenty feet from her. Tevi drew her sword.

"What the fuck are you doing?"

Shard did not answer. The dragon's mouth opened as it drew in a deep breath.

"*Fire!*" The warning voice of prescience sounded in Tevi's head.

Jumping left or right would be no help. Tevi had already observed the dragon's ability to track moving objects. Only one direction had any hope of safety. Tevi dived forwards. A blast of searing heat flowed over her back. The acrid stench of burning fur filled the air. The cloak would be ruined, but it had saved her from serious harm. Tevi hit the ground rolling and ended up between Shard's front legs. She doubted that the dragon would willingly roast its own stomach.

The grass was wet. With luck, it would put out any fire on the cloak, but Tevi did not have time to deal with burning clothes. She thrust her sword at Shard's soft underbelly. The well honed blade bit through the scales and crimson blood splattered on Tevi's face. However, from her prone position, she did not have the reach to stab more than eight inches deep. For a beast the size of the dragon, this was no more than a flesh wound. She tried to scramble up for a better strike.

Shard reared back on its hind legs and then lunged down, jaws agape. The dragon's mouth was lined with rows of dagger-like teeth. Tevi had got as far as her knees. She swung her arm across defensively and backhanded the dragon with her shield. The impact was so hard it sent tingling darts flying from her fingertips to her shoulder.

Shard threw back its head and roared, in either anger or pain. Tevi gained her feet and thrust forwards once more with her sword. This time, she connected with more force, at the base of the dragon's throat. Blood spurted out, but it was still far from a fatal injury.

The dragon's wings unfurled. With a second great roar, it left the ground. The wind from its ascent sprayed yet more of its own blood on everything below.

Tevi stared up. This would be the end, she knew. Shard could pour fire on her from far out of reach. Why had it brought her here to kill her? It made no sense. Nothing about the dragon had ever made sense. She remembered the words it had said before leaving its lair: *"We're going to be fighting once we arrive. You need to get yourself suitably equipped."*

At least Shard had not lied.

But then she noticed that Shard was not wheeling around for another attack. The dragon was flying away, laboriously, into the east. The flap of its wings was uneven. Its head was sagging. Its legs dangled limply beneath it. Everything about the dragon spoke of pain and defeat. Had she injured it more than she knew? Because unless this was just one more bit of incompressible dragon behaviour, Shard was running away, defeated. Tevi stared after it, bewildered.

The jolt as someone grabbed her round the waist caught Tevi by surprise. She looked down. The baby's mother was on her knees, her face buried in Tevi's stomach, sobbing in gratitude. More folk surrounded them. Then people appeared from all around in an ever-growing crowd. Some hung back shyly. Some patted her back. Some grabbed her hands and kissed them. Those farther away punched the air in rejoicing, and they cheered.

Everybody was cheering.

❖

The distant way station was blurred and faded in the dull grey light, as if it were melting into its surroundings. Jemeryl viewed the buildings from the top of a slight rise. In her estimation, it was just over an hour's walk away and should easily be reachable by nightfall. The station presumably marked one standard day's travel on horseback from Tirakhalod. It would be a good target to aim for. The rain had stopped for the while, but more would come before dawn, and a roof over her head would be nice.

Jemeryl adjusted the straps of her backpack and strode down the slope. All day, her mood had been lurching about. Maybe it was just as well that she had been alone. She was sure that anyone else would have thought her mad as she switched from hysterical sobbing to placid acceptance and back again in the space of a minute. Perhaps she was mad.

Her current chain of thought was playing along the lines of giving the talisman to Mavek. He would use it and probably destroy the world, but it would not be her fault directly. And if it did work, against all the odds, then she and Tevi would be together, just so long as Mavek's alterations did not change the past so much that the two of them had never met in the first place. Jemeryl shook her head at her folly. She would never willingly give up the talisman. Not unless someone caught her at the wrong moment. And anyway, if Anid had vented her anger on him, Mavek might no longer be around to give the talisman to.

Even so, she wished that Mavek was with her on the road. She could say sorry for what she had done to him. They could then sob on each other's shoulders about their lost partners and he could tell her how to survive through the years ahead. Tears started to stream down Jemeryl's cheeks again. She had given up wiping them away and now carried on, half blind, down the hill.

The light was fading rapidly as she finally approached the way station, but it was still good enough to reveal the details of the buildings. On one side of the road was a guard post, similar to the one back by the bridge. Beside it stood another stone-built shelter that was probably a blacksmith and farrier. Jemeryl spared a quick glance through the open doorway of the guard post. No one was about. No weapons or personal possessions lay scattered. The fire in the hearth was out. Next door, the furnace in the smithy was also cold.

Facing the guard post on the other side of the road was a two-story wooden inn. The walls were rough cut timber, crudely tacked onto the crooked frame. The roof was a mildew-covered thatch, coming adrift in the wind. This building also looked deserted. The windows were all shuttered, although the door stood half ajar. The tap room was dark and silent. No smoke issued from the chimney. Behind it were stables and a hay barn.

When Bykoda was alive, the inn would have been disguised by a glamour to make it seem luxurious. All who passed through would have been impressed by Bykoda's wealth, unless they had the gift to see through the magic. Now anyone could perceive the inn for the ramshackle heap it really was. With Bykoda's death, her Empire was falling into chaos, and Mavek would not be able to hold it together for long, even if he had recovered from the soul-shredding.

The thought produced a twinge of guilt, but Jemeryl's mood was currently in the numb, detached phase. She was incapable of any emotion. The empty inn would suit her fine. She did not want company. A jovial innkeeper and room service would have been wasted on her. Getting drunk sounded attractive, but was probably not a good idea. She felt terrifyingly out of control as it was. Alcohol could only make things worse. Fortunately, there was little chance that looters would have left any bottles of wine behind.

Jemeryl shoved the inn door fully open with her shoulder and stepped into the room. Immediately the smell of blood and death assailed her. The year was not advanced enough yet for the swarms of flies that bred on decay, but a scurry of rats spoke of other scavengers. Dead bodies lay in the tap room, and Jemeryl had the sure sense that they were human rather than animal.

While her eyes adjusted to the gloom indoors, Jemeryl stood in the doorway. However, her sorcerer senses were not dependant on light. She probed outwards through the fifth dimension, searching for threats and clues as to what lay before her. The results were confusing. Despite appearances, the inn was not deserted. Horses were in the stables and four people were alive in the next room.

Why had they not called out? They were standing so still that it had to be deliberate. Were they survivors of the trouble here, and frightened that she was one of the attackers, returned? Or were they the killers, anxious not to be caught for their crimes?

Jemeryl's eyes were now accustomed to the low light and able to assist her other senses. Two bodies lay at the side of the room. Jemeryl went and crouched by their side. One was a young boy of no more than six. The other was older. They were both northerners, with long blond hair and broad faces, but the likeness between them went further, enough to show shared family ties. The man was most likely the father, uncle, or elder brother. From the position of the bodies, he had died trying to protect the boy, and failed. Both had been run through with a sword or spear.

Jemeryl lifted the man's arm. The skin had a purplish tinge and the fingernails were pale, but there was no stiffening in the joints. He had been dead for only a few hours. She carefully placed his hand back over the boy's and then raised her head. She let her senses probe deeper.

These two were not the only murdered victims in the inn. At the rear of the tap room an open doorway lead to a storeroom beyond. More bodies were in there. Blood tracks on the floor showed where they had been dragged through from elsewhere in the inn. Somebody had been trying to clean up. Had her arrival disturbed whoever it was? And why hide the bodies rather than bury them?

Jemeryl guessed that she would soon be getting answers. The living people in the next room were moving. One was opening a door behind her very, very slowly and carefully, so as not to make a noise. The effort was completely wasted. Normally, Jemeryl blocked out the auras of people around her. Life would be far too distracting if she did not. But at the moment, the fifth dimension had most of her attention. The aura behind her was such a tense knot that following the person's actions could not have been easier. Jemeryl waited until the door was fully open before turning to face the sneak.

A woman stood there, dressed in shoddy remnants that had once been the uniform of Bykoda's army. She held a spear in her hands. From the bloodstained point and shaft, Jemeryl thought that she could work out what was going on, but it was best to make sure.

"Did you kill these people?"

The armed woman was visibly startled to be discovered and addressed, but she recovered quickly. "Me and my mates."

"Why?"

"Same reason we're going to kill you. We want your gear and we can't be arsed with arguing."

The woman's face twisted into a snarl and she launched herself forwards. Jemeryl let her take two steps before throwing out her hand and twisting the elemental forces of the sixth dimension. Green static rippled over the woman's body, crackling and hissing. Apart from this, she dropped without a sound.

Shouts erupted in the room beyond. "Shit! It's a witch."

"Run!"

The pounding of a panicked stampede faded to silence. By the sound of it, the fallen women's comrades were not coming to her aid. Heroism could not be numbered among their virtues. Though even if they had rushed into battle, it was too late for her. Jemeryl rose and followed. By the time she reached the rear door of the inn, three horsemen were disappearing from the stable yard.

Jemeryl considered sending a ball of fire after them. She even went as far as pulling back her arm, reaching through the sixth dimension, but stopped. Yes, they were murderers and thieves who were taking evil advantage of the anarchy. But it was not like her to go seeking blood. She had killed her attacker without thinking, and it had not been necessary. A harmless display would have sent them all running. In fact, had she made it clear that she was a sorcerer from the moment she entered the inn, she would never have been attacked in the first place. What had happened to her? Had she not caused enough hurt to others recently?

Jemeryl dropped her face into her hands and cried. She realised she had just spent a whole two minutes without thinking of Tevi.

When she was calm again, she returned to the tap room. Now three bodies lay on the floor, one solely on her conscience. The gang's scheme must have been to make the inn appear deserted and then ambush all unsuspecting travellers who entered, children included. They had not even had the courage for an open fight. Their preferred mode of action involved sneaking up and stabbing their victims in the back. But Jemeryl would put an end to their murderous trap so that they could not drift back and start again after she had left. The inn would make a fitting funeral pyre for the dead.

Jemeryl was about to leave the tap room when the woman on the floor caught her eye. The thief was about the same size as her. The clothes should be a fair fit, and the fleeing bandits had not taken their fallen comrade's horse with them. Jemeryl had already decided to claim it. Adding the uniform would help her blend in on the road. How many deserters were wandering across the plains? She would be just one more.

If Mavek retained anything of his sanity, and had not been killed by Anid, he would be looking for her. He would expect her to be disguised—which was one reason why she had made no attempt to change her appearance. The telltale trace of magical transformation might make her more conspicuous, if anyone was checking for it. But the simple switch of clothing would be undetectable.

Jemeryl quickly stripped the woman and went across to the guard post. She had no desire to sleep among the corpses in the inn. Yet the guard post had its own associations. The layout was too much like the one where she had spent three days waiting for Tevi. Each night she had gone to sleep hoping that the next day would see them reunited. She now had nothing more to hope for. There was nowhere on earth that she could go and wait for Tevi to arrive.

The pain gripped her with a physical force. Jemeryl sat on the edge of the bunk, arms wrapped around herself. Through it all, the talisman was a seductive force, tempting her, making each moment a fight and twisting the knife still further.

At last she slept through sheer exhaustion.

❖

The damage to Uzhenek was less severe than had at first seemed likely. Tevi learnt that torrential rain had fallen all morning before she arrived. The straw houses had been sodden. Those touched directly by the dragon's breath had burnt, but the fires had not spread. She'd had the chance to view the entire city as she was carried around, shoulder high. People crowded the streets to watch her pass. More food, drink, and gifts had been pressed upon her than she could possibly accept.

Night had fallen before the celebration showed signs of calming down. The crowd around Tevi thinned. The more sedate had gone to their beds. The more rowdy had passed out drunk, but an exuberant crowd still surrounded her. The first that Tevi knew of something new about to happen was when a ripple of quiet flowed across the gathering. The general carousing did not stop completely, but a nervous edge crept in.

The people nearest Tevi stood aside to reveal a group of three newcomers who wore the uniforms of officers in Bykoda's army.

"Greetings, stranger," one of the lieutenants addressed her.

"Greetings." Tevi wondered where the witches had been during Shard's attack. Although, if Altrun was a guide, they could not have done much to help.

"Captain Curnad asks for the honour of the Dragon Slayer's company. If you could spare him a few minutes."

The title was not accurate. She certainly had not killed Shard, but the epithet had attached itself to her during the afternoon. Tevi nodded. "Yes. Of course."

"Thank you. We will escort you to him." The officers were clearly being polite by not challenging her status, and regardless of how the request had been phrased, Tevi could not refuse.

The witches led her back to the centre of Uzhenek. Their destination was one of the stone-built survivors of the citadel. The walls were massive and the doorway was protected by a portcullis. The windows were high arrow slits. Tevi guessed that it had been a prison or an armoury. She was shown into a small room that held nothing apart from a rough table and four chairs. Only one of these was occupied.

Captain Curnad stood to greet her. He was a small wiry man of about fifty. His blond hair had been cropped close to his skull. The expression on his weathered face was stern and thoughtful but not hostile.

Once the other officers had withdrawn, leaving them alone, Curnad gestured for Tevi to take a chair and poured wine into two tin goblets. Possibly, while Bykoda was alive, the drinking vessels would have looked like gold. Tevi took a sip, remembering the last time she had shared wine with one of Bykoda's officers. She desperately hoped there would be no love potion this time.

From the moment she had entered the room, Curnad had been watching her intently. At last he spoke. "I think I should start by saying that I recognise who you are, Captain Tevirik."

The announcement was not a complete surprise. His face had been faintly familiar, although Tevi had been unable to place it.

Curnad went on. "I'm one of Anid's deputies. I was with her up at Tirakhalod not long ago. You were with the sorcerer Jemeryl at a gathering in the keep."

"Oh yes." Tevi remembered him. "Weren't you the one who threw wine at Ranenok's lieutenant?"

"I wouldn't waste good wine on any of them." Curnad relented enough to give a half smile, and then his manner became more purposeful again. "I assume you know about the news recently. We've heard that Jemeryl killed Bykoda, and Mavek is now in charge. I was thinking that Uzhenek would be out of the action, but then you show up, dressed like a hero from legend, just in time to deal with a very convenient dragon. I could dig out a message orb and tell Tirakhalod what has happened. But I'm wondering if it might be wiser for me to take the long-term view."

Tevi said nothing, waiting to see where he was going.

"If I could contact Commander Anid, I probably would, but I haven't heard from her since yesterday, and this morning I was told that Ranenok is now in charge of the entire army." Curnad put down his goblet. "If Jemeryl could defeat Bykoda, then she could whip any of the acolytes in her sleep. And we all know that Mavek won't be able to run the Empire. The way I read it, he's already had trouble with Anid and Yenneg."

His eyes fixed on Tevi shrewdly. "I'd heard that you're ungifted, but you're clearly not ordinary. After today's performance, you've got the whole city in your hand. It doesn't help that the townsfolk saw all of us running scared. And we were. I don't know where Jemeryl found the dragon, or how she got it to play along with the charade. But it just goes to show that she isn't someone to get in the way of. She's already got herself a strong base here with you as a figurehead."

"I'm not a powerful witch. I've got where I am by giving unquestioning loyalty to whoever was winning. The way I see it, in this current fracas the winner is going to be Jemeryl. So I'm going to play along with the game of you as the great Dragon Slayer until she arrives." He picked up his goblet again. "You are expecting her to get here soon, aren't you?"

Tevi's lips tightened in a wry smile. The only direct question he had asked her was one she could answer truthfully. "Yes. I am."

❖

The next morning, dressed in the rag-tag uniform, Jemeryl rode away from the burning inn. Ash from the inferno she had started rained down around her, and for miles along the road, the wind carried the smell of smoke.

CHAPTER THIRTEEN—THE HERO

Jemeryl awoke at the start of another grey day. She rolled onto her back and flung her arm over her eyes, trying to block out the world. The attempt was futile. Grief lived within her like a parasite, squeezing her lungs and filling her throat. Most of her had died with Tevi, and the fragment that was left had no desire to go on. Perhaps she should complete the job and then kill herself.

The idea was worryingly attractive. It had been sliding around the corners of her mind for the previous four days. Jemeryl opened her eyes, took a deep breath, and faced it head on. Why not? The best efforts of sorcerers had found no evidence for an afterlife. Probably there was none. But oblivion did not sound so bad at the moment, and regardless of what might await her, how could she be frightened to follow Tevi anywhere?

In her absence, Mavek would claim the talisman, unless somebody else got to it first. But the world she left behind would no longer be her concern, except for the faint possibility that Mavek might succeed in changing time. In which case, both she and Tevi would be alive again and none the wiser.

Jemeryl groaned and sat up. The idea of abandoning the talisman to Mavek, in whatever way, was a cowardly attempt to delude herself, avoiding reality. Even if he was still alive and sane, he did not have the ability to use the artefact. Why else put so much effort into intimidating the other acolytes if he did not want their help with the talisman? And what made Mavek think that a co-operative effort would work?

Jemeryl lifted the chain around her neck and pulled out the talisman. The stone disc lay cupped in her hands. Once it had seemed sinister and deadly. Now it was far more ambiguous. If anyone should attempt to use the talisman, it ought to be her.

Obviously, Bykoda had more experience than she did, but Jemeryl did not think she was being immodest by believing that she matched the late Empress in skill. And her Coven training gave her the benefit of knowledge and skills acquired by generations of sorcerers, which might help her to tackle a crisis.

As her extended sorcerer's senses tracked into the higher dimensions, Jemeryl's eyes fixed on the pattern engraved on the talisman. The trick would be to probe very delicately, without upsetting anything. In fact, until she had learned more, she must not do anything. She had to discover how the device worked, find out what principles lay behind it. And then she should experiment carefully, to see if she could identify the flaw that Bykoda had warned of.

Once she understood the problem she could then make an informed decision about what she should do. But for the moment, she was not doing anything. She was just looking.

"Jemeryl!" Klara's voice was a warning croak.

In shock, Jemeryl's hands clenched around the talisman and she bolted up straight. Then her head fell back and she closed her eyes. This was the second time that she had started to use the talisman. Without Klara as the voice of her subconscious, how far would she have gone? Would she have stopped at all?

Jemeryl thrust the talisman back inside her shirt and stood up.

In this region of the grasslands, the terrain was folded into a series of gentle rolling ridges. The damp wind rustled across the plains, carrying the scent of more rain on the way. Rolls of heavy cloud hung low overhead. Her horse stood nearby, grazing on the fresh grass.

The road was no more than parallel lines of hard-packed dirt, formed by the passage of wheels. In an emergency, and with a fast carriage, little sleep, and regular changes of horses, the distance between Tirakhalod and Uzhenek could be covered in two days. More normally, it took four times as long, which meant that Jemeryl was now at the midway point.

After her experience on the first night of the journey, she had avoided stopping at the way stations. Her supplies would last her until Uzhenek, where she could buy more. Jemeryl's mouth turned down at the corners; she was deluding herself again. At the rate she was going, the supplies would last her all the way to Lyremouth. She should try to eat more. Breakfast would be a good start, but her stomach felt tense and cold. Perhaps when she was on the road and fully awake she would be able to summon some appetite.

Jemeryl called the horse over and hoisted the saddle onto its back. While she worked, her head shook repeatedly in a combination of dismay and incredulity. She could not believe how close she had been to activating the talisman. Klara took a perch between the horse's ears and watched her attentively, somehow managing to convey both concern and reprimand. Jemeryl paused and met her familiar's eyes, although when she spoke, it was mainly to herself.

"If I want to kill myself, then that's my right. But I don't have the right to take thousands of other poor bastards with me." She bent to adjust the cinch strap. "It's quite simple. I take the talisman to Lyremouth, make sure it's safe, and then if I don't feel any better, I can kill myself there with a clear conscience."

❖

A boisterous entourage of children followed Tevi through the squalid streets of Uzhenek, shouting, jumping, and fighting imaginary dragons. The youngest was barely old enough to walk. The eldest was old enough to have known better. Over three-quarters of them were wearing identical plaited bands of blue and black wool, although there was no general agreement as to where the braid should be worn. Some had it around their arm as an amulet. Some around their throat as a necklace. The more extroverted used it as a hair band.

The townsfolk had decided that blue and black were Tevi's colours. With each day, more of them were sporting the token of their allegiance to her—a display that Tevi did not want and certainly had not asked for. She wondered whose idea it was and where the braids were coming from. Had the collapse of Bykoda's Empire stranded an enterprising merchant with a cargo of coloured wool, and he had seized on the chance to cut his losses?

As she passed by, people stopped whatever they were doing and waved at her. Some went so far as to shout and brandish their blue and black braids in the air. Tevi acknowledged the accolades with all the conviction she could muster. By the braids and the cheers they were declaring themselves as her followers, which meant that she was their leader, which in turn meant that she was responsible for them. With each day it was getting worse.

Tevi arrived at the western edge of the city. Ahead of her, the road carried on through farmland before crossing the river Kladjishe on a low wooden bridge. On the other side, the road turned north to Tirakhalod and ran in a straight line across the wide flood plain until it climbed the valley wall and disappeared over the top at a point maybe five miles distant from where she stood.

Half a dozen groups were visible on the road, all of them heading to Uzhenek. The city's population was growing by the hour, as reports of the mighty Dragon Slayer spread. The new arrivals brought stories of turmoil, looting, and slaughter, of property stolen or destroyed, of murderous gangs. They came hoping that the Dragon Slayer could protect them and put it all right again.

Tevi felt as if she were being physically crushed by the weight of their hopes. She had made no promises, but others made them on her behalf. The town was alive with wild stories of the things she had claimed that she was going to do, and even wilder stories of the rewards that her followers were going to receive. Not one of the claims had come from her lips. It was not fair that she should be the one left feeling guilty.

Increasingly, she shared Captain Curnad's belief that the battle with Shard had been a staged piece of theatre, designed to achieve just this result. Except she knew that the controlling force behind the display was not Jemeryl, but the dragon itself. Why had Shard done it? What was the dragon expecting to happen next?

Tevi's gaze travelled along the road, dotted with pitiful refugees, coming to her for sanctuary. Her only comfort lay in the hope that the dragon had told the truth when it said Jemeryl was also on the way to Uzhenek and would get there soon. This was not just from the desire to be reunited with her lover and reassure herself that Jemeryl was safe. Given all the ridiculous stories flying around, it would be nice to have someone on hand who really could slay a dragon.

❖

Jemeryl reached the top of a gentle hill. Ahead of her, the road dropped into a deeper valley with a river flowing through and a small town built on the far bank. Closer at hand was a sprawling collection of buildings surrounded by a high wooden palisade. From what Jemeryl could remember, the river was a tributary of the Kladjishe, and the town was called Rynrudth, or Redezth, or something like that. Uzhenek lay another eighty miles to the south.

The sun was dropping towards the horizon. If she wanted, she could spend the night in the town, or she could press on and cover another few miles by nightfall. Jemeryl urged her horse forwards, still trying to work out what would be best. She was finding decisions very difficult.

By the time she reached the wooden palisade, Jemeryl had just about made up her mind to wait and see what the town had to offer. She rode past the stockade gates with barely a glance at the six soldiers standing guard there until the sergeant hailed her.

"You! Where do you think you're going?"

The aggressive voice made Jemeryl stop and look over in surprise. Even before she was completely sure that she was the one addressed, her horse had been surrounded by a ring of soldiers, pointing spears in her direction.

"What is it?" Jemeryl tried to collect her thoughts.

"I said, where do you think you're going?"

"What busin..." The rest of the sentence died. Too late, Jemeryl remembered that she was wearing the clothes she had taken from the army deserter. By bad luck, it seemed that she had come across one of the few places in the collapsing Empire where military order still held. "Er...Uzhenek."

"On whose orders?"

"My captain's."

"Who is your captain?"

Only one name came to mind. "Tevi. Um...Captain Tevirik." Jemeryl knew that she was not sounding at all convincing.

The sergeant clearly thought so too. "Get off that horse."

Jemeryl hesitated. The soldiers would not be able to stop her if she made up her mind to continue, but she did not want to advertise her true identity. Fortunately, Klara had been flying on ahead and was able to settle down out of sight. But how best to deal with the soldiers? Jemeryl was considering tampering with their memories, when an officer arrived on the scene. The witch would still not present much of a challenge in a fight, but his memory would be better protected.

Jemeryl hopped down from her horse. At worst, she would end up spending a few hours in a cell. She could break out and make it look as if she had done it by conventional means. Nobody would bother Mavek with news about the escape of an ungifted common soldier.

"What's going on?" the witch asked.

"Sir. I suspect that this soldier is a deserter."

"Oh, that's ridic—"

"Speak when you're spoken to!" the witch shouted in Jemeryl's face.

The sergeant continued. "Sir, she came trotting down the road and was going to go straight past the gate without showing her authorisation. And she still has not given satisfactory account of herself, sir."

The witch turned to Jemeryl. "Now, soldier. What have you to say for yourself?"

"Would I—" She got no further.

"You start whatever you're going to say with 'sir.'"

Jemeryl grit her teeth. She would have to put more effort into her act. "Yes, sir. I'm sorry. I'm tired. I've been on the road a long time. What I was going to say is, would I have brazenly ridden past the gates if I were a deserter? I'm under orders to get to Uzhenek as soon a possible."

"Where is your authorisation?"

"I...I've lost it...sir." Jemeryl could not believe how inept she was sounding. "If you don't believe me, sir, you can contact my captain at Tirakhalod."

"Who is your captain?"

"Te...Tev..." Suddenly the weight of her grief hit Jemeryl. The name would not form on her lips. She dropped her head so that no one would see the tears in her eyes.

"I don't think we need to hear any more. Take her to the brig, sergeant."

Jemeryl shook her head, mainly in despair at herself. Talking her way out had been a complete failure. She hoped that her backup plan would work better. Once night fell, she would have to break out of jail. Fortunately, the cell she was dumped in did not look as if it would present much of a challenge. She could be out of it in seconds.

However, to Jemeryl's surprise, the sergeant returned less than an hour later with three subordinates, and in an unnecessary show of force, dragged her from the cell and frogmarched her to the large open parade ground in the centre of the compound. The escort then withdrew, leaving Jemeryl standing alone in middle.

The sun was setting, but it was still light enough to see normally. Jemeryl looked around in confusion. In front of her was the biggest construction in the compound, presumably either the army headquarters or the compound captain's home. On the other three sides stood ranks of common soldiers, maybe as many as two hundred in total. Two officers stood in the corners at the rear.

The sound of a door closing drew Jemeryl's attention back to the main building. Three more officers had emerged and now took up position facing the assembly of soldiers. The officer on the left of the group had slightly more embellishment on his uniform and a longer cloak than the rest, which Jemeryl guessed made him the one in charge.

The captain raised his voice to a shout. "We all know that there are temporary difficulties at the moment. And we all know that some people think they can take advantage of the situation. What I want everyone here to also know is that no one will get away with it as long as I am in command. All deserters will be executed on the spot. I want this to be an example to everyone here."

It took Jemeryl a moment to understand what was intended. "Hey! Don't I get a trial?"

The captain did not bother replying. He was engaged in knitting the sixth dimensional tensors into a power vortex. With a throwing action, he impelled the elemental rift towards Jemeryl. If it hit, it would result in a relatively quick, although very painful death. Fortunately, the attack was easy for a sorcerer to dispel. Jemeryl set up a counter-flow current and the energies discharged in a dazzling shower of sparks, ten feet from where she stood.

For three long seconds everyone on the parade ground was frozen in shock. Jemeryl opened her mouth, about to try taking control of the situation, when she sensed a new attack. One of the witches behind had launched a hail of ion darts at her. Jemeryl quickly raised a shield. Again, she averted the strike, but now the other witches had recovered from their surprise and were summoning their skills. Many of the ungifted soldiers were also charging into the attack, drawing their weapons.

The display of stupidity stunned Jemeryl. Surely everyone must realise that they had made a mistake and that it was time to talk? Individually, she could easily overpower anyone there, but surrounded and under attack from all sides, she was going to have to fight in earnest. Yet, still, she tried to make one last plea for common sense.

"Wait, I—"

The two witches standing beside the captain joined in opening a conduit through the fifth dimension, trying to rip her aura to shreds. Jemeryl had no time to defuse it safely. She diverted the flow away from her, but the wild shot flipped towards the corner of the parade ground where the ion darts had originated. The witch standing there had attacked through the sixth dimension, so it was no surprise that she was blind to the fifth and could not defend herself or those near her. Screams echoed around the compound. Jemeryl repelled another two bolts aimed at her, and again the deflected charges found defenceless targets.

Even then, the attackers did not stop. The ungifted fighters would be on her in an instant. With no time for anything non-lethal, Jemeryl hauled on the power tensors, focusing the energies. The nearest soldiers were smashed aside, crumpled and broken. She sent another burst towards the captain and his attendants. He was able to ground the discharge, but the subsequent explosion knocked all three of them off their feet. Now, at last, people started to retreat. The ungifted soldiers were the first.

The captain scrambled up and shouted, "Keep her pinned down. I'll be back." He dived through the doorway behind him.

The witches tried to follow his order. Jemeryl knew that she did not have the option to subdue them gently. Some of Mavek's creations could cause problems, even for a sorcerer. Whatever the captain had gone for, she dare not passively await his return. The captain's two attendants had used a fifth dimensional attack. Beneath them both, Jemeryl tore open drains in the elemental plane. The heat gushed from their bodies and they fell as frozen shells.

A final suicidal group of ungifted soldiers closed on her. Jemeryl blasted them to ash and looked around. The remaining witch had fled.

No one, apart from herself, was still standing in the parade ground, although screams and groans came from several of the fallen figures. Jemeryl raced after the captain.

The room she entered was clearly an administration office. She stopped and listened. A voice was speaking in the room to her right. Jemeryl pushed open the door and stepped through.

The captain was hunched over a table. "—must be a sorcerer. Yes, red hair. She just arrived in Redezth. We didn't—No, she's here!" The last three words were delivered as a panicked cry. He lifted a crossbow that had been lying on the table.

Jemeryl was very sure that it was no ordinary weapon. Before the crossbow could be aimed at her, she attacked. For an instant the captain was wreathed in green static and then he collapsed without a sound. The sudden silence was shocking.

Jemeryl's knees felt weak. How many people had she just killed? She stumbled to the table. A message orb lay in the middle of a sheet of satin cloth. Who had the captain been talking to? And could she explain that what had happened here was not her fault? Without stopping to think, Jemeryl focused her attention on the orb.

Mavek wavered into view. The blacksmith was not in the castle. Grassland reached to the horizon behind him, covered with soldiers and attendants setting camp.

"You!" Contempt filled Mavek's voice.

"Mavek. I'm sorry. I didn't mean—"

"I don't want your apologies."

"It wasn't—"

He cut her off again. His eyes grew wild, frenzied in anger. "What I want is to see you grovelling on your knees. I want to have your heart beating in my hand and squeeze the life out of it. I want to hear you squeal like a pig."

He hated her. Was she surprised? Confronted by his hostility—his quite justifiable hostility—Jemeryl felt herself grow calmer. There were things she had to say to him.

"Mavek, what I did to you was unforgivable, I know. You must believe that I'm truly sorry. But surely you remember what it's like when you lost your partner. I'd just heard about Tevi. I wasn't in my right mind. I'm..."

Mavek was no longer listening. His face had crumpled and he began sobbing. "Kenan. I've got to get Kenan back. You've got to give me the talisman."

"It won't work."

"It will, for both of us. You have to give it to me. We won't be alone. Nothing will..." Tears streamed down his face.

Jemeryl watched him in appalled pity. Her own eyes started to fill. "Mavek. The talisman isn't safe. It won't work. It will just kill more people and leave thousands of others like us, without the people they love. We can't do that."

Mavek's mood flipped again to sneering sarcasm. "Like you care about anyone other than yourself."

"I do. Just now, the people I killed here. I didn't want to, but they attacked me. I had no choice. You have to give up on the talisman before more people get killed."

"Never. I'll hunt you to the ends of the earth. And it doesn't matter what happens, because when I get the talisman I'll put it all to right. And then I'll have Kenan back, and we'll..." He was sobbing like a three-year-old again.

Jemeryl loosened the ties in the ether and the message orb returned to rest. Mavek was seriously deranged. The soul shredding had left him unbalanced, and it was her fault. Everything was her fault.

❖

On the outskirts of Redezth, heading south, Jemeryl passed what was unmistakably an inn. The frontage was shabby and unwelcoming, but daylight was fading fast and she might as well stop. None of the surviving soldiers had made any attempt to intercept her when she left the compound. She doubted that they would organize a pursuit of her. At least not until Mavek got there. Jemeryl was sure that he would be on the way.

Jemeryl dismounted in the rubbish-strewn yard behind the inn. The overweight landlord appeared after a lengthy wait. She scowled at the small silver coin offered, but shouted at a stable hand to take care of the horse and then led Jemeryl to a room on the upper floor.

"Will you be wanting a meal?"

Jemeryl shook her head. "No, I ate earlier."

Judging by her expression, the landlord thought that Jemeryl had done it as a personal insult to herself. Jemeryl wondered what the response would be if she also admitted that she was lying.

"If you want a drink, the tap room is downstairs."

Jemeryl could have guessed as much from the rumble of loud voices beneath her feet. Once the landlord had gone, she lay on the creaking bed and closed her eyes. There was no likelihood of sleep. Quite apart from the turmoil in her head, the voices from the tap room were clear enough to hear every word.

"Have you heard about over at the fort?"

"A massacre, Ronny was telling me."

"Hundreds dead, burnt, maimed."

"It's awful."

"Who was it?"

"A rogue sorcerer gone berserk."

"What I heard, it's the same one who murdered the old hag, Bykoda."

"Probably going to set herself up as the new Empress."

"So we swap one murdering bitch for another?"

"Bykoda never went around killing without cause."

"She wasn't blameless."

"Never said she was. But this one's worse." A general round of agreement followed.

"Oh well, I'm off home while I've still got one to go to."

"Me too."

After several boisterous good-byes, the noise below dropped to a soft murmur. Some locals remained, but the loudmouths had gone. Jemeryl swung her feet off the bed and sat up. She felt sick. Obviously the drinkers in the bar had not connected her with the evil sorcerer on the rampage. She wanted to run downstairs and explain that it was not her fault. She was trying to protect them. She was not evil.

But maybe they were right. She had taken part in a massacre. And she was to blame. How could she have been so stupid as to ride past a squad of soldiers, disguised as a deserter? If she had given it a moment's thought, she would have known to take a detour, or make herself invisible, or do anything that showed the faintest trace of intelligence.

Jemeryl curled forwards, overwhelmed by guilt. Everything she did only made things worse. She had treated Mavek with unforgivable savagery. She did not blame him for hating her. She had killed dozens of innocent soldiers. She had not saved Tevi.

Her shoulders shook with sobs. She was going through hell, trying to save the people downstairs, and they did not appreciate it. She could not go on as she was. She needed advice and only one person could help. She had to talk it over with Tevi.

Jemeryl pulled the talisman from her shirt. It swung before her eyes on its chain, taunting her. What options did she have? Mavek would be after her. He now knew where she was. One on one, she could defeat him and any of his followers. But as the recent battle had shown, when the odds started to stack up, even witches could pose a threat. She had got through this time unscathed partly because she had caught them by surprise. If they had known what she was from the start and coordinated their attack, things might have been a bit trickier.

When Mavek caught up with her, he would have dozens of witches under his command, and all of his weaponry armed and ready. The chances of her winning the battle were not good, and the slaughter in the compound would be nothing by comparison. Yet even this would be utterly insignificant next to what would happen if Mavek tried to use the talisman and it ruptured.

In all honesty, Jemeryl knew that she could not keep the talisman safe. She had to use it. Yes, it might cause massive devastation, but the odds were better if she was the one making the attempt. Even if the device was unflawed, Mavek would not be able to control its power. Not least because he was no longer of sound mind. Thousands were going to die, regardless of what she did. The people downstairs thought she was an evil murdering bitch, so why not act like one? And she needed to see Tevi.

Jemeryl swept her mind clear of the chaos and focused on the talisman, dismissing a flicker of complaint from Klara. The layers of the talisman opened as her senses probed deeper. The contours in time began to twist and resolve themselves. The links through the temporal currents acquired form and clarity. Tentatively she gathered in a few and examined them. She could see where to go. Like so many of Bykoda's inventions, it was breathtakingly simple.

The crash of the door downstairs shattered Jemeryl's concentration. Her contact with the talisman broke and she sat up, angry at the thoughtless interruption, and the shoddy inn design. How stupid to have bedrooms over the tap room.

"Hey! Have you heard the news?"

"The fight in the compound? You're too late."

"We were all talking about it earlier."

The first person spoke again, excited. "No. A rider just came in from Uzhenek. They had a dragon down there a few days back."

"Dragons!"

Jemeryl had been about to raise a shield to block out the irritating voices. She stopped. Another dragon. Was it just a coincidence?

The new arrival went on. "Folk were being burnt and ripped apart, and the whole town was about to be destroyed. But then a hero showed up. Damn near killed the dragon and sent it running."

"Who was it?"

"No one knows for sure. A woman. They say she has the strength of ten."

Jemeryl's hand tightened around the talisman, but her eyes were no longer on it. Her head and heart were reeling between distrust and euphoria. Did she dare to believe that it might be Tevi?

❖

The sunset was flaring to red on the horizon when Jemeryl caught her first sight of Uzhenek from the rim of the valley. As she grew closer, the light faded, swallowing the city before her eyes. By the time she stood on the bridge over the Kladjishe, the mass of squalid huts was just a darker patch of shadow on the valley floor, except for a few dozen torches, snapping in the cold wind. The lights served only to suggest the scale of the city. No clustering or order was apparent, indicating buildings of importance or main thoroughfares.

She can't be here. It isn't her. The words repeated in Jemeryl's head, as they had since she left Redezth. But the attempt to keep her hopes in check was futile. No matter how much she tried to prepare herself for the blow, Jemeryl knew that she would not be able to bear the pain if the hero turned out not to be Tevi.

Her horse's head was sagging, its hooves falling heavy on the road. She had made the journey from Redezth in two days, a hard ride even with the assistance of magic. Jemeryl suspected that she was nearly as exhausted as her horse, but she was too tense to be able to tell. Learning that Tevi was dead had been the worst experience of her life, and she was terrified that she was about to go through it all over again.

She can't be here. It isn't her.

As she reached the first torch on the outskirts of Uzhenek, Jemeryl saw four soldiers gathered in the light. Blue and black bands were knotted around their biceps and hung from the shafts of their spears, clearly the token of whoever was now in charge of the town. Jemeryl had abandoned the remnants of the deserter's uniform, and the sentries paid her little attention until she reined in her horse beside them.

"Excuse me. Is there any chance of meeting..." Jemeryl paused, not wanting to say Tevi's name aloud, as if giving voice to the possibility would deepen its power to destroy her. Her hopes rested on no more than the coincidence of a dragon and a strong woman.

"The Dragon Slayer?" One soldier finished the sentence for her. The woman grinned. "You'll see her, all right. She walks around and talks to folk. Doesn't stay hidden. Just keep your eyes open tomorrow."

Jemeryl swallowed and nodded. She could not wait until tomorrow, but she was not going to make a fuss. She did not need an audience to watch her break down when she found out that the Dragon Slayer was a stranger. At her urging, the horse plodded on.

Uzhenek was a shantytown. It did not deserve the name of city and never had, even when Bykoda was alive. Back then, her phantom citadel had cast a glamour over the site. Now the ethereal towers were gone, but the filth and the squalor remained. Overcrowding had been added to the mix. Refugees slept on the streets, huddling in whatever shelter they could find.

The townsfolk were marginally better off in their decrepit huts made of straw and dung. But surely these hovels would not be good enough for the heroic Dragon Slayer. Only one part of Uzhenek might provide suitable accommodation. Jemeryl steered her horse through the dark town towards the centre where the citadel had once stood.

The road she was on rose steadily until she emerged from the tightly packed slums onto the open hilltop. More soldiers were in evidence here, as well as large gangs of townsfolk. Jemeryl slipped off her horse and caught the reins. Several bonfires were burning on the hilltop with excited figures clustered around. Jemeryl started to approach the nearest but then stopped. What should she do? Demand to be taken to the Dragon Slayer? Now that she was so close, panic was threatening to overwhelm her. She might be within minutes of discovering that the hero was not Tevi.

She can't be here. It isn't her.

A faint commotion was going on some way off to her right, but getting closer. People at the bonfire turned to look. An undisciplined gang was crossing the hilltop, diffuse and turbulent on the outside, tighter and calmer closer in. Whoever was at the middle was hidden by the throng.

Jemeryl stared at the approaching mob, certain that the Dragon Slayer was at hand. Who else could it be? For an instant, a gap in the surrounding crowd opened, but all Jemeryl had time to see was an embroidered blue surcoat, glittering in the light from the bonfire. The gap closed again and hid the figure from view. Was it Tevi?

Jemeryl took a step forwards, ready to summon her magic and get her answer, when the crowd opened again. The person in blue, a woman, was looking back, talking to the man behind her. Then she turned her head and Jemeryl felt her heart stop. The whole world stopped. She could see nothing except Tevi strolling towards her.

Jemeryl's hand must have yanked on the reins, because her horse skittered and tried to pull back. The disturbance was just enough to draw a few glances. Tevi also looked across, and their eyes met.

Jemeryl could not have moved. She did not need to. Tevi broke away from the group and raced over. "Jem! You're here."

Arms enfolded her. Tevi's voice murmured in her ear. "Shard said that you'd come, but I haven't known whether I... I'm so pleased you're here."

Jemeryl collapsed into Tevi's embrace. A crowd gathered around them, but the people and noise scarcely registered. Someone took her horse. She and Tevi, arms wrapped around each other, were gently guided towards a stone building—or was Tevi the one leading? *Dazed* was not the right word for Jemeryl's mental state. Her warding mantra had fled, leaving only a hole in her mind that would not fill with coherent thoughts.

The mob lessened once they were inside the building, but a few stayed with them until they had reached their destination, a small room on the upper floor. Jemeryl was shaking and disorientated. Her legs managed to get her to a low bench before they gave out. While Tevi cleared everyone else from the room, she looked around, trying to drag her head together.

The townsfolk had clearly given the hero the best that they could offer, although this did not amount to much more than the solid rough-cut bench, a table and two chairs. A heap of fur rugs strewn in a corner was presumably Tevi's bed. Weapons were stacked in another corner. Bottles and an oil lantern stood on the table, and heat came from a glowing iron brazier.

Tevi slid onto the bench and hugged her. "Waiting here for you has been awful."

Jemeryl gave a tight nod.

"Are you all right, Jem?"

"I will be, I..." Jemeryl buried her face in Tevi's shoulder. More than anything, she needed to feel her lover's physical presence.

After a few minutes, Tevi pulled back and studied her face. "Are you sure you're all right? You look pale."

"I'm just tired. I haven't been sleeping well. I thought you were..." Jemeryl closed her eyes. She could not finish the sentence. "What happened to you? How did you get here?"

Tevi launched into her story, but Jemeryl found it hard to follow. Nothing could get past the mind-numbing realisation that Tevi was sitting beside her, alive. She found herself focusing on Tevi's lips, watching how they moved, but the words would not hang together in her head.

Tevi broke off her account. "Are you sure you're up to this?"

"Yes. I'm fine."

"You look like you're about to pass out. We need to make plans, but it can wait until tomorrow. Come on. It's late. You'll be better after a sleep."

Jemeryl nodded in acquiescence rather than agreement. She was beyond making decisions.

When she made no attempt to stand, Tevi pulled her to her feet, led her to the pile of furs in the corner, and helped her free of her clothes. Jemeryl stretched out on her back beneath the warm covers and tried to relax. She watched Tevi blow out the lantern and strip off her own clothes. And then Tevi was beside her in the bed, moulding to the contours of her body. Jemeryl grabbed hold of her hand.

"Is anything wrong?" Tevi's voice sounded unsure.

"No. You're here with me. What could be wrong?"

The backlog of emotion was sloshing around at the edges of Jemeryl's mind. But she did not want to think about it, did not want to deal with it. She wanted to forget everything about the previous seven days. Tevi was there with her. That was all she needed to think about.

Jemeryl rolled onto her side. One arm snaked around Tevi's back, pulling her in close. Her lips sought out Tevi's and their mouths joined together in tender combat. Jemeryl pushed her leg between Tevi's thighs and hooked it around the back of Tevi's knee, locking their hips together. She wriggled the arm that was squashed between them upwards until the backs of her fingers encountered the softness of Tevi's breast.

Tevi's response was slow, hesitant. She broke off their kiss. "Jem? What's up?"

"I want you."

"I thought you were tired."

"I missed you when we were apart. I need you."

Tevi stroked Jemeryl's hair and stared into eyes. "And that's all?"

Jemeryl twisted her head and began nuzzling Tevi's ear. "That's all."

Tevi chuckled softly. "Then I won't try to talk you out of it."

Tevi's hands began their own exploration, gently stroking the back of Jemeryl's neck and then brushing down her spine to the cleft of her buttocks. The effect of the touch shot through Jemeryl, familiar and wanted, and crashed into the knowledge that she had thought never to experience it again.

The breath caught in her lungs, but not from passion. Unexpected tears stung her eyes. Jemeryl tried to force the pain away. Tevi was here, in her arms. Nothing else mattered; nothing could be wrong.

She raised herself slightly, pushing Tevi onto her back, and lowered her mouth to Tevi's throat. The taste and the texture were so well known to her and so uniquely Tevi. With a conscious effort, Jemeryl summoned her desire to let it wash the memory of grief from her.

Jemeryl shifted her weight, so that her thigh pressed down harder between Tevi's legs. The gasp this drew from Tevi skipped across Jemeryl's memory, like a stone across a pond, bouncing off recollections of a hundred other times. It was the sound Tevi made. Jemeryl had thought that she would never hear that gasp again. The body beneath her was so very precious.

Tevi's breathing was becoming ragged. Jemeryl looked at her lover in the soft red light from the brazier, head thrown back, eyes closed, mouth open. No sight in the world was more wonderful, or more vital to her. Living without Tevi was impossible, yet for seven days she had carried on a pretence at life. The nightmare was over. She could forget it. She wanted to. She needed to. All Jemeryl had to do was force away the memory of pain with the sensation of the present.

Jemeryl shifted down, so she could take Tevi's breast in her mouth. But the anguish was too raw, and the wave of emotion could be held back no longer. A sob broke through. Tears dropped onto Tevi's skin.

"Jem?"

Her tongue worked against the hardness of Tevi's nipple, trying to force passion into her actions. But her nose was blocked and her breathing was out of control. Jemeryl had to raise her mouth to draw breath.

Tevi's hands gripped her shoulders, pulling her up. "Jem. What's wrong?"

Jemeryl met Tevi's eyes. "I thought you were dead. I thought you—"

The words shattered the last shred of Jemeryl's self-control. The pain ripped through her, welling up from her gut, contorting her face and choking in her throat. Her body convulsed with hysterical crying. "I thought you were dead."

"Oh, my love. It's all right. It's all right."

Tevi rolled Jemeryl onto her side and then wrapped her in a tight hug, holding her close and murmuring repeated nonsense words into her ear. Jemeryl could not speak. She clung to Tevi like an injured child while the agony of the previous seven days came out in a storm of tears. The process was unstoppable, working its way through her and leaving her drained. And all the while, Tevi held her secure, stroking her hair and kissing her gently.

At last Jemeryl fell asleep, worn out, with her head on Tevi's shoulder.

CHAPTER FOURTEEN—CAUSE AND EFFECT

The midday sky over Uzhenek was a rich unbroken blue. The clouds had gone and might not return until the autumn. In a good year, three or four cycles of rain fell during spring. In a bad year, none came at all, and by summer, the vegetation would be sparse and desiccated, the rivers reduced to a trickle, and the bodies of deer and wild cattle would be littering the grasslands.

Tevi sat with one leg hitched up on the balustrade that ran around the flat roof of the house. Uzhenek was definitely best viewed from above, and in sunny weather. The mottled thatched roofs looked quaint in the sunlight and hid the shoddy hovels underneath. The stench of decaying filth was more diffuse than it would be down in the mud-filled streets, although it was still stronger than Tevi liked.

However, the smell was not what was currently worrying her. Her gaze left the panoramic view of Uzhenek and returned to Jemeryl, who was sitting beside her. Although the night's sleep had wrought a considerable improvement, Tevi had never seen her lover so emotionally weakened. The tears had gone and in their place was a solemn calm. Maybe to others it would have given the impression of typical sorcerer's detachment, but not to Tevi, and she noticed how Jemeryl continually maintained physical contact between them. Even now, their knees were touching.

Once again, Tevi tried to imagine what it would have been like, had she spent seven days thinking that Jemeryl was dead. Her frown deepened. The mental acrobatics were not something that could deliver unequivocal answers, but she was left with the gut feeling that there was more that Jemeryl needed to tell her. While they sat on the roof, Jemeryl's eyes kept drifting northwards, and an expression of distress would cross her face. But whatever the issue, Tevi was willing for Jemeryl to speak when she was ready.

So far, their conversation had covered Bykoda's murder and the incidents at the guard post rendezvous up to the conversation with Anid when Jemeryl had got news of Shard's attack on the troops. Thereafter, Jemeryl's narrative had become more vague, skipping through the days. Was it simply that she was too upset to recount the details? Or had something else happened?

For her part, Tevi had just finished telling the full story of her dealings with Shard, including the effect of her dramatic arrival on the town's inhabitants.

"So what game do you think Shard was playing?" Tevi said in conclusion.

A half smile crossed Jemeryl's face. "There is a saying among sorcerers, 'Never try to second-guess a dragon.'"

"I know they aren't something you want to take chances with. Shard could have totally destroyed this place."

"There's more to it than that. Dragons don't perceive time in the same way that we do. For them time exists in two dimensions."

"Isn't it the same for sorcerers?"

"Not to the same degree. And not without going a bit mad if they have the gift too strongly. Humans don't have the mental equipment to deal with the viewpoint."

"And dragons do?"

"For them, it's the only way that they can imagine being."

Tevi's forehead knotted as she tried to remember everything Jemeryl had told her about two-dimensional time. "Does that mean that dragons can predict the future?"

"Sort of...except they don't see it like that." Jemeryl paused. "The best analogy I can give is that humans view their lives like a book, with one page following the next. It's one-dimensional and linear. Dragons view their lives like a painting, in two dimensions. It means that a dragon always knows everything that it is ever going to know, but there's no point asking it about anything else. They are aware of their entire life simultaneously, except that simultaneous is a temporal concept that doesn't make sense from their viewpoint."

"Mmmm..." Tevi pursed her lips, frowning.

"What are you thinking?"

"I'm trying to work out if my conversation with Shard would have made any more sense if I'd taken it backwards."

The first genuine laugh of the morning burst from Jemeryl. "I don't think it works like that. But if it's any consolation, you are now a member of a very small and exclusive group of people who have spoken with a dragon and lived to tell of it."

"Have you?"

"Oh no. I've never even seen one."

"I guess Shard was quite impressive to look at. But you haven't missed much in the way of talking. And even when Shard did make sense, it could be..." Tevi shook her head. "I guess evil is the word, except it didn't feel like that."

"Amoral?" Jemeryl suggested.

"Yes."

"I was taught that the dragon's time sense is incompatible with our ideas of good and evil. If you think about it, our concept of guilt is based on causality. If you do something knowing that it will result in evil, then you've done wrong. A bad act is one that has bad consequences. But to a dragon, effect does not follow cause. To them, everything is part of an inevitable pattern. If a human kills someone, you see it as terminating their linear story. If a dragon kills someone, nothing has changed. For them, in two-dimensional time, the person is still living, not yet born, and already dead."

"It was her time to die."

"Pardon?"

"It was the reason Shard gave for killing someone."

Jemeryl nodded. "And they are just as philosophical about their own deaths. It's part of the pattern of their life. They know when they are going to die, and they can't conceive of trying to change it. *Fatalistic* doesn't begin to go far enough in describing their outlook. For them, the thought of changing their destiny is terrifying. They don't—" Jemeryl broke off sharply. "Oh...of course, the talisman."

Tevi met Jemeryl's eyes in understanding. "I told you that I thought Shard was frightened."

"The talisman must scare the dragons witless. Just as humans don't have the mental capabilities to cope with two-dimensional time, dragons don't have the ability to handle the unknown. It's not something that they ever encounter."

"They can't bear having a surprise?"

"No. The effect of the talisman would be like suddenly discovering that someone has rubbed out part of their life painting and replaced it with something new."

"The first thing Shard said to me was, 'I don't know what's going to happen.'" Tevi frowned. "Except it knew that you were coming here."

"Perhaps it was just making a best guess. Or maybe all of the temporal options inherent in the talisman had me getting to Uzhenek."

Tevi chewed her lip, trying to remember everything that Shard had said. "Maybe Uzhenek was far enough away from the talisman for Shard to still be able to see the future." She immediately shook her head. "No. Surely distance wouldn't matter. If the future changes, it isn't dependant on where you are."

"It might. Time and space are far more interlinked from a dragon's viewpoint. Why do you think that distance might be involved?"

"Partly because Shard panicked at the idea when I suggested picking you up and flying us both over the Barrodens. And partly because, when flying here, Shard took an enormous detour that would make sense if it was avoiding the spot where you and the talisman were at the time."

Jemeryl looked thoughtful. Her hand moved to the front of her shirt, as if to feel the talisman through the material. "And Anid said that dragons had inhabited the northern Empire many years ago, but they hadn't been around for decades. Which might tie in with the time that Bykoda made the talisman." She grinned. "So not only was Bykoda the first sorcerer to successfully create a device to change time, she was also the first sorcerer to make a really effective dragon ward. No one has had much luck with them in the past."

"And Shard needs us to make sure that nobody uses the talisman, because it can't get close enough to protect the thing itself?"

"That's one possible interpretation of what we know."

Tevi turned to look out over the town. On the open hilltop below, the inhabitants were going about their business. No one was paying any attention to the roof of the house. This was thanks to Jemeryl's magic, which had hidden them from the eyes and ears of the ungifted. Otherwise, it was a safe bet that a horde of excited sightseers would be gawking up at them. After all the fuss that had surrounded her for the previous few days, being ignored was a very welcome change. However, the thought reminded Tevi of the effort Shard had made to install her as the Dragon Slayer. Something did not tie in.

"I don't see why Shard brought me here to Uzhenek. I mean, I'm grateful that it did, but you were heading back to the Protectorate anyway. Shard didn't need to get involved."

"Except Mavek had you prisoner and was taking you north. If Shard hadn't rescued you first, I'd have gone after you."

"Would it have made any difference in the long run?"

"It might. And it makes sense if Shard didn't want me to bring the talisman any nearer to its lair."

"But Shard could have killed me in reality. Which would have been just as effective in stopping you chasing after me, and would have saved it the trouble of flying me here and staging the battle. I don't see what setting me up as the Dragon Slayer achieved."

"If Shard had truly killed you, I'd have—" Jemeryl broke off and looked down.

From the guilt-ridden expression on her face, Tevi was sure that Jemeryl's reaction was due to more than remembered grief. The sorcerer was rubbing the palm of one hand, as if trying massage away stiffness. Her mouth worked, but no words came. Maybe one of the issues that Jemeryl needed to discuss was about to come up. Tevi shifted a little closer and put her arm around Jemeryl's shoulder, but left her to speak in her own time.

"I was going to use the talisman."

"When? And wouldn't it have..." Tevi was confused.

Jemeryl's face twisted in torment. "Um...yes. The talisman would have ruptured. And I'd have caused the deaths of tens of thousands... maybe laid waste to the entire region. But I wasn't thinking. I didn't care. I wanted you back. I couldn't..."

"Jem? You... After all you've said? Surely you wouldn't really have done it?"

"I would. At the very moment that the news of the Dragon Slayer reached me, I was about to try changing the past...to change things so that you hadn't gone on that last mission. I guess that's why Shard wanted to make you famous, knowing the story would spread. The idea that you might be the unknown hero was the only thing that stopped me from completing my attempt to use the talisman and killing everyone."

Jemeryl laid her head on Tevi's shoulder. "I know we have to take the talisman to Lyremouth. Even when I was about to use it, I knew that it was wrong of me and that I should take the talisman to be unmade. But I didn't care. And now, when I think of Mavek, I feel so hypocritical. I'm going to take the talisman away from him so that he can't do the very thing that I was going to do."

"But you didn't use it."

"Only because I got news that made me think maybe you weren't really dead. Mavek is never going to get the news that he wants. I have no right to judge him. I don't feel as if I even have the right to stand in his way."

"But we have to stop him. We have no option."

"True. But it doesn't make me feel any better about myself. And I've treated him so badly."

"No worse than he's treated—" Tevi felt Jemeryl flinch so violently that it was as if she had been slapped. "Jem? What is it?"

When no answer was forthcoming, Tevi shifted around slightly and tilted Jemeryl's head so that their eyes met.

"Jem?"

Jemeryl's face contorted in the effort to force out the words. Tears were forming in her eyes. "After Anid told me about the dragon taking you. I found Mavek alone. I attacked him."

"You used magic against him?"

"Yes."

"Did you hurt him much?"

"Oh yes. I ripped his aura to pieces. Torture would have been a soft option by comparison. He is so much weaker than me. He couldn't defend himself." The tears were now running down Jemeryl's face.

"He's not dead?"

"No. Just a little insane. Hopefully his memory of it will be patchy, but..."

Tevi pulled Jemeryl into her arms, but this was partly for time to sort out her expression. On the islands of her birth, only women were given the strength potion. The result was that she had been brought up to think of men as weak and needing protection. For a woman to attack a man was the action of a thug and a coward. Even after years on the mainland, Tevi could still feel her islander morality offended when she saw men mistreated.

Of course, she knew that the reaction was illogical. On the mainland, men were often stronger than women. However, in this case, Jemeryl herself conceded that Mavek had stood no chance. Tevi felt judgmental words forming on her lips. She fought them back. Jemeryl was neither a thug nor a coward, and her tormented expression showed that she was already berating herself more than adequately. Tevi hunted around in search of something reassuring to say. Her lover was in need of support.

"He was the one who started all this. He only has himself to blame."

"Oh no. I went far beyond what was justified. I'm worse than him."

"You haven't killed anyone."

"I have. On the way here...hundreds, maybe."

"What! Who?"

"Soldiers...people who attacked me."

Tevi did not know what to say. Cruelty and aggression were two things that she had never witnessed in her lover—two things that she would have said were totally absent from Jemeryl's nature. And she knew Jemeryl better than she had ever known anyone else, maybe even better than she knew herself.

She drew back and stared deeply into Jemeryl's eyes. Her confusion retreated. Whatever had driven Jemeryl to her actions, Tevi was certain that her lover was, if not blameless, then at least understandable and forgivable. Maybe in the future they might discuss all the issues; what was needed now was unequivocal backing.

"If you were attacked, then you're allowed to defend yourself."

"Mavek didn't attack me."

"He murdered Bykoda in cold blood. And he is consciously planning to use the talisman, which is as good as murdering thousands more."

"So was I."

"No. You didn't plan it out in advance. You didn't have months or years to make a decision. You weren't in your right mind when you did it...any of it."

"You don't know that."

"Yes, I do."

"How can you?"

"Because I know the woman I love."

❖

Captain Curnad bowed and left the rooftop terrace. Jemeryl watched until he had disappeared down the ladder and then turned her attention to the road from Tirakhalod. At this exact time one day ago, she had been riding down it approaching Uzhenek, alone and in dread. Today, she was reunited with Tevi and had, apparently, a dozen of Bykoda's ex-army witches as followers.

Curnad had just been trying to negotiate promises of a position in the new Empire in exchange for his support. In the end, Jemeryl had found it best to hint that the post of regional commander might be his reward. She had thought it safer than admitting she was planning on leaving Uzhenek before dawn.

In truth, Jemeryl would have preferred to stay a day or two longer in the city and recover from her exhaustion, but she dared not let Mavek catch up with her. Even the one day she had allowed herself was a luxury of questionable wisdom. In all honesty, Jemeryl knew that she had not been in a fit state to travel. And after the battle in the Redezth fort, she had pressed on at a pace that Mavek, with an army in tow, would not be able to match. However, with an uncertain future, every day's lead they had over him should be preserved.

Jemeryl sat on the balustrade and looked down. Curnad was marching back to his makeshift headquarters in the old armoury. Jemeryl smiled, noting that despite Curnad's talk of loyalty and trust, she and Tevi had been given rooms in a rather less secure building. A disturbance on the other side of the hilltop then caught Jemeryl's attention. Tevi was returning, surrounded by a enthusiastic mixed group of soldiers, refugees, and children.

As far as any of the townsfolk were concerned, the Dragon Slayer was ruler of the city. Only the witches were aware of who and what Jemeryl was, and from what Curnad had said, he was assuming that she was keeping Tevi as a figurehead as part of a devious plan to outmanoeuvre Mavek. Fortunately, he had not presumed to ask questions as to what this plan might be, and thus saved Jemeryl the job of inventing a plausible explanation.

In another couple of minutes, Tevi joined her on the rooftop. Jemeryl felt a small knot of tension in her stomach loosen. Even though her confidence was returning, she still wanted to have her lover within arm's reach. Jemeryl beckoned Tevi over to the balustrade and planted a quick kiss of greeting on her lips once she was seated.

"Did you have a nice walk?"

"Not really. Uzhenek is a dump and the people are too..." Tevi shrugged.

"Why did you go?"

"Because I feel that I owe it to them." Tevi indicated the town with a vague wave of her arm. "They think I'm going to protect them, and look after them, and make sure they're all fed and healthy and safe from harm. I feel bad knowing I'm about to desert them. And playing the hero game is making it worse."

"You're not responsible for them. You didn't volunteer for the job."

Tevi frowned glumly. "No. But I still feel guilty at the thought of abandoning them. I've been accepting their food and accommodation and everything. I shouldn't have gone along with the role of leader if I wasn't willing to accept everything that goes with it."

"If it makes you any happier, you are protecting them. They may not know it, but the greatest threat they face at the moment is Mavek getting his hands on the talisman." Jemeryl interlaced her fingers with Tevi's. "Surely it's a wise and noble leader who does what is necessary to save her people, even when she can't explain it to them and take the credit for her actions."

"Now you're poking fun at me." Despite her words, an amused grin grew on Tevi's face.

"Just a little." Jemeryl barged her gently with her shoulder. "Curnad was here, by the way."

"What did he want?"

"An important job in my Empire when I take over. I've offered him the post of regional commander. I hope you don't mind. You weren't expecting the job yourself, were you?"

Tevi's grin widened. "No. He can have it. Just as long as you have something suitable lined up for me."

"I was thinking about the Empress' official bed warmer."

"I'd like to think that I was overqualified for the post."

"Maybe, but it comes with a range of benefits that might interest you."

A noise from the hilltop interrupted any reply Tevi might have made. Several people were running towards their building, clearly bringing an urgent report. Tevi left the balustrade and crouched by the top of the ladder. In a few seconds more, Jemeryl heard excited shouts from the room below.

"I'm up here," Tevi called down.

A sharp exchange followed in one of the local dialects unfamiliar to Jemeryl, although Tevi appeared to follow it without difficulty. The news was clearly both unexpected and problematic. Tevi's expression became steadily more concerned.

"What is it?" Jemeryl asked.

Tevi shook her head, frowning. "They say there's a large army heading towards the city from the north."

"Mavek? How far away is he?"

"That's just it. They say only a few miles."

Jemeryl stood and went to the north facing side of the roof. The road to Tirakhalod cut diagonally across the valley floor and disappeared over the distant escarpment. How could Mavek have got to them so quickly? And why had there been no news of the army's approach until they were upon the city? There had to be some mistake. But even as she watched, she saw the first banners appear on the opposite valley wall.

"Is it Mavek?" Tevi asked at her shoulder.

"I don't see how it can be. I'm going to check."

Jemeryl summoned Klara to her wrist. In seconds, she had transferred her senses to the magpie and was off, flying over Uzhenek.

The first detachments of the advancing army, cavalry units, were already onto the valley floor and sweeping west, flanking the city. Jemeryl swooped low over the galloping horses. The riders were frantically spurring their mounts onwards, as if in a race. Jemeryl circled them once but could see no banner or face that she recognised. The leaders plunged into the Kladjishe without breaking stride and began to ford the river.

She turned back to the main body of the army. More and more soldiers were appearing. Who were they? And where had they come from? And then, among the leading squadrons on the road, Jemeryl saw the unmistakable form of the huge blacksmith mounted on a black horse.

Mavek and his escort were progressing at a steady canter along the road. But could these horses have come all the way from Tirakhalod? Unlike her own mount the previous night, they were stepping briskly, with no trace of tiredness. Jemeryl knew of various spells that could be used to invigorate animals, but they were short-term measures, and fiddly to apply successfully. Quite apart from any moral considerations, it would be impractical to cast them on every single horse and soldier in an army. How many troops did Mavek have with him?

Bewildered, Jemeryl flew north, climbing the valley wall and over the top. Now at last she could see the full extent of the army. Behind the cavalry units were rank upon rank of foot soldiers, thousands strong, all in full battle array, and all of them were running.

❖

Once night had fallen, the surrounding ring of campfires and torches made the extent of the encircling army apparent to everyone in Uzhenek. Tension rose in the besieged city, but as yet, the mood was defiant and the wearing of blue and black braids was even more in evidence. Some people had progressed to matching face paint made from soot and berries.

Tevi strode around the perimeter of Uzhenek, arrayed in armour and putting on a show of confidence for the benefit of anyone watching. She now had Ranenok's rune sword at her side, but otherwise was kitted in the clothes and equipment she had got from Shard.

She did not say much but would frequently send a condescending look in the direction of the nearest enemy position and then catch the eye of one of her sentries and smile, as if sharing a private joke. So far, the ploy was proving surprisingly effective. As she moved on, muttered comments behind her would invariably assert that victory was a forgone conclusion. Tevi hoped that they were right.

Ideally, she would have been with Jemeryl, making plans. However, Mavek was unlikely to do anything before morning, while the situation in the town might hit a crisis without warning. And so she was out rallying the troops while Jemeryl was engaged in placating talks with the officer witches. The planning could wait until everyone was as happy as possible and unlikely to do anything rash.

Time crept by. Tevi wished that she did not feel so much of a sham, but she could tell that her visible presence on the streets was having its effect. Many people were even feeling secure enough to seek their beds, and the streets were emptying. Nobody was panicking or spreading wild rumours. The soldiers standing sentry all were looking positive and disciplined.

At the side of town beneath the valley wall, she paused. This was the point where the two opposing lines were closest. Mavek's troops were occupying the high ground above her, little more than a furlong away. They were near enough to hear, and normally Tevi would have expected distant singing, officers shouting orders, the clank of steel, and the whinnies of horses. However, the enemy were unnaturally silent. Was this a good or a bad sign?

Her own side were far more typical of soldiers on the eve of battle. Her job in boosting morale was done. Tevi was debating whether she should make one last circuit of the town, or if she should check the armoury, when a young woman raced up. The girl was fifteen or so, with the blond hair and broad face of the plainsmen, and sporting no fewer than four blue and black braids.

"Ma'am. A herald has arrived from the enemy. Your consort suggests you might want to return and hear the message."

Tevi restrained her grin at the word *consort*. There was clearly no doubt in the townsfolks' minds as to which one of them was having her bed warmed. It also answered her question about what to do next. Tevi turned and headed back to the centre of town.

Presumably to give an air of formality to the audience, somebody had placed a high-sided chair in their room and draped it in fur and bright cloth to make it more throne-like. However, when Tevi entered, Jemeryl was still standing. She was also alone, apart from Klara perched on the chair's back. The sorcerer looked tired and agitated, but gave a warm smile.

"You got the message?"

"The herald? Yes." Tevi glanced around. "Where...?"

"He'll be here soon. Mavek is mind-riding an ordinary soldier. I thought it would be wise for Curnad to check him out for dart guns or other hidden surprises."

"Mind-riding?" Tevi understood the term. She had seen Jemeryl perform the trick often enough with Klara. The use of a human as the subject was what concerned Tevi. The ruthless abuse of magic was common in Tirakhalod, but not something she would have expected from Mavek.

"Obviously he wants to talk with me himself but is only prepared to risk putting someone expendable within striking distance of me." Jemeryl looked down, shamefaced. "I guess I can't blame him."

Tevi might have argued, but at that point, the door opened and the herald was ushered in. As Jemeryl had said, the man was a common soldier, dressed in the tattered and dirt-stained relics of Bykoda's uniform. The only thing to mark him as an official herald was the broken arrow he carried, a sign of truce.

However, the man's appearance was not without significance—if you knew what to look for. His manner caught Tevi's attention at once. His movements were jerky and his hands trembled. His lips had a blue tinge. The pupils of his eyes were too large and too dark. Bloody rags fringed the tops of his boots. Tevi caught her breath. The implications were appalling and she wondered whether Jemeryl would realise the significance.

Captain Curnad had followed the herald into the room and now stood by the doorway, looking hopeful. He clearly would have liked to stay for the discussion, but Jemeryl waved him away. As he left, he cast a resentful scowl at Tevi, although he made no complaint.

Jemeryl waited for a few seconds after the door was closed before speaking—possibly using her sorcerer senses to check that Curnad was not loitering outside. "Mavek, I don't know what you're hoping to achieve by this. You know I won't give you the talisman. It isn't safe to use."

"Bykoda used it all right. But if you're worried about safety, why don't you join me? You can monitor what I do with it to make sure there are no risks. Don't you see that it will work out well for both of us? If...if I have Kenan..." For a moment his composure faltered. "I've got to have Kenan. Then I won't have any reason to kill Bykoda, so you'll get your partner back as well. Nobody will be hurt. We'll both be happy." The herald's voice was at least an octave higher than Mavek's bass rumble, but the intonation was instantly identifiable as the blacksmith's.

Tevi guessed that he had not recognised her. Unsurprising, since she was still wearing her helmet. She tugged it off and cleared her throat. "Um...I'm not dead."

The herald's head jerked in her direction. "You? What...?" He spun back to Jemeryl. "No! It's not fair. How did you do it?" His voice broke into to a shout of outrage. "You used the talisman."

"I didn't. And it doesn't work like that. If I'd used the talisman then you wouldn't have known—"

Mavek was not listening. "You give that crap about the talisman not being safe. You used it. You changed time to get her back."

"No, I—"

"Not safe? You just want to keep it for yourself."

"It isn't safe. And if it ruptures it will kill thousands of people."

"Like you care."

"I do care."

"You didn't care about me." Tears glittered in his eyes. "No one has ever cared about me, apart from Kenan. She loved me. I love her."

"Mavek, I'm sorry. I'm really sorry."

"Don't say that!" He was screaming. "I'm going to get the talisman. You're surrounded, and I have you outnumbered. You can't beat us all. If you don't surrender, I'll destroy the town and kill everyone here, and prise the talisman from your dead fingers. I'm going to get it and you can't stop me."

Tevi had been listening with increasing concern. "There's no need to attack the town. The people here are innocent."

"So was Kenan." He flung an accusatory finger towards Jemeryl. "She says that she cares about other people. We'll see how much she cares when my troops are hacking their way through the poor townsfolk of Uzhenek. I swear, nobody will get out of here alive."

Tevi was appalled. "Mavek. What's happened to you? You weren't like this in Tirakhalod."

"She happened to me. But it doesn't matter what I do. Because once I get the talisman, I can change things so that none of it even takes place." He turned back to Jemeryl, advancing so that his face was mere inches from hers. "If I don't get the talisman, then all the people I kill will stay dead, and it will all be your fault."

The herald jolted as if he had been punched, and his eyes glazed. When they cleared again, his expression was one of fear and confusion.

His head jerked from side to side, clearly trying to work out where he was. Mavek had gone.

"You can go. As a herald you have safe passage from this town," Tevi told him.

Possibly, the man had some idea of what had happened to him. He nodded and scuttled from the room like a rabbit chased by hounds. As the door slammed shut behind him, Jemeryl sank onto the chair with her head in her hands.

"He's right. It is my fault."

Tevi moved to Jemeryl's side and put a hand on her shoulder. "No, it isn't. It's a stupid argument. Mavek is responsible for his own actions."

"Some of the blame is mine. I can't ignore the part I played in sending him over the edge." Jemeryl wrapped her arms around Tevi's waist and buried her face in Tevi's stomach. "He wouldn't be so bad if I hadn't hurt him."

"You don't know that for certain."

"I can't imagine the old Mavek threatening to wipe out Uzhenek."

"Can you stop him?"

"Mavek on his own, no trouble, even if he had another of the acolytes helping him. But I won't stand a chance against all six, and he'll have dozens of witches in support, and all his weapons ready." Jemeryl leaned back and looked up at Tevi. "I'm sorry. I know that you feel responsible for the townsfolk, but we're going to have to make a run for it. With luck, I'll be able to sneak us through the lines. Maybe he won't attack once he learns that we've gone."

"He'll attack at first light tomorrow before he has the chance to find out. And we've got no hope of outrunning him."

"Why not?"

"The state the herald was in. Did you notice his blue lips and the way he twitched?"

Jemeryl shook her head. "Not really. What does...?"

"It's one of Dunarth's potions. She calls it sleepstop. The troops have cruder names for it. When someone takes it, they don't sleep, they don't feel tired, they don't feel much pain. As long as they take the drug, they can run all day and all night until they drop dead."

"And that's how he got his army here so quickly. I'd been

wondering—" Jemeryl broke off, frowning. "It can't be safe."

"It isn't. Like I said, people will keep going until their hearts burst. But the really dangerous time is when the effect wears off, and the build up of exhaustion hits all at once. If his foot soldiers have run all the way from Tirakhalod, then I guess that two-thirds of them will be dead once they stop taking the drug, and the other third won't be far from it. I doubt that he has enough sleepstop to keep his army going for more than another day or two, which is why he's going to attack at the very first opportunity. He won't have an army left once the sleepstop runs out. But the only real use he has for common soldiers is to deal with large numbers of ungifted opponents. Once Uzhenek is massacred, he won't have any more need of them."

"Why did the soldiers agree to take it?"

"Because very nasty things happen to common soldiers in Bykoda's army who don't obey orders."

Jemeryl's grip on Tevi tightened. "Did anyone ever force you to take it?"

"No. They never give it to officers. The witches are too valuable to risk losing, and they wouldn't have wanted to upset you by making an exception in my case. But they give it to horses. Which is another reason why Mavek will attack early. We won't be able to outrun him if his horses don't need to rest. He'll want to conserve stocks so that if we escape from Uzhenek, he'll be able to keep the acolytes and witches on horseback for as long as it takes to catch us."

"So what do we do?"

Tevi closed her eyes. Through her mind ran images of the excited children chasing after her, the cheering soldiers wearing their blue and black braids, and the weeping mother clinging to her. "We can't abandon the townsfolk, but I don't see how we can protect them."

"At the moment, I don't see how we can do anything. I wish I'd never come to Tirakhalod."

Tevi cut off the self-recrimination. "This isn't your fault."

"Yes, it is. The only reason—"

"No. The only reason we're in this mess is because Bykoda wanted to rewrite her past mistakes. But the way you deal with your mistakes is to face the consequences, make what amends you can, learn, grow, and move on. That's what life is, growth and change."

"Do you really think that?"

"Yes."

Tevi knelt and pulled her lover into a hug. She had to get Jemeryl into a more positive frame of mind if they were to stand any chance. Her eyes flitted around the room, hunting inspiration, and then she spotted Klara, perched on the back of the chair.

"Could Klara take the talisman?"

"Kla—Where?"

"To Lyremouth. It isn't that heavy. Could she carry it and fly over the Barrodens?"

Jemeryl summoned her familiar onto her outstretched hand and considered the magpie thoughtfully. "I'd guess so. Certainly with a couple of spells to help her along. But it would be dangerous."

"More dangerous than the talisman staying here? If we sent her off now, by dawn tomorrow she'd be hundreds of miles away. Then we could tell Mavek that there was no point attacking Uzhenek, because the talisman was beyond his reach no matter what he did."

Jemeryl shook her head. "He's psychotic. He still might kill us. But I could fix it so that Klara would carry on, even after my death. Except she wouldn't have any protection. She'd be as vulnerable as an ordinary magpie. There are buzzards and hawks on the plains, and eagles in the high Barrodens. If she was killed, the talisman would be left lying around for anyone to pick up."

Klara ruffled her feathers. "Charming! For a moment there I thought you were worried about me."

Tevi grinned, mainly in relief. It was the first time that Klara had spoken since Jemeryl had arrived in Uzhenek. Playing with the familiar as her alter ego was the best sign yet that the sorcerer was getting back to normal.

Tevi dragged a second chair over and sat down beside Jemeryl. "We could keep it as a last resort, if we can't come up with a better plan. The risk of Klara getting attacked by eagles is still safer than the certainty of Mavek using the talisman."

Jemeryl nodded. "True. But there has to be another option. We just need to work it out." She rested her chin on her fist and stared at the wall opposite, but then her gaze returned to Tevi. "Come on. You're supposed to be the military tactical expert here. Haven't you got any good ideas from playing on your battle table?"

Tevi opened her mouth to deny having any worthwhile ability, then closed it again, frowning in thought. Similarities with various other battles leapt into her head, although none of them had a positive outcome.

"Well...as a straight battle, it's hopeless. So we need to come at the problem from a different angle. See if we can think of a way to attack that Mavek won't expect and won't have made plans for. The biggest mistake any commander ever makes is in letting the enemy pick the battle plan. We can't afford to merely react to what Mavek does."

"What sort of thing are you thinking of?"

"Nothing definite at the moment. But we need to really search our memories and make sure we aren't overlooking anything. Somewhere there has to be something we can use. And the more unconventional it is, the more likely that it will outfox Mavek."

Jemeryl reached out and took hold of Tevi's hand. At the touch, Tevi felt a grin grow on her face. The situation still looked grim, but working together, she was sure they would find a way through.

CHAPTER FIFTEEN—NIGHT SORTIE

Sunset was long past and the moon was low on the horizon. A cold wind gusted over the plains. Darkness in Mavek's camp was broken only by the flickering from campfires, each with its knot of soldiers huddled around, silent and unsleeping. Their eyes were fixed on the snapping flames. Most were standing, a few sat, but none lay on the ground, apart from the dead.

As Tevi marched by one group, a soldier collapsed in a shuddering heap and then was still. She glanced at him in passing—an older man, heavily built. It was always the ones with tired hearts who went first. His comrades dragged him away, to add to the piles forming out on the plains beyond. As yet, the number of corpses was small in relation to the size of the army, but once the sleepstop ran out, the situation would change. Who would be left to bury them all?

Tevi's teeth clamped together. For the moment, qualms about her mission faded. Cold-blooded assassination was not something she could ever feel happy about, but Mavek had to be stopped.

Jemeryl marched in line behind her. Tevi would have preferred walking side by side, and even holding hands for comfort, except that the action might compromise their pretence of being soldiers in Mavek's army. After considerable debate, Jemeryl had decided not to use magic, either to disguise them or render them invisible. The ungifted and most witches would not see through the cover, but in the case of the acolytes, magical disguise would alert rather than fool them. And the acolytes were the ones who posed the greatest risk. Anyone else, Jemeryl might have some chance of silencing without raising the alarm.

A simple spell had diverted the attention of the sentries when they infiltrated the enemy line. Apart from this, Tevi and Jemeryl were merely dressed in the uniforms of common soldiers with smears of mud across their faces for disguise. So far, it was working. No one was giving them a second look as they marched through the camp in search of Mavek's quarters.

Tevi had been tempted to ask directions at one of the fires. Was it unreasonable that in a camp of this size, some soldiers with a legitimate need to find the commanding officer might not know where he had based himself? However, there was no need to take the risk. Time was not an issue and they had only to march the full circuit in a purposeful fashion to locate their target.

Seen from Uzhenek, the campfires formed a perfect, unbroken ring. From in their midst, the situation was far more chaotic. Sentry points had been set at regular intervals encircling the city, but behind them, the fires were scattered at random, without planning or order. The gaps between them varied from a spear length to an arrow flight. The most distant were a quarter mile out into the plains.

Supplies and weapons had been dropped wherever the owners saw fit. Bows and swords lay unprotected in the damp grass. Some groups had made attempts to erect bivouacs, but few were completed, and none were in use. Tevi wondered at the mental state of the soldiers. In Ranenok's section of the army, sleepstop had been given as a last resort. In her time serving under him, Tevi had only seen it used twice. Both instances had been for short periods, but even then, the deterioration in the soldiers' ability to think and act rationally had been manifest.

These soldiers were clearly not in a normal frame of mind. If it came to battle, how would they perform? Could they still obey orders? Would they be able to fight at all? Or might they be reduced to acting like frenzied animals? That last possibility was obviously the most worrying.

Tevi gave a quick glance behind her. Jemeryl had been very keen not to take the lead, in case they were stopped and questioned. Not only was there slightly more chance of Jemeryl's face being recognised by someone with enough power to cause problems, but the experience at the fort in Redezth had shown the gaps in her experience. Leaving the talking to someone who could give the right sort of military answers was definitely a good idea.

Walking along, Tevi once again reflected in amazement on her lover's naivety. How long had Jemeryl thought a captured deserter would be allowed to live? If it had not been for the captain's desire to make a public example, Tevi doubted that they would have even bothered taking Jemeryl as far as the cell. Did Jemeryl not have the first idea of what the life of a common soldier in Bykoda's army was like?

A soft tap on the arm broke into her thoughts. Jemeryl was pointing furtively towards a distant collection of tents gathered around a high pavilion. A stacked bonfire blazed in an open space before it like a beacon. The skyline beyond was broken by the ominous silhouettes of huge catapults and trebuchets. A trio of banners flapping in the wind provided further confirmation that this was Mavek's headquarters. If he was not in the pavilion, then he would surely not be far away. Tevi changed course.

From some way off, Tevi could see a few figures gathered around the bonfire, clearly in search of warmth. However, unlike the common soldiers, these stood in relaxed poses. A flagon was making the rounds on the far side. Heads were turned together in conversation. Obviously the people here had not taken sleepstop, which meant that they were most likely officer witches.

Tevi's intention was to skirt around the headquarters area, avoiding the firelight, and then loop back behind the pavilion. Only when it was too late did she spot the two people standing alone in shadows between outlying tents.

Ranenok was facing in their direction, although his attention was focused on another person who had her back to them—Kharel. Tevi recognised the seer from her outline against the firelight. The pair were standing close and holding hands. Either they were taking chances, or Mavek was unconcerned about liaisons between his more powerful followers.

The path Tevi was on went within a few feet of where the two acolytes stood. And it was too late to back away. Such behaviour would only risk drawing attention to herself. Tevi marched on without a pause.

Her old commander was clearly unhappy. The stump of his left arm was tapping his side in a gesture she recognised as annoyance. Even in the darkness, the frown on his face was unmistakeable. The faint glimmer from the bonfire accentuated the downturn of his lips.

Tevi passed by close enough to hear him murmur to his lover, "I wish I knew what was going on in Mavek's head. Why ruin the army to attack a town like Uzhenek? What does he want from Jemeryl?"

For a second, Tevi was tempted to stop and answer the questions. She still respected Ranenok and would rather have him as an ally than an enemy. Maybe she and Jemeryl could tell him the truth and win him over, but the risk was not worth the chance. She carried on.

For his part, Ranenok did not even glance in her direction. At that time of night, few common soldiers were still occupied with errands, but enough were active to make the sight of two more marching through the camp unworthy of notice. The sound of his voice faded into the night behind her.

Beyond the tents lay an unoccupied region given over to engines of war. Tevi wondered why they had been dragged all the way from Tirakhalod. Was it just Mavek seizing the chance to play with his creations, like a child with a previously forbidden toy? Uzhenek no longer had any walls to batter down and no defences to justify using such overwhelming power.

On Tevi's right, the machines were a silent, deadly presence. On her left, the nearest campfire was more than fifty yards away. No one was around to see or hear them. Tevi checked to front and rear and then ducked into a gap between two carts. Here the darkness was total. She felt, rather than saw, Jemeryl slip into the space beside her.

"We've found his headquarters. What now?" Tevi asked.

"You could wait here while I go to tackle Mavek."

"No."

Jemeryl had not wanted Tevi to come on the night sortie and had initially tried to talk her out of it. Only Tevi's experience with the army had silenced her objections and cut short the argument, since there was no chance that Tevi would have quickly agreed to her lover going alone. She was not about to change her mind now.

Jemeryl sighed but did not try to restart the debate. "Well then. I guess that we sneak up carefully, find Mavek, and kill him."

Tevi could not bring herself to speak. She had liked Mavek, and now she was preparing to murder him. Restraining a groan, she let her head fall back and looked up. Black against the stars were the outlines of giant catapults mounted on carts. Their ammunition would be nothing so mundane as rocks. The vision of fire and acid falling on Uzhenek rose before her mind's eye. Tevi thought of the girl who had brought the message about the herald, with her trusting smile and coloured braids, and then imagined the sight, sound, and smell of the girl screaming as the flesh was seared from her bones.

Alternately, Tevi thought of Mavek claiming the talisman and destroying half the world. The scenario was less gruesome and violent, but far more devastating. The people would not merely die, but never even have existed. Their lives would be erased utterly.

Mavek had to be stopped.

"Did you hear what Ranenok was saying?" Jemeryl asked.

Tevi drew a deep breath and turned her thoughts away from images of death. "Yes. And I bet he's not the only one who's confused by Mavek's behaviour."

"None of the ordinary soldiers were talking."

"That's the sleepstop. At first it makes people jabber away, but as time goes on, they get quieter and quieter."

"Did you see any other acolytes around the fire?"

"No. I kept my eyes straight ahead. Why?"

"I wonder what happened to Anid. She can't have passed on what I told her to Ranenok or Kharel."

"Do you think she challenged Mavek?"

"She said that she was going to."

"Mavek is still here, so I guess he killed her before she got the chance to speak to the other acolytes."

Jemeryl only sighed in response.

"Whatever happened to her isn't your fault."

"You keep saying that about everything."

Tevi found Jemeryl's hand in the darkness and squeezed it. "Once we're safely back in Lyremouth, you have my permission to start wallowing in guilt, but not before."

"I may hold you to that."

Despite the words, Tevi could hear a smile in Jemeryl's tone. Tevi squeezed her hand once more and then let go. "Time to move?"

"Yes. I'll lead."

Jemeryl slipped past her and continued along the space between the carts. The darkness was too complete for Tevi to see anything, and she only realised that Jemeryl had stopped when she banged into the sorcerer's back.

"What is it?"

"There's a trap set here."

"Magical?"

"Yep."

"Can you disable it?"

"Of course. Hang on one minute."

Closer to five passed before Jemeryl took Tevi's hand and guided her on. At the end of the carts was a narrow gap, and then Tevi's elbow brushed against the round sides of stacked barrels. A tug from Jemeryl drew her right, left, and right again, past the huge wheels of more wagons.

"You need to duck," Jemeryl whispered.

"Another trap?"

"No. You're about to walk into the shaft."

Tevi reached out with her free hand and felt the wooden pole at nose height. She dipped under it. Jemeryl had once explained that her sorcerer senses did not allow her see in the dark, but if she concentrated, she could spot where things were. Tevi assumed there was a difference.

Twice more they stopped for Jemeryl to disable traps. This was clearly a region where the ungifted where not supposed to be wandering. At last, Jemeryl pulled her down into a crouch, between a final huge set of wheels at the end of a wagon. Tevi looked up. Blocking out the stars above her, like a gallows, was the towering frame of a trebuchet.

In front was a clear strip of trampled grass, twenty feet or more in width. The weak rays from the rising moon shed just enough light for Tevi to make out the rear of the pavilion at the other side. She was about to whisper a question in Jemeryl's ear when she heard the sound of footsteps. Three witches strolled into view. The one in the centre was carrying an oil-soaked torch.

She yawned loudly. "I think I could do with a dose of sleepstop."

"I'd rather have brandy."

"I'd rather be back in my bed."

"Alone?"

"To be honest, I'm too tired to care. Just as long as they don't steal all the blankets."

"War is hell." The other two laughed at the dry tone.

"Especially when your leader has lost his marbles."

The laughter stopped.

"I mean, hypothetically speaking." The speaker backtracked on his words.

"Yeah, right."

The three witches had now passed the point where Tevi and Jemeryl were hidden. Tevi was just starting to relax when one of them stopped and looked back. For a moment it seemed as if he was staring directly at her, but then he wiped a hand over his face.

"Dammit, I'm tired."

"We all are."

One of his colleagues looped an arm through his and towed him away. The witch went, unresisting.

Tevi looked at Jemeryl. The sorcerer had her hands up in a warding gesture. Only when the witches had passed from view did she lower her arms.

"That was close," Tevi said.

"Very."

"Now we cut our way into the tent?"

"Yes. And hope that plan number one works. Because I'm not so keen on either two or three."

Jemeryl darted across the grass, beckoning for Tevi to follow. The material of the pavilion shimmered like silk, even in the weak light. Jemeryl ran her hand over it and then drew her knife from her belt sheath. While she carefully unpicked a seam, Tevi knelt by her side, anxiously looking out for the return of the witches. Were they sentries walking a patrol, or just incidental passers-by? Would they be back?

The cutting of the row of stitches, one by one, progressed with agonising slowness, but Tevi trusted that Jemeryl had her reasons for not simply slicing the material. Presumably, magic had been woven into the fabric. Minutes trickled by before the gap was big enough to crawl though. Jemeryl went first. Tevi followed, after one final look back for the patrolling witches.

The rear of the pavilion had been divided into separate sections by hanging drapes. The space they entered was being used for storage. Several small crates were stacked to one side. A saddlebag had been dumped in a corner, and a mound of clothing was heaped in the centre. Through a gap in the curtain, Tevi could see into the central region of the tent where glowing iron braziers gave off both heat and light.

Jemeryl moved forwards slowly, placing each foot with care. At the opening, she stopped for a long time, studying the space beyond before she slipped through. Tevi made to follow, but an upheld hand caused her to freeze. Jemeryl shook her head sharply. Their eyes met in a silent argument. Tevi clenched her jaw but then nodded.

The likelihood was high that Mavek would have set traps and alarms. Tevi knew that she could do nothing except trigger them. This was a task that Jemeryl must tackle alone, but she could keep watch— for what good it might do.

The dull light from the braziers cast a red glow over the carpets and cushions on the floor and the tray bearing the half-eaten remains of a meal. A heavy curtain hung over the entrance. The bonfire outside threw huge shadows of the army officers over the front of the pavilion. Tevi's attention switched between the moving images and Jemeryl.

Step by step, the sorcerer advanced across the pavilion, avoiding some spots and stopping to weave patterns in the air at others. Tevi could feel her heart pounding as she watched. From outside the tent came the crackle of the bonfire and the murmured conversation of witches. The only other sound was the wind rippling over the roof of the pavilion.

By the central support post, Jemeryl halted and looked around. Her gaze fixed on some drapes partitioning off another section of the large tent. She looked back to Tevi and nodded slowly and with meaning. Mavek was there.

Jemeryl continued her stealthy progress. She was almost within six feet of the section when the curtain hanging over the entrance to the pavilion was pulled back and Ranenok appeared.

For a moment, everyone was frozen in shock, and then Ranenok drew breath.

Tevi leapt forwards. "Wait, listen."

Ranenok paid no attention. "Help! Intruders! To me!"

Shouts erupted in the night. The clamour was drowned out by the sudden roar of flame. Jemeryl had hurled a web of fire at the concealing drapes. From somewhere nearby Mavek's voice rose in a strangled scream, but the cry was of fear and surprise, not pain.

Burning tatters of material fell to the floor, revealing the blacksmith rising from his bed. And before him was a glowing blue screen. The chances had never been good that he would have gone to sleep unprotected. When he saw Jemeryl, his expression changed to one of raw, hysterical panic.

More officers burst in through the entrance behind Ranenok. Tevi was sure that Jemeryl would be able to break through Mavek's shield, but she would need time. Tevi doubted that she would be able to buy more than a second or two, but maybe it would be enough. She drew her sword and charged forwards.

Ranenok turned to face her. His eyes held a look of regret, even as he raised his hand. Tevi saw the cartwheel of sparks stream towards her. They hit, and then there was only blackness.

❖

Tevi came back to consciousness with a burning ache in her joints. Her face was pressed into the rough floor carpet and all she could see were boots moving back and forth in front of her eyes. Her arms were bent behind her—tied, she realised, when she tried to move them. Voices murmured in disjointed sentences.

Shouts reverberated in the distance, and then the sound of pounding footsteps became louder. Someone burst into the pavilion. "She's got away, sir."

Tevi's head cleared a little. Were they referring to Jemeryl?

"Where did she go?" The voice Tevi recognised as belonging to Dunarth.

"It doesn't matter." This time it was Mavek who spoke. "She won't go far."

"You hope."

"I know. Because she's going to want to talk to me."

A hand grabbed Tevi's hair and hauled her to her knees, and then wrenched her neck back. She was staring directly up into Mavek's face. The blacksmith's eyes still showed the fading traces of his fear. A tic jumped in his cheek, but his lips were set in a twisted leer as he studied her.

"We have a bargaining chip that Jemeryl won't be able to ignore."

❖

Jemeryl sat alone in the room with her head clasped in her hands, trying to fight back her despair. Assassinating Mavek had always been a long shot. Everything would have been so much simpler and less fraught had it worked, but she had to remain positive. Their plans were not totally in ruins, even though Tevi had been captured.

The most hopeful sign was that, although dawn was long past, Mavek's troops had not yet attacked. If Tevi was right about the limited supplies of the drug, this could only mean that Mavek had another scheme in mind. The most likely candidate for this new plan was some sort of negotiation involving Tevi, which had to mean that she was alive and in a fit state to be traded.

The next move was therefore up to Mavek. Jemeryl fought to remind herself that every hour of delay would be working to her advantage, but the waiting was torturous. Even so, the knock at the door was unwelcome. Regardless of how things went, the next few hours were unlikely to be pleasant, and the person wanting to see her might only be Captain Curnad ready to repeat the appeals for information that she had no intention of granting.

Jemeryl braced herself for the worst and called out, "Enter."

The face that appeared around the door did not belong to Curnad, nor to anyone else she knew. Had the captain and other witches abandoned her? Not that it mattered.

"Ma'am. An envoy from the enemy is here to see you."

Listlessly, Jemeryl signalled for the messenger to be shown in.

A few moments later the door opened again for the deputy blacksmith, Cluthotin, who looked no happier or less nervous than the last time they had met.

The two of them stared at each other in silence for a while and then Cluthotin cleared his throat. "Jemeryl. The Emperor Mavek wishes to speak with you in person and asks that you accompany me to see him." He looked at her significantly. "He promises that you will not be harmed."

The request was pretty much what she had been expecting. Jemeryl merely nodded and stood. The waiting was over. Now it was time to see how the game would play out.

The streets of Uzhenek were crowded but quieter than Jemeryl had ever heard them before, making the wailing of infants all the more noticeable. The adults gathered in small groups, heads together, muttering, or sat alone in doorways, huddled in sullen despair. Their faces held anger, bewilderment, and fear. Jemeryl knew that tales of the failed sortie had spread through the town. Her own blazing retreat had ensured that it could not be kept secret. Were the rumours also now spreading that the Dragon Slayer was captured, or dead?

Jemeryl looked at the squalid, rotting huts and mud-filled roads, the people dressed in rags and the half-naked children. Tevi was right. These people had so little, it was not fair if even this should be taken from them. The attempt to assassinate Mavek had been made on their behalf, to limit the risk of an all-out attack. Jemeryl thought about the gnawing of her own bad conscience. No matter how things went, Jemeryl understood why Tevi had been willing to take the risks she had, and respected her decision.

Cluthotin led the way to the side of town nearest the escarpment. When she emerged from between the last of the huts, Jemeryl could see that the valley rim was lined with a hundred or more people. These would undoubtedly be the massed witches and acolytes, Mavek's insurance that she would not use the opportunity for another assassination attempt. However, Mavek must be very certain that he had her in his grasp. He had to be sure that she would not try to explain to everyone assembled just how Bykoda's death had taken place and what was really going on.

Mavek's standard flew in the middle of the line, at a point where a slight projection from the lip of the escarpment made a natural platform. As she grew closer to the spot, Jemeryl easily identified the tall form of the blacksmith in a regal stance, flanked by three of the other acolytes. Anid was not one of them, she noted.

At Cluthotin's indication, Jemeryl stopped fifty yards below where Mavek stood. Close enough to see and hear, but not close enough to hope that a surprise attack might get through—not when the witches and acolytes were alert and ready to come to his defence. Jemeryl's escort backed away a few steps, leaving her alone.

She struck her own pose, hands on hips and head thrown back. "You wanted to talk."

Mavek took a half-step forwards. "No. I wanted you to surrender."

"You've already made the suggestion once. In case you've forgotten, I refused."

"I think you're the one with the bad memory. Have you so soon forgotten what happened last night?"

Mavek turned and gestured to the witches standing behind him. On cue, Tevi was dragged forwards and thrown to her knees beside him. Despite the circumstances, Jemeryl felt her heart leap to see her lover, alive and whole. Their eyes met across the distance, and momentarily the rest of the scene faded from her thoughts. Jemeryl took a breath. It was all going to work out all right. It had to. She looked back to Mavek.

"I hadn't forgotten. But in order for a threat to be effective, what happens when you refuse has to be worse than what happens when you give in. Tevi's life is far more at risk if I surrender."

"It's a debatable point. But even if it were true, there are lots of different ways to die."

Mavek gave another signal. This time, Dunarth stepped up to stand behind Tevi. She placed her hands on either side of the kneeling woman's head. For an instant, Tevi froze, and then her body bucked. A scream was torn from her throat.

"Stop that!" Jemeryl shouted. Regardless of the forces gathered above her, she could not prevent herself from reacting. Her hands moved, summoning the elements.

All along the line of witches, there was an immediate response, arms and staffs at the ready. Jemeryl froze. The battle would be hopeless, and no matter what else, Mavek would surely not allow Tevi to die right now. She forced her hands back to her side.

For another minute, Tevi's screams rang out over the valley. Each one ripped through Jemeryl—more potent than any injury inflicted on herself. And then, at last, Dunarth released her grip and stepped back. Tevi collapsed to the ground in a ball, shuddering convulsively. Jemeryl's eyes could not pull away from the sight. Her stomach felt as if it held needles of ice, while the remainder of her insides had turned to water. Her knees shook, threatening to give way.

"Jemeryl!" Mavek's shout barely reclaimed her attention. "Do you want to think again about surrendering?"

In all her planning and calculating, Jemeryl had not expected to be quite so completely overwhelmed by impotent fury. Controlling her breath enough to reply was beyond her. Jemeryl was aware that

Cluthotin had returned to her side. Slowly, she turned her head towards him. The witch was holding out an iron collar. Jemeryl's gaze travelled up to Mavek, then on to Tevi's crumpled form, and finally back again to Cluthotin.

Wordlessly, Jemeryl took the collar from his hand, lifted it up, and snapped it shut around her own neck.

❖

The inside of Mavek's pavilion showed evidence of clearing up after the previous night's battle. Somebody had hastily patched the gash in the wall that Jemeryl had created during her escape and removed the damaged braziers. The floor had been swept clean, removing any scraps of burnt cloth, although the scorch marks were still there.

Jemeryl squinted at her surroundings through half-shut eyes—not that it helped. Her eyes were not the problem. The energy tensors of the sixth dimension streamed through the iron collar. They covered her head in a chaotic vortex of power that blinded her to anything beyond. The auras of the fifth dimension were shifting and untouchable, like shadows falling on water. Time was linear, locked, and unbranching.

She felt so vulnerable, worse than ungifted. Her sorcerer's senses were now a liability, not an asset. In an attempt to stave off the panic, she concentrated on her ordinary senses. Tevi coped with just four dimensions under her control. She could do the same. She had to. The impending conversation with Mavek was too critical to make a mistake, and she had mere seconds to compose herself while he ordered his followers to leave.

Mavek waited until Jemeryl and he were alone before speaking. He smiled at her in triumph. "It's time for you to give me the talisman."

"I can't."

"You're not in any position to refuse."

"I don't mean I won't. I mean I can't. I don't have the talisman to give you."

"You're lying."

"No. Last night, before we left Uzhenek on the way to your camp, I dispatched the talisman to Lyremouth with my familiar. You remember, Klara the magpie? We knew that the attempt to kill you was not certain to succeed, so we wanted the talisman safely away from here. Of course, if the attempt had succeeded, I would have called her back before she had gone too far."

Mavek grabbed Jemeryl's shoulders. His fingers dug painfully into her joints. "You're lying."

Jemeryl shook her head in answer.

"Call it back, now."

Jemeryl jerked her jaw upwards to emphasise the iron collar around her neck. "Even if I wanted to, I couldn't with this on."

"It's all a trick to get me to take the collar off."

"No."

"Well, I know how to check." He stalked to the entrance of the pavilion and called to the people outside. "Bring the other prisoner here at once."

"There's no point in hurting her," Jemeryl said quickly.

"I won't...much."

A minute passed before the curtain opened and Tevi was brought in by two witches. Her eyes were still glazed from the punishment she had received at Dunarth's hands and her feet stumbled. She seemed oblivious to where she was. Jemeryl felt her stomach clench at the sight. Mavek gestured for the witches to leave. With them gone, he then advanced towards the bound prisoner.

"Please," Jemeryl begged. She could not bear to see Tevi hurt more.

Mavek ignored her. He placed one of his huge hands on Tevi's head. With the other, he drew patterns in the air, spell-binding his victim. The effect was less dramatic than the previous magical assault. At first Tevi did no more than shudder. Then she gasped loudly and her eyes closed. When they reopened, they were utterly blank and devoid of life.

"Last night, when you left Uzhenek, what were your plans?" Mavek demanded.

"We were going to kill you." Tevi's voice was an apathetic monotone.

"And what did you do with the talisman?"

"Jemeryl sent it off to Lyremouth with Klara. She would only call Klara back if you died."

Mavek swore and shoved Tevi away. She fell limply, without any attempt to save herself and then lay, unmoving, where she landed.

"You're going to call it back." Mavek snarled the words at Jemeryl.

"I don't even know if can. By now, Klara should be halfway through the Barroden Mountains."

"If you can't, you are going to regret it. I swear. You will regret it." He loomed over Jemeryl, pinning her against the central support post. His voice softened. "I won't harm you. But I'll hurt her." He pointed at Tevi's unconscious body on the floor. "I'll hurt her so much that she'll beg for death. In the end, you'll kill her yourself as an act of mercy. And then I'll leave you to live with that knowledge for the rest of your life. Do you understand?"

Jemeryl nodded, appalled by the intensity of anger in his eyes.

Mavek continued. "I'm going to get Dunarth in here and get her to take your poor sweetheart over to the far side of camp with a large escort. You're then going to have five minutes to establish contact with your familiar and get her to return. If you don't, or if you attack me so I can't send Dunarth the right message, then I'll make sure that she has some suitable instructions to implement. Is that clear?"

"Yes."

"And do you agree?"

Jemeryl could feel tears forming in her eyes. She looked at Tevi, who was starting to stir. At that moment, their plans were irrelevant. Everything was irrelevant except Tevi's safety. She dare not risk further defiance; she could only hope.

"Yes. I agree."

❖

Jemeryl gasped in relief as the whirlpool of forces around her head dissolved.

Mavek stepped back, holding the open iron collar in his hands. "Hurry up. You don't have long. And I'm going to be monitoring what you're doing, so you'd better get back in contact with your familiar and don't try anything clever."

Jemeryl nodded. Any show of aggression on her part would be futile. Apart from Dunarth holding Tevi as assurance of her good behaviour, Ranenok and Kharel with two dozen witches were just outside the pavilion, armed with a selection of weaponry. They would spot any attempt to overpower Mavek.

However, Jemeryl wondered if they had noted that a sorcerer who could so spectacularly defeat Bykoda needed such elaborate protection against her. And what conclusions might they draw? However, there seemed little hope that they would come to her aid or mount their own challenge to Mavek.

Jemeryl knew that she was on her own, and she had to make sure that she gave Mavek no grounds to further mistreat Tevi. A show of instant obedience was wise. She closed her eyes and started to focus her thoughts, opening pathways through the upper dimensions. Her projection shot along waves in the ether, as she sought the small avian aura that was intimately bound to her own.

The blacksmith's aura was a shadowy presence, skittering around the edges of her search, but Jemeryl knew his claim to be monitoring her interaction with Klara was a bluff. The blacksmith, with his weak grasp on the fifth dimension, could not hope to follow her. Even Dunarth would have found it impossible. The bond between sorcerer and familiar was the strongest that magic could forge and impenetrable to anyone else. In a very real sense, Klara was her. As long as they were both alive, the ties between them could not be broken.

The bonds reformed and she melded with Klara enough to sense her surroundings and know that the magpie was not flying, but underground.

"No!" Jemeryl jerked back, ducking as if from a blow.

"What is it?"

"Klara. She's been attacked."

"By what?"

"An eagle, at the edge of the Barrodens."

Mavek leaned across and grabbed Jemeryl's jaw in one hand, squeezing in her cheeks. He forced her head up and his eyes searched hers. "You're playing tricks with me."

"No. I swear it."

He let go of her. "And?"

"Klara. I...I think her wing is broken, but she managed to escape. She's in a rabbit hole, hiding. We have to get to her."

"Has she still got the talisman?"

"Yes. Of course."

For a moment, it looked as if Mavek would strike her, but then he snapped the collar back around Jemeryl's neck and pulled her forwards until their faces were mere inches apart.

"All right. We'll go south. After all, time isn't an issue. But if you're playing games, then you will end up being sorry. I promise you. Death will be an easy option."

CHAPTER SIXTEEN—CALLING IN THE STAKES

D ry coughs rasped in the woman's throat. Her fingers were curled like birds' claws over her chest. Her body contorted in the fight to draw air into her lungs, but it lacked the strength to succeed. As Jemeryl watched, the woman's battle ended. Her last breath escaped in a sigh and her fingers relaxed. Another dead soldier.

Horrified, Jemeryl fixed her gaze on the horizon. The scene was being repeated all around Uzhenek. The effect was so much more pitiful in that the soldiers died quietly, without thrashing around or screaming for help. They had no reserves of energy left to carry them through the period of the drug's withdrawal.

Jemeryl's horse tossed its head and shuffled nervously, unsettled by the scent of death. The orderly who was holding the reins swore and gave a sharp tug. The action was far more forceful than was necessary to stop the horse wandering. Jemeryl guessed that the young man was feeling on edge. How could he not be? He was an ungifted soldier who for some reason had been spared the fate of his fellows. His survival was probably due to nothing but chance. The officers needed cooks, stable-hands, and lackeys to perform various menial tasks, and therefore a few common soldiers had not been given sleepstop.

The orderly's eyes were locked on the horse's neck. Was it a deliberate attempt to ignore what was happening around him? Was he feeling guilty about his good luck? Or was he dreading spotting someone he knew and cared about?

Jemeryl's eyes shifted back to the soldier who had just died. In witnessing the unknown woman's end, Jemeryl had been angry at the cruelty, despairing at the pointlessness, and saddened by the tragedy. But somewhere there must be people who had loved her. For them, she would not be just a dead human being. They would remember the person she had been and the hopes for what she should have become—the parents, waiting for their daughter's return, and close friends and lovers, who had wanted the dead woman to be a part of their future. To them, she would have a name, and when they learnt that she was gone, their grief would burn with raw agony.

At the thought, Jemeryl's jaw clamped shut. She had only been playing at sympathy. She forced herself to look at all the bodies littering the ground. This time she made herself remember how she had felt when told that Tevi was dead and then tried to imagine the same scene played out ten thousand times, when the news of the dead at Uzhenek was carried back to the homes they had left. Jemeryl bowed her head as the mental picture constricted the pit of her stomach, and sudden tears burned her eyes.

"I'll take charge of the prisoner." Mavek's voice made her flinch. She had not heard his horse's approach.

The orderly handed over the reins and scurried away. Jemeryl looked up. The remains of Mavek's army were mounted and ready to depart, formed up in four columns. She and Mavek were at the head of the largest. Tevi was also in their section, although positioned well towards the rear. Ranenok, Kharel, and Dunarth each led one of the columns. Their prominent roles were in keeping with their status, but Jemeryl suspected the main reason was to give none of them a chance to talk to the prisoners.

The other two acolytes, Anid and Yenneg, were not present. In total, Jemeryl estimated that the reduced army consisted of about one hundred and fifty witches and a couple dozen ungifted orderlies. The huge war machines were being abandoned and would doubtless soon be used as building material by the townsfolk of Uzhenek.

Mavek urged his horse forwards. Jemeryl's kept pace beside it, and the rest of the column followed on.

"Why did you do it?" Jemeryl asked, once a small gap had opened up between them and the two riders behind.

"What?"

She indicated the dead and dying soldiers. "Why did you even bother to bring them? They'd have been no use in catching me."

Mavek shrugged. "They might have had a role to play."

"You murdered them on a faint off chance?"

"I didn't murder them."

"You ordered then to take a drug that killed them. Isn't that murder?"

"It doesn't matter."

Jemeryl turned and stared at him. "You can't believe that."

"Once I get the talisman, then none of this will have happened. They'll all be alive, so I won't be guilty of anything and neither will you."

Mavek's careless disowning of his own actions stunned Jemeryl. Even if the talisman worked, no mere artefact could bestow such total absolution from guilt. "No. I've made mistakes. I regret lots of things I've done. But fixing things so that I never had the chance to go wrong won't change what I am, or what I'm capable of. I've done what I've done, and that is what I must accept the blame for."

Mavek snorted in derision. "Now you sound like Anid."

"She was right." Jemeryl glanced over her shoulder. "What happened to her, by the way?"

"Dammed fool."

"What did she do?"

"Not her. Yenneg."

Jemeryl frowned. "What did he do?"

"He killed her."

"When?"

"That night...at the...after the guard post exploded. Before you..." He was struggling for words. Tears formed in his eyes.

Jemeryl hung her head. Mavek was clearly more focused than when she had spoken to him via the message orb at Redezth, but he was still not healed from the assault she had inflicted on him. He probably never would recover completely, and regardless of what had caused her to do it, she was guilty of a crime.

"Yenneg lay in wait for her with the golems?" Jemeryl suggested to help him out. Now that she thought about it, she could remember the sound of fighting from the north, just after Anid had left her.

"Yes. Bykoda always used to keep the military commanders at each other's throats. Anid and Ranenok didn't let it overcome their common sense. But Yenneg...stupid oaf." Mavek snarled and then continued muttering under his breath.

"What did you do with him?"

"I...um...he's locked in a cell in Tirakhalod." Mavek's eyes drifted away, as if he had lost interest in the conversation.

They rode in silence for a few minutes while Jemeryl held her eyes on the plains ahead and tried to plan out her words. Eventually she turned to him again.

"Mavek, I'm sorry that I attacked you at the guard post. It was very wrong of me, and I regret it. I'm ashamed and angry at myself. I wish it hadn't happened. I wish I'd been a better person. I'll try to be one in the future."

Mavek's shrug looked more like a nervous twitch. "It doesn't matter. Once I get the talisman it won't have happened."

"It matters."

"Not to me."

"But it matters to me because it tells me something about myself that I don't like."

"And you want to live with this self-knowledge?" Scorn underlay Mavek's voice.

"Yes. It's a question of morality."

"What's so moral about leaving a wrong un-righted when you have the chance?"

"It's to do with lying to yourself and pretending that your actions aren't evil."

"You think I'm an evil person? I'm not. I never hurt anyone if I can help it. If I didn't know that I could undo the deaths of those soldiers back there, then I would never have given them the sleepstop."

"The talisman won't work."

"It has to. What's wrong? Do you want Kenan to stay dead? Don't you—"

Jemeryl interrupted gently. "Mavek. I understand how you feel. I was once on the point of using the talisman myself—back when I thought that Tevi was dead. And I'm even more ashamed of that than I am about attacking you. Please believe me. You shouldn't try to use the talisman."

Mavek reined in his horse and sneered at her mockingly. "Do as I say, not as I do?"

"Just because I sound hypocritical doesn't mean I'm wrong."

"You're lying. You used the talisman to get your lover back."

"I didn't. Please believe me. The talisman will rupture if you try to use it. It's unstable, but even if it wasn't, you shouldn't use it. From seeing the changes in you, I've realised that the whole concept of the talisman is wrong. We have to accept the responsibility for our actions, here and now. If we can deny the consequences of what we do, then we can deny guilt and blame, and without them, there is no way to measure good and evil."

"Nothing noble about living with your mistakes. The talisman just gives the chance to make things right. I'm going to get Kenan. We're all going to be happy. It's all going to be all right."

Jemeryl shook her head. "When Bykoda told me about the talisman, I thought so too, and the only problem was that it had become unstable. But now, I think it is evil—not in itself, but in its effect on people. You didn't used to be heartless. But you've let the thought of the talisman blind you to the truth of what you're doing. It's made you think that right and wrong don't matter. It's destroyed the good person you used to be."

Mavek held Jemeryl's gaze for the space of ten heartbeats and then spurred his horse forwards across the plains, heading south.

❖

By the seventh day, the Barroden Mountains were filling the skyline ahead of them. White capped peaks stretched across the horizon. The grasslands rose and fell in waves, leading up to the foothills.

They stopped at midday to rest the horses. Jemeryl stood in the spot directed, fingering the iron collar. Adding to her loathing of the device were the raw sores it had chafed around her neck. The mayhem in the higher dimensions no longer disturbed her quite so much, but she was still at the level of the ungifted. In a fight, she would be unable to hold her own against a third-rate witch.

Whenever Mavek was elsewhere, a detail of witches stood guard on her. Supposedly, they were to prevent her escaping or attempting to remove the collar. Jemeryl suspected that their true purpose was to prevent any of the other acolytes from having a private talk with her. She had noted that a similar guard was kept on Tevi.

On all sides, the witches milled around, stretching their legs, or gathered to talk in small groups while the ungifted orderlies prepared lunch. Jemeryl scanned the crowd, trying to pick out Tevi. They had not been able to speak since leaving Uzhenek. As far as she could tell, Tevi was not enthralled and had recovered from the magical assaults on her aura. On the one occasion that she had got close to Tevi, the eyes meeting hers had been alert and focused, and a ghost of the familiar smile had touched her lover's lips.

Finally Jemeryl spotted Tevi walking a few dozen yards away, surrounded by her guards. Tevi's head and shoulders were slumped. She looked tired and dispirited. Jemeryl hoped that nothing other than the long journey was to blame and that Tevi was not being subjected to any abuse.

As if in answer, just then, one of the witches cuffed Tevi around the head and she stumbled to her knees. The witch drew back his foot for a kick. Despite the iron collar and her escort, Jemeryl would have rushed over, but Ranenok's voice rang out. The army commander strode over to the group around Tevi. He looked nearly as furious as Jemeryl felt. She was not near enough to hear what was said, but from the demeanour of the witches, Ranenok was leaving them in no doubt that he did not want to see his ex-captain mistreated and was keeping a protective eye on her.

Jemeryl had barely calmed down when another angry voice was raised. She turned around. Mavek was bearing down on her.

"How much farther to this rabbit hole?" he screamed

"Not far." Jemeryl wondered what had provoked the query, although Mavek was still volatile enough that the cause might be nothing at all noteworthy. Perhaps he had just seen a rabbit.

"You seriously expect me to believe that your magpie flew all this way in a single night?"

"It's only about two hundred miles, and I enhanced her speed and stamina."

Mavek came close and glared into her eyes. "You better not be playing tricks."

"What trick could I be playing?"

"Thinking you can escape and flee over the Barrodens."

"This is where they are highest. There is no way that I could manage it. Even if I got this off." Jemeryl indicated the collar.

"So where is the talisman?"

"It's not far. I've only got the brief impression from Klara to go on, but I'll recognise the spot when I see it."

"One day away? Two?"

"Two should do it, I'd hope. But I can't say for certain."

Mavek grabbed her shoulder and pulled her closer still. His voice dropped to a dangerous whisper. "You better hope. You've got your two more days. If I haven't got the talisman in my hand by then, I'm going to see if I can find a way to improve your memory."

❖

Tevi sat on the ground, flexing her neck and shoulders as much as her bound hands would allow. It had been another long day in the saddle. Her back ached and her thighs felt like they had been kicked. She hoped she would be allowed a decent night's sleep, but it would depend on whoever had guard duty. Most witches acted as though she was unworthy of notice. Unfortunately, there were a few who had evidently been affronted by her previous status as a captain and were now venting their spite. So far, she had suffered no serious injury, nothing more than a few bruises and petty humiliations. But were it not for Mavek's orders that she be kept safe, and Ranenok's protection, Tevi knew that things would be far worse.

The wind had dropped and the cloudless sky was yellowing with evening, although sunset was still an hour away. That night they were making camp a little earlier than normal. The hilly terrain had been tough on the horses, and the animals had been gently weaned off sleepstop. They would be needed for the return journey.

The campsite selected was in a wide basin just below the crest of one of the higher hills. The vegetation was coarser than on the plains, cut by swaths of bracken and dotted with spindly trees, the first Tevi had seen for days. To the south, the high Barrodens were a towering presence, so close they seemed to be hanging over them.

As she looked at the scenery, Tevi found her eyelids starting to close, and a yawn crept up on her. After attempting to fight it back for a short while, she gave up, flopped onto her side, and closed her eyes. Why not take a few minutes' sleep if she had the chance? The grass was damp, but not enough to bother her. She was just drifting off when a shadow fell across her face and a foot connected sharply with her ankle.

"You. Get up. You're wanted."

Tevi opened her eyes and looked up. The seven witches surrounding her were not her normal guard detail, and if anything, their expressions were a fraction more contemptuous. None of them offered her help to rise, despite her bound hands. Once she was on her feet, they turned without another word and led her through the camp.

The party crossed the hollow and began to climb the slope behind. From the line they were taking, Tevi guessed their destination would be the crest of the hill overlooking the site, but she doubted that she was being escorted there simply to admire the view. From some way off, Tevi saw two figures waiting for them. Both were instantly identifiable from their outline. No one could match Mavek for size, and Tevi could always recognise Jemeryl. The two were clearly arguing, but not until she grew close could Tevi make out the words.

"Mavek, please. This won't achieve anything."

"We'll see."

"The talisman is near. I know it is."

"But it isn't in my hand, and your two days are up."

The escort of witches came to a halt a few yards from where the two sorcerers stood. Tevi's eyes fixed on Jemeryl with mixed emotions. It was good to be close to her lover and hear her voice, but Jemeryl was clearly very upset about whatever Mavek was intending. When Tevi added in the possible reasons for her own presence, she felt a cold knot tighten in her stomach. The signs did not look good.

The level top of the hill was about twenty feet wide and covered only in grass. Rabbit holes pitted the surface. A fallen tree lay just at the point where the hill started to drop again on the side away from the campsite. The trunk was no thicker than Tevi's waist and its life on the windswept hilltop had left it twisted and bent like a corkscrew so that it now rested on three points along its length.

Mavek strode to the tree and indicated the highest section where the wood was two feet clear of the ground. "This will do. Bring her over here."

Tevi looked at Mavek. He was clearly referring to her, yet he would not call her by name. He had not done so since he murdered Bykoda. Was this his true nature coming through? That despite the kindly face he had once shown, he had always truly regarded her, the ungifted warrior, as unworthy of acknowledgement? Had he only acted friendly as a ploy? Or was he now, deep inside, ashamed of his actions? Was he only able to push himself to continue by denying that the people he hurt were the same ones that he had known and liked before?

"Mavek, please!" The panic in Jemeryl's voice was unmistakeable, and it made Tevi's skin prickle. Something unpleasant was about to happen.

Tevi's hands were untied and she was shoved to her knees beside the tree. The biggest of the witches twisted Tevi's left arm up her back and clamped his elbow around her neck to hold her still. One of his comrades on the other side of the tree grabbed hold of her right wrist and stretched her arm over the trunk. She wondered if everyone realised that the display of physical intimidation was a sham. With her strength, Tevi could easily pull free, but it would serve no purpose. The witches would only counter with magical restraints.

Mavek approached the tree. In his hands he held a large war axe, making a show of hefting it like an executioner.

"Mavek!" Jemeryl screamed the name hysterically.

The blacksmith stopped and looked back at her. "I told you that you had two days to find this rabbit hole. I think you're playing tricks, but I'm going to be generous and give you another four days."

From her kneeling position, Tevi looked up at Mavek's face. The tone and expression she recognised as the smug cruelty of an overconfident thug, and as such, more worrying than honest anger. Mavek had slipped over the edge. His hint at a concession was a game, and a game he was now enjoying as he learnt to savour the power he held over his victims.

Jemeryl also seemed to realise that Mavek's words were purely to taunt her. She stared at his face in horror and disgust. "Mavek, you know you don't—"

He cut her off. "Well, sort of generous. Your ungifted friend has four limbs. Today she loses her right arm. Tomorrow her left. After that she had two legs. Don't worry, I won't let her die of blood loss. But if I don't have the talisman by then, she loses her head. And then she'll be gone, which might give you a bit more motive to find the talisman."

"No!" Jemeryl's voice was soft, desperate. She grabbed at the collar around her neck. "Please. Take this off. I only had a brief link with Klara. Maybe if I could make longer contact it would help me find her quicker."

Tevi's lips sealed in a tight line. The pleading was pointless. She would not play along with Mavek's game and add her voice to Jemeryl's. Tevi turned her face away. The witch behind her had a tight lock around her throat, but Tevi had just enough free movement to look along the length of her arm. It was part of the body she had lived in for twenty-four years. How would she cope without it? The image of Ranenok and his stump shot before her eyes.

Tevi flexed her fingers, felt the tendons shifting in the back of her hand, the muscles bunching in her forearm. The rough bark of the tree scratched the skin on her bicep, even through the thickness of her shirt. Her thumb rubbed along her fingertips. She wanted to remember what it all felt like.

She heard a gasp from Jemeryl and a grunt from Mavek and then the whistle of a blade, cutting the air. In reflex, Tevi's eyes scrunched shut. The thud of steel biting into wood sounded louder than she would have imagined. The trunk shuddered from the impact. The witch behind her flinched and a sliver of bark hit Tevi's face, but she felt nothing else.

Tevi opened her eyes. The axe was embedded in the tree, six inches from her arm. An involuntary gasp broke from her lips, but the sense of relief died in an instant. This was not a reprieve, just Mavek drawing the tension out, twisting the knife. He released his grip on the shaft and turned to Jemeryl. Tevi's gaze followed his.

"Please." Jemeryl was staring at the gap between axe and arm. Her face was bloodless.

Mavek swaggered slowly across the hilltop to where she stood, but the melodramatic posturing was so overdone that it would have been funny had it not been for the circumstances. Tevi's lips curled in contempt. Mavek was a joke when it came to projecting authority. He would never be able to dominate by the force of his personality alone. Bykoda could have been more menacing when combing her hair. True ruthlessness did not need an axe.

Mavek paced around Jemeryl, raking his powerless opponent with his eyes. After one complete circuit, he stopped in front of her and then slowly and deliberately slipped an iron key loose from a ring on his belt. The key was tiny, lost in his huge hands, but the right size for the lock on the collar around Jemeryl's neck. He held it up between thumb and forefinger and waved it in front of Jemeryl's face.

"You want me to take this off?" He tapped the key on the collar, making a faint metallic clink. He paused, sneering at her. "You must think me stupid."

Mavek palmed the key and spun away, returning briskly to the axe. The tree juddered as he wrenched it free from the wood. The blade rose again.

Tevi looked up, wanting him to meet her eyes, to have him acknowledge her as a person, his victim who had once been his friend. But Mavek's face was strangely emotionless. His eyes were fixed only on her arm, judging his aim. She might have been no more than firewood for chopping. His hands on the shaft tightened, ready for the downswing. Tevi clenched her teeth, bracing herself for the strike.

The eruption of shouts and screams from the campsite came without warning. All heads turned. The grip on Tevi's neck loosened as those holding her craned to see what was happening. A couple of witches who were only onlookers moved to the brow of the hill, seeking the cause of the disturbance below. However, the direction they needed to look was not down, but up.

Huge bodies were falling on the campsite, eight or more in number, serpentine necks outstretched, wings pulled back, jaws open. The snap of leathery skin slicing the wind sounded clearly, and then came the thunder of erupting flame. Agonised screams cut above the bass roar. Smoke billowed up against the pale sky. Before anyone on the hilltop could react, a dragon shot by, low overhead. Huge claws plucked one witch from the group around Tevi and carried him away, leaving only a stream of blood splattering in its wake.

Chaos erupted. The dragons swooped and dived around the campsite like monstrous seagulls around a beached carcass. More waves of fire cascaded down, crackling and roaring, but now it was answered. For an instant, one dragon blazed white and then dropped lifeless from the sky.

The remaining witches in the escort broke from their frozen shock. Two turned and fled, but the others raced down the hill to the camp to join their comrades. Mavek dropped the axe and strode to a better vantage point overlooking the battle. His hands began to swirl, drawing patterns in the air.

Tevi seized her chance. Most likely, Mavek had never seen a dragon before, and at first sight, they were distracting enough to claim anyone's attention. Now he had his back to her and the axe lay near at hand. Quickly, she grabbed it and charged forwards. The distance between them was less than a dozen steps. Tevi lifted the axe up over her shoulder. Her fists, clenched around the shaft, were level with her head.

At the last second, Mavek must have sensed her presence. He spun around. His hands shot out in her direction.

"*Duck left,*" the voice of prescience yelled in Tevi's head.

She threw herself sideways, hitting the ground hard. Blue lightning ripped through the air where she had been. The dead tree trunk behind her exploded in a hail of burning splinters.

Tevi rolled onto her stomach. Mavek's legs were only two feet from her head, but she did not have time to rise. Already his face was turning in her direction. His arms started to move. One-handed, Tevi swung the axe around in a loop. From her prone position, the awkward slash was impossible to control or put any real power behind. Still the blade connected with Mavek mid-calf, cutting into the bone, maybe even breaking it.

With a yowl of pain, Mavek collapsed. Both hands grasped at his wounded leg, and as they did so, a small key dropped onto the grass. Tevi scooped it up and shoved herself to her knees. She glanced back. Jemeryl had been coming to join in the fight but was still several yards away. Tevi tossed the key to her. Before she could do anything else, she heard new sounds from Mavek.

Despite his injury, Mavek was trying to struggle up. Tevi had lost hold of the axe. Rather than hunt for it, she swung a two-fisted punch into his side. Judging by the sound, some of his ribs fractured at the blow. The force sent him spinning sideways. His head cracked on a stone as he crashed to earth again. Blood was soaking through his leggings from the axe blow. Lying flat on his back, he appeared semi-conscious, but if he had time to recover, he would be more than a match for her, or any ungifted person. Tevi dare not give him the chance.

The axe lay on the grass a yard away. Without rising from her knees, Tevi snatched it up and scrambled to Mavek's side. She hoisted the weapon.

Mavek's eyes were hooded, barely open. His face was blank. But then, suddenly, his gaze fixed on the blade and awareness leapt into his expression. His fingers twitched, summoning magic to his defence, even as the axe began its downward sweep.

His focus shifted, locking eyes with Tevi. The instant dragged out to eternity. In Tevi's hands, the axe descended in slow motion, as if it were sinking through treacle, while points of ominous red lights appeared on Mavek's fingertips, directed at her heart. The axe fell. The lights glowed brighter.

Then Mavek froze. His flesh shimmered, rippling as if seen through a heat haze. His face contorted in a spasm of pain, and static leapt between the teeth in his open mouth. His fingers relaxed and the lights on them faded at the very moment that the axe completed its arc, smashing through his skull. Mavek's body slumped lifeless. Blood made a red halo around his head in the grass.

Tevi looked up. Standing in the same spot as before was Jemeryl, with the open collar in her hands. Their eyes met.

"You did that? The shimmering?"

Jemeryl nodded.

Tevi stood up. "Which one of us actually killed him?"

"It doesn't matter."

Tevi went to Jemeryl's side and hugged her tightly. "True."

For a moment they stood there, arms around each other. Tevi rested her head on her lover's shoulder. The solidity of the body in her arms was enough. Nothing else really counted.

Then together, they turned and looked down on the campsite. The battle was already over. Fires burned in the bracken, and the basin was littered with blackened corpses. None of Mavek's army remained, although dozens of figures could be seen fleeing down the hillside. Two dragons lay among the dead, but high overhead, seven more circled the field of battle like carrion crows.

"We're lucky they arrived when they did," Tevi said, looking up.

"Luck didn't come into it."

"It didn't?"

"Nope. I'd say that plan two worked perfectly."

"Plan two?"

"Would you like your memory back?"

"What?" Tevi brought her gaze down to Jemeryl.

"I altered your memory before you were captured. And don't look at me like that. You agreed to it." Jemeryl grinned. "So, do you want it put back straight?"

"You took some bits out of my memory?"

"Yes. And put other bits in that are false."

"Why?"

"We knew Mavek would want me to wear an iron collar. But in some ways it protected me. With that sort of disruption so close, he wouldn't be able to get inside my head. So it was a safe bet when I said Klara had taken the talisman away, he'd use magic on you to check. Before we set out to try and kill him, I changed your memories so he'd just see confirmation of what I told him. Mavek was too weak in the fifth dimension to spot my tampering. If he'd got Dunarth to probe your head, she might have noticed, but she'd also have learnt some things that Mavek didn't want her to know."

Tevi felt swamped by confusion. "You didn't send Klara off with the talisman?"

"No."

"So where is she?"

"Back in Uzhenek. Look, it will be much quicker if I just return your memory."

Jemeryl lifted her hand to Tevi's head, but before she could do anything, Tevi caught hold of her wrist. "Hang on. Before you start changing things, I want to be clear on what's happening."

"But it will—"

"Just humour me."

Both relief and affection showed in Jemeryl's smile. "All right. We had three plans. Plan one was the attempt to assassinate Mavek in the camp. It would have been easiest if it had worked. But if it failed, plan two was for you to get captured and for me to surrender and then tell him that Klara had flown off with the talisman."

Tevi frowned. "Wasn't that risky?"

"Very, but it was your idea. You remembered something Shard had said to you. *'When you can get him away from it, we will all come.'* We'd worked out that the dragons couldn't get close to the talisman. However, as long as I had the talisman and Mavek was chasing me, then the dragons couldn't help us. We had to lure Mavek away from where the talisman was. Before we went to Mavek's camp, I put Klara into an enchanted sleep, with the talisman tied to her. And then hid her in a magically sealed underground chamber so she was safe from the townsfolk."

"And plan three?"

"Plan three was, if I got killed, spells would come into play with Klara, so the chamber would open and she could try to get back to Lyremouth on her own."

"Oh."

"Any more questions?"

"No."

"Then would you like all your memories back?"

Tevi was now feeling more surprised than confused. She merely shrugged as a reply.

"I'll take that as a yes."

Jemeryl placed her hand on Tevi's forehead. For Tevi, the resulting sensation was rather like a hiccup in her thoughts. Something popped, and then there had always been a knowledge that had not always been there the moment before. She staggered and then shook her head.

"Are you all right?" Jemeryl asked.

"Um...yes. I think so."

They began to walk down to the remains of the campsite.

Tevi spoke again. "Jem."

"Yes?"

"You were right. It would have been quicker if you'd just given me my memories back."

Jemeryl laughed. "I did say."

"But you can't expect..." Tevi's voice died.

Two bodies lay on the ground nearby. Their clothes were burnt and their skin and hair was charred black, but it was easy to see that they had died with their arms around each other. Or, in the case of one of the bodies, an arm and a severed stump. Tevi bent down and turned them over gently.

Where their faces had been protected from fire by the other's head, Ranenok and Kharel were still recognisable.

"Kharel foresaw that she would not outlive Bykoda by long," Jemeryl said softly.

Tevi stood up and looked around the carnage of the battlefield. Smoke drifted across the scene from burning bracken, although most of the fire had gone out in the damp grass. "I wonder where Dunarth is."

"Either dead or running."

A rush of wind grew loud. They turned around as a dragon swooped low across the hillside. It banked over where Mavek's body lay and then came back towards them and slowed. The back draft of its wings whipped up a blinding cloud of ash. When Tevi could see again, Shard was standing before her on the scorched grass.

The dragon lowered its head closer to Tevi. "I said you'd understand in the end."

"It wouldn't have hurt if you'd explained it better in the beginning."

"It wasn't necessary, and I didn't know how."

"And you left your arrival to the last minute."

"I thought humans appreciated dramatic timing."

"In stories, but not when we're about to lose an arm."

"But you didn't." The dragon turned to Jemeryl. "You can call me Shard as well if you want."

"Um...thank you." Jemeryl looked bemused.

"You're going to take it away?"

"Yes."

Shard stared at Jemeryl for a long time. Its neck twisted left and right, as if it wanted to view her from several angles. "I don't generally like sorcerers. You can never be completely sure of them, but I think that you're going to be all right."

"Sorcerers don't generally like dragons. And I don't know if I want to form a judgement on you yet."

"If you wait until morning, some of the horses will make their way back here. That will mean you can get to Uzhenek and away more quickly. I want it gone." The dragon looked again at Tevi. "You can keep the armour I gave you. We won't meet again."

Shard spread its wings and sprung upwards. The other dragons swooped around it and then together they swung off towards the northwest. The sun was setting as the flight of dragons faded into small dots above the horizon.

Tevi shaded her eyes to watch them vanish. "They don't go in for big emotional good-byes, do they?"

CHAPTER SEVENTEEN—THE COVEN
AT LYREMOUTH

Seated at a window, high in the Guardian's tower, Tevi rested her head against the glass and looked down on the scene outside. Billows of soft drizzle were sweeping across Lyremouth harbour. The sounds of the city were muted in the damp air. The sea was leaden. Even the surf looked grey in the fading light. Pennants on the ship's masts flapped soggily. The view was not exactly cheery, but Tevi found it very relaxing and safe.

The noise of a door opening drew her eyes away from the harbour. A row of senior sorcerers filed into the hallway from the chamber beyond and proceeded towards the exit. Three of them frowned at Tevi disapprovingly as they passed by, but most ignored her. Only one gave a friendly nod of recognition.

The Coven authorities did not approve of relationships between their members and the ungifted. Some of the senior sorcerers clearly felt that Tevi was a problem that should be dealt with in some way. Fortunately, Gilliart, the elected leader of the Coven, did not share the view. But regardless of what even the Guardian might want, Tevi was a free citizen with the right to life and justice, and she could not be simply disposed of.

More than anything else it symbolised to Tevi the difference between the Protectorate and Bykoda's Empire. There, Jemeryl's refusal to give her up would be seen as the problem. In the Protectorate, Tevi could be a problem in her own right.

Jemeryl was the last in the line of sorcerers. Her expression was pensive, but it changed to a smile at the sight of Tevi waiting. She wandered to the window and also took a seat, shifting sideways to face her.

"You could have come to the meeting," Jemeryl said, once the last of the seniors had gone from the hallway.

"I got the feeling that some didn't want me there."

"True, some didn't. But Gilliart was quite happy, and with the Guardian on your side the rest don't matter much."

Tevi shrugged. "I wouldn't have understood most of what was said, and I've had quite enough of talking to sorcerers recently."

"Me included?"

"That depends on what you want to say." Tevi grinned as she spoke.

Jemeryl countered the teasing with mock-seriousness. "I could tell you what was discussed at the meeting."

By way of answer, Tevi gave an exaggerated groan of despair. Since their return to Lyremouth, they had been dragged through a succession of debriefings, private interviews, reviews, and interrogations where a dozen different people all wanted to know the same things. Why not have just one big meeting with everyone there and get it all over with at once?

This last meeting had dealt with plans for exploring the talisman's design. Tevi had been informed that she did not need to attend because there was nothing that she could contribute. While this was probably true, the condescending delivery of the message had irritated Tevi and she had almost decided to go out of perversity, but in the end, she could not face another four hours of tedious debate.

"Oh, go on. You want to know what was said," Jemeryl said, teasing.

"Do I?"

Jemeryl wrinkled her nose. "Well, maybe not. It was mainly a lot of manoeuvring about who's going to be in the group that reviews the proposals for suggested research strategy. I'm sure you'd have understood most of what went on. There was more politics than magic."

"I'll try to live with my regrets at missing it."

"The only thing everyone agreed on was that nothing should be done until we understand the risks. It will be years before anyone is allowed to touch the talisman. Maybe never. Some seers have made a preliminary examination and agree that it would definitely rupture if anyone tried to use it." Jemeryl's expression became troubled and her head dropped. "I haven't told anyone that I was about to."

"You might not have."

"I was—"

"You can't say for certain. Even without overhearing the news about me, you might have changed your mind before any damage had been done."

"But—"

Tevi leaned forwards and took Jemeryl's hand. "No buts. There isn't a person alive who couldn't be pushed into doing something awful by the wrong set of circumstances. Guilt or innocence can be a question of luck. You don't have to confess to what you might have done if things had been different."

"What about attacking Mavek?"

"All right. Own up to that if you want."

"I did."

"And?"

"They all agreed it would have been better if I hadn't, but nobody seemed overly upset on his behalf."

"He'd embarked on a course that could destroy the world. Are you surprised it lost him sympathy?"

"But he didn't succeed. Doesn't the hypothetical innocence apply to him as well?"

"Are you determined to beat yourself up over this?"

Jemeryl pouted like a three-year-old. "You said you'd let me wallow in guilt when we got back here."

"Um...I did, didn't I?" Tevi sighed in exasperation, but then she caught Jemeryl's eye and smiled. "Anything else of interest?"

"One thing that could affect us. A delegation from Horzt arrived yesterday. They're petitioning to join the Protectorate."

"Horzt? I thought they were all for independence."

"It's amazing what effect an infestation of dragons can have. Now that the northern plains are overrun, the people of Horzt are having second thoughts about wanting protection."

The innocent remark gave an uncomfortable jab to Tevi's conscience. She grimaced and looked out the window.

"That worries you?" Jemeryl asked.

"Not Horzt itself, but I wanted to protect the people in Uzhenek. I know I never claimed that I could, but I felt responsible."

"You saved them from Mavek's army and from him getting the talisman."

"But now their lives are ruined."

"That's open to argument. Uzhenek will be abandoned, which is no bad thing. The people will go back to being nomadic hunters. I'm sure that when they talk about the old times, they'll romanticise Bykoda's reign, but I don't know if they'll be any less happy than before."

"Except they've got dragons killing and eating them."

"It won't happen often. Dragons aren't really that keen on eating people. We tend to wear indigestible bits of metal and stuff. Plus there isn't as much meat on us as there is on wild cattle and deer, and there's enough wildlife on the plains to share. Hunters can co-exist with dragons quite well. The only time we get into conflict is when it comes to gold."

"Shard had quite a hoard."

"Dragons love gold and gems. Maybe it's because they don't decay or age. For a dragon they're one thing that never changes in its life view. Perhaps the consistency gives them stability. Whatever the reason, they'll do anything to collect it. Which is another reason Horzt wants to join the Protectorate. Most of Horzt's money comes from trade over the pass. Merchants carry gold, so until something comes along to drive the dragons away, caravans will be taking other routes. With less money coming their way, Horzt won't have to pay so much in taxes to the Coven."

"And you said it might affect us?"

"If Horzt joins the Protectorate, they'll need a town sorcerer. If I want the post, then Gilliart has said it's mine for the asking. I have experience of the plains. And I know the characters left over from Bykoda's regime."

Tevi studied Jemeryl's face. She could tell that something was bothering her lover. "Do you want it?"

"Do you?"

"It isn't me who'll be taking the post."

"But would you mind?"

"Why should I?"

"Because, when we went to Tirakhalod, it was all my idea. And I know that you didn't enjoy it. It doesn't seem fair if I get to say where we go next."

Tevi turned her head again to look out the window. A rain-swept dusk was falling over the sea. Given the choice, where would she go? She had been exiled from the island of her birth, but she had never felt that she belonged there anyway. Lyremouth was all right, but it did not feel like home, and nowhere else had any sort of claim on her at all. She looked back to Jemeryl.

"If Horzt joins the Protectorate, then the mercenary's guild will be setting up a proper guild house in the town. Like you, I know the northern plains. And I've ridden on a dragon. I'm sure the guild would be very happy to offer me a permanent job. Maybe even deputy guild master. But however it goes, it won't be like Tirakhalod."

"And you'll be happy?"

"Of course, because I'll be in the only place I really want to be."

"Where? Horzt?"

"No. By your side."

APPENDIX

THE LEGEND OF THE WITCH'S DEMON AND THE DEATH OF BYCODA

As told by the hunters of the Northern Plains

Long, long ago, this land was ruled by a great sorcerer called Bycoda, who was as wise as she was virtuous. Her Empire was a time of peace and plenty for all. Famine was unknown. Fair, well-appointed cities and mighty castles graced the land. The people passed their days in ease and contentment, protected by Bycoda's brave captains, who were all wielders of great magic in their own right. They rode far and wide with the soldiers of her army, enforcing her laws and protecting her subjects from harm.

Bycoda held court at the palace of Tiracholon. Eternal summer reigned over the lofty towers of her home. The scent of blossom was forever carried on sweet winds, and the sounds of music and laughter filled the air. Never have a people been so fortunate, and all this was Bycoda's doing. Her people's love for her was such that any would have gladly died for her sake.

Yet this blessed time was doomed to end. Far to the south, in the foothills of the Barrodens, lived an embittered, solitary witch, called Yemeril. She loved no one and no one loved her. Each day she went about her business, gathering herbs and bones, and cursing anyone who crossed her path, although folk avoided her whenever they could.

One day, it happened that Yemeril went in search of a rare plant, and she wandered far from her normal paths. At nightfall, she was many miles from home, and so she lay down to sleep beneath the shelter of a twisted old yew tree.

Now, Yemeril knew it not, but this yew was the home of a shape-shifting demon, named Teir-Varek. That night, the demon took the form of a beautiful woman and lay beside Yemeril and seduced not only her body but also her mind. Although, in truth, this was no great feat, for the witch's unfriendly ways had left her apt for mischief.

Many days and nights passed as Yemeril stayed at the yew tree with her demon lover. And when they were not satisfying their desires, they spoke idly of many things, as lovers will. In this, the demon had the most to impart, for her travels in the netherworld had granted her much secret information. Amid the stories, Teir-Varek told of a talisman owned by Bycoda that allowed the wielder to command the allegiance of dragons.

"Oh, my love," said Yemeril when she heard this. "If only we had that talisman. Then the whole world would bow down before us, and we could live as Queens."

"Why should it not be ours?" the demon replied. "All it would take is firm resolve and a little guile."

So the pair plotted to take the talisman from Bycoda. At last, when their plans were complete, Yemeril left the mountains and travelled north to Tiracholon. Once there, she went to Bycoda and made a show of friendship.

"Noble Empress," Yemeril said, smiling to conceal her intent. "I have come from a land far away, yet even there, stories of your wisdom are told. Therefore I am here in the spirit of sisterhood, that we might share our knowledge, for I also am greatly skilled in the magical arts."

"Then as a sister you will be welcome in my halls," Bycoda replied.

And so, for many months, they spoke together of matters arcane, revealing the magical knowledge they had acquired.

One day, as the two were talking of the many perils that lay beyond the borders of the realm, Yemeril said, "Dear Bycoda, I wonder that you are so well able to defend your Empire."

"That is due to my brave captains, who lead my army against all monsters and villains who would harm my people."

"Perhaps in this I may assist you. I know of a great warrior who would willingly join your captains in protecting your land. Furthermore, she is dear to my heart, and it would bring me joy to have her close beside me."

"Then you should summon her forthwith, and I will grant her the rank of captain in my army, and show her fitting honour, for your sake."

By these means, did the demon, Teir-Varek, gain access to the palace. And ably did she fulfil her role of captain, for she had the strength of a dozen men, although in all other ways she disguised her true nature and appeared as an ordinary mortal.

Another year passed while the two plotters remained in Tiracholon, until they judged that it was time to move on with their evil scheme. Then Yemeril went to Bycoda and said, "I have seen how your captains battle with ordinary dangers, but how is it that no dragons assail your lands? Surely your captains, no matter how brave, could not defeat such powerful foes."

"The dragons stay away by my command," replied Bycoda. "For I have a talisman that can bind them to obey my will."

"But where do you keep the talisman, dear Empress? For surely it is open to misuse and must be kept safe."

"Indeed. It is kept in a chest at the foot of my bed, that may not be opened by any manner of magic, and the one key I keep on a chain about my neck." With these innocent words, Bycoda forfeited her own life, for now the plotters knew they must murder her in order to take the talisman.

Now, Bycoda had the custom that twice a year she held a great festival in her palace, when all her captains and nobles came to do her honour. At these gatherings, the feasting and revelry would last from daybreak until sunset. Music would fill the hall to the rafters, and the fountains in the gardens ran with sweet wine.

As the time for the spring gathering approached, Teir-Varek spoke thus with the witch. "My love, the time for us to act draws near. We should kill Bycoda and take her talisman on the night of the festival when all her supporters are assembled in Tiracholon."

"But surely this is the worst time, when she is surrounded by her loyal attendants," Yemeril said.

"No. For she will think herself secure, and her guard will be unwary."

Yemeril was afraid and asked, "How shall we kill her? For I have spent much time with her. I have seen that she is a mighty sorcerer, and I do not think we can defeat her, even if we join our powers."

"Again, we will use guile. Did you not know that I have made a great study of poisons? I will give you one that will end Bycoda's life in an instant."

"Suppose she will not drink it?"

"She will not need to. It is a venom so potent that one small scratch from a coated pin will cause her death. Wait until after Bycoda retires at the end of the festivities and go to her room. Her followers will have drunk themselves witless and will not be alert. Say you have brought her a brooch as a gift. When you give it to her, pierce her skin with the pin, as if in accident, and that will be enough."

So the treacherous plan was agreed, and on the evening of the festival, Yemeril went alone to Bycoda's chamber with the poisoned brooch.

"Dear Empress," the false witch said. "I have brought you this as a token of my love for you."

Bycoda, thinking no harm, held out her hand to receive the gift, and as she did so, Yemeril pressed the brooch down on her hand so that the pin on the clasp pierced Bycoda's finger.

"Oh Empress, forgive my careless action," Yemeril cried, as if all had happened by mischance.

Bycoda held up her hand, and saw but a drop of blood on her finger, but then she felt her heart lurch, and a blackness rose up before her eyes. In sudden understanding, she knew that she had been deceived by Yemeril and Teir-Varek, and that she would now die by the witch's treacherous hand. Yet, with her last breath, Bycoda cursed her murderers and swore that both would gain only death in return for their betrayal of her kindness and trust.

As Bycoda died, a wave of grief swept over the Empire. Brave soldiers threw down their weapons and wept. The trees in the garden lost their blossom and a cold wind ripped through the eternal summer of the court. Across the land, all were overwhelmed by a feeling of loss, and sorrow consumed them, although as yet, none knew the cause.

Once the cruel murder was done, Yemeril took the key from around the dead Empress's neck and stole the talisman. Then Teir-Varek set fire about the palace and the evil pair fled, heading back to their home. However, standing between them and the Barroden Mountains was the great city of Uzhenec, led by Bycoda's loyal captain, Curnad. He had been warned in a prophetic dream not to attend the gathering in Tiracholon and to be alert for the murderers. So he remained in the city, ever vigilant, and would not let them pass.

When she heard of his defiance, Yemeril took the talisman in her right hand and summoned a dragon to destroy the city. Fire and death rained down from the monster's jaws, until Uzhenec, once the fairest of cities, lay half in ruins, but still Curnad would not surrender. He took his sword and shield and summoned his strongest magic to his defence, and for six hours he fought the beast until he slew it and struck off its head. At this, the entire city hailed him as their hero and gave him the title Dragon Slayer.

When she saw her attack had failed, Yemeril was despairing, but Teir-Varek said, "My love, have I not shown you that guile may often win where crude force fails? Now we will try a new plan."

"What will you do?"

"Remember, I am not bound to this form and may appear however I choose." At these words, the demon's shape began to shift, and in a few minutes she had the likeness of one of Curnad's most trusted soldiers. In this form, the demon walked boldly through the streets of Uzhenec until she found the heroic Dragon Slayer, supervising the city's defences.

Feigning an excuse, she led Curnad to a secret place and then basely stabbed him in the back and hid his body. Once this was done, the shape-shifter again switched form, most deceitfully, into the likeness of her victim. Pretending to be the murdered Curnad, she secured her control of Uzhenec and summoned Yemeril into the city.

Scarcely could the two restrain their glee at the success of their plan. The good folk who had stood against them now did their bidding. For alas, the people of Uzhenec did not know that the one they called the Dragon Slayer was none other than a false demon. Yet many folk wondered that the witch Yemeril was now an honoured guest in Uzhenec, and that Curnad, who had been so bold and cheerful, now skulked around the city with never a smile for any he had once called friend.

Meanwhile in Tiracholon, great had been the lamentation when the death of their beloved Empress had been discovered. To see the tears and wailing that filled the palace would have broken the hardest heart. Never had there been such an outpouring of sorrow.

But at last, Mavec, the most loyal and valiant of all Bycoda's captains, stood and addressed them thus: "The loss we have suffered is beyond bearing, and our woe shall know no end. We should take no shame in our tears. Yet it seems to me that we would have great shame if the foul assassins who have murdered our dear Empress should live to enjoy the benefits of their crime. Therefore I swear to hunt them down, to the ends of the earth and beyond. And never shall I turn aside from this task until their bodies lie dead before me."

At these words, the assembled captains roused themselves from their weeping and joined the hero in his oath. And so Mavec led Bycoda's army in their quest for revenge. Across the plains they went, and so bitter was their grief, and so savage their anger, that they ran for three days and three nights, without pausing for sleep or food, until they surrounded the city of Uzhenec, where Yemeril and Teir-Varek were resting, unaware of the forces coming against them.

When the two murderers awoke the next day, they saw the city surrounded by a ring of fair banners fluttering in the wind. The dawn sunlight reflected off the ranks of keen-edged swords and sharp spears. The faces of the soldiers were stern and fearless, seeking only to avenge their dead Empress. So strong and noble an army had not been assembled before in the history of the world.

At this sight, Teir-Varek took great fear and deserted her lover. Again she changed her shape, this time turning herself into a magpie, and then she flew off with the talisman. The witch, Yemeril, was thus alone and abandoned, and had no hope but to throw herself on the mercy of her enemies. Bound in iron chains, she went before them, and confessed to all that she had done.

When they heard her story, many of Bycoda's loyal captains were stirred to fury and would have killed her on the spot, but Mavec stayed their hands.

"You have been most wicked," he said to her. "And your life is certainly forfeit. But yet your death may be either slow or quick. So tell me this, where is the tree under which you first encountered Teir-Varek? For, by my magic, I know that the demon will return to her home. Furthermore, I know that unless both the tree and the demon's mortal body are destroyed, then Teir-Varek cannot be utterly banished from this plane of existence, but will ever return to cause strife in the world."

At these words, Yemeril's face turned pale, and she said, "I shall willingly show you where the tree is, that you may destroy my former lover, for in truth she has deserted me and my heart has broken from the pain of it."

So the army set off again across the plains, until they reached the foothills of the Barroden Mountains. Then Teir-Varek moved against them, but ever the demon preferred trickery to honest fight. She poisoned their food and water, so that nine soldiers out of every ten died. Yet the survivors were not in the least swayed from their revenge; rather did it inflame them to fulfil their oath and rid the world of the evil demon.

And so at last, with Yemeril's guidance, the old twisted yew came in sight, and standing beneath it was the demon, surrounded by her hell-spawned allies. When Teir-Varek saw that her former lover had led the army to her, she gave a great cry of rage. Then did Teir-Varek take the talisman in her right hand and raise it high in the air and summon the dragons to her defence. And it is told that the first to die was Yemeril, killed on her vengeful lover's command.

Then was the battle fully engaged. Swinging his great war-axe, Mavec led the assault on the demon's lair. Great was the fight, and many a mighty deed was done, and many a brave soldier fell. Always in the forefront of battle was Mavec, yet no harm came to him, as if his life were charmed. He fought his way through blood and fire to the yew, and with a single great blow, struck off the demon's right arm, so that the talisman fell to the ground.

Now the dragons were freed from the demon's will, and in a frenzy they turned on both sides of the conflict. The largest dragon of all swept down and unleashed a river of fire, consuming Teir-Varek, Mavec, and the yew in a single pillar of flame, destroying them all utterly. Thus was Bycoda's murder avenged. The demon, Teir-Varek, was banished for all time from this world, and Yemeril, who had struck down the good Empress, lay dead by her lover's hand.

Yet, the triumph was not joyous. Many good warriors died in the battle that day. It would take a year to recount the noble deeds of the fallen. Of Bycoda's captains only two lived to see nightfall. The valiant Yernag returned to Tiracholon, and tried to hold back the onset of chaos, but he died within the year, defending the tomb of his beloved Empress. The soothsayer Dunort also survived, but her grief and horror at what she had seen turned her mind, and she spent the end of her days as a wild thing upon the plains, and none might speak with her.

With the battle over, and the army in ruins, the dragons now had the run of the land. They took great delight in tearing down all signs of Bycoda's Empire. The cities and castles they razed to the ground, so that scarcely one brick remained on another to show where once the fair cities of Uzhenec, Krewco, or any of the others had stood. We who have come after can only wonder at the glory we have lost.

But of the talisman, the reason for this sad tale, a story of hope is told. In the last seconds of his life, Mavec saw the dragon descending and understood that he was about to die. For himself, he knew he could die with honour and his Empress' death avenged, but he foresaw a bleak future for the lands, with no way to defeat the dragons. At his feet, he noticed the talisman lying on the ground, still in the demon's severed hand. So at the instant of his death, Mavec took the talisman and thrust it into a rabbit hole, that it might not perish in the dragon fire.

And so it is foretold, that one day the talisman will return to the lands. One day a traveller will find the burnt stump of an old yew tree, and by its roots a rabbit hole. And in there, where Mavec placed it, will lie the talisman. Then shall a new hero arise, and the dragons will be banished from the land and once again a time of peace and plenty will be ours.

❧❧

About the Author

Jane Fletcher is a GCLS award winning writer and has also been short-listed for the Gaylactic Spectrum and Lambda awards. She is author of two fantasy/romance series: the Lyremouth Chronicles—*The Exile and The Sorcerer*, *The Traitor and The Chalice*, and *The Empress and The Acolyte,* and the Celaeno series—*The Walls of Westernfort*, *Rangers at Roadsend,* and *The Temple at Landfall*. In her next writing project she will be returning to the Celaeno Series with *Dynasty of Rogues*.

Her love of fantasy began at the age of seven when she encountered Greek Mythology. This was compounded by a childhood spent clambering over every example of ancient masonry she could find (medieval castles, megalithic monuments, Roman villas). Her resolute ambition was to become an archaeologist when she grew up, so it was something of a surprise when she became a software engineer instead.

Born in Greenwich, London in 1956, she now lives in south-west England where she keeps herself busy writing both computer software and fiction, although generally not at the same time.

Visit Jane's website at www.janefletcher.co.uk

Books Available From Bold Strokes Books

Sleep of Reason by Rose Beecham. Nothing is as it seems when Detective Jude Devine finds herself caught up in a small-town soap opera. And her rocky relationship with forensic pathologist Dr. Mercy Westmoreland just got a lot harder. (1-933110-53-8)

Passion's Bright Fury by Radclyffe. When a trauma surgeon and a filmmaker become reluctant allies on the battleground between life and death, passion strikes without warning. (1-933110-54-6)

Broken Wings by L-J Baker. When Rye Woods, a fairy, meets the beautiful dryad Flora Withe, her libido, as squashed and hidden as her wings, reawakens along with her heart. (1-933110-55-4)

Combust the Sun by Andrews & Austin. A Richfield and Rivers mystery set in L.A. Murder among the stars. (1-933110-52-X)

Of Drag Kings and the Wheel of Fate by Susan Smith. A blind date in a drag club leads to an unlikely romance. (1-933110-51-1)

Tristaine Rises by Cate Culpepper. Brenna, Jesstin, and the Amazons of Tristaine face their greatest challenge for survival. (1-933110-50-3)

Too Close to Touch by Georgia Beers. Kylie O'Brien believes in true love and is willing to wait for it. It doesn't matter one damn bit that Gretchen, her new and off-limits boss, has a voice as rich and smooth as melted chocolate. It absolutely doesn't. (1-933110-47-3)

The 100ᵗʰ Generation by Justine Saracen. Ancient curses, modern day villains, and a most intriguing woman who keeps appearing when least expected lead Archeologist Valerie Foret on the adventure of her life. (1-933110-48-1)

Battle for Tristaine by Cate Culpepper. While Brenna struggles to find her place in the clan and the love between her and Jess grows, Tristaine is threatened with destruction. Second in the Tristaine series. (1-933110-49-X)

The Traitor and the Chalice by Jane Fletcher. Without allies to help them, Tevi and Jemeryl will have to risk all in the race to uncover the traitor and retrieve the chalice. The Lyremouth Chronicles Book Two. (1-933110-43-0)

Promising Hearts by Radclyffe. Dr. Vance Phelps lost everything in the War Between the States and arrives in New Hope, Montana with no hope of happiness and no desire for anything except forgetting—until she meets Mae, a frontier madam. (1-933110-44-9)

Carly's Sound by Ali Vali. Poppy Valente and Julia Johnson form a bond of friendship that lays the foundation for something more, until Poppy's past comes back to haunt her—literally. A poignant romance about love and renewal. (1-933110-45-7)

Unexpected Sparks by Gina L. Dartt. Falling in love is complicated enough without adding murder to the mix. Kate Shannon's growing feelings for much younger Nikki Harris are challenging enough without the mystery of a fatal fire that Kate can't ignore. (1-933110-46-5)

Whitewater Rendezvous by Kim Baldwin. Two women on a wilderness kayak adventure—Chaz Herrick, a laid-back outdoorswoman, and Megan Maxwell, a workaholic news executive—discover that true love may be nothing at all like they imagined. (1-933110-38-4)

Erotic Interludes 3: Lessons in Love ed. by Radclyffe and Stacia Seaman. Sign on for a class in love…the best lesbian erotica writers take us to "school." (1-933110-39-2)

Punk Like Me by JD Glass. Twenty-one year old Nina writes lyrics and plays guitar in the rock band, Adam's Rib, and she doesn't always play by the rules. And, oh yeah—she has a way with the girls. (1-933110-40-6)

Coffee Sonata by Gun Brooke. Four women whose lives unexpectedly intersect in a small town by the sea share one thing in common—they all have secrets. (1-933110-41-4)

The Clinic: Tristaine Book One by Cate Culpepper. Brenna, a prison medic, finds herself deeply conflicted by her growing feelings for her patient, Jesstin, a wild and rebellious warrior reputed to be descended from ancient Amazons. (1-933110-42-2)

Forever Found by JLee Meyer. Can time, tragedy, and shattered trust destroy a love that seemed destined? When chance reunites two childhood friends separated by tragedy, the past resurfaces to determine the shape of their future. (1-933110-37-6)

Sword of the Guardian by Merry Shannon. Princess Shasta's bold new bodyguard has a secret that could change both of their lives. He is actually a *she*. A passionate romance filled with courtly intrigue, chivalry, and devotion. (1-933110-36-8)

Wild Abandon by Ronica Black. From their first tumultuous meeting, Dr. Chandler Brogan and Officer Sarah Monroe are drawn together by their common obsessions—sex, speed, and danger. (1-933110-35-X)

Turn Back Time by Radclyffe. Pearce Rifkin and Wynter Thompson have nothing in common but a shared passion for surgery. They clash at every opportunity, especially when matters of the heart are suddenly at stake. (1-933110-34-1)

Chance by Grace Lennox. At twenty-six, Chance Delaney decides her life isn't working so she swaps it for a different one. What follows is the sexy, funny, touching story of two women who, in finding themselves, also find one another. (1-933110-31-7)

The Exile and the Sorcerer by Jane Fletcher. First in the Lyremouth Chronicles. Tevi, wounded and adrift, arrives in the courtyard of a shy young sorcerer. Together they face monsters, magic, and the challenge of loving despite their differences. (1-933110-32-5)

A Matter of Trust by Radclyffe. JT Sloan is a cybersleuth who doesn't like attachments. Michael Lassiter is leaving her husband, and she needs Sloan's expertise to safeguard her company. It should just be business—but it turns into much more. (1-933110-33-3)

Sweet Creek by Lee Lynch. A celebration of the enduring nature of love, friendship, and community in the quirky, heart-warming lesbian community of Waterfall Falls. (1-933110-29-5)

The Devil Inside by Ali Vali. Derby Cain Casey, head of a New Orleans crime organization, runs the family business with guts and grit, and no one crosses her. No one, that is, until Emma Verde claims her heart and turns her world upside down. (1-933110-30-9)

Grave Silence by Rose Beecham. Detective Jude Devine's investigation of a series of ritual murders is complicated by her torrid affair with the golden girl of Southwestern forensic pathology, Dr. Mercy Westmoreland. (1-933110-25-2)

Honor Reclaimed by Radclyffe. In the aftermath of 9/11, Secret Service Agent Cameron Roberts and Blair Powell close ranks with a trusted few to find the would-be assassins who nearly claimed Blair's life. (1-933110-18-X)

Honor Bound by Radclyffe. Secret Service Agent Cameron Roberts and Blair Powell face political intrigue, a clandestine threat to Blair's safety, and the seemingly irreconcilable personal differences that force them ever farther apart. (1-933110-20-1)

Protector of the Realm: Supreme Constellations Book One by Gun Brooke. A space adventure filled with suspense and a daring intergalactic romance featuring Commodore Rae Jacelon and a stunning, but decidedly lethal, Kellen O'Dal. (1-933110-26-0)

Innocent Hearts by Radclyffe. In a wild and unforgiving land, two women learn about love, passion, and the wonders of the heart. (1-933110-21-X)

The Temple at Landfall by Jane Fletcher. An imprinter, one of Celaeno's most revered servants of the Goddess, is also a prisoner to the faith—until a Ranger frees her by claiming her heart. The Celaeno series. (1-933110-27-9)

Force of Nature by Kim Baldwin. From tornados to forest fires, the forces of nature conspire to bring Gable McCoy and Erin Richards close to danger, and closer to each other. *(*1-933110-23-6)

In Too Deep by Ronica Black. Undercover homicide cop Erin McKenzie tracks a femme fatale who just might be a real killer…with love and danger hot on her heels. (1-933110-17-1)

Erotic Interludes 2: Stolen Moments by Stacia Seaman and Radclyffe, eds. Love on the run, in the office, in the shadows…Fast, furious, and almost too hot to handle. (1-933110-16-3)

Course of Action by Gun Brooke. Actress Carolyn Black desperately wants the starring role in an upcoming film produced by Annelie Peterson. Just how far will she go for the dream part of a lifetime? (1-933110-22-8)

Rangers at Roadsend by Jane Fletcher. Sergeant Chip Coppelli has learned to spot trouble coming, and that is exactly what she sees in her new recruit, Katryn Nagata. The Celaeno series. (1-933110-28-7)

Justice Served by Radclyffe. Lieutenant Rebecca Frye and her lover, Dr. Catherine Rawlings, embark on a deadly game of hide-and-seek with an underworld kingpin who traffics in human souls. (1-933110-15-5)

Distant Shores, Silent Thunder by Radclyffe. Doctor Tory King—and the women who love her—is forced to examine the boundaries of love, friendship, and the ties that transcend time. (1-933110-08-2)

Hunter's Pursuit by Kim Baldwin. A raging blizzard, a mountain hideaway, and a killer-for-hire set a scene for disaster—or desire—when Katarzyna Demetrious rescues a beautiful stranger. (1-933110-09-0)

The Walls of Westernfort by Jane Fletcher. All Temple Guard Natasha Ionadis wants is to serve the Goddess—until she falls in love with one of the rebels she is sworn to destroy. The Celaeno series. (1-933110-24-4)